masked sins

USA TODAY BESTSELLING AUTHOR
AMANDA RICHARDSON

Masked Sins
Amanda Richardson
© Copyright 2024 Amanda Richardson
www.authoramandarichardson.com

Copy/line editing: Marion Archer at Making Manuscripts and Jenny
Sims at Editing4Indies
Proofreading: Michele Ficht
Cover Design: Moonstruck Cover Design & Photography
Cover Photography: Rafa G Catala
Cover Model: Ignacio Ferrari

BLURB

**"Where pain and pleasure converge ... her *submission*
becomes my darkest playground."**

Orion
As the youngest Ravage brother, I've spent too much
time partying and drinking away my life.
Now that I'm sober, I've learned to channel my need for
control. And I share my knowledge online, as a masked
persona.
The last person I expect to message me is Layla, the
daughter of the man my mom married.
She's always been my greatest temptation, and when she
unknowingly confides in my alias, her deepest fantasies
become my new obsession.
Behind the mask, I teach her the art of surrender—and
she's eager to learn every lesson.
And when the mask comes off, her resistance only fuels
my desire to break and corrupt her.

Completely.

Layla

As a ballet dancer by day, everyone sees me as the
epitome of grace and innocence.
But beneath the good-girl facade, I have dark, hidden
desires I've never told anyone about.
Connecting with a mysterious masked man online seems
like the perfect solution.
He dominates me from behind a screen, making me his
willing student.
But Orion's return to my life only complicates matters—
and our forbidden chemistry is impossible to ignore.
I'm caught between the stranger's sadistic magnetism
and Orion's intoxicating charm.
As it turns out ... they both revel in sculpting my desires
with skilled hands and cruel smiles that promise *both*
heaven and hell.

Masked Sins is a full-length, "his mom married her
dad" billionaire romance with intense themes. It is
book four in the Ravaged Castle series. All books can
be read as standalones.

Warning: This book contains a possessive, jealous
antihero who's a sadistic Dominant, explicit sexual
situations, and strong language. Despite that, our
guy is a bit of a cinnamon roll for Layla. There is no
cheating, it is *not* a love triangle, and there is a HEA.

There once was a castle, so mighty and high,
With large, gilded gates, it rivaled Versailles.
To all those below, it was splendid and lush,
But to those inside, it was ravaged and crushed.
Five Ravage boys born amongst old, rotted roots,
Their father ensured they'd all grow to be brutes.
Some said they were cursed, sworn off of desire,
But they turned into men and found what they required.
Forbidden, illicit, they had to work for that love,
They questioned that castle when push came to shove.
The curse and the rot gave way to unsavory tastes,
Dark proclivities and sick, messed up traits.
Five stories of five men with sinfully dark tales,
The Ravage brothers prove that love does prevail.

AUTHOR'S NOTE

This book contains themes that may be problematic for some people. However, please note that Masked Sins is not a dark romance.

For a complete list, please visit my website here:
www.authoramandarichardson.com/triggers

Happy reading!

For all the bookworms who think praise and degradation kink should always go hand in hand.

else they could do. None of us were surprised when she stopped walking or when she needed around-the-clock oxygen.

I'm already a burden to my brothers, Layla, and especially Scott, the man who married my mom ten years ago. He had rules about drinking and living under his roof, and I'd been breaking those rules a lot lately.

I want to scream all of this at him, but Gary is a decent guy. He's Scott's best friend, and I realize now that I should've gone somewhere else in Crestwood. Choosing the bar owned by someone who's known me since I was fourteen probably wasn't the smartest idea, considering I planned on getting rip-roaring drunk today.

Except it's hard to find a place that doesn't know me —either because of my father and the Ravage name or because of what recently happened to my mom.

"Listen," he says, his voice gentler now. "I get it. I really do."

Pressing my lips together, I glare at him. "You have no fucking idea, *Gary*."

"I do, actually. And I'm sorry for your loss—"

Before he can finish his sentence, I grab a nearby glass and throw it down onto the floor. Another person screams, and rage boils just beneath my skin.

Stop feeling. Push it down. Keep going until you don't feel thing.

"You all really need t-to come up with a better s-logan," I slur. "I'm so sorry for your loss. Your family is my prayers. We're thinking about you during this

PROLOGUE
THE AUDITION

Orion

Seven Years Ago

Breaking glass pulls me out of my stupor. Someone says my name, but I hardly hear it. Everything sounds like it's underwater—hollow and vague. I know I should look around to make sure no one is hurt, but the room is spinning. I'm going to be violently ill if I move too quickly.

Lifting my head, I slowly track the bartender gesturing at me. I can't hear him. I only hear the beating of my own heart. He points at my hand as someone brushes up against the side of my body, lifting my arm. I startle at the sight of the blood and turn to face the person touching me. That's when I see the shattered glass around my seat and the lines of blood tracking down my forearm.

I pull away from the person helping me, stumbling

off the stool as my pulse whooshes in my ears. *How much did I drink?* My boots crunch glass as I make my way to the back of the bar. Each step is unsteady, the room spinning slightly as I push through the haze. My vision blurs at the edges, and the floor feels like it's shifting beneath me. I stumble over the threshold of the small bathroom, barely managing to catch myself on the sink. The lock clicks into place with more force than I intended, echoing in the tight, grimy space.

I can't tell if it's the alcohol or something darker clouding my thoughts, but I feel disoriented, as if the world has slowed down around me. When I close my eyes, the only sounds are my own labored breathing and the faint, distant hum of the sports game on the television out front—a reminder of the world still moving beyond this door while I struggle to keep my footing.

Someone pounds on the door.

"Orion, open the door," Gary yells, the handle rattling as he tries to break the door down. "We should get you checked out. Come on, man."

"Fuck off," I yell, stumbling as I turn on the tap. "I'm f-fine. Jus' going to clean it up."

Running the water, I clean my arm and pull out the shard of glass embedded in my palm. It doesn't feel like my arm. It feels like someone else's arm. Like I'm having an out-of-body experience.

I don't feel a single fucking thing.

Once the water runs clear, I turn the tap off and pat the thick cut with paper towels, pressing into the wound until the paper blooms red.

"Orion, I swear to God," Gary bellows, hammering on the door.

I grumble as I toss the paper towel and open the door. "'S okay," I tell him, patting his large chest with my good hand. "S-s-top worrying about me."

He sighs heavily, running a hand down his long beard. "I'm sorry, man. You've gotta leave."

"'S fine," I reply, nodding. "I have s-somewhere to b anyway."

He follows me, and when I get back to my usual se the broken glass is gone—as is my drink.

"Where'd you put it?" I ask, slowly turning to him and nearly falling over in the process.

"You're drunk off your fucking ass, Ravage. Go h Sleep it off. I already told Scott to expect you."

I rub my mouth with my hand as anger begi bloom inside me. "Scott."

"Yeah, man. Come on—"

"And why the fuck would you do that?" I as voice cracking. "He already has enough fucking deal with. His wife just *died*, asshole," I hiss.

His wife—my mom.

Technicalities.

Gary's face softens.

I fucking hate the look he's giving me. *Pity.* F me. Why the fuck would he pity me? It's not didn't know my mom was going to die. No, we years to get used to the idea. We all did. None o surprised when she started declining. None o surprised when the doctors told us there wa difficult time. For fuck's s-sake, who came up with those?" I shout, stumbling backward.

Gary reaches out and takes my hand, but I can tell by his flared nostrils that he's pissed off. *Good.*

"I broke things too, kid. But you'll soon find out that while it can feel good to break something, it doesn't make up for the broken heart you get when you lose someone."

The instant the words are out of his mouth, I feel remorse for what I did. Not only did he know my mom well, but he also lost his wife a few years ago.

Of course he can relate, and here I am, acting like a fucking teenager throwing a tantrum.

Shame casts a web around me, suffocating me. It feels like every fucking thing is falling apart around me.

Every *single* thing.

I pull out of his grip and twist around, storming to the exit and shoving the door open. I don't turn around, but I keep walking down the street past all of the familiar shops and storefronts in downtown Crestwood. It doesn't matter that it's raining. I can't feel it—just like I can't feel the open wound on my palm.

I hate this. I hate everything about this town except for one person. The one thing that keeps me tethered to this earth is the one person who grounds me. My cheeks are hot and wet, and I realize I might be crying.

Fuck this.

Everything spins around me as I pull my phone out, and I have to steady myself on a nearby wall. After requesting a ride on my phone, I sit on a nearby bench.

My phone is almost dead, so I open the text that Layla sent a few minutes ago.

Wish me luck!

My heart skips several beats when I open the picture. It's a reflection selfie. Her hair is in a tight bun, and she's in her black leotard, posing in front of a large mirror. And just like every other time I've laid eyes on her, my throat catches. The raw beauty, the large smile, the way I know she's nervously chewing her nails down to the quick ...

I go to text her back and let her know that I'm on my way, but my screen goes dark.

"Fuck," I mutter.

I tuck my phone away as I begin to shiver. It's cold for March, and I don't have a jacket. Inspecting the wound on my hand, I decide it doesn't need immediate attention. When a red Toyota pulls up, I assume it's my car, and I stumble into the back seat.

"Orion?" the driver asks, dark brows pinching as he takes in my soggy, drunken appearance.

"Yeah," I answer gruffly. "Hey man, do you have a phone charger?" I slur.

"No, sorry."

"'S okay."

"West Hollywood?" he asks, checking the address of Layla's audition on his GPS.

"Yeah."

The rest of the drive is quiet despite the pelting rain. I let my left cheek rest against the cool glass, dozing on

PROLOGUE
THE AUDITION

ORION

Seven Years Ago

Breaking glass pulls me out of my stupor. Someone says my name, but I hardly hear it. Everything sounds like it's underwater—hollow and vague. I know I should look around to make sure no one is hurt, but the room is spinning. I'm going to be violently ill if I move too quickly.

Lifting my head, I slowly track the bartender gesturing at me. I can't hear him. I only hear the beating of my own heart. He points at my hand as someone brushes up against the side of my body, lifting my arm. I startle at the sight of the blood and turn to face the person touching me. That's when I see the shattered glass around my seat and the lines of blood tracking down my forearm.

I pull away from the person helping me, stumbling

off the stool as my pulse whooshes in my ears. *How much did I drink?* My boots crunch glass as I make my way to the back of the bar. Each step is unsteady, the room spinning slightly as I push through the haze. My vision blurs at the edges, and the floor feels like it's shifting beneath me. I stumble over the threshold of the small bathroom, barely managing to catch myself on the sink. The lock clicks into place with more force than I intended, echoing in the tight, grimy space.

I can't tell if it's the alcohol or something darker clouding my thoughts, but I feel disoriented, as if the world has slowed down around me. When I close my eyes, the only sounds are my own labored breathing and the faint, distant hum of the sports game on the television out front—a reminder of the world still moving beyond this door while I struggle to keep my footing.

Someone pounds on the door.

"Orion, open the door," Gary yells, the handle rattling as he tries to break the door down. "We should get you checked out. Come on, man."

"Fuck off," I yell, stumbling as I turn on the tap. "I'm f-fine. Jus' going to clean it up."

Running the water, I clean my arm and pull out the shard of glass embedded in my palm. It doesn't feel like my arm. It feels like someone else's arm. Like I'm having an out-of-body experience.

I don't feel a single fucking thing.

Once the water runs clear, I turn the tap off and pat the thick cut with paper towels, pressing into the wound until the paper blooms red.

"Orion, I swear to God," Gary bellows, hammering on the door.

I grumble as I toss the paper towel and open the door. "'S okay," I tell him, patting his large chest with my good hand. "S-s-top worrying about me."

He sighs heavily, running a hand down his long beard. "I'm sorry, man. You've gotta leave."

"'S fine," I reply, nodding. "I have s-somewhere to be, anyway."

He follows me, and when I get back to my usual seat, the broken glass is gone—as is my drink.

"Where'd you put it?" I ask, slowly turning to face him and nearly falling over in the process.

"You're drunk off your fucking ass, Ravage. Go home. Sleep it off. I already told Scott to expect you."

I rub my mouth with my hand as anger begins to bloom inside me. "Scott."

"Yeah, man. Come on—"

"And why the fuck would you do that?" I ask, my voice cracking. "He already has enough fucking shit to deal with. His wife just *died*, asshole," I hiss.

His wife—my mom.

Technicalities.

Gary's face softens.

I fucking hate the look he's giving me. *Pity.* He pities me. Why the fuck would he pity me? It's not like we didn't know my mom was going to die. No, we had two years to get used to the idea. We all did. None of us were surprised when she started declining. None of us were surprised when the doctors told us there was nothing else they could do. None of us were surprised when she stopped walking or when she needed around-the-clock oxygen.

I'm already a burden to my brothers, Layla, and especially Scott, the man who married my mom ten years ago. He had rules about drinking and living under his roof, and I'd been breaking those rules a lot lately.

I want to scream all of this at him, but Gary is a decent guy. He's Scott's best friend, and I realize now that I should've gone somewhere else in Crestwood. Choosing the bar owned by someone who's known me since I was fourteen probably wasn't the smartest idea, considering I planned on getting rip-roaring drunk today.

Except it's hard to find a place that doesn't know me —either because of my father and the Ravage name or because of what recently happened to my mom.

"Listen," he says, his voice gentler now. "I get it. I really do."

Pressing my lips together, I glare at him. "You have no fucking idea, *Gary*."

"I do, actually. And I'm sorry for your loss—"

Before he can finish his sentence, I grab a nearby glass and throw it down onto the floor. Another person screams, and rage boils just beneath my skin.

Stop feeling. Push it down. Keep going until you don't feel a thing.

"You all really need t-to come up with a better s-slogan," I slur. "I'm so sorry for your loss. Your family is in my prayers. We're thinking about you during this difficult time. For fuck's s-sake, who came up with those?" I shout, stumbling backward.

Gary reaches out and takes my hand, but I can tell by his flared nostrils that he's pissed off. *Good.*

"I broke things too, kid. But you'll soon find out that while it can feel good to break something, it doesn't make up for the broken heart you get when you lose someone."

The instant the words are out of his mouth, I feel remorse for what I did. Not only did he know my mom well, but he also lost his wife a few years ago.

Of course he can relate, and here I am, acting like a fucking teenager throwing a tantrum.

Shame casts a web around me, suffocating me. It feels like every fucking thing is falling apart around me.

Every *single* thing.

I pull out of his grip and twist around, storming to the exit and shoving the door open. I don't turn around, but I keep walking down the street past all of the familiar shops and storefronts in downtown Crestwood. It doesn't matter that it's raining. I can't feel it—just like I can't feel the open wound on my palm.

I hate this. I hate everything about this town except for one person. The one thing that keeps me tethered to this earth is the one person who grounds me. My cheeks are hot and wet, and I realize I might be crying.

Fuck this.

Everything spins around me as I pull my phone out, and I have to steady myself on a nearby wall. After requesting a ride on my phone, I sit on a nearby bench.

My phone is almost dead, so I open the text that Layla sent a few minutes ago.

LAYLA

Wish me luck!

My heart skips several beats when I open the picture. It's a reflection selfie. Her hair is in a tight bun, and she's in her black leotard, posing in front of a large mirror. And just like every other time I've laid eyes on her, my throat catches. The raw beauty, the large smile, the way I know she's nervously chewing her nails down to the quick ...

I go to text her back and let her know that I'm on my way, but my screen goes dark.

"Fuck," I mutter.

I tuck my phone away as I begin to shiver. It's cold for March, and I don't have a jacket. Inspecting the wound on my hand, I decide it doesn't need immediate attention. When a red Toyota pulls up, I assume it's my car, and I stumble into the back seat.

"Orion?" the driver asks, dark brows pinching as he takes in my soggy, drunken appearance.

"Yeah," I answer gruffly. "Hey man, do you have a phone charger?" I slur.

"No, sorry."

"'S okay."

"West Hollywood?" he asks, checking the address of Layla's audition on his GPS.

"Yeah."

The rest of the drive is quiet despite the pelting rain. I let my left cheek rest against the cool glass, dozing on

and off. All I want to do is see her. All I need is ... *her*. As
we pull off the freeway, my injured hand begins to throb.
Great.

The driver pulls up to the large white building forty-
five minutes later, and I pull a couple hundred dollar bills
out, throwing it to him despite already paying for the
ride in my app. It's raining even heavier here, so I
stumble toward the awning. There are posters across the
double front doors, and it takes me a second to fully
process what they say.

The Paris School of Ballet: Auditions TODAY only.

I swallow as bile works up my throat. Paris. Which is
in fucking *France.* Shaking my head, I pull the double
doors open. Signs point to the waiting room, but I stand
near the doors to stay out of the way. When I pull my
phone out, the screen is black. *Fuck, I forgot.* Looking
around, I wonder if I should ask someone for a charger,
but then I decide to just stay put until Layla finishes. Her
audition is at four, which—according to the clock—is in
an hour. I'll see her when she comes around the front.

Pacing in front of the glass double doors, I watch the
traffic on Santa Monica Boulevard stop and go at the
nearby light. Despite still being drunk, my walking back
and forth helps with the nausea. I sit down after a while,
feeling shaky as everything begins to spin. Ballet dancers
come and go, most of them around Layla's age. None of
them notice me or care that I'm just some random drunk
dude hanging out at a dance audition for high schoolers.
Once the nausea passes, I stand again and look around.
It's now four fifteen, and despite knowing these audi-

tions can last hours, anxiety claws up my spine. What if she's already done and waiting for me somewhere else? *Maybe there's another exit.* I walk down a nondescript hallway. The arrows for the waiting room take me to a white door, and when I push it open, about fifteen young girls are doing all kinds of poses—but no Layla.

I back away and continue down the hallway. Murmured voices catch my attention, and I steady myself on the wall as I slowly walk closer. It's a mix of hushed French and British accents, and I'm just about to walk away when I hear one of them say Layla's name. Sneaking closer, I silently stand just outside of the door to try to understand what they're saying about her.

"... never make it in Europe, let alone Paris," a woman says disdainfully.

"Her credentials are impressive," a man says, his British accent low and droning.

"What good are her credentials when she doesn't look the part of a ballerina?" the first woman retorts, her tone disgusted.

I curl my fists and continue listening—my chest both aching for her and also burning with rage. *This is her dream, and these people are making fun of her?*

"Times are changing, Jean. I think we should watch her performance and see what she can offer."

"Times may be changing, but she's twenty pounds too heavy. Do you really think our male dancers will want to pick her up? Perhaps she could make the cut with diet and exercise, but she'd have to starve herself all summer. Did you see the audition song? It's uncultured and cheap. I suspect she'll have trouble fitting in with the elegance of the *Paris School of Ballet*, her weight notwithstanding."

The man sighs and murmurs something unintelligible, and I want to break this fucking door down and scream at them for insulting Layla.

Fuck this school. Layla deserves better.

With the alcohol from earlier still coursing through my veins, I somehow manage to find a back entrance to the audition stage. I'm just about to find a hiding place when a flash of red hair catches my attention.

The music starts—Layla's music—that is most fucking definitely *not* uncultured and cheap.

"Take Me to Church" by Hozier.

Pride fills me as I slowly walk closer to the side of the stage. She's worked so *fucking* hard for this. She's practiced for hundreds of hours in the tiny dance studio in Scott's house, using the techniques she's perfected since she was three. And it all leads to this pinnacle moment—this one audition.

My eyes find the judges—two men, two women.

They're hardly watching. Instead, one of the women shakes her head and starts quickly talking to one of the men.

I glare at them as my chest burns with anger. They don't deserve her. I take a step closer to the stage as the chorus begins, and Layla jumps and twirls into the air. Her leotard hugs every inch of her perfect body—her narrow hips, her small breasts, her long legs ... how can they not see how perfect she is? I take another step closer until I'm on the edge of the wing—just a foot away from exposing myself to the judges. The bright lights cause me to blink rapidly, and the music swells through the room. You can't even hear Layla landing on the stage floor. She'd practiced her landings for six months in order to do that. My eyes rove down to her feet, to her pointe shoes with ribbons criss-crossed tightly around her ankles.

I've always been in awe of how she does it—of how much she changes when she dances.

Gone is the insecure teenager, replaced by a confident professional who gets lost in the music. Her taut muscles hold her elegant form with every movement, and I lick my lips as she lands a few feet away from me, her body bent in half with her arms out to her sides. When she raises her head, the movement of me running a hand over my mouth must catch her attention because she snaps her eyes to mine, causing her to stall and miss her next move.

Fuck.

Instantly, pink blotches run down her neck to her exposed chest. Her chest rises and falls as her eyes widen, and it takes me two full seconds to realize that I fucked up.

Royally.

She's panting but otherwise not moving—just staring at me with a mix of outrage and surprise.

That's when I hear one of the judges make a tsking sound, and I lose control.

When I step forward onto the stage, the bright lights

practically blind me. The music swells as Layla's fists curl at her sides, and as I get closer, her nostrils flare.

"Sorry," she tells the judges, not looking away from me. "He's my stepbr—"

"Excuse me." The snobby one—Jean, I assume—shakes her head again and stands up.

"Don't do this," I say slowly.

"Ri," she growls, chest still heaving.

"Don't move to Paris." My voice cracks on the last word.

The words startle her, but before she can even rear her head back, the music stops completely.

"Excuse me," the woman repeats, her French accent thick and judgmental.

"Sorry, please give me one second to start over," Layla says gracefully. Her eyes begin to water as she glares at me again. "Leave. *Now*," she urges, her voice low enough for only me to hear.

I hold my hands up, but in doing so, I stumble to the side. *Fuck.*

Her eyes widen even more before she lets out a cruel laugh. "Oh my God. You're drunk, aren't you?" she whispers, though it sounds more like the hiss of a viper.

"Layla," I whisper, an unknown emotion filling every cell in my body. I can't place what it is. It's a mix of guilt, shame, and desperation for her to stay. To not move five thousand miles away from me. *Especially* not when these fucking assholes can't even appreciate her. "You can do better than this," I say, even though I know the words are ash on my tongue.

The Paris School of Ballet is the most elite dance school in the world.

And they were making fun of her.

I can't tell her that, though. I'd never be able to forgive myself if I did.

If *I* caused her pain.

At least right now, she just thinks I'm drunk and stupid. I'd gladly take the blame to keep her from getting hurt. If she knew what they said about her, she'd give up. She'd get more restrictive with her food. It would break her because I'd heard her mutter those same sentiments about her body after eating.

"We're going to have to ask you to leave," the man bellows from the judges' table.

"Fine," I growl, looking at him. "I'll go."

"Both of you," the woman adds, crossing her arms.

Layla lets out a tiny gasp before looking at the judges' table. "Please. I can start over—"

"I'm afraid the audition is over, with or without this blatant interruption," the woman says simply, looking back and forth between us. "Not only is your song choice unconventional and inappropriate but you simply don't fit the image of a Parisian ballet dancer."

Shame, embarrassment, and anger flit across Layla's face. Tears gather in her eyes, and she storms past me. My reflexes must be slow because even though I reach out for her, I miss grabbing her wrist by half a second. Turning back to the judges, I narrow my eyes.

"You're going to regret this decision for the rest of your life."

I don't wait for their response. Following Layla through the backstage door, I stop walking and stumble into a nearby garbage can just as she whirls around and snarls at me.

"You ruined everything," she hisses, tears streaming down her face.

"I'm sorry," I tell her, stepping closer. Her smell—*God, she always smells so fucking good, like wild strawberries*—invades my senses, and I use my hand to press her body into the wall.

She's all skin and bones—*and would collapse if she lost another twenty pounds.*

I've taken time to learn about her restrictive eating habits, trying to understand the emotional and psychological challenges involved. I wanted to be more informed. I wanted to be compassionate. And I know her well enough to know exactly what triggers her—and that's any negative comment about her body. I've been so mindful of avoiding those topics or situations, and I try to create a safer environment for her.

The thought of her hearing those words when I know how sensitive she is cuts somewhere deep and dark inside me, and I'm fucking *glad* she wasn't able to audition. Fuck them—fuck all those people.

To me, she's flawless.

"Sorry?" she cries, her voice cracking. "You fucking asshole." She shoves me, but I hardly move. I'm too surprised. In the ten years I've known her, I've only heard her swear a couple of times.

"You never would've been happy there," I tell her,

even though I know my words are empty. *Trust me,* I want to say. *You deserve better than a company that would tell you to starve to death.*

She huffs out an anguished sound. "This audition was *everything* to me, Ri. You knew that," she sobs. "And instead of waiting for me like a respectable brother, you arrive drunk and cause a scene—"

"I'm not your brother," I murmur, mesmerized by the way the black mascara tracks down her pale skin. Mesmerized by her freckles and delicate nose, her long lashes, her full lips …

I don't ever want her to think of me as a brother. As I dip my head so our faces are closer, her sharp air intake is all I need to know.

"No, you're not," she hisses, baring her teeth. "You're *nothing.*"

She's trembling now, making me wonder what she would do if I pressed my lips against hers—if I showed her just how *not* brotherly I could be. Her eyes dip briefly to my lips, and it's all the confirmation I need.

She feels it, too.

I thought I was going fucking crazy. We were as close as real siblings, and these feelings didn't start until about a year ago. But of course, being six years her senior, I shoved them aside.

Her pupils bloom dark, and I scrape my nails against the cinderblock wall behind her to keep from touching her.

"I hate you," she says, her voice shaking.

"No, you don't," I murmur, letting my face dip an inch lower. "But it would be easier if you did."

"Did you interrupt my audition because you're drunk or because you don't want me to go to Paris?"

I let out a soft chuckle. "Both."

"You need help," she says through gritted teeth, but I don't miss the way her eyes flick to my lips so, *so* briefly.

"I know," I say quietly.

The anger slowly leaves her, and the tears that wet her cheeks begin to dry as she sniffles. Looking up at me, she has something in her expression that I can't place— an exasperating war wages behind her beautiful hazel eyes. Her eyes dance between mine, and the crease in her forehead deepens.

Don't kiss her. Don't do it—

"Do you really want to move to Paris?" I ask her.

"Yes," she whispers. "I do."

Guilt heats my cheeks, and I let out a long, slow breath. "You can try again—"

"No, I can't. It was my last chance for a callback and getting an invite to the private auditions." Her voice cracks, and she breaks eye contact to look down. *Fuck,* I'm an asshole.

"Next year," I tell her, digging my nails into the wall even harder to keep from brushing a small strand of hair away from her eyes. "Next year, you'll kill it, Layla."

Her eyes begin to water, and when she finds my eyes again, I see the expression on her face for exactly what it is—resignation and sadness.

Before I can react, she shoves me backward. I stumble

back unsteadily, and then she walks away from me. My hand throbs where I cut it because I'm starting to sober up, but I ignore it.

"Layla," I call out, jogging after her.

She twists around, and *fuck,* fresh tears flow down her cheeks. Her hands are clenched at her sides, and her face is scrunched with despair.

"Stay away from me, Orion. I never want to see you again."

It feels like someone's stabbing me in the chest— repeatedly—with a serrated knife, pulling my nerves out with each withdrawal. My hand even moves to my chest to make sure I'm not *actually* being stabbed.

"You don't mean that," I tell her, my voice a little bit too loud.

"I do. How can I ever forgive you for this? I should've known ... all you do is drink and think about yourself. You're the most selfish person I know. I've been working toward this moment my whole life." Her chest's heaving. "It was three minutes, Ri," she whimpers, dejected. "Three minutes to prove something to them. And yeah, maybe they would've rejected me, but at least I would've *tried*. I'd have given it my all. But you ruined it. Just like you ruin everything." Her face crumples.

Fuck, the pain is worse now.

I want to defend myself.

I want to tell her she's wrong—that I'm not selfish because I think about her way more often than I think about myself.

I want to tell her that it all worked out in the end because they were rude as fuck, and she deserves better.

I want to tell her that if I hadn't overheard them or seen their judgmental faces, I would've hidden in the shadows and waited for her to finish.

But I suppose that wasn't my decision, and now I'll face the consequences.

"It's pathetic," she adds, lips curling. "You're twenty-four. You're supposed to be an adult, and instead, you're getting drunk on a Tuesday afternoon." I clench my jaw and look down at the floor, knowing exactly what's coming next. And it's made worse coming from *her*. "I know your mom died three months ago. I know you've been having difficulty keeping a job because of it. I get it. I loved her too, Orion. She raised me. Out of everyone, *I get it*," she adds, almost pleading with me.

"Stop," I whisper, my voice hoarse.

"That's why this hurts so much," she adds, and I snap my eyes up to look at her. "Because out of everyone in the world, I thought you had my back. I thought I had your support."

"You do," I tell her, taking a step toward her.

You have more than my support. You have everything I can give. As the alcohol slowly burns through my system, I get more sober with each word out of her mouth.

She steps back—*away from me.*

"No, I *thought* I had your support. But I was wrong," she says glumly.

"Layla, I'm sorry about today—"

"It's not just today."

Her declaration causes my heart to actually stop, fluttering for a second and causing me to sway on my feet.

"What the fuck do you mean?" I ask, growling the words out.

She sobs and covers her mouth. "I can't do this. I looked past everything that happened with Derek—"

"Derek? You mean the guy who *assaulted* you?" I grit out.

"You put him into a coma for three months," she shrieks. "It's not healthy, Orion."

I grind my teeth together as I take a deep breath. "What are you saying, then?"

She shifts her weight and crosses her arms, looking down at the floor. "I meant what I said earlier. I don't ever want to see you again."

Fuck. Anything but that.

"Look me in the eye and say it," I command, curling my fists. "I dare you."

She cries harder. "This isn't easy for me, you know. You're my best friend. You're more than just my step—"

"Say. It," I grit out, shaking. "If you're going to make such a large declaration, at least have the courage to say it loudly."

Her face crumples again as she looks up at me with large, tear-filled eyes. "I can't do this anymore. I can't be your friend while you ruin your life. I can't keep excusing your unhinged behavior. Get your freaking life together, Orion."

I wince and swipe at my mouth. "It's going to be pretty hard to avoid me when we live under the same roof." My nostrils flare as I shake my head. "You know what? I'll make it easier for you. Consider me gone," I tell her, ignoring the way my voice trembles.

Her expression is indifferent, and that feels worse than her telling me she never wants to see me again. I expected anguish or regret—but instead, she just watches me as I take a step backward.

"Goodbye, Layla."

She lets out a cracked sob. "Goodbye, Orion."

I turn and walk away. I have to actively place one foot in front of the other, over and over and over, until I'm pushing a fire door open.

An alarm sounds behind me, but I continue walking down Santa Monica Boulevard, feeling numb.

Feeling *nothing*.

I don't even attempt to stay away from more alcohol. Walking through the doors of a bar, I sit down on the stool and order a triple whiskey. My breaths are coming in quick pants, and my hands shake enough to make the amber liquid slosh over the side when I bring it to my lips.

"Another," I tell the bartender.

He nods and grabs the bottle again, not caring that pretty soon, I may have to be carried out via ambulance.

Let her hate me.

It's better than her ever hearing those unkind words.

Let. Her. Hate. Me.

And I will drink to cauterize the wounds.

For as long as it fucking takes to erase the burning pain in my soul.

CHAPTER ONE
THE DINNER

Layla

Present, Seven Years Later

"That's it, Olivia. Spine straight. Good. Lift your arms higher," I say slowly, observing my student's posture. Her wiry arm begins to tremble, and I clap once. Everyone drops their arms. "Very good. I know it hurts after a while, but I promise, it gets better," I say gently.

"Miss Rivers?" Olivia asks, brows furrowed. "Is it snack time yet? I'm hungry."

I press my lips together as I squat down to meet my twelve-year-old student face-to-face.

"How do you feel about chocolate?" I smirk as I pull a chocolate bar out of the pocket of my zipped-up hoodie.

All the kids squeal, and I smile as we walk over to the bench. They're restless now that they know they're getting a treat, and I chuckle as I dole out a generous amount for each of them, followed by string cheese. Growing bodies need all the nourishment they can get.

"My mom says I'm not supposed to eat chocolate anymore," Jenicka says, brown eyes downcast.

I sigh and crouch down in front of her. "You are a strong athlete. You practice some of the hardest dances in the world. Your body needs to replace all of the lost energy, Jen. Did you know that Olympic athletes need to eat extra food when they compete?"

This gets everyone's attention. "A lot of extra food, in fact," I tell them. "Chocolate has carbohydrates, which our body needs to perform well."

"My mom says carbs are bad," Olivia says timidly.

"They can be for some people, such as if you have uncontrolled blood sugar issues or are allergic to wheat. But for the majority of us, carbohydrates feed our brains and muscles."

I could continue. I could tell them how female athletes are looked at differently—specifically dancers and especially ballet dancers. Where male athletes are lauded for eating a lot to perform, females are told to stay thin, to restrict, to make themselves *smaller*.

And I'm so sick of little girls getting told this message.

"Some people may say that because that's what they were taught," I tell Olivia seriously. "Do you remember what I told you all last week?"

"Don't make ourselves smaller for other people," Jenicka responds, happily chewing on her chocolate.

"That's right. A lot of silly people will insist that you

have to be less, but I'm telling you now that you can be *more*. You can be big and loud. You can take up space. In fact, it's your right to do so. Do you understand?"

Twelve identical nods tell me that I'm at least—*hopefully*—getting through to them. There's no way in hell I'd let these babies think the things I did about myself at their age. I went through hell and back combating those thoughts, and I'm finally in a good place with food. I won't tolerate any negative talk in my class. I just have to hope they're taking some of what I teach them back home. If I could hand them a shield from the world, I would. But since I can't protect them, my words will have to suffice.

Olivia's and Jenicka's moms could shove that chocolate right up their behinds, for all I cared.

As the kids finish their snacks, I walk over to my purse and pull my phone out. Zoe and Remy have been blowing up our group chat, and I quickly tell them that I'll respond once this intensive is over in a couple of hours. I glance up to check on my students, but they're all still happily eating and talking in excited whispers.

I love this age group—twelve to thirteen. They're still young enough to be optimistic and sweet but old enough that I can get real with them sometimes. I'm sure they won't think I'm cool in a couple of years, but they adore me for now. And I'll hold on to that as long as I can.

I look down at my phone, seeing as I have a minute to let them finish eating. A text from my dad comes through just as I'm scrolling through my favorite dark romance Facebook group, so I open it really quick.

DAD

Still on for dinner tonight? I'm making
steak.

> Sure. Sounds great! Be there around 6.
> Just need to shower after intensive.

DAD

Okay, sweetheart. I invited Orion too. It'll
be nice to have you both under one roof
again.

My breath catches like it always does whenever
anyone mentions him.

> That's fine.

I lock my phone and put it away, taking a couple of
calming breaths. I haven't seen Orion since Zoe and
Liam's wedding—my best friend and Orion's oldest
brother—who got married last year. It just so happened
to be the same wedding where we kissed for about ten
seconds at the rehearsal dinner.

That's what I get for drinking too much tequila.

Somehow, despite vowing to stay away from him,
we'd managed to circle each other like toxic sharks for
seven years, both out for blood. I still hadn't forgiven him
for the audition he ruined, which made for volatile
reunions whenever we were together. If we didn't end up
arguing, it was something else—such as him punching
my date or showing up at my friends' parties unan-
nounced. It wasn't healthy, and I hated what our relationship had become. If we weren't bickering or glaring

at each other, we were usually both quiet and brooding around the other.

Except when we kissed.

But that was just the tequila. It meant *nothing*.

After returning to my students, I guide them through turning preparations before demonstrating pirouettes. It's not every day that a professional dancer can teach them. Though I hardly consider myself professional despite dancing for the Los Angeles Ballet last season and then recently being cast by the Pacific Ballet Company as Odette in *Swan Lake* a few months ago. It still seems surreal that I get to do this as my job.

I'm a work in progress when it comes to being proud of myself and my accomplishments.

All the dancers for the Pacific Ballet Company are on hiatus until the next season starts in a couple of weeks, so I'm currently spending my days volunteering to teach ballet intensives for kids.

"Miss Rivers?" Bradleigh, a girl in my class, says quietly, crossing her legs and arms.

"What's up?"

She shuffles her feet. "Is it okay if I come to class in a t-shirt over my leotard next week?"

I furrow my brows. "Of course." I don't continue, instead waiting for an explanation if she chooses to share one.

Bradleigh started the class two years ago, and she went by a different name back then.

She uncrosses her arms a bit. "Thanks. It's just until my mom can get me my medicine."

I smile. "Whatever makes you comfortable. Okay?"

She nods. "Okay. Thanks," she answers, seeming brighter than before.

She joins the others, and I feel silly for not considering her comfort. Of course she might want to cover herself up right now, especially since puberty is hitting them all around now.

Secretly, Bradleigh is my favorite student—resilient, talented, and kind. She's alluded to having a hard time at school sometimes because of how she identifies, yet even at twelve, she remains positive and willing to learn.

She's also the only student who signed up for all my intensives through the summer.

Checking the clock, I see that we're nearly at the end of class, so I clap my hands three times to get their attention.

"That's the end of class. Please practice your pirouettes and balancés. You're doing great, so be sure to remember that, too."

"Thanks, Miss Rivers," they all say at the same time.

"What's our mantra?" I ask, holding a hand behind my ear.

"My body is unique and beautiful just the way it is," they shout.

Grinning, I clap. "Wonderful. Have a good weekend, everyone."

Everyone turns to me for révérence. Then they file out of the studio, and I follow them, making a beeline for Olivia's and Jenicka's moms, who happen to be friends.

"May I have a word with you both?" I ask.

They smile. Jenicka's mom says, "Sure. They looked great today."

Oh good, a positive. That helps.

"They did. They've worked so hard. I'm so proud of them," I say genuinely.

"How can we help?" Olivia's mom asks.

I actively have to keep myself from wringing my hands together because confrontation like this makes me uncomfortable. However, for the sake of my students, I have to do it.

Both moms are young—they can't be much older than me. I have to hope that it was just an honest mistake.

"First, I love having both girls in this group. Their enthusiasm is infectious, and they're so talented. I thought I'd ask about something they both said when I served them a piece of chocolate earlier." They look between each other before turning back to face me, and I school my face into gentle concern. "Olivia said that she's not allowed to eat chocolate, and Jenicka mentioned that carbs are bad."

Jenicka's mom winces. "I didn't think she'd heard that. I'm on a diet and was talking to a friend about it."

I smile. "I understand. With little kids especially, we have to be mindful of how we talk about food. They hear everything," I add, rolling my eyes. Both moms laugh, which is a good sign.

"And we're just trying to limit sugar," Olivia's mom says. "I didn't mean she could *never* have it." She seems mortified.

I nod. "I know you're doing your best," I assure them. After all, if they think I'm attacking them, they might not be receptive to learning and doing better. I've taken many nutrition classes over the years, so I feel well-versed on the topic. "Would it be okay to send you both resources for how to talk about food in front of children?" They both nod enthusiastically. "Great. I'll send it over tonight."

"Thanks, Layla, that would be helpful," Olivia's mom says.

"Yeah, thank you. See you next time," Jenicka's mom adds.

"See you both next class," I say, watching as my students filter out of the dance studio, checking the clock. I have an hour to get home, feed Sparrow, and walk to Dad's house. It's convenient living two blocks away from him in Los Feliz.

After tidying the studio, I slip into my flats, lock up, and head down to the parking garage in the studio's basement. Looking around, I hold my pepper spray and walk to my BMW X3. It's my pride and joy—something I bought used, in cash, with my own money. I don't make a great salary, but last year, I was lucky to get a mortage on a fixer-upper listed well under the market rate. I'm financially comfortable, so I count it as a win.

It's a cold day for March, and despite seldom raining in LA, of course it decides to pour the entire drive home. The traffic is horrendous, and by the time I get to my two-bedroom bungalow, I have about fifteen minutes to get ready.

Hopping out of my car, I jog to the door and unlock it. My cozy house greets me, and I relax instantly. My eyes skim over the houseplants and fairy lights, as well as the small fireplace and reading nook nestled along the back window.

Because I live alone, I turned my guest bedroom into a library with built-in shelves. I've been slowly organizing the titles by author name, but it's a daunting task I've been putting off since I moved in last year. As a self-professed bookworm, I have over a thousand books, and I spend almost all of my free time at home, getting lost in a new world.

The bungalow is small—just under 800 square feet —but I converted a small studio in the backyard into a dance studio for practicing.

Despite being perfect for me, I've made minor changes, such as the light pink wall color in the library and the flowers I planted all around the perimeter of the sage-green exterior.

It's my oasis—my happy place.

And seeing as how I loathe dating, I'll probably die here all alone as an old cat lady.

A low-pitched yowl sounds through the 1930s cottage, and I smile as I squat down to pet my ragdoll cat, Sparrow. I named him that when I was a teenager and obsessed with Jack Sparrow. It didn't help that he'd had an eye infection for a few weeks as a kitten and looked like a pirate with one eye swollen closed.

He's an old man now, but he's the best part of my day.

"Hi, Row Row," I croon, setting my purse down and walking into my small kitchen to feed him. "I'm sorry, but I have to go to Dad's house for dinner. I'll be back later, okay?"

An urgent meow is the only response I get. I bang around the small wooden cabinet that houses his food, and as I set the wet food down for him, he purrs appreciatively. I pet his thick fur, smiling down at him for a second. He's *so* fluffy—he practically gets swallowed up by his fur until I get him groomed in the summer months.

Standing, I grab a glass from one of the floating shelves and fill it with water. This kitchen is what sold me on the house. Everything had been restored to its former glory. Whoever owned the house before me took great care in keeping the house's character, which included the exposed brick behind the black vintage stove. I *loved* this house, and now that I'd stuffed a plant in every free crevice and corner, it felt like I was walking into nature whenever I came home.

After finishing my glass of water, I set it down and walk to my bathroom, undressing quickly. The leotard and skirt end up in a pile on the tiled floor as I start the shower—mounted above the restored claw-foot tub—and as it heats up, I turn to face myself in the mirror.

"You are beautiful. You are perfect just the way you are. Food is nourishment, not the enemy."

I inhale and let my eyes drag down the reflection of my naked body, telling myself out loud all the things I appreciate about my body today—such as how strong I feel and how my hair just so happened to dry nicely, with the waves cascading down my shoulders and arms.

When I'm finished, I take the world's quickest shower without getting my hair wet before pulling on a baggy cream-colored sweater and a pair of wide-leg jeans. I swipe some moisturizer on my face and take my contacts out, donning my round, wire-framed glasses.

Since it's raining, I pull my hair up into a clip and slip into a pair of platform UGG slides. When I'm finished, I clean Sparrow's face off. If I don't, his smelly food will get everywhere, thanks to his fur. He meows and rubs against my legs as I wash my hands.

"Be a good boy, okay?" I tell him, grabbing my purse and opening the door.

The rain has stopped, but it's still cold for LA, so I grab my long camel coat and pull it on as I step outside. Closing the door, I begin the trek to my dad's house, only remembering that Orion will be there as his parked bike comes into view in the driveway.

"Crap," I mutter, looking down at my casual, baggy outfit. Shaking my head, I stand taller. "You're not here to impress him," I tell myself.

Taking a deep breath and faking a confident, neutral expression, I walk up to the front door and open it. My father's booming voice resounds through the house. I take my coat off and drop my purse onto the chair by the door, quietly walking toward the kitchen.

My dad has his back to me, and the smell of fried meat fills the air. He normally uses the grill out back, but since it's raining, he's using the stove. He's in his usual printed button-up—this one with bright purple hibiscus flowers—and cargo shorts. I let my eyes wander to the man standing against the counter beside him, and my mouth goes dry.

Honestly, *how* is it possible that Orion looks better every single time I see him? It's unfair.

And frankly, it's inconvenient.

It's much easier to hate someone when they don't look like every dark romance book boyfriend I've ever been obsessed with over the years.

Short, dark brown hair that's tousled in a way that makes it seem like he makes zero effort yet completely complements his sharp cheekbones, straight nose, and full lips. His thick eyebrows are defined and slightly arched, giving him a villainous look and framing his face to give him a commanding presence. He's wearing a dark gray thermal pushed up to his elbows, black pants, and motorcycle boots. Whorls of black ink snake down to his left hand, and I don't know how it's possible, but he somehow looks even more jacked than the last time I saw him.

His muscles pull on the fabric of his thermal shirt, and I give myself a second to admire his narrow waist and muscular thighs. The way the muscles fill out the pants is—*to use a term from my romance books*—something that makes my heart skip a beat.

Just as I move my eyes back up to Orion's face, his lips quirk up slightly, and he slowly turns to face me with darkened pupils.

Kill me now ...

He totally caught me checking him out.

I clear my throat and walk into the room with my arms crossed.

"Hello," I say to him, pressing my lips together in my best impression of a scowl.

"Hello."

My dad turns around and grins. "La-La," he says, wiping his hands before opening his arms for a hug.

I smile and walk over to him, letting my cheek rest against his shoulder for a second too long.

Nothing is like a hug from your dad.

He's all I had when I was really young, considering my mom left us when I was two. Well, until he met Felicity, Orion's mom. Since she passed, my dad's been … okay. Alone and bored, but okay. I'm just glad I live nearby so I can see him a few times a week.

"Hi, Dad," I say, pulling away.

"I hope you're hungry." He gestures to the three massive steaks popping and sizzling next to him.

"Starving," I practically moan. It's true—I'd eaten lunch, but that was hours ago. I glance back at Orion, and his eyes snap up from my legs.

"How are you?" he asks, crossing his arms.

I do the same and lean against the opposite counter, arching a brow. "Fine. You?" I say politely. I somehow manage to keep my voice even despite the fact that my heart is galloping a mile a minute.

Did he get taller? Has he always been this tall? Is that even possible?

I'm tall for a girl—nearly five foot nine—but he practically towers over me at six foot four. And since he seems to have consumed *only* Goliath-approved protein powder for the past three months, he also seems bigger than that now.

"Yeah, I'm good," he answers, running a hand behind his neck.

His shirt pulls up slightly, exposing a sliver of his abdomen. My eyes practically twitch as I keep them on the counter above his left shoulder. I should *not* be thinking these things about him.

Don't look, don't look, don't look—

"Ri, can you grab the beers and bring them to the table?" my dad asks as he plates the steaks.

Orion smirks at me before he pushes off the counter and walks to the fridge. Once he's gone, I inhale three times rapidly, like I've somehow forgotten how to breathe.

"La-La, can you grab the potatoes and green beans?"

"Sure."

I grab the bowl of creamy mashed potatoes and the platter of green beans sautéed with garlic and olive oil. My mouth fills with saliva, and I take my usual place at our decades-old dining table. My dad sits at the head, and I sit to his right while Orion sits to his left.

Across from me.

Just as I sit down, he kicks my shoe.

I glare up at him, and he sits up straighter with that same smug smirk as before.

The thing with Orion is that he *knows* exactly which of my buttons to push to get me to lose my cool. I can't decide if he's just that much of an asshole or if he's trying to get my attention for another reason. He only has one mode around me, and that's unhinged.

Jealous, cocky, brutish ...

I've seen him with others, and I know he's only like this around me. It must be that we grew up together. Despite not talking, he defaults to playful brother behavior every time we're together.

Zoe loves him, and I've seen the way his brothers talk about him. How my *dad* talks about him. But for whatever reason, he acts out around me.

It drives me insane.

Mostly because he's *so* hot and cold. He punched my date once for getting too handsy, and I didn't see him again for months. When we kissed at Zoe and Liam's rehearsal dinner, it was ten seconds of insane passion, followed by him pushing me away and leaving the venue early. I think most of that was because I was inebriated, but still. Nothing after both instances—nada. Not a call or text. It's not that I wanted him to reach out to me after those events. Seven years ago, I made it very clear that I didn't want him to be a part of my life anymore, so I don't know why I was surprised when he was doing what I asked him to do—to leave me alone.

It's just that sometimes he looks at me like he either hates me or wants to push me against the wall and ruin me forever.

Shivers work down my spine at the thought.

I don't have long to dwell on the complexities of my

Orion Ravage, however, because a second later, my dad plops a steak on my plate.

We all engage in casual conversation as we help ourselves to the sides. I grab a beer and ask my dad about his new prediabetes regimen. He was diagnosed last year, which meant that he's now working out at the local gym four times a week, as well as watching what he eats. It's also why I took a nutrition class to help him plan his meals.

As I chew the delicious steak, my dad asks Orion about his soon-to-be newly opened club. Orion stays mum about it, only saying it's different from anything else he's ever done. That piques my curiosity, and I make a mental note to ask Zoe about it the next time we have a girls' night.

"And how's ballet intensive?" my dad asks.

I can feel Orion's eyes on me as I finish chewing. "It's great. The kids are so grown this year, and they've improved a lot since last year."

"They're lucky to have you as their teacher," my dad replies, smiling at me.

"Thanks, Dad."

I avoid glancing at Orion.

"And when do you return to PBC?" he continues, referring to Pacific Ballet Company.

"In two weeks."

"Well, put me down for a ticket for every Saturday show."

I beam at him. "You know you don't have to come every weekend, right?"

He scoffs. "Please. I'm retired now. What else do I have to do with my time?"

"And what will happen when I go somewhere else? Are you going to follow me?"

At this, I see Orion stiffen in my peripheral. I let my eyes rove over to his face for the first time since we sat down, and his eyes bore into mine with such intensity that I nearly choke on my mouthful of mashed potatoes.

He holds eye contact while he raises his water glass, sipping slowly so that I have no choice but to watch as it bobs down his throat. He has a bit of scruff shadowing his jaw and neck—much shorter than he used to wear it —and it takes me a second to realize he's drinking water. *Not* alcohol.

In fact, I can't remember the last time I saw him with a drink. Even at Zoe and Liam's wedding a few months ago, he had a bottle of sparkling water.

"We'll see. Maybe Ri and I will fly out to whatever exotic place you'll be next. Austria. France. Sweden."

I huff a laugh as I sip my beer, finally breaking eye contact with the person I once considered a brother by circumstance.

"I think Orion has enough on his plate."

I allow another look at him, and he's watching me with narrowed eyes. He looks like he wants to say something—like he has a secret he's dying to spill—but he shrugs and takes another sip of water.

"Whatever you want to do, Scotty," he drawls, looking at me before looking at my dad.

They start talking about Orion's newest bike—a

sleek black something or other out front. My dad rode
Harleys before I was born, so they've bonded over bikes.
Once we all finish eating, and before I can protest, my
dad stands up and begins clearing the table.

As he leaves the room, I feel Orion's eyes on me
again.

"Ice cream?" he asks, cocking his head. "I brought
your favorite."

He knows strawberry is my favorite and one of the
only things that can win me over. Many of our childhood
fights were solved with a sneaky cone of the creamy pink
ice cream.

"Okay. Um, I'll get it," I say quickly. *Anything* so that I
don't have to be alone with him.

Inside the kitchen, I pull down two bowls. "Are you
having ice cream, Dad?" I ask, though I already know
what he's going to say.

"No thanks, La-La. Sugars are still on the downslide,
so I'd like to keep it that way," he adds, giving me a rueful
but jaunty smile.

"You should be proud of yourself," I tell him, placing
a few generous scoops in each bowl for Orion and me. "I
know how much you love sugar, so this can't be easy."

He walks over to me and kisses the top of my head. "I
do, but I love the idea of watching my grandchildren
grow up even more."

I snort. "That's presumptuous. I don't even know if I
want kids, Dad."

"Orion does, so at least I'll get some with him," he
adds casually.

I go still at his words. They've had conversations about kids? I never would've guessed that Orion wanted any. For so long, he could barely hold down a job. He was the epitome of a party animal, never even coming close to settling down. In fact, I recently ran into him with a leggy blonde while I was out with Zoe.

"Orion wants kids?" My dad nods and begins to whistle, quickly rinsing our plates off and loading them into the dishwasher. "Leave those. I'll do them when I'm done with my ice cream."

"Nah, I have nothing else to do. It makes me happy to feed and care for you again."

I smile warmly and pick the two bowls up. "Okay. I still wish you'd accept Orion's offer to pay for a house cleaner."

Orion and I hardly ever talk unless we have to, but trying to get some help around the house for my dad is one thing we agree on.

He guffaws. "And what would I do while they're here? Sit on my goddamn ass and watch them vacuum? I don't think so. I promise, I'm fine."

As we walk back into the dining room, I see Orion texting someone on his phone. He quickly locks and pockets it, and I set his bowl down a little too hard.

I swear I hear him chuckle under his breath.

He and my dad talk some more about motorcycles, and then somehow, they get on the subject of a family vacation we'd taken to Yellowstone when Felicity was still alive. It was a tradition. Every year, the four of us would pick a place somewhere in the continental US and go for a week around Easter. He argued that most places were warm enough to visit then, but not summertime hot. We'd trek to places like the Grand Canyon, Boston, New Orleans, Sedona, or Montana.

Those trips were some of my favorite memories growing up.

I remember feeling like a *real* family when Orion and Felicity joined my dad and me. And having four bonus siblings by marriage who no longer lived at home? Even better. Being young without a mother figure was hard on me, and I envied all my friends who had a traditional two-parent household. Not that gender mattered—one of my best friends growing up had two moms. I felt like I was missing out on many things growing up. My dad worked long hours at the bar with his best friend, Gary, and I craved a parent picking me up from school instead of going to after-school care. I craved someone to sing me lullabies and braid my hair. My dad tried both, and though it was a valiant effort, he never quite succeeded.

And then he met Felicity, and a few short months later, I was suddenly a part of this wonderful nuclear family.

I loved Felicity like a mother—it was hard not to. She was beautiful, devoted, and kind. I don't exactly know what happened between her and Charles Ravage, Orion's father. I just know it was a bad situation. After having five sons, she was grateful to raise me.

I finally had someone to sing me lullabies and braid my hair.

That is, until we all lost her when I was eighteen.

But I had her for ten lovely years.

I swallow as I look over at my dad, who is talking animatedly about how I'd gotten stung by a bee when it flew into the car when I was sixteen.

Turns out, I'm allergic to bees.

"Oh, you should've seen Orion's face. I swear, he was white as a sheet the entire ambulance ride to the hospital. I thought he was going to pass out."

I look over at Orion, and he's running a finger over the rim of his glass.

"I don't remember that," I say slowly.

"Sweetheart, he was worried sick—quite literally, if I remember correctly."

"Yes, well, it's not every day that you see your step —" He swallows. "You were struggling to breathe."

Mixed feelings surge through me. He was always attentive growing up, but I guess I only remember the drinking and the way we push each other's buttons now.

He looks away pointedly, and my pulse begins to spin when the hand resting on the table curls once.

"Aw, it was sweet," my dad says, oblivious.

He has no idea what happened between us. I've never told him—never told anyone, in fact. Zoe and Remy have an idea of what occurred, but no one knows what actually happened at that audition.

It's for the best.

After my dad and I chat a bit more, I head home early. It's been a long day, and my whole body aches from the repetitive movements I had to do for the students today. I've also been slacking on keeping myself in shape, so starting tomorrow, I'll have to wake up early to get my practice in. If I don't, I won't be able to play Princess Odette in *Swan Lake*—a coveted role I worked my ass off for.

As I say goodbye to Dad and grab my purse and coat, I see Orion whisper something to him and follow me to the foyer.

"Um, what are you doing?" I ask as he reaches around and opens the door for me as I slip my second arm into my coat.

"Walking you home," he says matter-of-factly.

I roll my eyes and look up at him. "Thanks, but I'm perfectly fine walking alone." He smells like... *home*. This close, I can see the yellow specks in his crystal-blue eyes.

His jaw hardens, and he nods once. "Fine."

I push the door open and begin walking, huffing out a frustrated sigh as I go. It's not until I'm a few houses down that I hear a rumbling sound behind me. Twisting around, I see Orion slowly trailing me on his motorcycle.

"I said I was fine," I yell, glaring at him.

He flips the visor up, and I get a peek at his playful smirk. "You said I couldn't walk you home. You never said I couldn't follow you some other way." He snaps the visor back in place and continues trailing me.

And that *freaking* helmet ... combined with that fitted leather jacket and his thick thighs hugging the seat of his bike ...

I've been watching too many hot biker videos and imagining Orion with his tattoos and that helmet, gripping his handles, flexing those muscles, watching those veins in his arms pop.

I curl my fists inside my pockets as I walk up my driveway, not even looking back at Orion as I let myself inside.

The roar of his bike reverberates through the neighborhood, and I smile as I lock my door and reach down to pet Sparrow.

"What a jerk," I whisper, thinking of my stepbrother.

CHAPTER TWO

THE INFERNO

Orion

My boots thud heavily against the wood floors as I do a final walk-through of my new club. Neil, the builder—an older man in his fifties—waits patiently in the corner of the room.

Though he'd never admit he's nervous, his feet shuffling every few seconds tells me something entirely different. Despite using him for my other two locations, the Ravage last name still makes people jumpy. Stella, my sister-in-law married to my second-eldest brother, Miles, had done a good job telling everyone how wonderful our family was to anyone who would listen. She'd smoothed over a massive public relations shit show a couple of years ago, but our reputation still tainted almost every aspect of our lives.

"This is great," I tell Neil as I face him.

He visibly sags and lets out a quick breath, like he was expecting me to say something else.

I'm used to it now, but I hate that my family name still weighs on me, even today.

"Amazing." He bends down and grabs his work bag. All his workers have left already upon completing the club, and he gives it a once-over. "It's a strange setup for a bar," he muses, completely aloof as his eyes wander upstairs before they shoot to the door that leads down to the basement. *That's because it's not a bar,* I think. "But seeing as this is number three, you must know what you're doing."

I chuckle. "Or maybe I've just gotten lucky thus far." I glance at the basement door. "This one will be a bit different from the other places."

"Right. Well, I'll have Barbara send the bill on Monday. Maybe I'll take the missus for a night out when it opens."

I smile and nod, thinking of Neil and his *missus* here when I unveil the kinkier sides of the club. Who knows what kinds of things they're into—maybe they'd enjoy it. Being in the lifestyle had taught me that kinksters came in all shapes, sizes, ages, ethnicities, and backgrounds.

"Of course. Have a good weekend, Neil."

Once I hear the front door close, I do another walk-through of the club, ensuring it's all set up before I bring the furniture in and start training the staff. I take another quick tour of the upstairs—or what will be known as *Paradise*. Then I walk down into the dungeon—or what will be known as *Purgatory*.

The building hasn't been used since the 1950s, and before that, it was an old lumberyard just on the outskirts of downtown Crestwood, California. Instead of rooms for different kinks, I'd chosen to keep it simple. Those seeking or wanting to give pleasure could go upstairs to *Paradise*.

And those seeking to receive or administer pain—like me—could go to *Purgatory*.

It was a choose-your-own-adventure club with the same exclusivity that my brother, Chase, used with The Hunt. Though I wasn't into the primal kink like he was, I liked the idea of starting small and growing. I don't want to exclude people, but I also know that running a place like this will mean ensuring everyone—from the employees to the invited guests—stays safe.

From the outside, it will be a nondescript building. The bar itself will be called *Inferno*. Upon entering, customers must be vetted by the community or personally known to me. Unlike most clubs that require membership and ID, this venue ensures only trusted individuals are allowed in. Once inside, guests are shown through a coat room to the main bar area, where they can choose to go upstairs or downstairs, depending on their mood.

Before I forget, I pull my phone out and the skull balaclava from my back pocket, popping the hood of my sweatshirt over my head when I'm done. Setting my phone on a windowsill, I hit record and walk backward with my arms spread. The recording cuts off after fifteen seconds, and I save the video to upload across all social media channels and type out a caption.

Will you be my good girl and kneel for me? Stay tuned for my next video on communication and safe words.

I triple-check that no identifying factors are in the video before hitting upload. Unlike how select friends and family know about Inferno, no one knows I'm also Starboy1997 across multiple social media channels.

It started as a way to educate people about kink without showing my face and thereby inviting speculation about our family, and over the past few months, the fans have gone a bit rabid. Every time I upload a new video, it's akin to fanning a flame, but I enjoy it.

Women can be too casual about kink, and my mission is to ensure people stay safe and that it stays consensual for all parties. Aside from enjoying myself, I hope I'm also helping people make safe decisions, educate themselves, and maybe enjoy the view while they learn.

I pull the mask off and stash it in the pocket of my dark jeans before letting my eyes sweep over the place. Grabbing my helmet, I pull the door closed and lock it.

It's still cold as fuck for March, so I pull my leather jacket and helmet on before unlocking my bike, swinging one leg over the seat, and moving the kickstand up.

It's half past noon, so I have an hour to get downtown, and as I gun the throttle, my bike sends me flying down the main street in Crestwood. My fingers are already frozen through, so I grab the leather gloves stashed inside the bike at the next light.

By the time I get downtown and park my bike, it's five minutes to two. I take the stairs two at a time as I wave at the Stardust Playhouse security, sliding through a back door and taking a hallway to one of the box seats overlooking the stage. There are twenty seats up here, and I purchased all of them for the entire season.

Though it's only been a little over a week, I haven't missed a single day of Layla's performance.

Pulling my hood over my head, I lean back as the lights dim and the ballet begins. At this point, I could write a book about the ballet since I've seen it over a hundred times. The show starts with Prince Siegfried planning his twenty-first birthday with a royal ball. Soon after, his mother tells him he must choose a woman to marry, and he unhappily tells her he'd rather marry for love. He goes out into the forest with his new bow and arrow, where he sees a group of swans on a nearby lake.

This is where I sit up straighter—leaning forward over the balcony as Layla appears. She stands up to full height, turning from a Swan Queen into a woman named Odette. My whole body warms at the sight of her in a white bodice and tutu, her pale skin glistening and maneuvering in a way that transfixes me every time. She dances with Siegfried, and despite knowing the male dancer's husband, I still feel envious of how he touches Layla—how his hands grip her waist and how he looks at her like she's the only person in the world.

Layla's tiara sparkles as she turns and turns—a pirouette, if my research is correct. I don't know much about ballet, but I've been trying to learn because I can't resist the urge to know everything about her. *Even though she told me all those years ago to leave her alone.* But that was an impossible ask. She'll never know how close I've actually stayed. Always on the sidelines.

The music swells, captivating everyone in the audience.

I still can't hear a Tchaikovsky piece without thinking of Layla.

My favorite part of the ballet begins next. Layla comes out in a black costume instead of a white one. She's now the evil Odile, and I watch as she confidently seduces Siegfried. *Fuck,* she has no idea how entrancing she is. When she plays Odette, she's shy and docile. But when Odile comes out? She's bold, unyielding, and steps into that role easily.

I take a deep breath and sit back. Only a few more minutes are left of the show, and I can't risk being seen by her when they do the curtain call. However, I can't seem to take my eyes off her even though I know this part by heart. It's where she dances her final dance with Siegfried—dressed in all white once again.

It's the happy ending.

The one part that makes me dread returning to my real life since the woman dancing this part wants nothing to do with me in real life. For these two hours, I can pretend she's dancing for me just like she used to. The secret smiles, the searching eyes ... for ten years, she danced for *me.* It was platonic back then, but I still felt connected to her.

Plus, when she's on stage, she's not stiff and robotic

like she so often is around me. She's in her element, and I get to witness the real Layla again—temporarily, at least.

I think of our encounter at Scott's house a few weeks ago. I haven't seen her since except to watch her ballet performances, and on the days she has off or there's no performance scheduled, I feel it.

My whole body feels off—and I get irritable, antsy, and argumentative.

I need her like I used to need alcohol. One vice for another, yet I'm not sure which is worse.

My old obsession with alcohol.

And now my obsession with my stepsister.

Step*sister.*

We grew up together, so I know I shouldn't house these fantasies for her.

It can never happen, and I've come to terms with that, but it doesn't dull the obsession.

If anything, it makes me want her more.

And this obsession isn't new. I've craved her for years. Mostly from afar, but I wanted her even back when she didn't hate my guts.

The sound of clapping stirs me out of my stupor, and I quickly turn and walk out of the box just as Layla and Siegfried hold hands and smile out into the audience.

I take the stairs two at a time to beat the crowd and am on my bike two minutes later. Waiting in a nearby alley for Layla's white BMW to pull out, I pull my gloves on and grit my jaw against the cool breeze. I hate that she always walks to her car by herself, especially considering she has overzealous fans due to what she does.

Carrying pepper spray won't do much if she's physically overpowered.

If I don't watch out for her, who will?

I'm the only one here, though—so what does that make me?

About an hour later, the white SUV drives out of the parking garage, and I wait a few seconds before following her through downtown, three cars behind her so she doesn't know it's me. I don't typically follow her like this, but today's a special occasion. Zoe let it slip during our weekly munch—a meetup for people in the lifestyle—that Layla has a hot date tonight. I couldn't ask where or with whom without arousing suspicion from Layla's best friend, so I decided to find out for myself.

I was grateful for Zoe's intelligence. She'd gotten married to Liam, my eldest brother, last year. We were close before they got together, seeing as the two of us were oftentimes in the same friend groups due to being into kink. She's the reason I know so much about Layla's life, and I willingly inhale every crumb and morsel she gives me about my stepsister.

Just after seven, Layla pulls into the valet line for The Angry Squirrel, a high-end restaurant in Santa Monica. Traffic was horrendous the entire drive over, and based on the way she scurries into the restaurant, I'd say she's late.

I am *very* interested in seeing who she's meeting.

Parking my bike a couple of blocks away, I lock my helmet up and pocket the keys, casually walking up to the host stand and skimming the restaurant. Layla is seated in the back, and across from her is some blond guy in a suit. I roll my eyes and turn to face the hostess.

"I don't have a reservation, but I'll give you a thousand dollars in cash if you seat me in one of the seats in the back," I murmur, leaning in close to her and pointing at seats behind Layla. She won't see me unless she turns around and actively looks for me.

The hostess's eyes go wide as recognition sweeps over her features. "Of course. This way, Mr. Ravage."

The one time I can use my name to my advantage.

Smirking, I follow her to the table and sit down facing Layla's table, pulling the cash out of my wallet and discreetly handing it to the hostess before she walks away.

A female server asks if I'd like water or anything to drink.

And just like every other time I'm asked, I resist the urge to say, "Double whiskey, neat."

Instead, I politely smile and say, "Sparkling water. Thank you."

She returns a few minutes later with a large bottle of Aqua Panna. "What brings you to The Angry Squirrel, Mr. Ravage?" she asks while pouring.

"I was in the neighborhood," I tell her quickly. The longer she's here, the higher the chance Layla will get curious and look behind her. I need to be discreet and blend in.

"Can I please get some bread when you get a chance?" I ask.

The server nods. "Certainly. Whatever you want," she practically breathes, lashes fluttering. After a second of uncomfortable eye contact, she turns and walks away, and I sigh in relief.

While waiting, I slowly sip my sparkling water and watch my stepsister flirt with a stranger. A complete *imbecile,* if I'm being honest. His smile is goofy, and his hair is too perfectly coiffed to be taken seriously. My eyes narrow when she laughs at something he says because I know her well enough to know that *that* laugh was forced. I let my eyes drag over her tailored cream-colored trousers, matching vest, and blazer. The way her hair is still pulled into a tight bun at the back of her head tells me she didn't have time to wash it. Her glasses sit perched on her nose. Her hands are clasped together on her lap, and she hasn't touched her wine.

Of course she hasn't. She hates wine, you asshole. Tsk, tsk.

Who is this guy, anyway? I bet he ordered the wine without asking her what she prefers.

When the server comes back with the bread, I thank her. When she doesn't immediately move to leave, I lean forward slightly and give her a flirtatious smile.

"Can you please send a cosmopolitan to the woman in the cream blazer? Belvedere vodka if you have it. Don't tell them I sent it," I tell her, winking.

The least her date can do is provide a drink she'll enjoy.

She nods, brows furrowed. That probably wasn't what she expected me to say.

"Of course, Mr. Ravage."

She scurries off, and I continue to watch Layla.

Her date won't stop talking. She can't seem to get a word in—not that she's trying. No, she's too polite for that. At the end of the night, she'll thank him politely and probably never speak to him again. From what Zoe tells me, Layla has trouble connecting to her dates and hardly ever goes on a second date. My pride and arrogance both *fucking* love that fact, and I sit back and smile as a runner walks over to their table and sets the cosmo down in front of Layla.

Just as her spine stiffens, I pull a menu up and hold it in front of my face in case she turns around. It's not like she'll *know* I sent it—but she might suspect it and look around. When a minute has passed, I lower the menu slowly and smirk as I watch her sip the drink I sent her.

Just as I'm about to order, my phone buzzes in my pocket.

Pulling it out, I see that it's a +33 number.

My father.

I hit the talk button. "Hi," I say, voice low and rumbling.

"Orion," my dad says weakly. "Have you given any more thought to my proposal?" Typical. Straight to business.

No *how are you* or questions about my life.

"Do you mean the proposal in which you defy the boundaries my brothers have clearly set? No, I haven't."

"Did you tell them my predicament?" he asks, voice cool and businesslike.

"They are aware of the diagnosis," I practically growl.

He's quiet for a moment, and I have to hold my

tongue so I don't say anything cruel. Like all the other times he calls me, I wonder why I even bother to pick up the phone.

"And they're aware that I'm simply trying to divide my assets before it's too late? Miles especially should be thinking about the future of his daughter."

I grind my teeth together. He's so fucking manipulative. Being the only son who still speaks to him means I've become the mediator. Miles used to until our father screwed Stella's father over financially. Chase, Liam, and Kai—my other brothers—all vowed to cut contact as adults, and to be honest, I don't blame them. Now that he's dying, he thinks he has a right to weasel his way back into their lives despite them having very clear, very valid reasons for their estrangement. I was too young to comprehend the harmful things that happened growing up at Ravage Castle, plus I ended up moving in with Layla and Scott at fourteen. By that point, my mother and brothers had taken it upon themselves to shield me from the worst of it in the years prior.

I often contemplated cutting contact with him to support my brothers, but then he got sick, and the youngest-child guilt took over, so here we are.

"I'm sure Beatrix will be taken care of," I answer, speaking of Miles and Stella's daughter and his only grandchild. "She does have four doting uncles—myself included—and a plethora of aunts."

Plus, our mother made sure my brothers and I had access to our trust funds before she left him. None of us had any interest in his wealth—the art and cars, mostly

—that he wanted to leave to us upon his death. We'd been more than financially independent from him for almost two decades. It was just an excuse; a massive guilt-trip from a father who never bothered to arrive for us or put our best interests first.

"And what about you? Have you found a suitable wife yet, or are you still lusting after Scott's daughter?"

"That's none of your business."

"Of course it is. I was the same way with your mother, mind you. She resisted me for years until I finally wore her down."

The bread I'd chewed on turns to lead in my stomach. Like many things having to do with my parents and my childhood, I didn't know that about their relationship. I was young when the problems began, and my older brothers protected me from almost everything that happened.

"And then she left you," I add, wanting to drive the point home.

"Of course she did. I never let her breathe. I never let her have her own life. I was always watching her. I was *obsessed* with her. Despite the fact that she left me for someone else, and even though she's gone, I will always love her." He's quiet for a few seconds as my heart pounds. Layla laughs at something her moron date says across the room, and then my father says something that turns my blood to ice. "You remind me of myself. Rebellious. Determined. Business-savvy. You can't tell me it's a coincidence that your mother was a ballet dancer too—"

"Right. Well, Dad, goodbye." I hit the end button

before he can get another word in, swallowing a couple of times to tamp the bile down.

I never let her breathe. I never let her have her own life. I was always watching her. I was obsessed *with her.*

I can hardly breathe as I look at Layla across the restaurant. Squeezing my eyes shut, I run a hand over my face. Why is it that he always unnerves me and knows just what to say to get me to question everything I've ever done?

Seven years ago, when Layla told me she never wanted to see me again, it was easy not to take her words to heart. We still lived under one roof, and despite moving out shortly after our argument, I still saw her regularly at Scott's house. There were dinners and family functions, and my brothers had always been mindful of including their stepsister in anything important—despite hardly knowing her. When our mother remarried, I was the only one still living at home, so we became the closest.

When Layla started dancing for the Los Angeles Ballet and then more recently Pacific Ballet Company, I used it as an excuse to support her from afar. But as my drinking got worse, it became an unhealthy obsession. She pulled away—started dating, stopped going to Scott's when I was there—and stopped talking to me altogether. She bought the house in Los Feliz down the street from Scott, and our lives stopped intersecting so much.

I tried moving out.

I tried staying away from family functions I knew she'd be at.

I tried—for years, I made an earnest attempt at staying away.

But I couldn't do it.

I felt like I couldn't breathe, and I needed a way to be around her.

And now, I don't give a shit if I'm too obsessed.

Because she's *mine*.

It takes me a minute to realize the server has been asking me a question for several seconds.

"... steak? Or perhaps you'd like to try one of our specials? The mussels are new to the menu, and the lamb is served with couscous and marinated eggplant ..."

Her words float in and out of my ears, and my eyes find the back of Layla's head.

"I'll have the mussels. Thank you."

She nods and smiles. "Would you like to keep the menu?"

"Yes, please."

The next hour passes with me slowly eating my mussels while Layla—to my delight—eats the same dish as me. Her date doesn't stop talking the entire time, and when I see the server walk back over and ask them about dessert, he shakes his head.

Layla's spine sinks *just* barely, and when I look back down at the menu, I see blackout cake served with fresh strawberry ice cream.

Smirking, I make eye contact with the server, and

when she comes over, I ask her to send a cake with extra ice cream to their table.

Just like last time, I hold the menu in front of my face when the runner brings the cake to their table, knowing there's a much higher chance of her thinking I'm here. Especially now that she's been brought two separate things she didn't order.

When I lower the menu, Layla eagerly eats the cake and ice cream while her date talks and talks some more. Between bites, she tries to hide her yawns behind a hand. She also spends three minutes inspecting her spoon. He doesn't notice of course.

Fucking bastard.

She's probably wishing she was at home reading a book and snuggled up with her cat.

Without thinking, I pull my phone out and text her.

My chest aches when I realize the last time we texted was two years ago when Scott was admitted to the hospital for a suspected stroke. He ended up being fine, but Layla and I had been cordial as we coordinated when to visit him in the hospital and for how long. There had been thousands of times when I wanted to text her.

Damn, I miss her.

These past few years have been painful, knowing that I couldn't talk to the person I considered my best friend. *Not* talking to her feels unnatural—like an acute sense of loss. We were always calling and texting before that fateful audition seven years ago.

Not a day passes that I don't think of texting her.

I don't think she realizes how desperately I need her.

I'm not sure why I feel like today is the day to break the silence, but something about watching this asshole talk over her all night has my mind spinning with fury.

> I ordered you an extra scoop.

As soon as I hit send, I pull the menu back in front of my face and angle my body behind a beam so she won't see me unless she looks. Peeking over the top of the menu, I smile when I see her pull her phone from her purse.

My smile widens when I see the way she stills—how her legs instantly uncross like she's been discovered. She looks around quickly as her date drones on and on without even realizing she's not paying attention.

I wait for her to respond, but of course she doesn't.

> Do you think he'll be hoarse later after all that talking?

This time, she says something to him and stomps to the bathroom, phone in hand. I lean back in my chair and watch three dots appear once before disappearing.

Is she texting me in the bathroom? Did I get under her skin that badly?

> You should probably get back to your date. He looks bored.

LAYLA

Are you watching me?! Are you here?!?!

No. You know what? I don't care.

Then why'd you run off to the bathroom?

LAYLA

I had to pee.

Bull. Shit.

LAYLA

What do you want, Orion?

You?

I blow out a breath before responding.

A "thank you" would be nice.

LAYLA

Seriously? God, you're so freaking
arrogant.

How was the cosmo?

LAYLA

Unbelievable. Get a life, Orion.

You are my life, I type out before erasing it. Glancing at the hallway with the bathrooms, I stand and leave enough cash for a 200 percent tip. As I approach Layla's table, her date eyes me warily.

I'm used to it—the dark hair, tattoos, and muscles tend to make people squirm.

He jerks backward when I place my hands on the white tablecloth and lean in close to his face.

He looks terrified, which only amuses me further.

"There's a small chance she'll be nice and give you a second date." I lean closer and practically snarl my next sentence. "But just so it's crystal fucking clear: if you so much as *touch* her tonight, there are worse things than death."

Her date scowls up at me. "Is that a threat?"

"I don't make threats."

Before Layla can catch me, I push off the table and give him a menacing stare. He startles when I throw my hands up, and I chuckle as I walk out of the restaurant.

My phone vibrates a minute later, and I already know who it is.

LAYLA
Did you scare my date away?

I may have said hello.

LAYLA
You are such an asshole.

I know.

LAYLA
Why are you doing this?

He didn't order you dessert.

Three dots appear and disappear several times, but she doesn't respond.

I'm still smiling by the time I get on my bike.

Sometimes I miss drinking, but other times, like now, it's much more fun to be sober.

CHAPTER THREE
THE MESSAGE

LAYLA

Kitty, the makeup artist, finishes my face with setting spray and uses a small comb to control my flyaway hairs. I thank her, sit back in my chair, and grab my phone. I've already spent an hour warming up and have a few minutes before I have to change into my costume. Kitty rummages around in her bag as the other dancers get their stage makeup put on by other artists. I scroll social media as she does. My feed refreshes, and suddenly, I'm watching a video from a masked creator named Starboy1997.

He's not speaking—just standing in what looks like some sort of dungeon. There's text laid over his video, along with music.

Rachmaninoff's "Isle of the Dead."

Huh. Classical music is an interesting choice for a masked thirst trap.

It instantly piques my interest because I love all things Rachmaninoff, Tchaikovsky, and Mozart.

He's wearing a black hoodie and jeans, and his mask is a black balaclava with a white skull image on the front. I'm no stranger to masked creators. They've taken the internet by storm recently, and being a dark romance bookworm, I've had certain fantasies about these masked men. However, this one is different somehow.

For one, he's fully clothed. Most of the others are shirtless or wearing clothes that leave little to the imagination. Starboy1997 is wearing a black hoodie. Something about his stance is so ... commanding. And "Isle of the Dead" is a beautiful piece. It's not my favorite Rachmaninoff work, but it's close. It's haunting and ethereal. Third, he seems to be teaching something, and when my eyes skim over the text, my heart pounds.

Three examples of rules I've given my submissives before:

They will address me with respect.

They will kneel until they are told to get up.

They will communicate with me if they are unhappy in any way.

Remember, the rules exist for two reasons: for my submissive's benefit and for my pleasure.

The video ends a second later and loops back to the beginning.

I watch it seven times.

"He's so hot," Kitty says from behind me, and I jump, locking my phone.

"Who?"

"Starboy. He's everywhere. His videos are really good, too. He's not just a hot guy account, either. He's informative."

I take in the information as Kitty helps me out of my makeup chair. "Why the mask, then?"

Kitty shrugs, blowing a piece of short black hair out of her face. "Anonymity? I dunno. Maybe he's famous." She checks her watch. "Go get ready! You're on in fifteen."

I return to the dressing room and quickly change into the white Swan Queen costume. I'm just putting my toe pads on when Kitty walks back in with the tiara.

"I almost forgot." She fits it on my head, securing it tightly. "Merde," she adds, blowing me a kiss.

Like the minutes before all shows, my stomach erupts in nervous butterflies. I mindlessly start stretching, admiring the new, large bouquet of peonies my father sent today. It's a bunch of twenty-six stems—one for each year I've been alive, I assume. The peonies are always so lovely, perfectly blooming upon every delivery.

They must cost a fortune.

I make a note to chide him for the lavish gift. He doesn't need to send them *every* day. The entire theater is practically overflowing with peonies by the last performance of the week, not that I mind. Still, he's on a budget and shouldn't be spending money on such frivolous things.

When I pick up my phone to text him, the video of Starboy1997 from earlier pops up, distracting me. His location is different in all of them, but they're all darker spaces that are hard to identify. In one of them, he's not wearing a hoodie but a long-sleeved black shirt. It clings to his muscles, and without thinking, I hit "like." His videos are educational and simple. He's not trying to turn people on, though somehow his presence turns *me* on—a rare feeling.

That doesn't stop the commenters, though.

Here we gooo. Another masked man to obsess over.

Daddy? Please?

How do you stand so still? And why is it so hot?

Starboy, pls, I am working.

Another video to bring to my therapist.

It's a damn CRIME that I'm not your sub.

I'm smiling as I scroll. Sometimes Starboy responds, and sometimes he doesn't. His replies are usually generic, but every once in a while, he throws in some praise or degradation, which makes me chew on my lower lip.

Yes, you did, pretty little cockslut.

That's right. Well done.

Look at you … such a willing cum rag.

I'm so proud of you.

Who is this guy? And where can I find one in real life?

Someone might be surprised that my biggest sexual fantasy is to be called names. To be corrupted by someone with more experience.

Too bad I hardly ever feel attraction to the men I *actually* go on dates with.

A quick internet search tells me I'm not the only one

curious about Starboy's identity. With over two million followers, of course people are curious about him. But there's nothing except that he resides somewhere in the Los Angeles area. And *that* was only discovered because of the skyline in one of his videos.

A light knock on my dressing room has me locking my phone and turning it face down on my vanity—as if the person on the other side will be able to see through my locked screen.

"Ten minutes," someone calls from the other side.

I take a deep breath and check my appearance once more before exiting my dressing room and walking toward the stage. There, I forget about the outside world —about everything except what I'm about to do. I wrap my hand around the handle of the stage door when the side door opens, startling me.

To my surprise, my dad pushes the door in— followed closely by Orion.

My heart flutters slightly at the sight of him, but I don't hold eye contact, instead walking over to my dad and giving him a careful hug.

"I forgot you were coming tonight," I say quickly, breathless for some reason that has nothing to do with my stepbrother. *Nothing at all.*

"It's Saturday, isn't it?" he asks, grinning widely. "And I brought Orion. He hasn't ever been to a show."

I glance behind my father, locking eyes with light blue ones. His lips twitch, and his eyes gleam with mischief. His hair is a bit neater than usual, and he seems to have less scruff than normal. He's wearing a white button-up rolled to his elbows and fitted black trousers with black Converse High Tops. No tie, but it's formal for Orion. Unlike his brothers, I don't think he owns a single suit. If he does, I'm not sure I could handle it. We haven't spoken since last weekend when he threatened my date out of nowhere, and I'm still not sure what his intentions were that night. The fact that he'd texted me … I'd stared at his responses all weekend, even going so far as to memorize them.

He didn't order you dessert.

For years, we haven't spoken except when we happened to be in the same room.

What changed recently?

Why was he there last weekend? Was he watching me? The thought of him skulking around in the back of the restaurant creeps me out and also makes everything inside me turn to jelly. Lance had left shortly after I'd gotten back from the bathroom. I'd looked for Orion, but I didn't see him anywhere in the restaurant, and my brain had the audacity to be disappointed.

I'm blaming all of the dark romance books I read.

"Hope that's okay," he says slowly, holding up two tickets.

Front row seats. I'd be able to see him the entire time I was dancing.

My skin breaks out in a cold sweat, and as his eyes track over my heavy makeup and tiara, something inside my stomach flips upside down.

"It's almost time for me to go on," I tell them.

My dad gives me a quick peck on my cheek. "I know.

We'll go get seated, but I just wanted you to know that I'm so proud of you, La-La."

"Thanks, Dad. Oh, that reminds me, I really appreciate the beautiful flowers, but you don't have to send them every day."

He pulls away, and his brows knit together, but before he can respond, Orion claps a hand on his back.

"We should go sit down, old man."

"You're right. I'll go and give you two a minute," he says quickly, walking out of the door they came in through.

That leaves Orion and me alone.

At first, it looks like he's going to turn around and walk after Dad, but instead, he takes a step closer to me.

"I'm sorry for last weekend," he says, his voice a low murmur.

I cross my arms and hold myself taller. Even when doing so, he still towers over me.

"You should be."

His lips twitch, and to my chagrin, he takes another step closer so that he's in my personal space. He smells good—like leather and tobacco, though I don't think he smokes. My expression falters, and I take a step back. He chuckles, running a hand over his mouth. I follow the movement of his hand, and my eyes unintentionally drag over his mouth.

"Are you still thinking about that cake? Is that why you're so unfocused right now?" he asks, fully grinning like he's won some bizarre game I had no idea we were playing.

My nostrils flare, and I huff out a frustrated breath. Before I can respond, he turns around, leaving me alone with only a few minutes to spare.

I close my eyes and take a few steadying breaths, attempting and failing to quell my nerves.

Pretend he's not watching you. Pretend it's any normal day, and your hot stepbrother is not in the front row with that arrogant smirk splashed across his face.

Somehow, I'm able to relax my breathing and focus on stretching for the next sixty seconds. The soft notes of Tchaikovsky float through the air, and I continue stretching my calves and hamstrings. I also do breathing exercises to warm my lungs, and the last thing I do before one of the coordinators finds me is stretch my ankles and feet. Despite doing pointe for over a decade, it still doesn't one hundred percent come naturally to me. After every performance, I still have to ice my feet and bandage my toes to prevent blisters, but I welcome the pain. I'm used to pushing my body beyond the boundaries I set for myself week in and week out.

Or maybe I'm just a masochist, I think derisively.

I'd given up all outside activities and committed to dancing full-time when I was fourteen, and it had been full steam ahead since then—with a few setbacks.

I welcome the challenge of giving everything I have during a performance because anything less has the power to end my career. No matter how skilled I am, I know I'll eventually hit a ceiling where I'll no longer be able to put my body through such extremes. Being twenty-six, that day might come sooner than I expect.

It all works out in the end, though.

Dancing is my safe space—the place where I can let go and be vulnerable and let my body feel the music completely.

The woman in the headset ushers me farther into the wing, and when it's my cue, I float onto the stage and drown everything else out.

I can't quite describe what happens when I perform, but I go somewhere I can only access on stage. It's like I *become* Odette, and then later, Odile—and nothing else matters except conveying the story correctly. Prince Siegfried—played by Raphael Beaufort tonight—is the ballet dancer I interact with most on stage. He's professional on stage, and we've never had an issue with compatibility while playing our roles, but he still avoids me backstage.

Orion punched him at a Halloween party a year and a half ago for getting too handsy with me.

The thought of what happened that night makes me stumble slightly on my next landing. Not enough for anyone in the audience to notice, but Raphael's brows arch ever so slightly when he holds his hands out for me to jump into for our next move.

The rest of the performance goes smoothly, and once we come back onto the stage for the curtain call, I see Orion doing a slow clap with that same damn smirk splayed all over his face.

"He has a lot of fucking courage to show up here," Raphael grumbles into my ear with his French accent.

Of course Orion has to arrive during a show when

Raphael performs—usually Tuesday, Friday, and Saturday, instead of Ivan, his alternate, who performs on the other nights.

Orion's eyes flick from me to Raphael, then they narrow slightly.

Once we finish our curtain call, I walk to my dressing room and change. Both Orion and my dad await me when I get to my car in the underground parking garage.

"What a wonderful performance, La-La," my dad proudly says as if he wasn't here last Saturday and the one before that.

"Thanks, Dad." I turn to Orion. "I need to talk to you."

"I'll give you kids some privacy," he says cheerfully. He begins walking to his Subaru, which is parked next to a sleek, black motorcycle.

Once he's inside his car, I turn back to Orion. "Do you want something from me? Why is it that I don't see you for months after—after—" I can't say it out loud, but the way his eyes twinkle tells me that he knows exactly what I'm insinuating.

"Still thinking about our kiss?" he asks, choosing that exact moment to lean against my car, crossing his legs and arms like he doesn't have a care in the world.

I ignore his question even though my brain is flustered and trying to keep up. "And now, all of a sudden, I see you every weekend? What do you want from me?"

"Did you go on another date with Mr. No Dessert?" he asks, biting his lower lip.

My fists curl at my side. "No, actually. Turns out, he

doesn't care for being threatened with something *worse than death*," I grit out.

Orion laughs. "He told you."

"You're worse than Sparrow marking his territory," I add, voice shaking. "At this point, I'm going to turn into an old spinster with fifty cats—" The blood drains from my face. "Wait, the guy from a few months ago who never called me back ... was that you?" I accuse, taking a step forward.

"Listen, Layla. I just so happened to be at the same restaurant as you last weekend. I saw what happened and wanted to have a bit of *brotherly* fun." He holds his hands up and gives me a placating smile. "I overstepped, and I'm sorry."

A pang of disappointment works through me. *Wait ... did I want him to stalk me? What was wrong with me?!*

"So you didn't say something to the other guy from a few months ago?"

He dips his head, and something dark passes behind his eyes. "Scout's honor."

I stand straighter and clear my throat. "I should get home. See you later."

Orion doesn't move. Instead, he rakes his gaze over my face as if he's searching for something.

"You're really good," he says slowly. "On stage."

His compliment startles me. "Oh. Thanks."

He pushes off my car. "See you next week," he adds, winking.

My stomach nearly bottoms out. "Next week?"

"*Phantom of the Opera*, remember?"

I clench my jaw. I'd forgotten about that—and most importantly, I'd forgotten that *he* was going. Zoe and Liam had two extra tickets to see a Tuesday night show, and I happened to have the night off from PCB. Zoe also knows it's my favorite—I guess I should've known I'd be into masked men because of how much I loved the book.

Little did I know that the fourth ticket would be going to Orion.

"Right. Yeah. See you then," I say quickly, feeling flushed and flustered.

He walks away just as I go to unlock my door, and once I'm inside, I close my eyes and lean my arms on my steering wheel to rest my head and calm my racing heart. It's not until I hear Orion's bike engine tearing down the street that I truly exhale. I grab my phone and unlock the screen to text Zoe and Remy about our upcoming girls' night, and when I do, I realize I never exited Starboy1997's profile earlier.

I scroll for a few minutes, watching and pining over his videos as I squirm in my seat. It's the mystery of *who* he could be. If he's in Los Angeles, have I stood behind him in line at the grocery store? Does he get stuck on the 405 every afternoon like I do? I check for clues that he's married or maybe even a perv, but so far, he seems legit and knowledgeable. And thanks to the books I read, I'm intrigued by the topic of kink and BDSM.

The things I fantasize about are things I've never even told Zoe, who's in the kink lifestyle. I'm not anywhere near as experienced as she is, though, so I never feel like I can chime in and talk about how I want to be choked or held down and called a *whore*. I didn't even know I'd like stuff like that until I started reading about it. Who knows—perhaps if someone did those things to me in real life, I wouldn't enjoy it. Sure, I got turned on while reading about it, but that didn't mean I'd be into it personally, right?

Starboy is exactly who I've been searching for. A safe space to explore my interests. I scroll all the way down to his first video, and it's the same as all the other videos—him standing or sitting with spread legs as classical music plays and text pops up on the screen. At the end of the video, it says:

My DMs are always open.

I should send him a message.

I mean, he probably gets thousands of messages a day with two million followers. The chances of him seeing it are slim to none, but I suppose I should shoot my shot. I fumble over what to say, but eventually, I decide to keep it simple.

LITTLEDANCER

I'm really interested in a specific kink. But I've never done it in real life … I've only read about it. I'd like to learn more, but I'm a total noob, and I don't know where to go from here. Thanks! I love your videos.

Sighing heavily, I click out of his profile and set my phone down.

He probably won't respond, but at least I tried.

As I drive out of the parking garage, I imagine

Starboy seeing my message and clicking over to my profile. *Shit, I'd put that I'm a ballet dancer in my bio.* He might put two and two together and figure out who I am. My full name is there, and an internet search would show me as the company dancer for Pacific Ballet.

I imagine him coming to a show—sitting in the front row with his hood up.

I imagine those large, veiny hands running up and down his thighs as he watches me dance for him—a dark mystery full of secrets and power.

I imagine what his voice would sound like. Would it be deep, rough, a low purr? Would he ask me to kneel for him after? Would he sound just as commanding as he looked, with long, muscular legs and large, beautiful hands?

How would those hands feel on *me*, doing the things I've only dreamed about for the past couple of years?

By the time I get back to my house, the space between my thighs aches and pulses with need. I say a quick hello to Sparrow, who stretches on his pillow by the front window as I walk inside and throw my bag onto the floor.

Shutting my bedroom door, I don't even bother removing my clothes as I climb into bed and quickly rub one out by slipping one hand under the waistband of my sweats. My orgasm crashes over me quickly and powerfully, and my back arches as I pant heavily, imagining it's Starboy's hands instead of my own. When I'm done, my legs shake, and I can't stop laughing as reality sets in.

This *never* happens. Being turned on by a stranger?

Not ever. But there's something so ... fresh and real about this guy. It's not the hot body that turns me on. It's the way he makes his videos, the music he chooses, and the words that flash over some of my favorite music.

It's like he *gets* me on a deep, visceral level.

All the guys I date assume I'm a prissy ballet dancer with my tight bun and prim posture. They assume I don't want to put out, and one even joked once that he only went on the date to see if he could get into my pants. If it's not that, it's guys making disgusting comments about how flexible I must be.

That's what I deal with on a day-to-day basis, and *that's* why I don't date a lot.

This guy, though ... I have a feeling he'd tempt me to no end.

The mystery of who he really is only adds another element of intrigue.

As the post-orgasm haze dissipates, my smile falls off my face.

Masturbating to some guy I found online is a new all-time low.

Ugh, what the heck is wrong with me?

I don't check my phone for the rest of the night.

CHAPTER FOUR

THE REPLY

ORION

"Where is pretty girl?" Earl asks, squawking from his aviary.

I sigh and set my keys and wallet on the side table before walking over to Earl's elaborate setup. When I bought this penthouse from Chase a couple of years ago, I made sure I could put Earl somewhere safe. I'd hired a professional to build him a state-of-the-art aviary complete with a small pond, an actual, live tree, heating and cooling, as well as plenty of room to fly around. It even has automatic shades for nighttime. He also gets the fanciest pellets and seeds as well as spring water.

He is the most spoiled African grey out there—and probably the smartest, too.

Before we lived in downtown Crestwood, I'd rented a large loft in downtown Los Angeles. I was drinking a lot at the time, and I'd talked about Layla once when I'd gotten home from seeing her, calling her *pretty girl.* Earl remembered—and now he asks me whenever I come home.

Somehow, my fucking bird managed to imprint on my stepsister, sight unseen.

Damn the intelligence of parrots. It's fucking creepy sometimes.

"She's not here," I tell him, walking over to the door of his aviary. Unlatching and opening it, he squawks again.

"Thanks, Master," he says, flying off somewhere.

On top of building him an aviary fit for a king, I also hired the best trainer to ensure he doesn't leave the penthouse and only goes to the bathroom in his designated place in the aviary. I have to admit, it's very convenient.

I turn the lights on and walk to the kitchen, which is located at the back of the penthouse. I hadn't changed anything after Chase moved out, and though it was a nice enough place, it didn't quite feel like home. Still, being so close to all my businesses is convenient: two regular bars and now Inferno, the kink club, all in or near downtown Crestwood.

Opening the refrigerator, I grab a strawberry sparkling water and sip it while leaning against the counter. The clock on the oven tells me it's just past ten p.m. Still early, yet too late to go out for anything *good*, per se.

I crack my knuckles—a nervous habit I picked up after I gave up alcohol—before pulling my phone out from my pocket. I click over to the app where I last posted a video. I'm inundated with notifications—thousands of comments already, shares, likes, and reposts. My messages are always at "99+" because I don't have the time or energy to read all of them, but I still open it from time to time.

I understand the appeal of Starboy1997. The "no speaking" thing is mysterious, as is my all-black outfit. I'm a *safe* Dom in their eyes because I've given my followers signs to look out for with fake Doms. They have a parasocial relationship with me. They know Starboy. They trust him. And in a world of men constantly taking advantage of women, that's important. I never want to betray that trust because what I do—and the things I teach—matters.

Clicking over to the messages, I scroll through all of the inappropriate requests and photos, the kink-shaming religious nuts, and the requests for interviews. I quickly scroll down to make sure I didn't miss anything important, and then my heart nearly jumps out of my chest when I see a message request from someone with the username of LittleDancer.

Layla.

I know it's her because, of fucking course, I check out her profile. Maybe not every day, but close.

There's no fucking way—

My thumb clicks through to the message request quickly, and before I know it, I'm slamming my La Croix down. My heart pounds as her words appear on my screen. I verify it's actually her profile, and everything inside me tenses.

Running a hand over my face, I slowly read my stepsister's message to Starboy.

> **LITTLEDANCER**
>
> I'm interested in a specific kink. But I've never done it in real life … I've only read about it. I'm interested in learning more, but I'm a total noob, and I don't know where to go from here. Thanks! I love your videos.

I'm grinning, and my face is burning by the time I finish reading the short message. She loves my videos? Well, fuck. How long has she been following me? If I'd known …

Before I can think, I'm typing out a response.

> Hello, little dancer.

I hold my breath, waiting for a response, but after several minutes, it doesn't come.

Holy fuck. Layla messaged me—

Except she doesn't know it's *me*, does she?

Leaning my head back against the cabinet, I quickly shoot a text to my brother Kai.

> You up?

> **MALAKAI**
>
> Is this a booty call?

> I haven't eaten yet, and I was going to grab some tacos from the truck down the street.

All my brothers know that if I ask to hang out—especially at random times—it's likely because I'm bored. I never really feel the urge to drink myself into oblivion anymore, but I think they're always worried I'll fall down that rabbit hole again if left to my own devices.

Curse of being the youngest sibling who used to have a drinking problem, I suppose.

I almost always reach out to Kai first because he lives half a mile away in a condo just outside of St. Helena Academy, where he works as the headmaster. He moved to downtown Crestwood a few years ago when he took the job.

MALAKAI

20 min?

> Sure. I'll grab us the usual.

I stand and walk over to the dining room, where Earl perches on the mantel, cocking his head at his reflection in the large mirror above the fireplace. On top of being a smart-ass, he's also incredibly vain. He spends hours studying his reflection, and I make a mental note to look into getting him a bird friend that he won't brutally kill. I looked after Captain Sushi, Zoe and Liam's serval cat, while they were on their honeymoon. During those two weeks, Captain spent most of his time hiding in my

MASKED SINS   83

closet because Earl had scared him so much. Given
Captain's size, you'd think it would've been the other
way around, but I've seen Earl scare off humans before,
so I wasn't surprised.

Fucking birds.

"I'm going out for an hour. Are you going to be good,
or do you need to return to your cage?"

"Earl is a good boy, Master," he crows.

I huff a laugh. "Okay. See you soon."

Walking to the elevator, I push the button to head to
the lobby. The taco truck is only a few blocks away, so I
walk instead of taking my bike. I wave to the security
guard as I exit the building. Pulling my leather jacket
tighter, I check my phone for a response from Layla
about fifty times before I walk up to the white food truck.

I shake hands with the cook and order for Kai and
me, paying with cash and leaving a hefty tip. Grabbing a
table under a string of bistro lights, I refresh my message
requests at least a dozen more times before Kai claps me
on the back.

"Hey," he says, taking the seat opposite of me.

He's in a dark gray T-shirt, a black jacket, and jeans,
and despite knowing he's not as religious as everyone
thinks—not anymore at least—it still startles me to see
him dressed so casually.

The chef calls our number, so I jump up to grab our
tacos and sodas. When I sit back down, I push his basket
closer, but I can feel his eyes boring into me.

"What's wrong?" he asks, squeezing lime over the
carnitas, cilantro, and chopped onions.

"Nothing," I lie, doing the same to my tacos and taking a massive bite so I don't have to answer.

Kai smirks as he takes a swig of his soda. "Mmm. Okay. I think you forget that your face is very expressive."

"I'm just hungry," I grumble, shoving more food into my mouth.

My brother shrugs and eats his tacos, and while we eat, I think he'll drop it. Except his discerning nature always wins in the end, and after wiping his mouth and hands, he leans back and looks me straight in the eye.

"Is sobriety bothering you?"

His question catches me so off guard that I can't help but laugh. "No. Aside from the random cravings for whiskey, I haven't missed alcohol at all."

Despite being sober now, I didn't stop drinking because I was an addict. Not in the true sense of the word, at least. I tend to have an addictive personality, but once I put my mind to something, I could overcome pretty much anything. My therapist, Dr. Ludlow, had told me it was because I was the youngest, and the youngest children were always scrappy and resourceful. He'd also told me that because of my narcissistic father, who rarely displayed physical affection and was habitually cruel, it meant that I often thought of myself as a burden to others.

That checks out.

But no, I hadn't given up drinking because I couldn't stop.

I'd given up drinking because I wanted to get my life together.

For so long, I had trouble identifying what I wanted. I put my needs last, always worrying, always trying to please everyone. I didn't know what healthy boundaries looked like, and I struggled with vulnerability and intimacy.

I'd walked straight from a bar into a munch, and kink had very quickly replaced alcohol.

The feeling of topping someone, of commanding them ... it was exactly what I was looking for. I've always been drawn to nurturing people, and having that mutual respect moved me in ways I couldn't otherwise find.

I spent a lot of time learning how to do kink the right way. I took college courses on consent and sexuality. I made sure to attend talks and conferences when I could. It was a hobby for Chase and Liam, my two brothers in the lifestyle. But for me?

It was my lifeboat.

Becoming a Dominant saved me in more ways than one.

"Dad's in the hospital again," I tell him slowly, peeling the label off the soda bottle.

Kai sighs and leans forward. "Is that what's bothering you?"

I narrow my eyes as I look down at the table. "Not really. Maybe a little. It should. I mean, it's fucked up that our father has cancer, yet I can't figure out how to care."

"I'll tell you what I told Miles. I hope our father finds peace within himself for his actions."

I scoff. "How can you be so righteous about him? After everything he's done?"

Kai chuckles darkly. "Righteous? I'm not righteous. I never said I don't wish him pain for what he did to us or to Mom. Some days, I secretly hope he suffers. That doesn't make me very holy, does it?" He pauses, balling his hands, which are resting on the table. "But I don't want to talk about him anymore. Not right now." His gray eyes bore into mine. "Tell me what's bothering you."

"I'm worried I'm turning into him," I admit.

Kai's brow furrows. "I don't see it. For one, you're a lot nicer than him, even when you're being a jackass."

"Very funny."

"Why do you think you're turning into him?" Kai asks, expression curious.

Aside from the fact that I'm the last single brother left, besides Kai?

Besides the fact that, unlike Kai and St. Helena, I have no idea what my future looks like?

At least Kai has God.

I have no one.

I blow out a heavy breath of air. Here goes nothing ...

"Because I'm in love with her," I tell him, heart hammering in my chest. "With Layla. *Our* stepsister." His face remains expressionless, and only the twitch of his lips has me sitting up straighter. "Why are you looking at me like that?"

Kai bursts out laughing, covering his mouth as he

leans back in his seat. "Wait, is this supposed to be a surprise, Ri?"

"What the fuck do you mean?" I frown.

"I thought——" He shakes his head. "No offense, little bro, but it's been obvious for a very long time. I think the only person who *doesn't* know is her."

"Wonderful," I mutter. "But you agree. I *am* obsessed. Just like Dad was obsessed with Mom."

"No, that was different," he says slowly, but I can see the puzzle pieces clicking away.

"Really? Was it? Older man with power and money lusting after a younger woman who just so happens to be a ballet dancer? I mean, fuck. Copy and paste," I add, shaking my head.

"So that's what's eating you up? You're worried you'll push her away like Dad pushed Mom away?"

I shrug. I can't tell him about Starboy or the message from Layla, a.k.a. LittleDancer. I started doing those videos to educate people without the reputation of our family following us in a very public way. I wanted something *for me* that no one else knew about. Being the youngest means my life is always under a microscope from my four older brothers. My masked persona is a way to be myself, away from their influence.

I do tell Kai about attending all the ballet performances and interfering with her dates. Kai just listens— his eyes on me the entire time I talk. His intensity is alarming sometimes, but at least I know he's genuinely listening and concerned. I'd always been the closest to Chase and Liam, but I've gotten closer to Kai over the past couple of years since sobering up and opening the bars. He pushes me to be honest and open. He challenges me. He sees me as an equal.

Not that my other brothers *don't*. It's just that, in their minds, I'll always be their little brother.

"You want my advice?" he asks, placing both hands behind his head.

"Do I?" I ask, smirking as I finish the last of my soda.

"Maybe you should stop stalking her like Dahmer and instead try getting to know her."

"I do know her—"

"No, you don't. You *knew* her. A lot of things can change in seven years. I know you guys had that falling-out, so maybe now's the time to repair your relationship with her."

I scowl down at the table. "She doesn't want anything to do with me."

He shrugs. "Don't give her a choice."

"Can't believe I'm taking relationship advice from the brother who doesn't date."

Kai gives me a lopsided smile as he stands. "Who told you I don't date?"

A few minutes later, I'm walking back to my penthouse alone. I get ready for bed, check my messages fifty more times, and after tucking Earl into his darkened enclosure, I fall right to sleep.

———

The following morning, as light seeps through the corners of my blackout curtains, I reach for my phone and instantly check my messages again.

There's a reply from LittleDancer.

I sit up quickly and click through to Layla's response.

> **LITTLEDANCER**
>
> Wow. I didn't expect you to respond.

I want to laugh, scream, pump my fist.

> Guess you're just special.

She responds immediately.

> **LITTLEDANCER**
>
> Does that kind of flattery work on everyone?

> Why? Did it work on you?

> **LITTLEDANCER**
>
> Maaaybe. Also, hi.

> To answer your question, I'd need to know what you mean when you say you've read about a specific kink. I need to know what I'm working with.

> **LITTLEDANCER**
>
> It's a specific kink I've read about in romance books. I've also researched it extensively, and I think I'd enjoy it in real life, but I don't know for sure. I'm single, and I don't exactly date much. I figured you might be able to advise me on how I should (and could) move forward.

I smile at the fact that she doesn't date much. Fucking *good*.

What the hell kind of books does she read? She was always an avid reader growing up. Fantasy and science fiction, if I remember correctly. Half her wall space in Scott's house was books—massive-looking bookshelves we bought for her fifteenth birthday.

I'm suddenly so curious about what this specific kink is and why she felt the need to message a stranger about it. If she follows my page and *loves* my videos ... does that mean she's interested in BDSM? Does she have experience with it?

What are you hiding under that good-girl persona, Layla?

She wants advice from Starboy, and I can give it to her, but it feels like a glaring breach of trust. I know her, yet she doesn't know the man behind the mask. My entire page is about consent, and here I am, getting her to spill her deepest, darkest secrets to who she thinks is a stranger.

If she found out, she'd never forgive me.

Not unless I gave her a reason to like Orion, too.

My mind spins with possibilities.

Doing this would mean taking advantage of her and betraying the trust she's given this stranger.

Then again ...

She might never forgive me for what happened, and I'd never get the chance to be inside her head like this again. On one shoulder, my curiosity begs me to do this, and on the other, my morality begs me to walk away.

To be able to wield her desires like a weapon ... is fucked up, but the temptation is too great.

I'd like to think I'm a good person, but when it comes to Layla, I'd gladly unravel her innocence, thread by thread.

Suddenly, I can't imagine saying no. It's wrong and fucked up and wholly deceptive, but ...

If I can only have her like this, it's better than nothing.

> Can you tell me a little about yourself?

The thought of speaking to her—and one day possibly *showing* her what a healthy BDSM relationship could look like ...

I could make her crave my dominance, the sting of my touch, and the echo of my commands, all while knowing exactly what to do to make her come undone under the weight of my control.

The things I could do with her.

And the things I could do *to* her.

My mind runs fucking wild.

LITTLEDANCER

I'm female, 26, and a professional
dancer. I have a cat and live down the
street from my dad … although, even
typing this out makes me feel lame. I
have almost no social life aside from
meeting up with friends for drinks once
or twice a month. All the guys I date are
just blah. I've given up, and I'm going to
be a cat lady forever.

I smirk. I shouldn't love this so much, but I do.

Cats are cool, though. I don't blame you.
There are lots of creeps out there.

LITTLEDANCER

Hopefully, I'm not talking to one of
them …

It depends on who you ask. :)

LITTLEDANCER

Ha ha.

So these books … what kind of kink are
we talking about?

LITTLEDANCER

It's hard to type out. I don't know if the
things I think I'd like are … normal. Or if
they're depraved. God, I can't believe
I'm confessing this to a stranger on the
internet.

Things such as?

She doesn't respond right away, so I send another
message.

> I want this to be a safe space for you. If you want to open up a conversation with me, we need to trust each other, and I need to know what your limits are and where your desires lie so I can help you.

LITTLEDANCER

I think I'm just nervous to speak my desires out loud.

Fuck. It's like I have a back seat to her mind right now, and though I know it's wrong, I respond by changing our chat to vanish mode.

> I changed our chat to vanish mode. That way, at least you'll know if I take a screenshot. Okay? I want you to feel safe. That's what I'm here for. Feel free to send and unsend if you need to.

LITTLEDANCER

Thanks. I wasn't worried, by the way. It's why I messaged you specifically. I can tell you aren't here to take advantage of women.

My heart skips a beat, and guilt washes over me.

If only she knew my favorite thing was pushing people to the edge—breaking them so completely with pain and pleasure that they become a trembling mess on the floor, begging for more.

She's not worried, but maybe she should be.

> There are more than enough predators out there. It's my job to help.

The sting of the lie works down my throat. I don't enjoy lying, and especially not to her. But my curiosity gets the better of me.

LITTLEDANCER

Here goes nothing …

Everything inside me pounds with anticipation as I wait for her response. While waiting, I pull a shirt on and leave my bedroom. Every few seconds, I look down at my unlocked phone to see if Layla has responded. I'm smiling as I open the curtains to Earl's aviary.

"Good morning, Master," he says, cooing as I open the latch to his enclosure. When I'm home, I like to let him have his freedom.

"We've talked about this. You don't have to call me Master."

"Okay, Master," he adds, flying away.

I make a mental note to never bring a submissive back here again because he's already picked up certain phrases and terms, such as calling me Master. There's also, *there you go, that's it,* and *good girl,* which are all commonly used throughout the day.

And then of course, he loves to pull out the degrading ones.

Such a good little fuckdoll is one of his favorite phrases, as is *my pretty little cumslut,* which makes having company interesting sometimes.

A lot of people think birds can't understand context, but I have a feeling Earl is much smarter than he lets on.

I walk to the kitchen to make some coffee.

Just as I press start on the machine—which is fully automatic—Layla's response comes in the form of a long paragraph. My mouth waters with the possibility of knowing what makes her tick, what gets her off, and what she has yet to explore, and I decide to savor it once I head outside. I grab my coffee, my phone, and head out to the pool.

When Chase left, this was a large patio where he used to host his infamous parties. Since I'm not really a party guy—anymore, at least—I decided to put a pool in, and most mornings, I swim laps for thirty minutes. It's sunny today, and the warm heat beats down on my arms as I take a seat on one of the lounge chairs. The pool is long and narrow, and the infinity edge overlooks Crestwood and Los Angeles beyond it. It's my little slice of solace.

Once I'm seated, I pull my phone out of my pocket and read Layla's response in full.

LITTLEDANCER

I started reading dark romance novels a
few years ago. Until then, I would've told
anyone that I was vanilla. And I'm sure if
you asked anyone in my real life, they
would bet money that I'm vanilla.
Innocent. Pure. My best friends are in
the lifestyle, and I've been observing
them for a few years, but it wasn't until I
read a certain book with a scene that I
realized ... I wanted to do what the
characters were doing. I did some
research and found out that I probably
have a degradation kink as well as a
corruption kink. As in, I want someone to
corrupt *me*. I understand that these
desires are normal, but I guess I just
want someone to show me so I can
know for sure if this is what I want.

I'm hard before I can even finish reading her
response, and I read it about twelve times without
moving at all before the information settles over me.

Fuuuuuuuuck.

A sliver of regret washes over me. Why did I respond
to her message? Why did I think knowing any of this
about the woman I craved would be easy? I'm proud of
her for being honest, but also turned the fuck on. And
that small kernel of guilt flashes through me again
because she'd never tell Orion—her stepbrother—any of
this.

She's only telling Starboy because she trusts his
anonymity.

I can't think about that, though. Now that I know ...
I can't walk away from this. The opportunity is too

great, and I can practically taste all the ways I'll savor her.

> Thank you for telling me. Have you researched these kinks?

LITTLEDANCER

Probably more than is normal.

I take a deep breath and rub my mouth with my hand. I haven't even touched my coffee, but my heart is racing.

> And this scene ... which book is it from?

LITTLEDANCER

Oh God. Do I actually have to give you the title?

> You never have to do anything you don't want to do. But I'm more than happy to read it and give you my advice, if you want. If it looks legit, I can point you toward resources, and we can talk about it some more. If it's problematic ... well ... we can cross that bridge when we get to it.

LITTLEDANCER

a.k.a. you'll suggest I see a therapist? ;)

I'm grinning. Talking to her is *fun*. I'd forgotten how quick and witty she could be because she's sullen and closed off whenever she's around me.

I'll have to change that.

> Very funny. Still waiting on the title.

LITTLEDANCER

It's called His Doll by ME Osborn. It's fan
fiction, so you won't have to buy it or
anything.

> Thank you for telling me. How about
> this? I'll read the book today, and we can
> discuss it tonight. Sound good?

LITTLEDANCER

Sure. Please don't judge me.

> I'm the last person to judge someone for
> where their desires lie.

LITTLEDANCER

Okay. Looking forward to hearing your
thoughts. *cringes*

I huff a laugh and like her message, and after down-
loading the fanfic to my phone, I quickly stand and walk
to my en suite bathroom, where I unsheath my cock.
There's no way I'll be able to get any work done knowing
that Layla might enjoy being degraded and corrupted ...
and that she just might be the perfect submissive for me.

Stroking myself, I think of commanding her to kneel
in front of me ... of degrading her by coming on her face
or calling her names. Of taking someone so innocent and
tearing her down. Breaking her. Splintering her resolve
and making sure she ends up a sobbing, soiled mess on
my hardwood, begging for more.

The fact that she might want that, too? *Fuck.* To
imagine Layla with mascara running down her face as
she chokes on my cock ...

To imagine her with a chapped ass, to take her from

behind like an animal, to slowly but effectively break down every barrier she's constructed over the years ...

To slide my cock between her perfect tits. *Fuck*, I'd give anything to touch her. *Anywhere*. I'd take whatever she gave me, inhaling her sickly sweet scent that always reminded me of summertime. To touch the soft skin, to look into those deep hazel eyes, to watch her mouth drop open and that tiny furrow between her brows to deepen as I unloaded inside her—

I come in record time, groaning as I close my eyes, as pleasure sparks from my balls to my throbbing cock, as thick jets of cum coat the glossy marble floor. The last of it leaves my body. After cleaning up the mess, I change into my swimsuit and walk back to the pool, take a sip of my now-cold coffee, and swim for more than double my usual time to try to get rid of all my pent-up sexual energy.

CHAPTER FIVE

THE REGRET

LAYLA

Oh God.

What have I done?

Right now, a random stranger on the internet is reading one of the filthiest books I've ever read (and that's saying a lot), and soon, we're going to discuss the themes to see if what I want to try is even feasible. Which ... it probably isn't because the book is about a vampire and his human doll. It's raunchy with no plot, but I've read it at least a hundred times. Sol, the protagonist, and Drake, the vampire, could be considered family members at this point. Is it *Twilight* fan fiction? Sure. But it's well-written—and I want to try some of the things Sol and Drake do with someone in real life. I'm just not sure if it's realistic.

Every time I stop and think about Starboy reading it, I cringe.

What the hell was I thinking?

I have the day off from performing and the hour-long intensive I run two days a week, so I walk to my dad's house in order to take my mind off a stranger reading lines such as:

I want you to be addicted to this kind of pleasure, little doll.

I'm looking forward to turning you into my slutty little toy so that you exist only to bring me pleasure.

Is that what you want? To be my fuckbunny?

Bend over and spread those creamy thighs. Good girl ...

Doesn't this feel nice? You were scared for nothing. Let Daddy take care of you and fill your pucker with my cum.

The thought of someone else reading how affectionately cruel Drake is to Sol ... the things they do together ...

I put my phone on Do Not Disturb as I walk up to my dad's house. To my surprise, Orion is sitting on the front porch. He doesn't see me at first, enraptured with something on his phone. I debate turning around because the last thing I need is to get into it with my stepbrother. But just as I take a step back, his head snaps up.

"Hey," he says quickly, pocketing his phone and standing.

"Hi," I reply, waving as I walk up. "Why are you out here?"

Orion shrugs, smirking. "It's a nice day. Scott's out getting burgers. Want me to text him to grab you one?"

Do I?

I mean … I wasn't planning on spending my afternoon with Orion, but I also don't want to give up an afternoon spent with my dad. I can do this. I'll need to get used to him again at some point. For half a second, I let my eyes wander down his white T-shirt, the tattoos on his right arm, and the way his hair is artfully messy. He's in dark jeans and those damn motorcycle boots again.

I can handle this.
I can handle this.
I can handle this.

"Yeah, sure."

His eyes linger on my bare legs for a minute before he gives me a coy, little smile and pulls his phone back out, sending a text to my dad. When he's done, he gestures for me to sit down.

"Care to join me? I was just reading."

"What are you reading?" I ask, crossing my arms and not moving from the front yard. If I get closer, I'll only be more tempted to stare at him up close.

"Just doing a little research for someone special."

White-hot jealousy spikes through me so intensely that I physically rear back. "Oh? I didn't know you were dating someone." There's a bite to my words, and Orion definitely notices because his eyebrows shoot up.

Sometimes I think he's forgotten that I grew up with him and that I can read him like the back of my hand. His expression flicks between a few different emotions—confusion, amusement, and then he hesitates. Like he's measuring me up. And then he schools his expression into something wary and uncomfortable.

"Do you want something to drink?" he asks, squinting at me and rubbing the back of his neck.

What I *want* is to know who he's dating because, as far as I know, Orion doesn't date. *Ever.* Then again, me being jealous is hypocritical. I have no right to be jealous of anyone he may be seeing.

"Uh, okay," I say slowly.

"Let's go inside."

Following him inside, my mind is ringing with curiosity.

Just doing a little research for someone special.

I know from Zoe that he's in the lifestyle like her and her husband, Liam.

My stomach clenches with both envy and fascination at the thought of Orion being into something kinky. I don't know much about any of it, aside from what I've researched about the kinks that interest me, but I'm curious.

Over the past couple of years, Zoe had implied that he wasn't interested in dating, but I suppose I should've known better. As I recall, he was a player in high school, and when I got older, I remember seeing him with different women every week. Even last year, at Zoe and Liam's wedding, he'd been chatting up some brunette woman.

It makes sense that he'd be dating someone.

Orion walks to the fridge and pulls out two sodas for us, and I quickly thank him.

Leaning against the counter, neither of us says anything as we sip our drinks. After a minute, he pretends to go through the mail lying on the kitchen island, and I let myself study him from behind.

What is he into? Zoe never told me, but now I'm curious.

And why do I want to know something like that about my stepbrother?

"How's the new bar?" I ask, hoping to cut through the awkward silence.

"Fine," he answers with his back still to me.

"What's it called? Maybe I can go with Zoe for our next girls' night," I offer.

His whole body stiffens before he turns around. "It's not exactly a girls' night establishment," he replies, lips twitching before crossing his arms.

My brows furrow. "Oh?"

All of a sudden, the front door opens, and my dad hollers into the house. "Hello! I come bearing cheese-burgers."

I don't look away from Orion as he huffs a laugh and walks out of the kitchen.

What the hell was that?

Pulling my phone from my pocket, I text my friends as I hear Orion helping my dad unpack the cheese-burgers in the dining room.

> What's Orion's new bar called? Maybe we can go for our next girl's night.

REMY

Omg.

ZOE

umm …

> What?

REMY

It's a kink club.

My heart stutters. Orion's new bar is a kink club?!

> I'm not opposed to that.

REMY

It's called Inferno.

Inferno … like the place Starboy1997 posted about last week? He'd given a list of safe places to explore kinks on one of his posts, and that was one of them. I remember it because I was surprised Crestwood had a kink club.

> I've heard of it.

ZOE

you have? *wide eyes emoji*

> Yeah. I follow this influencer who talked about it.

REMY

Please tell me that my sweet baby Layla is a Starboy fan …

> You know him?

ZOE

i dont think there are many people in the
lifestyle who dont know him

> He seems nice.

REMY

If you call whips and chains nice, sure.

My heart is beating so fast that I'm panting. I'm
taking in this information like a sponge, eager to absorb
all the information I can about the mysterious Starboy.

> I sent him a dm, and we've been
> talking...

ZOE

hold on ... you and starboy are talking?
about what?

> *smirking emoji*

REMY

My mind is officially blown.

ZOE

im honestly offended we werent notified
immediately but okay *eye roll emoji*

I laugh, and just as I type out a quick response with a
promise to tell them everything the next time I see them,
someone clears their throat from the doorway.

"Ready?" Orion asks, studying me as I pocket my
phone. "The food is here."

I want to ask him if he knows Starboy.

What exactly is his new kink club all about, and why

did he open one? I always assumed he was casual about it, but then again, no one ever told me anything. Zoe, bless her, called me her little vanilla bean.

My mind is bursting with unasked questions, but all I can do is nod. "Okay. Be right there."

The conversation flows easily as we eat, and I even manage to steal a few of Orion's fries when I finish mine. He rolls his eyes before handing the rest to me, and I realize with a start that I haven't stolen food off his plate since before we stopped talking.

"Read any good books lately?" my dad asks me.

Oh God. Talking to my dad about books is always super awkward. My reading tastes have evolved since I lived under his roof, and despite our similar love of books, our reading tastes couldn't be more different.

He likes historical fiction, and I like books where the hero tells the heroine, *I love seeing my pretty little slut mouth take my cock.*

"Oh, you know I always defer back to the classics. I'm rereading *The Hobbit*."

Orion coughs, drumming his fist against his chest a couple of times. "Went down the wrong pipe," he says, clearing his throat.

"That's nice. Orion said you're going to *Phantom of the Opera* next week. That will be nice for the two of you."

I nod, picking at the soggy lettuce I took out from my cheeseburger.

"Is it still your favorite book?" Orion asks pointedly, his head tilted slightly as if genuinely curious.

Growing up, I was *obsessed* with *Phantom of the Opera.*

I had posters, I dressed as Christine, the main female character, four Halloweens in a row, and even had parts of the book memorized by heart. I owned a few special editions of the book, too. I hadn't seen the play in years and couldn't wait to geek out over seeing it performed live.

If only Orion wouldn't be there to bear witness to my enthusiasm. I could already imagine the smirk on his face when he saw me mouthing along to the lyrics or getting misty-eyed during "*All I Ask of You.*"

"Yes. I may or may not be stalking a first edition worth thirty-two thousand dollars."

Orion lets loose a long, slow whistle. "That's a lot of fucking money for a book."

I sit up straighter. He doesn't understand. "No harm in looking, right?"

My dad clears his throat and changes the subject. "How's my catson?"

I roll my eyes. "You don't have to call him that," I tease, thinking of his affectionate name for Sparrow.

"I know. I'll have to come over and give him some scritches soon." He sets his shake down, and I narrow my eyes. He's not supposed to be drinking milkshakes, but I don't want to micromanage, so I don't say anything.

"That reminds me, I need to call Gary back," my dad mutters, pushing away from the table.

"How'd he go from Sparrow to Gary?" I mutter to Orion.

"I'm not sure I want to know."

I smile, thinking of the bearded guy my dad's been

best friends with for thirty-five years. They owned a few bars across the Los Angeles area together before they both retired a couple of years ago. Now, they spend their time doing things like fishing and golfing.

"I worry about him sometimes. I can't really help out with my measly salary."

"I have it covered, Layla. I'm more than capable of taking care of my family."

My family.

There's that warm, tingly feeling again.

"Thanks. That's nice of you."

Something shutters behind his eyes before he clears his throat and stands. "I should get back to reading. Will you be around today, or are you heading back home?"

That now-familiar pang of jealousy is back, and I clench my jaw to dispel the tense, anxious feeling inside me.

"I'd planned to hang around."

"Movie?" he asks, smiling slightly.

The way his lips lift casually ... his stance as if he's waiting for me ... it feels so familiar.

Like old times.

"Sure."

I stand and follow him to the living room, and we take our usual seats—me on the left recliner, him on the right one. He whistles and turns the TV on, and a few seconds later, my dad ambles back into the room.

"*The Mummy*?" Orion suggests, flicking through options.

"A classic," I answer, leaning back in my seat.

My dad takes his usual spot on the couch, pulling the ottoman over and placing his bare feet on top.

It feels so normal—almost like the last seven years never happened.

I can't remember the last time I allowed myself to just *be* around Orion without wanting to start a fight, and as the beginning credits begin to roll, I think about why I always seem to pick fights with him.

He ruined my audition seven years ago, but it's more than that—it felt like a *betrayal*. He was the one who helped me pick the audition song. The one who promised he'd be there for me. The one who watched me practice for hours—hundreds of hours, probably. He would choose to help me through insecurity and doubt about my repertoire rather than go out with his friends.

Growing up, I always wanted siblings, but of course my mom and dad only had me before my mom ran away. Then my dad met Felicity a few years later, and all of a sudden, I had stepbrothers.

It was the best day of my life, and from that point forward, my entire axis tilted slightly.

My world *completely* revolved around Orion.

And then, in one instant, he ruined everything. My future, my trust … it shattered around us that day, and every time I saw him, it felt as though I was opening those wounds all over again.

I sip my soda and watch as Rick O'Connell—a.k.a. Brendan Fraser—meets Evelyn from the comfort of his prison cell. The cast is beautiful, and I'm not ashamed to admit that I once wrote terrible fan fiction based on Rick, Evelyn, and Imhotep.

Pulling my phone out of the pocket of my shorts, I glance down at texts from Zoe and Remy, as well as a new message from Starboy1997. I take it out of Do Not Disturb mode. Looking around discreetly, my dad is already asleep with his head back, and Orion is fixated on his phone, so I swipe the message open.

> STARBOY1997
> This is actually pretty good.

I smile before quickly schooling my face into neutrality, lest Orion see me grinning at my phone like a maniac.

> Oh? Well, that's good.

> STARBOY1997
> So far, what I'm reading is fairly common in the community. Nothing stands out as unrealistic or over the top. The author did their research.

> I'm glad you're enjoying it.

He doesn't respond despite me waiting several minutes, and it takes me a minute to realize that I've been nervously chewing on my nails.

"Everything okay?" Orion asks, looking up from his phone.

"Yeah. Fine," I say quickly, ignoring him while I look at the screen. Even though I could probably recite this entire movie by heart, I'm having trouble concentrating.

My phone vibrates.

I fumble, trying to unlock it, and Orion huffs a laugh.

My heart leaps into my chest when I see another message from the mysterious, masked man.

STARBOY1997

Is that you in your profile picture?

I bite my lower lip, thinking of this guy looking at my profile. It's private—a decision I made when I started dancing professionally. Suddenly, a friend request comes through, and I nearly squeak out loud.

"You sure you're okay?" Orion asks, breaking me out of my stupor.

"I'm fine," I practically growl.

I glance at him quickly before looking down at my phone, totally engrossed in the conversation with Starboy.

I confirm the friend request on my phone and wait—scrolling through months and years of my life. There's everything from pictures of my dad and me, Zoe and Remy on random girls' nights, *lots* of pictures of Sparrow, and random other things like my pointe shoes, peonies, my library and reading nook, and sometimes pictures of what I'm reading—the PG ones, that is. Just as I'm about to lock the screen again and focus on the movie, I get another message.

STARBOY1997

You're beautiful. I hope someone tells you that often.

I know I shouldn't be blushing from what a stranger told me on the internet, but I am.

> Thanks. And no, there's no one. I'm pretty invisible.

STARBOY1997

> You sure? Because it's hard to believe you just walk through life without anyone noticing.

I nearly drop my phone as my heart sputters inside my chest. No one's ever said anything like that to me. Yes, I'm a ballet dancer, but when my shoes are off, I usually wear sweatpants and glasses at home. Plus, I've spent the past ten or so years battling crippling self-loathing and horrid thoughts about my body.

To have someone call me beautiful right off the bat ...

"Are you still watching?" Orion asks, sounding almost annoyed.

My dad is snoring now, and I look over at my step-brother, who has his phone resting on his lap.

"You've been on your phone, too," I accuse.

"You're right. I have been," he confesses, grinning. "I'm getting another drink. Want one?"

"Just water for me," I tell him absentmindedly.

He stands up and walks out of the room, and I unlock my phone again, staring at Starboy's message.

You sure? Because it's hard to believe you just walk through life without anyone noticing.

Oh, he's good.

I'm smiling as I reply.

> No one I notice, at least.

STARBOY1997

Ah, I see. Well, I can guarantee people are noticing. You said before that you don't date much. Is there a reason?

I chew on my lower lip while I debate how to answer him, because I'm still trying to figure it all out myself.

What the hell.

> Do you know what demisexual means?

STARBOY1997

I do.

> That's how I identify. I need to develop feelings for someone before I can be sexually attracted to them. Makes it hard to date when feelings usually develop long past when other parties lose interest.

STARBOY1997

I understand completely. I'm going to keep reading. I'll message you when I finish.

> Looking forward to it.

My cheeks are hot as I lock my phone and pocket it again. I try to concentrate on the movie, but my phone vibrates with another notification.

Starboy has posted a new video, and my thumb hovers over the notification. As much as I want to watch it right here and now, I'd die of mortification if Orion found out. I'm tempted to leave—to walk to my house and watch the video in private like I want to—but I'm also enjoying the rare camaraderie with Orion, and it wouldn't be fair to my dad if I ate and left. I'd intended to spend the day with him, and though I wasn't expecting Orion to be here too, I can't help but miss the way we used to hang out like this.

"Here you go," he says, handing me a glass of room-temperature water with a lemon slice.

I snap my eyes to him. "You remember how I like my water?"

He shrugs. "Of course I do." I notice he's drinking water too, and curiosity gets the best of me, so I ask the question I've been thinking about for weeks.

"Are you not drinking anymore?" I ask as casually as I can.

"I haven't had alcohol in over two years."

My eyes go wide. "Really? I had no idea."

"I'd rather not repeat the hell that was rehab," he admits, looking at the TV rather than me.

"Do you miss it?" I ask without thinking. "Sorry, that's really personal. You don't have to answer," I add, looking away from him.

"It's okay. And not really. I miss not thinking and not feeling. But I fucked a lot of things up when I was drinking. I ruined job opportunities, friendships, relationships ... I mean, I'm still living with the consequences of my actions while I was drinking around the clock," he says, turning to face me.

His regret is so evident that it almost feels like physical pain. I sip my water to dispel the emotion clogging my throat—to distract myself from the absolute hurt and longing that lay naked in his darkened eyes.

"I'm proud of you."

"Thanks, La-La," he murmurs. *La-La. He hasn't called me that in years.*

I give him a small smile, and he looks surprised for a second before he smiles and turns to the TV.

I don't know what, but something between us just shifted.

On the one hand, I'm still livid about what he did all those years ago. My future was wide open for me, and some nights, I lie awake and think of what my life would be like had I gone to Paris. I love dancing for the Pacific Ballet Company, and the fact that I've managed to snag the lead role after only a few years of dancing professionally is practically unheard of. I enjoy being close to Dad. But a small part of me wonders if I'd be happier in Europe, and blaming Orion for all of it was just easier.

He was my best friend, and it wasn't the ruined opportunity that hurt the most.

The betrayal—the breach of trust—made it unforgivable in my eyes.

Showing up drunk. Breaking into my audition. *Embarrassing* me.

On the other hand, it's been seven years. While I doubt we'll ever be best friends again, maybe I can work toward forgiving him.

For so long, I begged the universe that he'd get sober. Watching a loved one go down that path was … horrific.

But if he's been sober for over two years—a feat that astounds me—maybe I can try to be cordial with him. Perhaps I don't always have to decline invitations to events I know he'll be at or roll my eyes if Zoe brings him up. Maybe next week at *Phantom of the Opera* wouldn't be so bad, after all. It *was* my favorite book. The possibility of being cordial—even friendly—is tempting.

He's trying, so I can make an effort, too.

Maybe it's time to let go and see where forgiveness can take us.

CHAPTER SIX

THE SELFIE

ORION

I can hardly concentrate for the rest of the afternoon. Every time Layla looks at her phone, I hold my breath and wait for her to cave and watch Starboy's new video. After all, I posted it on the fly specifically *for her*. And once she sees it, she'll know it's for her.

The selfish bastard part of me wants to be sitting right next to her when she watches the video I took this morning—me wearing my mask in a dark room with text straight from her book laid over me.

And music from Tchaikovsky's "*Swan Lake*."

"*Don't you dare touch me. I scratch and bite.*"

"*You'll learn to crawl and beg too, darling.*"

I know Layla will lose her shit, and I'd sell my soul to watch her eyes take in the words from her filthy book and know Starboy posted for her.

However, she has more self-control than I expect. She's still at Scott's when I have to leave to work at Inferno's bar.

I say a quick goodbye to Layla and Scott—the latter of whom took a solid two-hour nap—and head to downtown Crestwood. The ride is long due to traffic, but it doesn't matter because I feel on top of the fucking world.

One smile.

She smiles at me for the first time in years, and I feel invincible.

I run home quickly to change and say hello to Earl, ensuring he's happy and content in his aviary.

"Hello, Master," he squawks. "Pretty girl?"

I stop walking. "Soon."

After grabbing a water, I walk to my bedroom, shedding my T-shirt and jeans and swapping them for a black button-up and black slacks. I quickly freshen up while checking my phone—my messages, specifically.

LITTLEDANCER

Don't mind me. I'm just over here melting over your latest post.

My pulse quickens as I smile, deciding to flirt just a bit.

Prove it.

I know I've now opened a can of worms. This started as an innocent question on her part, but somehow, things feel more serious now.

I can't fuck this up. This might be my last chance to get close to her. I have to play this right or risk losing her forever. I should feel guilty, but I don't. Not really. I know I can't continue under the Starboy alias forever. There will come a time when she'll figure out we're one and the same. But until that time comes, I'll do everything in my power to make her mine, once and for all.

When the time comes for the mask to fall, I'll have to be sure she wants me just as much as I want her.

I'm taking the elevator down to the street when her response comes in.

> LITTLEDANCER
>
> *attachment*

My thumb hovers over the hidden image—and my heart thrills with anticipation. I press down, and a picture of Layla lying in bed appears.

It's not revealing at all—in fact, it looks like she has the covers up to her chin. But it's her face, her eyes dark and sultry eyes behind her glasses, her lower lip between her teeth.

Fuck.

My cock twitches, and I let out a long, slow breath.

> You follow directions so well.

> LITTLEDANCER
>
> Guess you're just special.

Fuck. She's throwing exactly what I said to her this

morning back at me, and her clever wit is really fucking hot.

> I have somewhere to be right now, but we can talk about the book later. How does 10 p.m. sound?

LITTLEDANCER

Okay. You already finished reading it?

> I read all day.

> And just so you know, I think you're beautiful. Even more so when you're "melting."

LITTLEDANCER

Are you flirting with me?

> What would you say if I am?

LITTLEDANCER

Between this and the video ... *hot face emoji*

The elevator doors open, and I walk out onto the street toward Inferno, which is a few blocks away. I should be shutting this conversation down. I should tell her I can't help her with her discovery—I'm not a teacher. I'm a *Dom*. There's a difference. A Dom who claims to want to teach is usually considered predatory. I am my own worst enemy here since I teach people how to look out for people like me. I expect my submissives to be educated, well-versed, and knowledgeable about their limits, likes, and dislikes.

I never get involved with fans as Starboy.

I never let myself get too interested in the messages I receive—in fact, Layla's was the first I'd ever responded to.

However, when it comes to my stepsister, I'm ready and willing to break all the rules.

If I'm going to break the protocol I've set for myself, I might as well do it with her.

> I need to know something before we continue.

LITTLEDANCER

?

> If we continue talking like this, will it be within the boundaries of BDSM, or are we just friends? I don't want to overstep or coerce you into anything.

I walk two blocks before she responds, and I nearly run into several people checking my phone every other second.

LITTLEDANCER

I'm not sure. I'm not experienced like you, but I think I'd like to try it. You're not coercing me. If anything, I'm coercing you.

> That's why I stress that you do your own research and talking with other submissives in the community. Do you have a submissive mentor?

LITTLEDANCER

I have two friends in the lifestyle who are also submissives.

Okay, good. And we can start slow.

LITTLEDANCER

Do you do this often?

Never.

LITTLEDANCER

blushes

I need to know you're confident enough
not to agree to things or ideas you don't
like. Later on, we can establish a safe
word if we engage in any sort of play,
whether online or in person.

LITTLEDANCER

I am, and I agree.

I'm grinning as I walk up to the front door of Inferno,
hanging back a bit as I say goodbye to Layla.

I have to go, but we'll talk tonight.

LITTLEDANCER

Have a good night. :)

Here's my number in case you'd rather
text me.

attachment

Thanks. :)

I sigh and lean against the external wall of Inferno,
running a hand through my hair.

Now I had to pick up a burner phone—because if
Layla and I were going to actually do this, I couldn't use
my real number.

Once I'm inside, and after walking through tonight's events with the general manager, I make my way behind the bar and start to pour drinks for anyone who wants their first and only drink. Due to the nature of the Paradise/Purgatory levels, excess alcohol and kink don't exactly go hand in hand, so all patrons are limited to one drink. I've kicked out more than a few patrons who thought they could be sneaky with flasks, and they've since been banned. The rules are in bold in numerous places, as the safety of everyone here is paramount.

It's busy tonight, and I greet everyone who comes up to the bar for a drink, asking them what they think of the establishment. I like talking to the people who inhabit my places—and this one is no different. I recognize a couple of people from the local munch Zoe and I host every week at the pub down the street, but otherwise, word has spread organically over the last few months within the local lifestyle community. People are eager for a local safe space, and I'm more than happy to provide it.

The bespoke furniture, the dark and haunting atmosphere, and the low, classical music give it an almost ethereal vibe. Upstairs in *Paradise,* it's bright and white—lots of gold, mirrors, rounded corners, and soft things, like fur. There's a voyeur room, a game room, a room where toys can be purchased in order to be used, a feather room, a food room, and private rooms that can be booked.

In *Purgatory,* it's the exact opposite. Because the building used to be a lumberyard, there's a large cellar with vaulted ceilings and old coal storerooms. We decided not to add any windows—instead, outfitting the entire section with dim red lights and black flame candles. There are lots of iron fixtures and black paint, manacles and chains everywhere, and sharp edges. There's a wax room, a rope room, a chain room, a prison room, a spanking room, and a medieval torture room.

Neither floor is obligated to adhere to sadism or pleasure—in fact, we encourage people to explore both. I've hired the best dungeon monitors who are here for safety, watching over all play to make sure it's safe and that the right tools are on hand. They also ensure that safe words are obeyed and are first aid trained should the worst happen.

There are also House Doms and Dommes—experienced tops that are here to give people suggestions or advice, tasters, and demos.

I pay them all triple what they'd make elsewhere.

Observing is encouraged, and before playing in any room, nondisclosure agreements must be signed, as well as safety waivers so that Inferno isn't liable if anything happens. While people are welcome to play with the House Doms and Dommes, the rooms are also available for private booking.

A steady stream of people crowds the bar to replenish fluids with non-alcoholic drinks or for a breather between scenes. I say hi to those I know, and I introduce myself to those I don't. I make sure all the people who are curious about kink know about SSC (Safe, Sane, and Consensual) as well as RACK (Risk Aware Consensual Kink). Most of the people here are experienced enough to know the basics, but we do get some people, like Layla, who read a scene in a book and get curious. Because we welcome those new to kink, I try to do my part. Vetting my people with multiple, thorough background checks and community references is the hardest part of this job.

By the time I leave at half past nine, I'm exhausted. I say goodbye to Jack, the bouncer, and we bump fists.

"You're heading home early," he muses, wiggling his eyebrows. It's true—Inferno usually stays open until two in the morning, and most nights I'm locking the place up.

I shrug. "I have an important call."

I've attempted to keep my cool all night, but now that I get to discuss Layla's biggest fantasies *with* her … I wipe my palms on my slacks.

I had a woman ask to play with me tonight, and I didn't even entertain the idea before declining. In fact, I haven't done a scene with a sub in … *weeks*. My heart just isn't in it.

"Ah, I see. Well, enjoy your *call*," Jack says, smirking. "She must be someone special."

I smile and walk off without answering because he has no fucking idea.

Stopping in a convenience store, I'm in luck when they have both a burner smartphone and a dry-erase board—so that I can communicate with her without having to disguise my voice. I head back to my penthouse, and at five minutes to ten, I send LittleDancer a message.

> Should I call you? Or would you rather speak here?

It takes her a minute to answer, so I quickly pull my button-up off and throw my mask and black hoodie on.

LITTLEDANCER

Sure. We can do video or... not? Sorry I've never done this.

> Don't apologize. We can do video, but I'd like to keep my face and voice disguised. I have a dry-erase board so that we can speak. How does that sound?

LITTLEDANCER

If only you knew sign language. ;)

I stare at her message. Does Layla know sign language? Fuck, that's news to me.

> I do, actually. I had a sub for over a year who was hard of hearing. You know sign language?

LITTLEDANCER

Yeah ... my best friend in elementary school was deaf so I learned for her. Granted, it's been ... decades ... but I'm sure we can get me back up to speed.

Which friend? I ask before quickly erasing it. Racking my brain, I don't recall her having a friend who was deaf, so it must've been before I moved in.

> Most of my fluency is concentrated
> around BDSM terms and
> directions/commands.

LITTLEDANCER

Like I said, we'll get me up to speed. ;)

Fuck.

I'm hard already.

> Give me a minute. I'll call you.

For the first time in months—*years*—I wish I could take a couple of shots of alcohol to calm my nerves. Then again, I want to remember everything about this, and being drunk would mean I couldn't think clearly and offer sound advice.

I adjust my erection and pull the burner phone out of the box, activating it in just over a minute and creating a place for it on my bookshelf so that there's only a white wall behind me. Grabbing the dry-erase board just in case, I dim the lights slightly, grab my desk chair, and set myself up. I also make a mental note to disguise my handwriting in case Layla recognizes it.

Taking a deep breath, I ensure my hood and mask are on correctly before dialing Layla's number.

Here goes fucking nothing.

CHAPTER SEVEN
THE VIDEO

LAYLA

My phone rings with an unknown number. I make a note of the local area code, and despite trying, I can't seem to steady my erratic pulse. Despite my nerves, anticipation and excitement make it feel like my heart is being jump started.

I'm currently sitting at my two-person dining table and my phone is propped up on my fruit bowl. I smooth my hair and sit up straighter before answering, and when I do, it takes a second to connect the video. I don't take a breath until it does, and when he comes into view, I try to swallow down the nerves, but my mouth is too dry to do anything but stare.

Starboy is on mute and sitting in a chair against a nondescript white wall. He's wearing black pants, and a black hoodie is pulled over his signature skull balaclava.

The lighting is dim enough that I can't make out any distinguishing features like eye color, though his biceps are pronounced well, and I can see them through the thick cotton fabric of the sweatshirt.

My eyes skirt to the small rectangle that shows my video feed, and I realize with heated cheeks that I've just been staring at him wide-eyed. I'd changed into sweatpants, and my hair is loose and wavy around my shoulders. I'd debated wearing something *sexier*, but I didn't want to give him the wrong impression, and also, I'm not exactly known for my sex appeal. When I wasn't dancing, I was just Layla—a single cat lady who spent her Saturday mornings grocery shopping and her evenings reading about women who got railed by thousand-year-old demons.

I hadn't even bothered putting in my contacts, so he was getting the real me with glasses, no makeup, and an old shirt that said *"Men are better in books."*

Do I say something first? Should I use sign language?

Crap, I've even forgotten how to say hi in sign language. In fact, I've forgotten how to do anything but stare at the person on the other end of this call.

He leans forward and grabs something, and it takes me a second to see him set a small dry-erase board on his lap and write something out. A second later, he holds it up.

Hi.

I blush. "Hi," I answer, wincing. "Can you hear me?"

He nods and moves his hands, and it takes me a second to realize he's asking how I am in sign language. Fortunately for me, sign language has always been easy for me to observe and interpret. I think it's because I learned it at such a young age, but whenever I see it in real life, I can usually decipher it. I had a student a couple of years ago who was hard of hearing, and I picked it up again really quickly then, too.

"I'm good," I tell him, slowly signing. "I'm definitely rusty with sign language." I laugh. I swear he smiles, but I can't really tell with the mask covering his face. "How are you?" I ask, signing. It helps me to speak the words as I sign.

He shrugs and grabs the dry-erase board, rubbing the previous words off before writing something new. His handwriting is bold and blocky—all caps.

TIRED, BUT BETTER NOW THAT I'M TALKING TO YOU.

My mouth opens and closes. My heart gallops inside my chest, but I decide to play it cool and resist melting into a puddle on top of my dining room table.

"Same," I say lamely.

He signs something else, and I squint, trying to decipher it. He repeats the motions, and I realize he's telling me about the book.

"So … the book. Can you tell me about which parts, exactly, you'd like to act out?"

I swallow. "Umm, all of it."

His shoulders shake, and I realize he's laughing.

God, I wish I could see what he looks like when he laughs.

He leans forward slightly. *"Let's start with the first few chapters,"* he signs.

"Okay," I agree, signing.

"Drake meets Sol in college while he's posing as a student," Starboy signs. *"In chapter four, another man flirts with Sol when she's out in another city with some friends. That causes him to kidnap Sol and hold her captive against her will."*

"Well, it's not *exactly* against her will," I explain. "Her consent is dubious but very quickly turns enthusiastic."

Can you tell me which parts, specifically, you want to try?

My tongue feels thick as I respond. "Umm ... I like the idea of being controlled. Of someone telling me what to do and what not to do. I don't know. Something about being owned like that ... not having to be in control, learning to trust someone implicitly ..." Again, I don't bother signing this time.

"You want to be controlled?" he signs. *"As in power exchange?"*

"Maybe," I sign.

Starboy sits quietly for a minute before pulling the dry-erase board closer, erasing the last phrase and writing something else. It feels like he's writing forever, and I fully expect him to say something like *This was a bad idea. I never want to talk to you again.* I chew on my lower lip as I watch his hand grip the marker and the veins pop along his large palm and long fingers. Finally, he holds the board up, and it takes me a minute to read what he wrote.

> **LOOK, THE FOUNDATION OF ANY BDSM DYNAMIC IS CONSENT. POWER EXCHANGE IS, AT ITS CORE, A GAME OF PRETEND. WHEN I SPANK A SUBMISSIVE OR PUNISH HER IN ANY OTHER WAY, I'M DOING IT BECAUSE SHE'S LETTING ME. LIKE I SAID, IT ALL COMES DOWN TO CONSENT. I ONLY HAVE THE POWER I'M GIVEN. I DON'T TAKE POWER, AND ANY CREDIBLE DOMINANT KNOWS THAT RESPECT IS EARNED.**

"*I understand,*" I sign.

"*Good,*" he signs back. "*I think we should start slowly. I can establish some ground rules, and you can see how you feel following them for a few days.*"

I squirm in my seat when I think of being controlled by Starboy—of knowing *he* gave me rules to abide by. A small, dormant part of me relishes in the idea of pleasing him. Like most women who were straight-A students in high school, the idea of doing a good job for him is a turn-on.

"*How does that sound?*" he asks.

I nod.

"*I need to hear you say it, little dancer.*"

"*That sounds good,*" I tell him, signing. My hands shake as I move them to form the right words. "*What exactly are your ... rules?*"

Starboy spreads his legs slightly, and I can't help but

admire how good he looks leaning back in his chair with his mask.

"Let's use chapter six of the book. When Drake doesn't let Sol touch herself. I don't want you to touch yourself until I give you permission," he signs almost too quickly for me to interpret.

I suck in a sharp breath. "W-when will you give me permission?"

His shoulders shake again. *"That's for me to know and for you to obey."*

Holy hell.

"And then what?" I sign.

"Let's see how it goes for a few days. I'd like you to check in every day. You have my number now."

I swallow as excitement races through my veins. "Okay."

"If this goes well, we can discuss the next steps," he signs. *"And if you follow my directions well, you will be rewarded."*

I shift in my seat as ideas of *how* I'll be rewarded float through my overactive imagination.

"One last thing," he signs. *"I expect full monogamy while we're doing this. I will abide by the same rules, and I won't take a romantic partner or submissive while we're involved."*

"Of course," I nearly sputter out. The idea of dating someone else while talking to Starboy already feels wrong. An image of Orion flashes through my mind uninvited, but I very quickly push it away.

Orion is my stepbrother, and *that* can and will never happen.

"Good girl. If this goes well, we can try something else from the book next week."

"Okay," I nearly whisper. "And you're sure you want to do this with me?" I'm suddenly feeling insecure. "I mean, I'm just some random stranger from the internet."

Starboy's eyes bore into the camera, and I swear he's reprimanding me with a dark, silent glare. Grabbing the dry-erase board, he uses his sleeve to erase the last block of text and write something else. Again, I worry he's going to call this whole thing off, and I take a few deep breaths to quell the anxiety.

> **THIS IS THE FIRST TIME I'VE EVER DONE SOMETHING LIKE THIS. BUT SOMETHING ABOUT YOUR MESSAGE MADE ME WANT TO HELP YOU. CAN I BE HONEST WITH YOU?**

My breathing hitches. "Yes, be honest," I tell him a little breathlessly.

He watches me for a second before looking down and adding to the text on the board.

> **IF I KNEW YOU IN REAL LIFE, I'D ASK YOU TO BE MY SUBMISSIVE. FULL STOP. I'M HOLDING BACK. SO LET ME DO THIS. FOR YOU, BUT ALSO FOR ME.**

I've completely lost the ability to speak, so instead I think of how to sign what I'm feeling.

"That's really nice," I tell him with my hands.

"Trust me, I'm not nice," he signs in response.

I chew on my lower lip while I think of how to respond. *"I don't think I want nice,"* I sign slowly. "I read dark romance because I always fall for the villains. I want someone whose intentions are good, but instead of buying me flowers, he cuts off my ex's hands. Nice guys are just that—they're *nice*. But I want someone who will be all-consumed by me no matter what."

Starboy hangs his head and rubs the back of his neck, and the gesture reminds me *so* much of Orion ... I squeeze my eyes closed. *Why* the hell am I thinking of him right now?

Grabbing the board, he erases the last block of text and writes something new. My heart pounds as he holds it up for me to read.

> **WELL, TO BE FAIR, YOU CAN HAVE BOTH—THE GUY WHO BUYS YOU FLOWERS AND CUTS OFF YOUR EX'S HANDS.**

He looks up at me, and I swear I see a devious gleam in his eyes.

> **YOU WANT SOMEONE TO CORRUPT YOU. AND I'M MORE THAN HAPPY TO OBLIGE IN A SAFE, SANE, AND CONSENSUAL WAY. IF YOU'LL HAVE ME, THAT IS.**

Wow.
We're really doing this.

Starboy writes something else on the board, and I hold my breath.

I'M ALL IN.

"Me too," I tell him, signing at the same time.

"Please send me your address or PO Box. I'd like to send you a few things over the next week. I will also need your email address so that I can send over a basic contract," he signs.

"Okay. What would you like me to call you?"

Online, I'd seen that Dominants sometimes wanted to be called Sir or Daddy.

His head snaps up, and I swear his eyes widen just slightly. He takes the board, erases the words, and writes new ones.

YOU CAN REFER TO ME AS MASTER. AND YOU?

My blood thrums with arousal. This is crazy. I've never done anything like this before, yet I can't believe I waited this long to experiment. Zoe and Remy talk about being in the lifestyle every once in a while, and it's been interesting.

However, I've never been captivated like *this*.

I'm starting to suspect it has nothing to do with Drake and Sol but instead has something to do with the commanding way Starboy just established his dominance over a video.

"Yes, Master," I say softly. "My name is Layla, but you

can call me anything. And I don't think I know the sign for Master."

Starboy makes two fists and then extends his hands in a downward motion, and I copy him a few times before he signs, "*well done.*"

He grabs the board and writes some more.

1. Check in with me every day.

2. Do not touch yourself unless you get permission from me. I'll know if you do.

3. Sign the contract.

On paper, it sounds simple enough. Nothing too crazy, and it'll be a good way to get my toes wet. I'm still doubtful of why he wants to help *me* of all people, and then I remember what he said.

I'm holding back. So let me do this. For you, but also for me.

"Okay. I agree," I tell him verbally.

"*Stop overthinking,*" he says, signing slowly.

I huff a laugh. "I'll try."

He cocks his head. "*Fuck, you have no idea how much power you have over me, do you?*" he signs. "*I should go. We'll talk tomorrow at 10a.m.*"

I sit up straighter. "Yes, Master."

He shakes his head, but it doesn't look displeased. It looks ... in *awe.*

How is it that this powerful and important man is in awe of me?

"Good night, Layla," he signs, and the call disconnects just as his words float through my distracted mind.

If I knew you in real life, I'd ask you to be my submissive. Full stop. I'm holding back. So let me do this. For you, but also for me.

So let me do this. For you, but also for me.

For me.

Me.

Without thinking, I text Starboy. I don't care if I sound needy. Communication is key, right?

> I'm still trying to figure out what's in this for you.

STARBOY1997

> You've given me the honor of consenting to this. The reason you relate to Sol so much is because you're a natural submissive. You're also beautiful and intelligent, and you seem to understand me better than any of my other two million followers.
>
> Is that sufficient? ;)

My stomach flutters with something I haven't felt in ... years.

I occasionally meet men who are mutual friends or whom I meet online while perusing one of the horrid dating apps. But I've never felt anything close to something like this for any of them. Before my falling-out with Orion, I did feel like this around him, but that was because he was older and cool—unlike me, a wallflower in high school.

Most men are just not my type.

I tried dabbling in dating a woman once, but that felt all wrong, too. That's when I did more research and discovered the asexual umbrella. From there, I found the definition of demisexual. Something clicked in my mind and I stopped trying to fight against the tide of bad dates and zero chemistry.

I'd slept around a little bit—with three guys, all of whom were my friends—but it never led to anything serious. Sometimes I wondered if I'd ever find someone or if I was meant to live my life alone forever. If I needed feelings before feeling sexually interested, that just made it that much harder to find a guy who would understand and be willing to be patient, especially in today's dating environment.

I had a high sex drive, but I just didn't feel that sexual attraction very often.

Until now.

> That's more than sufficient.

STARBOY1997

I have a question now.

> Okay ...

STARBOY1997

What made you reach out to me?

My fingers hover over the keyboard, and I have to think of how to word the truth. It's not like I've been a follower of his for months but saying it out loud sounds even crazier.

> Truthfully, I found your profile the day I messaged you. I hadn't been a follower before that, but I wish I'd found you sooner.

STARBOY1997

Or maybe you found me at the perfect time.

I'm smiling as I heart his message, second-guessing it and wondering if I should do a thumb's up instead when another text pops up below his last message.

STARBOY1997

You overthinking? Don't. I liked the heart.

Damn.

> Caught me. Can I ask one more question?

STARBOY1997

Go ahead.

> How old are you? And what's your first name?

Three dots appear and disappear several times, and I chew on my thumb as I wait for him to respond. Finally, he answers.

STARBOY1997

To you, I am Master. I'm not opposed to giving you my real name, but it's unique and would be easy to identify. As for my age ... let's say I'm older than 30 but younger than 35. ;)

My mind is spinning with the new information. Okay, so he's not sixty, but he's older than me by a few years. And a unique first name ... hmm.

Thank you for telling me. I just wanted to be sure I wasn't falling for someone who's a grandpa.

STARBOY1997

If we're getting technical, a 35-year-old could feasibly be a grandpa.

I laugh out loud, startling Sparrow who is lounging on the couch a few feet away. Covering my mouth, I shake my head.

Fair enough.

STARBOY1997

Sleep tight, Little Dancer.

I heart his message before I let my head fall forward onto the table, groaning and smiling and asking myself what the hell I've just gotten myself into.

CHAPTER EIGHT

THE CONTROL

Layla

I sleep in the following morning, forgoing my morning exercise routine. I attempt to do some barre every morning, as well as some basic cardio and weight training, but I was up late reading over Starboy's contract. I also spent at least an hour tossing and turning, wishing I could get rid of the pulsing between my legs. Alas, I wasn't desperate enough to break the rules on night one, but it definitely left me feeling empty and burning until I finally fell asleep around two.

The contract was simple and basic. For a minute, I considered asking Zoe for help, since she was more experienced in all of this. However, after some thought, I decided I'd talk to her about it in person the next time I saw her.

The contract didn't touch on anything other than

what we discussed, though there was a clause about safe words. It explained the stoplight system—how the word "red" was to be used to stop all play, "yellow" to pause and communicate, and "green" to keep going. I couldn't envision a scenario where I'd need to use it, especially since our play would be online and mostly to gauge what I liked by taking it slowly.

The part that kept me up was the in-person meeting part, which was marked with an N/A.

Not applicable.

Except I *do* want to meet him in person, and the need to do so is strong, which surprises me. But if he only sees this as an online thing ... I shouldn't be getting so attached so soon.

It would almost certainly lead to my heart being broken.

Also, *this isn't me.*

I don't get attached to men. I just don't. Emotional connection takes a long time to establish, and to me, it's not really worth it. I'm never interested like *this*, or if there is a small inkling of curiosity about a date, they usually ruin it by bringing up my dancing or trying to get into my pants before I'm ready. In my very narrow experience with okay sex, it only happened once I'd made friends with someone, and even then, I was never truly into it.

Society places such a strong emphasis on physical attraction and sexual chemistry as important parts of dating and relationships. Being demisexual, I so often feel out of sync with the norms, which leads to me feeling isolated and misunderstood.

So why am I so into this stranger on the internet?

What is it about Starboy that appeals to me?

Is it just that we bonded quickly and deeply? Or is it because Starboy wasn't placing pressure on me?

Once, before I knew what demisexuality was, I'd dated a guy who was kind, patient, and willing to wait for my feelings to develop. And they did—a little bit, at least. His name was Erik, and him taking the pressure off helped immensely with letting things happen organically. It didn't work out in the end, but it was very difficult to find men who were so willing to wait for me in that way.

Perhaps it's because Starboy and I are only talking online, which means the societal pressure of instant attraction is off the table?

Except I was attracted to him immediately.

And I suppose I was curious to see if that attraction would translate in person or if he was actually just some online creeper.

I hope not, since I'd sent Starboy my address.

My nerves are all over the place because I gave a strange man my home address. But my dad had helped me install a state-of-the-art security system when I bought the place, so I am at least protected that way. Besides, I hate to admit it, but if Starboy broke in wearing his mask, I'm not sure I'd be scared.

I think I'd be turned the hell on.

What is happening to me?!

Groaning, I roll over and cover my face with my hands. Sparrow purrs on the pillow next to me, and I reach over to him, pulling him into my chest.

"What am I going to do, Row Row?"

Sparrow meows his answer and purrs louder, nuzzling into my neck.

Suddenly, my phone rings, scaring Sparrow enough to send him jumping off my bed.

My heart leaps into my throat when I see it's Starboy —or *Master,* as I'd renamed him in my phone.

I frantically sit up, pull my glasses on, and smooth my hair, running my tongue over my lips and teeth so I don't look like I just woke up.

Crap, crap, crap.

I hit the answer button, hoping the still-dark bedroom will work to my advantage. Starboy is muted again, and today, he's wearing his mask but no hoodie— just a black, long-sleeved shirt. The balaclava covers his whole head, though, so I can't even tell what color his hair is.

His video is also just as dark as last night.

"Morning," he signs.

"Morning," I croak.

"Did you just wake up?" he asks, signing.

I smile sheepishly. "Yes. I was up late envisioning a masked man breaking into my house because I stupidly gave a stranger my home address."

His shoulders shake with laughter. "*A nightmare or a daydream?*"

I smile. "A little of both," I say.

He laughs again. *"There's a package waiting for you at your door."*

Perking up, I tilt my head. "Already?"

He shrugs. *"You don't live far from me."*

I get out of bed and hold the phone up as I walk to the front door. "Is this the part where you start stalking me?"

He cocks his head. *"Would you like that?"*

I smile. "It depends. Hold on one second."

Setting the phone down, I open my front door to see a small, matte black box with a black ribbon and bow. Butterflies erupt inside me when I retrieve it, and I can't help but grin as I pick my phone back up and walk to the kitchen table.

I'm wearing a white cami and dark purple boy shorts, so I set the camera up to show myself from the neck up as I sit down and open the box.

"You didn't have to get me anything," I say softly.

I untie the bow and pull the ribbon off the box, and then I lift the lid up.

A dainty gold bracelet is clasped around a black, small velvet pillow, and I smile even wider when I realize there's a small, golden disk with a diamond constellation in the middle.

Stars for Starboy.

"Do you like it?" Starboy asks, leaning forward.

My throat constricts slightly. "This is really nice. Thank you."

"You're welcome."

I unclasp it and put it on. The thin, golden chain

hangs delicately around my wrist, and it's discreet, so wearing it won't annoy me.

"I like to get my submissive a gift when they sign the contract," he says slowly. *"You don't have to wear it if you don't want to, but I thought it would be a good way for you to remember who you belong to."*

Arousal pierces through me, and I look down at the bracelet. "Thank you."

"I should go, but let's talk tonight at 10p.m."

"I had one question about the contract," I blurt quickly. He leans forward, waiting for me to continue. "You marked N/A for the in-person parts of the contract ..." I look down, suddenly embarrassed to ask the question that's eating me up.

When I look up, he has the dry-erase board again, and he's writing furiously.

My heart pounds as he holds it up, fully expecting him to give me a reason that we can never meet in person.

MY IN-PERSON CONTRACTS ARE MUCH MORE DETAILED. IF/WHEN WE REACH THAT POINT, I'LL HAVE YOU SIGN MY REGULAR CONTRACT.

Relief washes over me. "Okay," I breathe out.

"Do you want to meet in person?" he asks.

I nod.

"Words, Layla."

Something hot slithers through me at his command. *Do I like this? I think I do.*

"Yes. Eventually."

He sits back and crosses his arms, watching me for a few seconds. My cheeks grow hot as he takes a deep breath. It's as if he's trying to cool himself off, too.

Is it possible that he's just as aroused by all of this as I am?

He uncrosses his arms. *"I'd like you to do some research today."*

I nod eagerly. *"Sure. What kind of research?"*

He signs again, and my brows knit in confusion because I don't know the word. He starts signing the letters.

S

A

D

I

S

T

I suck in a sharp breath, staring at Starboy as I squirm in my seat.

"Sadist?" I ask.

He nods, and then he grabs the board again.

I AM WHAT YOU'D CALL A SADISTIC DOM. I DERIVE PLEASURE FROM INFLICTING PAIN, SUFFERING, AND HUMILIATION. THIS USUALLY PAIRS WELL WITH SOMEONE WHO'S INTERESTED IN YOUR KINKS, LIKE DEGRADATION, BUT I WANT YOU TO KNOW EXACTLY WHAT YOU'RE GETTING YOURSELF INTO WITH ME. IS THAT CLEAR?

I take a deep breath. "I think so. But I can let you know for sure later tonight after more research, Master. I'm ready to learn."

A shock wave goes through Starboy's body, and I swear he's smiling as he writes something else on the board.

You're going to wish you didn't just say that, Little Dancer.

I smirk. "Doubtful."

"I'm not a good person. If you're looking for a pleasure Dom or a soft Dom, you'll need to look elsewhere."

I tilt my head and smile. "Sounds like you're trying to scare me off."

His eyes—which I can't really see—stare at the camera for a few beats before he looks down at the board and writes some more.

I don't pleasure my subs. I break them.

My heart pounds against my ribs, and the space between my legs pulses with each beat. My hardened nipples brush against the soft fabric of my cami. Even if I'm not experienced in this stuff, my body responds positively.

"Trust me. It takes a lot to break me after what my mind put me through for years, and I've already been at rock bottom. So you can try, but you won't succeed."

His eyes widen for a fraction of a second, and then he shakes his head and looks down.

When he looks back up again, he looks almost ... pained.

"Where have you been my whole life?" he asks.

"Waiting for you," I tell him.

"We're going to talk about your past when you're ready."

My past.

Right.

He leans back and runs a hand over his masked face, and I almost ask him to remove it.

This exchange got intense quickly, and I want to see the person I'm getting attached to. I want to see what color their eyes are, the color of his hair ... if he shaves every day, or if there's scruff. I want to run my hand over that face, but I don't even know what it looks like.

"Tonight, 10p.m."

"Okay. Thanks for the bracelet," I tell him.

"My pleasure. Don't forget to abide by my rules."

"Yes, Master." My voice is low and a bit more sultry than normal on purpose, and it has the intended reaction.

His body sags in resignation once again, and then he shakes his head before he disconnects the video call.

I set my phone down and take my glasses off, rubbing my face with my hands again.

Before I forget, I grab my phone again and text Zoe and Remy.

Still on for drinks tonight?

Zoe responds right away.

ZOE

like id miss hearing about starboy ... pls.

> Ha ha.

REMY

Same place as last time?

I think back to the last girls' night a few weeks ago. We'd gone to a new bar in Huntington Beach, but I don't feel like finding parking or sitting in traffic on Pacific Coast Highway tonight. Plus, my curiosity is piqued about Orion's new place.

> Hear me out ...

ZOE

omg u want to go to inferno, dont u?

theres limited alcohol. one-drink rule

orion will lose his shit if he finds out

on 2nd thought, id love to see that

REMY

How about a compromise? We go to Inferno, see what it's all about, and then we'll walk down the street to one of the other bars?

> I'm in.

ZOE

you are a chaos gremlin and i love it

REMY

Okay, I'm in. Inferno first. Someone
needs to be on Orion watch though,
because if he finds out Lay is there …
pretty sure he'd ravage everyone inside
the building.

Very funny.

REMY

Thanks, I try.

ZOE

im on it. going to have liam invite himself
over 2 orion's place and distract him

So what if he knows I'm there?

REMY

scared face emoji

No, really. Screw him. This isn't the
1800s where my older brother has to
look out for my every move.

ZOE

stepbrother

And?

ZOE

just saying … kissing your brother is ick,
but kissing your stepbrother isnt

REMY

YOU KISSED ORION?!

I'm going to kill Liam.

ZOE

have to go, im under deadline for
this book

REMY

Let's meet at my place at 6.

I heart Remy's text while chewing on the inside of my
cheek.

*Great, so now my best friends know that I kissed Orion a
few months ago.*

Liam had seen us kissing, and he'd obviously
told Zoe.

Ugh.

The night I kissed Orion at Liam and Zoe's rehearsal
dinner was the best kiss of my life … with the worst
person ever.

I'd been ignoring the obvious for months now—that
I was attracted to my stepbrother. It's wrong, and I hate
myself for it. Obviously because we used to have a close
bond, it could lead to emotional intimacy. It doesn't
matter, though, because it's wrong. Besides, he'd walked
away after that kiss. I've tamped down my feelings for
him because I don't even know if they're valid or if I'm
crossing some ethical line. I couldn't exactly talk to Zoe
and Remy about it. They know how I identify, but still,
it's *Orion*.

It can never happen, and now I have another person
in my life to give my attention to.

Nervous flutters begin working in my stomach when
I think of tonight. A kink club could be the perfect place

to actually *see* if this lifestyle is something I'm interested in pursuing with Starboy.

Walking to my coffee machine, I turn it on and grab a mug. When it finishes, I add some milk and sugar and sit back against the counter. Closing my eyes, I enjoy the sweet, rich taste of the coffee. It's only been in the last couple of years that I've allowed myself to enjoy things like full-fat milk and sugar. For so long, I used food as a punishment, and that meant restricting when I'd been bad. It wasn't until I collapsed on stage one night when I was dancing for LAB that I realized I'd been given a once-in-a-lifetime chance to start over.

Two years ago, I found my therapist and started working on my food issues. I was diagnosed with body dysmorphia and EDNOS—eating disorder not otherwise specified. I wasn't anorexic or bulimic, but I was abusing "healthy" food to the extreme. As a teenager, the only person who ever bothered to help me was Orion. My dad didn't understand, and at the time, he was still reeling from Felicity's cancer diagnosis. But Orion noticed. He used to take me out for meals. He wouldn't say anything. He'd just ask me what sounded good and order it for me. He never made me eat anything or said anything when I didn't or commented about what I ordered.

Over time, he became my safe space—until he started drinking heavily, that is.

I finish my coffee and make a second cup, pulling things out to make a veggie omelet. Cooking doesn't come naturally to me, but I enjoy fueling my body with foods that make me feel good—which means I just listen to what I want to eat. Sometimes that means Coco Pops for breakfast, and sometimes it's boiled eggs and a tangerine. Letting go of the power food held over my head for so long was the key, and I now happily eat whatever I want until I'm satisfied.

Sparrow meows and slithers between my legs, and I open a can of cat food, scoop it into his dish, and set it down for him.

A few minutes later, I'm eating while I stand in the kitchen as I scroll through Reddit posts that talk about sadistic Dominants. My skin pebbles as I read a firsthand account of what it's like to be the submissive of a sadistic Dom.

When I'm with him, I don't have to think. I just have to exist. It's amazing, but it's also terrifying.

The concept of a sadist unleashing their rage upon a willing victim can be a dangerous situation.

The lack of control is a surefire way for things to go horribly wrong.

I'm not sure how common it is for Doms to work out their rage issues through kink. It's safe when it's consensual. Communication is paramount.

Paired with the right masochist ... a sadistic Dom can be FUN.

It's like a fresh chocolate chip cookie hot from the oven ... you know you're going to get burned when you bite into it, but you will love every moment of the glorious agony.

It takes a lot of self-discipline to let the sadism out but still keep control.

A sadist might enjoy causing you pain, but it's structured around what you want, what you can handle, and what your needs are. That's the difference between a sadist and an abuser.

I set my phone down and finish my breakfast, unease sliding through my core.

What kinds of things does Starboy enjoy doing? Is it all to fuel his sadism, or does he enjoy giving pleasure, too?

I don't pleasure my subs. I break them.

Placing my plate and mug in the dishwasher, I walk to my bathroom and run the bath. I'm feeling antsy and nervous, and as I wait, I do some more research on sadistic Doms.

All in all, it seems ... fine to me.

Liberating, even.

In my research, I'd come to learn that I was probably a masochist. I enjoyed pain—I always had. When others complained about their feet hurting, I *craved* the sting because it meant I was progressing.

I could control the pain, in a way. It was physically real, something I could manage however I wanted to, and that helped me reclaim a sense of control.

That was especially important to someone with an experience of feeling helpless.

Taking my cami and underwear off, I pull my hair into a high bun and step into the scalding-hot water, hissing as I lower my body into the steaming water.

I always used to joke with friends that things like scalding baths *hurt so good.*

I mean, you don't get a VCH—vertical clit hood—piercing unless you crave that kind of pain, right?

Smiling, I sink lower into the water. It's something I did last year after reading about it in a book. It was crazy, and not something I'd ever considered doing before. Not even Zoe or Remy knew I had it, and it felt like my dirty little secret.

Taking control of my sexuality is a part of my healing process, and the piercing was a big part of that. Despite not exactly being sexually active, I do find it boosts my confidence and makes me feel powerful—something I didn't feel after ... *after my power was stripped from me*.

Literally.

Before then, I'd never believed I'd be a victim of sexual assault—no one does—but it had broken me. It resulted in fear of men for years. Self-doubt. Self-loathing.

Through long and helpful therapy sessions—*I wouldn't have survived without those dark days*—I realized my fear was their power, and I took that power back.

It certainly helped when Orion had beaten the guy to within an inch of his life, and of course his father, Charles Ravage, paid the judge off so that Orion wasn't charged with assaulting a minor.

I close my eyes as I remember that week.

How everyone at school turned against me because he was a popular football player, and I was a nobody.

How I almost gave up dancing.

How I turned to books to stay sane.

How I hardly left my house for years unless Orion was with me.

The idea of handing myself over to Starboy doesn't scare me.

I've seen and experienced enough shit to know what real pain feels like. I've isolated myself, mentally beat myself up more than I thought possible, and experienced such crippling self-doubt that I could barely get out of bed some days. Mixed with the restrictive eating?

I was in a bad place for a very long time.

I felt completely disconnected from my body.

Perhaps that's why I enjoy pain now—as a way to reconnect with my body. To experience intense physical sensations that bring me back to a controlled environment, to help rebuild a sense of physical presence and ownership over my autonomy.

For so long, I felt stigmatized and, even now, a bit isolated in my sexual identity.

Starboy, despite being a literal stranger, makes me feel like I belong. Like my desires are normal and accepted.

Doing this with him feels cathartic, and I'm excited to see just how far he thinks he can push me.

CHAPTER NINE

THE WITNESS

ORION

I take a deep breath and stare at the hospital room door, wondering if I'm brave enough to push it open. Dread curdles in my stomach when I double-check the number, but how could I be wrong when this is the nicest private suite at Cedars? Who else would be in here other than my father?

My phone vibrates, so I step away from the door. Liam's name flashes across the screen, and I quickly answer the call.

"Hey."

"How are you doing?" he asks. I can tell from his tone that he's in a good mood.

"I've been better."

"Everything okay?" he asks, his low voice tense with genuine worry.

The last thing I want to do is worry him. I spent half a decade worrying him, and I vowed to myself when I got sober that I'd never do that to him again.

I could tell him about our father—about how he's declining more rapidly than the doctors originally predicted. About how his doctor suggested he be transferred to hospice later today. But then I think of how that news would ruin his mood, and how he knows better than all of us how fucked up our father is because he's the eldest brother.

"Just busy with the new club," I lie.

"Ah. Well, I'm calling because of that, actually." I flick my eyes up to the door to my dad's room when a nurse exits, smoothing her pants and looking flustered. My silence prompts Liam to continue. "Zoe informed me earlier today that she's going to Inferno later for girls' night."

I switch the phone to my other ear. "No problem. I'll inform the security guards so they can keep an eye on her."

"Ri, she's bringing Layla."

I close my eyes and sag against a nearby wall. "Of fucking course she is."

"I've already told her that she's going to give you an aneurysm, but she insists that Layla is just curious. I guess she's been talking to some BDSM influencer, and she wants to learn more."

Fuck.

How did I not see this coming? Layla is naturally

curious, and now there's a new kink club open that her stepbrother happens to own.

Like a moth to a flame.

"Thanks for letting me know."

"Sure. And hey, maybe now's your chance to give her some space."

"She can have all the space she wants, but I'll be damned if she thinks I'll give her space inside my club."

He chuckles. "Okay, I should go. I'm on my way to the donut shop. Zoe hasn't left her office for a few hours, and I want to make sure she's alive. Donuts should lure her out of her cave."

"Writing deadline?" I ask.

"Yeah. This one is brutal. She called me by her male character's name last night, and when I went to correct her, her eyes just glazed over, and she walked out of the room without responding, mumbling something about the third-act breakup."

I laugh. "Tell her good luck."

"Do you need backup tonight? I'd be happy to come and mitigate it."

"No. I'll be fine. We hung out yesterday, and it was … good. I think the ice might slowly be melting between us."

"Finally."

"Yeah, yeah. I was a total ass to her, so I don't blame her."

"I'm glad you're on speaking terms again. It means we can all hang out without the awkwardness."

"That might be giving us too much credit."

"Right. Well, maybe I'll see you later. Try not to kill anyone who talks to her."

The call ends, and I take a deep breath as I'm faced with my current reality again. I crack my knuckles before slowly pushing the hospital door open and walking inside the suite. It's basic and nothing like a hotel suite but bigger than a normal hospital room. Plus, the window seems bigger, and there's a flat-screen TV.

My father is sitting up in bed reading the newspaper, and when he notices me, he sets the paper down on top of his frail body, squinting.

He doesn't recognize me.

I know it's a symptom of brain cancer, so I hold my hands up. "Hi, Dad."

"Orion?"

I nod once.

Growing up, my father was tall, handsome, and robust. He towered over all of us at six four, and his striking black hair and green eyes won him a lot of attention when I was young. My brothers and I all share certain traits. Chase has his sense of humor, Miles shares his good looks, Liam shares his protectiveness, and Kai shares his mysterious, secretive side. And me?

I share his possessiveness and obsessive tendencies.

The strong man I knew as my father has been withering away for months, and the man before me looks almost nothing like him, save for the dark hair and the eye color. His face is swollen. The thick black hair he always wore long is thinner and cut short. His shoulders used to be massive, but now they're narrow without their usual muscles he was so diligent about maintaining.

Tamping down the sick, sympathetic feeling of watching my father die, I clear my throat and stand straighter.

"How are you feeling?" I ask, taking a seat in one of the nearby chairs.

He shrugs. "Could be worse." Training his critical eyes on me, he lets them wander over my leather jacket and black pants before giving me an approving nod. "You look well."

I don't respond. Instead, I look up at the television, which is playing Bloomberg and running over the financial market news of the day. Something about knowing he's checked in even though he's dying ... I swallow. Even at the very end of his life, my father is apparently relentless in his pursuit of making money.

The idea makes me feel empty—and it makes me feel bad for him.

"Have you spoken to your brothers?"

I steady my breathing and turn back to face him. "No."

Anger flashes over his expression. Even now in his seventies, even sick with terminal brain cancer, he still has a temper.

"And why not?" he practically spits.

"Because they don't want to talk to you, Dad."

There. I said it out loud—the thing I've been insinuating ever since Miles cut him off a couple of years ago.

I've managed to brush him off every time we talk, but he deserves the truth.

"Then I'm ashamed to call them my children. I am *dying*. Doesn't that count for something?" he growls.

I shrug. "Their reasons are valid."

"Then tell me, why the hell do *you* still talk to me?"

I study his face—the scowl and the furrowed brows. The clenched fists at his sides. The flared nostrils. His anger completely distorts his face. A quick flash of a memory pierces through my brain. I've worked so hard to forget my life before I turned fourteen—telling myself it's for the better. But the memory plays before my eyes like a sick movie I don't consent to watching.

Kai, Chase, and I were sitting at the dining room table, and my mom was upstairs with one of her headaches—which I now know was her only way to get away from her verbally abusive husband. It was about a year before Mom left Dad. My dad is on his fourth drink, and he's slurring as he asks eighteen-year-old Malakai about his first-semester college exams. Chase is sixteen. I remember that he was usually at Jackson Parker's house, but tonight, he was home. And I was eleven or twelve.

By this time, Liam and Miles had moved out of Ravage Castle, but the three youngest brothers remained.

"I'm dropping out of college."

Dad goes still, and his hand grips the crystal tumbler tightly. "And why the hell would you do that?"

Kai puts his napkin on the table. "God has been speaking to me lately, and He says we need to turn this family around. I want to help. I want to help you, us—"

"No son of mine has an ounce of holy blood in their bodies," he growls.

Dad's face twists with hatred. He slams his fists on the dining table, making Chase and me jump in our seats. *"But do you know what we do have? Money."*

"I don't care about money," Kai grits out. *"I just want to do some good in the world to rebalance the scales."*

"You want to do some good? Good things come to those who work hard, Malakai."

"I don't need money or material things. Julian says that discontent is not satisfied by material things—"

"Julian?" my dad hisses. "Do you mean that flamboyant boy you constantly surround yourself with—"

"I hope you don't expect me to sit here and let you insult my best friend." Kai, who is usually so even-tempered, instantly pushes away from the table.

"Very well," my dad muses. "You are welcome to leave."

"Fine," Kai sputters, throwing his napkin down.

"Don't think that you can ever come back with that attitude."

My mouth drops open, and when I look over at Chase, his eyes are wide as they flick between our dad and our middle brother.

"Very well. I'll go say goodbye to Mom and pack my things."

As Kai storms off, my father takes another sip of his straight vodka. Pointing a steak knife at Chase, his face is still transfigured with brute anger.

"Eat your steak, Chase. Don't let it get cold."

I look down and eat as my father and my older brother do

*the same, knowing that for the rest of my life, I will have to
regulate my emotions and the emotions of my father, or risk
being ostracized.*

I think back to my father's question: "Then why the
hell do you still talk to me?"

My father's a narcissist, and I know that now.
Growing up, we were enmeshed as a family—always
touting closeness but never really having it. We were
stuck together in an unhealthy dynamic until my mother
chose to leave him right after Chase went to college,
taking me with her. It wasn't until I was older that I
began to look at my dad as someone who gave me life
rather than a father figure. We weren't close, but we
weren't *not* close either.

And I suppose I always felt like I had to keep that
tether to him because he'd never done anything to give
me a reason to walk away from him. I know my brothers
feel differently, but I always justified it because of that.

One of the first realizations when I got sober was
that my seeing him probably hurt my brothers, and I'd
been too deluded with alcohol to see it. I never really
stopped to consider why they had to walk away from
him. If they did, they must've had damn good reasons for
doing so.

I still hadn't had the courage to have a real conversation about it.

Maybe one day, I'd ask what happened to make them
walk away.

"You're so much like her," my dad adds, shaking his
head. "Your mother. Always worried about hurting my

feelings. At least have the balls to walk away like your brothers did."

His voice changes tone in the last few words, and he looks away.

"You think I'm scared to go no-contact like them?" I ask incredulously. "You don't scare me, Dad."

He turns to face me with narrowed eyes. "Then why are you here, Orion?"

It hits me then—yes, he's cruel, but he's also *scared.* Knowing that ... makes him seem so much smaller than I've ever seen him.

"Because you're dying," I say simply. "Even the worst criminal doesn't deserve to die alone."

He huffs a laugh before breaking into a coughing fit. The cancer is in his lungs now, and he's been coughing up blood for days.

"You're a better person than I am," he says after a minute, closing his eyes.

"I know," I tell him.

I'm not sure I believe it, but I'm working on it.

"And how's the ballet dancer?" he asks, looking away.

Grinding my jaw, I look down at my hands. "She's fine."

"Such a pretty, little thing," he murmurs wistfully.

"I don't want to talk about her with you," I grind out.

"Come on. Man to man. I can appreciate a fine specimen when I see one, and she's—"

I stand abruptly, nostrils flaring as I glare down at

the man before me. "I said I'm not going to talk about her with you."

"Layla," he says slowly. "That's her name, right? I met her once, you know. Attended one of her performances a long time ago. Even got to go backstage to meet her and the other performers."

I'm seething.

I didn't know this, but the thought of my father anywhere near her makes me sick.

"Stop," I growl.

"Perfect fucking tits," he adds, and I see red.

"Goodbye, dad."

I don't even care when the door slams behind me on the way out.

———

A few hours later, I'm brooding and walking toward Inferno with an extra angry bounce in my step. I know my father only says this stuff to spur me on, but it doesn't matter. Since I'm the only child still in contact with him, all of his attention falls on me. And since he's adamant that Kai won't ever settle with someone, that leaves me for him to focus on in his final days.

After I'd left, I'd gone on a two-hour bike ride around LA. Now that it's well past six, I make my way to Inferno in order to intercept Zoe, Remy, and Layla. I've already spoken to my security team, so I know they've just arrived.

Layla will expect me to lose my cool.

For years, I took it upon myself to ensure she was safe, healthy, and happy. The role of big brother came easily to me, and growing up, I wanted to cage her to keep her safe. And then that asshole of a football player touched her without permission—cornering her and violating her. It makes me sick to think about it.

He got what he deserved, and I've dedicated a lot of my free time ensuring he's as miserable as possible.

And hearing my dad talk about her like that … it made my blood boil. The way he let those words slip out, like he had any right to speak about her that way …

It made me want stake my claim even harder.

She's mine, not his—not anyone else's.

The thought of anyone else even imagining her that way is enough to make my fists clench. She belongs to me, and I'll make sure everyone, including him, knows it one day soon.

But I have to admit, even though I feel this posses-siveness, I know deep down I don't really have the right to think of her as mine anymore. We're not as close as we used to be, and she's her own person now. Kai was right; that's the Layla I used to know. Even if I've kept track of her since our falling-out—*then tasted her only months ago* — she's blossomed into a woman I don't fully recog-nize. She doesn't need my protection anymore. She's fully capable of looking after herself. And while I really fucking hate the idea of her possibly getting approached tonight, I know she's here because she's really good at following directions. *My* directions. I'd told her to do research, didn't I?

She's going to expect me to be mad.

But ... what if I'm not?

She's getting closer to Starboy, but I can't let that overshadow whatever we had between us as Orion and Layla. Because if I've learned one thing about us, it's that there's ... *something* there. It's not all one-sided as I assumed for so long. She feels something, too.

Perhaps it's time she confronts the feelings she has for her dear stepbrother.

She can't hide the stares and ogling for very much longer.

As I get closer, my foul mood begins to dissipate. By the time I walk through the back door, I'm practically grinning.

I have the perfect plan, and it includes charming her as Orion.

She thinks she likes Starboy?

I'll have to show her a bit of the man behind the mask.

CHAPTER TEN

THE DISREGARD

LAYLA

I'm not sure what I thought a kink club would look like, but I do know it's not this.

We enter through a nondescript door, and then we're taken to a small office—something that looks like the set from a bad '90s office rom-com. My eyes skirt over the drab office decor before finally landing on the woman behind the desk.

"Welcome, Ms. Arma. Nice to see you again," she says to Zoe, who thanks her.

She presses a button and the coat closet door opens. The coats that are hung up begin to part down the middle, revealing a door that leads to a bar.

"Thank you," I tell her, following Remy and Zoe through the coatrack and into the bar area.

"There's a one-drink rule," Zoe explains. "After

ordering, you're given a wristband that you have to keep on until you leave."

"Also, when doing a scene, one shouldn't be inebriated," Remy adds.

"I know that. I mean, I assumed," I say quickly.

In the back of my mind, I know I should've briefed them on what was going on with Starboy on our walk over. He mentioned submissive mentors, and Zoe and Remy could easily be that for me. But something stopped me. Maybe it's the fear of speaking about it too soon? That it could all be too good to be true? Still, I don't want them to think I'm a total noob.

"I do know *some* things, you know," I add.

Zoe looks up at me with honey-brown eyes. "My little vanilla bean isn't so vanilla after all, is she?"

I swat her shoulder playfully, but I don't elaborate.

I'm here tonight to observe and to see if there's anything here for me. If tonight goes well and I decide to move forward with Starboy, I'll explain everything to them.

"Let's grab our drinks," Zoe says. She and Remy both look incredible in their bondage-style dresses.

Meanwhile, I'm wearing a light blue, fitted denim dress that I recycled from a date three years ago. Compared to them, it feels way too innocent and demure, but my wardrobe is 95 percent lounge clothes, so it would have to do.

"Yes," I acquiesce, knowing that a bit of liquor will take the edge off my nerves.

"Is *he who shall not be named* here?" Remy asks, referring to Orion and looking around.

Orion's overprotectiveness feels like second nature now. I know he does it to piss me off and intentionally tries to get a rise out of me. As a teenager, I resented him for always looking out for me and being too paranoid. But when he nearly killed the football player who almost raped me ... I was grateful.

As an adult, I've learned to live with it, though I know if I talk to a guy and Orion is there, he'll do everything in his power to throw me off my game in a big brotherly sort of way.

Or maybe it's not so brotherly after that kiss a few months ago ...

I shove the thought into the back of my mind like I do with most thoughts about Orion.

We order our drinks and take a seat at the bar as we secure our wristbands. "All right, ladies. Are we going to Purgatory, or are we going to Paradise?" Zoe asks, crossing her legs. "I vote Paradise."

Sipping my cosmo, I raise my brows. "Do those two things entail what I think they do?"

"I don't think we're going anywhere," Remy murmurs, and I follow her line of sight to see my stepbrother bursting through the door we just came out of.

I brace myself. Zoe mentioned that Liam probably told Orion we were coming tonight, which can only mean one thing.

Sitting up straighter, I wait for him to notice us, but instead, he casually saunters over to the other end of the bar. He's wearing a black T-shirt and worn-in jeans with those boots he loves. His hair is messy, so he probably had his motorcycle helmet on most of the day. His dark scruff highlights his jawline and disheveled demeanor. He leans forward, his biceps popping as he smiles *that* smile and takes a can of Coke from the bar. Bringing it to his lips, he takes a long, deep sip. His throat bobs, and it's not until Remy nudges me that I realize I've been staring.

"Yeah, we're in big fucking trouble," she says.

"Shh," Zoe hisses. "If we're quiet, maybe we'll blend into the wall like those lizards who go transparent when scared."

"Not with *his precious* standing right here," Remy mumbles under her breath.

"Hey," I warn, sipping my cocktail.

Before we can argue further, Orion pushes back from the bar and walks right past us.

Once he's several feet away, Zoe lets out a slow breath of air. "That was close."

Remy's eyes narrow, and she moves her curly auburn hair off her shoulder. "I don't buy it."

"What do you mean?" I ask.

"He knows we're here. I'm sure of it."

"Maybe not." Zoe shrugs. "We'd just walked in when he got here—"

"Hey, Orion!" Remy says loudly.

He turns around, and I brace myself again. Slowly—ever so slowly—he flicks his eyes between the three of us, nodding once before continuing his walk deeper into the club. *Without* saying hi or losing his shit or ... *caring.*

I let out a shaky breath.

"That was weird," Zoe murmurs, brows furrowed.

My cheeks heat as Orion finally disappears around a corner. I feel like a child about to throw a tantrum because his possessiveness drives me crazy. But when he doesn't act like a savage brute, I apparently can't compute it, and it makes me burn with humiliation.

I hate him.

Crossing my arms, I attempt to appear nonplussed. "Whatever. Should we go see what each floor entails?"

Zoe and Remy share a look, but eventually, Zoe nods. "Yeah. Up or down?"

I glance toward where Orion disappeared, and then a sickening, not-so-fleeting thought enters my mind. Is he here to see the person he's dating?

Is that why he didn't say hi? Because she's here?

"Let's go down to Purgatory first," Remy offers. "*Just* looking. No participating for Bambi here."

I scoff. "I don't appreciate the nickname."

Zoe chuckles. "Okay, let's go after we finish our drinks."

"I'm just looking out for you," Remy adds, taking my hand and squeezing it once.

"I know," I tell her, bringing it to my lips and kissing it. "Thank you."

Once we're done with our drinks a few minutes later, we follow the hallway around a corner and down a winding staircase that leads into what seems like a dungeon. There are signs that phones are not allowed, so I tuck mine away in my bag.

Zoe goes down the stairs first, followed by Remy. I'm the last to make the trek downward, and as I do, the hairs on my arms stand on end.

The lighting gets dimmer the farther we descend into the depths of the club. It's not empty, but it's also not swarming with people. A lot of people are dressed in leather, and a woman walks around in high heels, carrying a whip. Several rooms that look like prison cells line the perimeter of the large room. Sconces with real flames line the walls, and the flickering, orange light casts a warm, almost eerie light on everyone's faces. Screaming metal music plays at a low volume through speakers I can't see.

Several seconds after getting to the bottom of the stairs, the crowd in front of us parts slightly, and my heart drops somewhere down low when I see Orion is the one drawing observers.

I walk over to the prison cell while holding my breath, attempting to remain behind enough people that he doesn't see me. He stands in the cell, shirtless, with only his pants hung low on his hips and his boots on his feet. He's leaning over an old stove, and a low flame flickers underneath what looks like a cauldron. A piece of his dark hair falls in front of his face, but he doesn't move it out of the way. It makes this whole thing so much more cryptic.

I'm *fascinated*.

"What's he doing?" I ask no one in particular.

"Wax play," Remy answers from next to me.

My eyes immediately dart to the other person in the

cell—a woman with long blond hair. She's facing away, so I can't see her face, but this must be her—the other woman.

Everything about her makes me *burn* with rage and jealousy.

My fingers tingle, and it feels like my whole body was plunged into ice-cold water when I realize I'm watching Orion with the woman he chose. *Well, he clearly doesn't want you, Layla.*

My knee-jerk reaction is to leave, but I'm also compelled to watch.

Orion takes a wooden ladle of what I presume is hot wax over to where the woman lies down on top of a black leather couch. Every heavy thud of his boots against the stone floor sends a shiver down my spine. She's scantily clad—in a plaid miniskirt and mesh bralette—but she's not naked. She's lying down on the couch, and he walks up to the back of it and begins to drizzle hot wax along the back of one of her thighs unceremoniously. His expression is completely indifferent, too—nothing to indicate he's enjoying this.

His muscles contract and relax with every movement, and I take in every inch of his bare chest and abdomen. The familiar black tattoos are stark against his skin, and my mouth goes dry when I see a new one above his left pectoral, but I can't make out what it is.

The woman hisses as Orion drizzles more wax onto her bare calf. His jaw is clenched, and when the woman moans, his nostrils flare, and he takes a step back.

"Who is she?" I ask Zoe, who came up next to me a few seconds ago. "Is that the woman he's dating?"

Zoe lets out a quiet laugh. "Dating? No. Haley is a regular at our munches. Trust me, Orion is not interested, and I think she prefers older guys anyway."

I furrow my brows. "So they're not dating?"

Zoe turns and looks at me. "Who told you Orion's dating someone?" Her lips twitch like she wants to say something else, but then she closes her mouth and must change her mind.

"He did. He mentioned it the other day at my dad's house."

Her brows arch upward. "Huh. Must be new."

I grind my jaw and look back at Orion. He's holding a paddle made of black leather in his left hand now and snaps his fingers loudly.

Haley jumps up and immediately crawls onto her knees on the couch, facing the back and bending over slightly. Her chest rises and falls, and I can see the flush on her chest from where I'm standing.

"Sometimes it's just fun to play with people," Zoe adds. "Haley and Orion trust each other. Orion likes to do certain things, and vice versa. They both have limits. For example, I know Orion's scenes are almost never sexual. But he enjoys inflicting pain, and Haley enjoys receiving it."

I watch as Orion slowly walks over to the front of the couch. Like before, he doesn't touch her—he just raises the paddle before bringing it to the back of her thighs, which are still caked with wax. *Ouch.* I squirm where I'm standing, wiggling my toes in my boots to dispel the arousal sinking to the space between my legs.

I shouldn't be turned on by watching my stepbrother spank his friend, but here we are.

Haley cries out after the first thwack of the paddle, and I look up at Orion for his reaction. His nostrils flare again, and his free hand curls into a fist. I hold my breath as he brings the paddle up again, and just as I'm about to release it, he snaps his eyes directly to me.

His pupils are nearly black as he brings the paddle to the back of Haley's thigh again, all while glaring at me. The room begins to spin, and I release a shaky breath as Orion breaks eye contact, and he continues to paddle Haley.

I adjust my stance again, ignoring the temptation to squeeze my thighs together. Crossing my arms, I feel the bracelet that Starboy sent me snag on my dress, and guilt washes over me.

I should not be lusting after Orion when I promised Starboy earlier today that I would remain monogamous.

"Please, Sir," Haley begs, voice breaking. "No more."

Orion's lips pull away from his teeth as his free fist curls again. "You'll do as you're told. Color?"

"Green."

He makes a low, growling sound before looking up at me again. It's not anger on his face. It's something darker. Something far more sinister. He seems to be directing his rage toward me—for simply being here or for another reason, I'm not sure. He looks back down at Haley.

"You can take more," he says, his voice a low purr.

"Please, Sir—"

He smacks her again, and this time, she screams. I'm practically panting, watching as sweat forms on Orion's skin, glistening beautifully and exaggerating the cut of his muscles. After several more smacks with the paddle on the other leg, I see him lean down and whisper something into Haley's ear. Even knowing that they're just friends doesn't matter. White-hot envy flows through me as his thumb brushes her cheekbone affectionately. He drops the paddle suddenly and picks her up, carrying her across the room and to a back door. They disappear through it, and I feel like I'm going to vomit.

"Where are they going?" I ask, feeling uneasy and restless.

"Aftercare," Remy explains, arms crossed.

"What does that entail?" I know what it entails on paper. Almost all the research I did involved discussions about aftercare, but I want to know specifically what Orion and Haley are doing because right now, my emotions are all over the place as I imagine them cuddling in a bed somewhere.

"For Haley, probably a warm cloth to remove the wax. Soothing lotion. A cuddly blanket, or a dark room. Maybe some food, water, juice ... It depends on her preference. Orion will also want to check in on how she's feeling about the scene."

I tamp down the burning jealousy. *What the hell is wrong with me?* A heavy ache settles inside my chest, and it takes me a second to realize that I miss him taking care of *me.*

"Do you want to stay?" Zoe asks me, grabbing my hand. "Or shall we check upstairs?"

I look back into the room Orion just exited. I *want* to stay and watch more of what he did, but I can't say that.

"Sure," I tell her, giving her a fake smile despite feeling sick.

Once we ascend the stairs, I glance back at the room to make sure Orion hasn't returned, but he hasn't. He's still off somewhere with Haley, doing who knows what.

I rub my chest as we make our way up to Pleasure, and I spend the trek up two flights of stairs shutting Orion out of my mind.

I promised Starboy exclusivity, which means the best thing I can do is walk away from my stepbrother—despite still being able to feel his eyes burning into mine while he paddled another woman.

CHAPTER ELEVEN
THE TEMPTATION

ORION

I hold my hand out and give Haley a low five. "Don't forget to tend to your skin," I tell her, tugging her arm forward and pulling her into a tight hug. A couple of seconds later, I pull away and shove my hands in the pockets of my pants.

"I know, I know. This isn't my first rodeo," she drawls, giving me a wry smile. "But it's nice that you still worry about me."

I roll my eyes. "Someone has to, Hales. You sure you don't want me to help with aftercare?"

"I'm okay. It was a short scene. Just enough to take the edge off," she adds, wiggling her brows. "I have to go. Hot date tonight."

"Be safe," I tell her, crossing my arms.

"I always am." Flipping her hair and giving me a

small wave, she walks out of the staff area before turning back to face me. "Hey, you okay? You seemed ... off tonight."

I take a wider stance as I rub my mouth with my right hand. "Fine. Just a lot on my mind."

"I saw Zoe was here with some friends. Anyone you know?"

I narrow my eyes. "What has dear Zoe told you?"

Haley smirks. "Oh, nothing. Just that your stepsister happens to be a leggy redhead, and that's exactly who I saw watching us earlier."

I shrug. "She's an adult. She can do as she pleases."

"Very convincing." She rolls her eyes. "Good night, Ri."

She leaves the employee room before I can respond, and I walk over to the couch where I'd given Haley some water and snacks fifteen minutes ago while checking in with her. We don't play together often, but it's always fun and wholly platonic when we do. Others at the club usually do scenes with me, but I haven't been an active participant for weeks. I haven't been in the mood. It wasn't until I saw Layla standing at the bar in that tight little dress that something had to give. I thought doing a scene would distract me, but instead, all I can think about is how different that scene would've been with Layla on that couch.

First and foremost, I would've dragged her to a private room so that I could savor her pleading cries all to myself. I would've watched her thighs bloom with color when I dropped the hot wax on her soft, unmarked skin. Her *perfect* skin—the creamy, unblemished thighs. How sore they'd stay for hours, how she'd have to remember the pain I inflicted every time she sat down or performed in front of three thousand people.

My cock begins to swell when I think of how badly I want to bend her over and paddle her ass for showing up tonight.

I could show her the darkness she thinks she craves until she's begging for more.

I could *taste* her innocence as I savor every breathless gasp of her surrender.

Fuck.

I stand and pull my shirt back on, adjusting my hard-on before quickly exiting the employee room. The club is busier now, and I have to slide past people to make my way down to the dungeon. I don't plan on confronting Layla, but I do want to keep an eye on her.

I can't help myself.

After circling the room several times, I don't see her down in Purgatory. Grumbling, I ascend the stairs toward Paradise.

It's more crowded up here. Pleasure more easily entices people, and who doesn't want to feel *good*? Once I'm on the floor, I scan the small crowd, spotting Layla standing with Zoe and Remy by the feather room, and I stand at the back as I watch my stepsister observe the participants.

One of Inferno's Doms stands over a woman sprawled over a fluffy white bed. She's completely naked, and he's running a large, white feather down her abdomen. She arches her back and moans as he gets closer to her hips, but he stops a few inches away from where she wants it. Narrowing my eyes, I cross my arms and watch Layla observe the scene.

Even from where I'm standing, I can tell she's turned on. Her neck is flushed, and her chest is rising and falling rapidly. Her denim dress clings to her slim, muscular body, perfectly accentuating the narrow curve of her waist and hips. Her long ponytail brushes against her back, and I fight the urge to walk up behind her and bite the creamy flesh of her slender neck.

Compared to everyone else, she seems so out of place here. Innocent. Young. *Yet to be corrupted.*

And on her delicate right wrist is the bracelet I sent her.

Poor, angelic little stepsister ... so turned on and not able to do anything about it because she was instructed not to.

And I know she'll obey me. *Well, Starboy.*

She's a good girl—always has been.

Just as I think it, she turns her head and looks right at me. I give her nothing—no smile, no scowl—before turning and walking to the other side of the room, hidden by the small group forming.

Being a Dominant, I've taught myself how to read cues and interpret looks and sounds. If my submissive is too far gone to use her safe word, I have to know to stop the scene.

I learned that the hard way.

And one failsafe thing I know for sure from experience is that people hate being ignored—especially when you've given them no reason to do so. Layla *expects* me to lose my shit because she's here. She *expects* me to lose my shit if she brings a date to a family party, just like she *expected* me to punch that fucking dancer in her company a couple of years ago.

Even if she doesn't realize it, she came here to get a rise out of me, but I won't give her that satisfaction tonight.

I watch for ten more minutes. The crowd begins to thin as they move onto the voyeur room next door. I stay exactly where I am, pretending to be engrossed in what I'm watching.

The scent of fresh strawberries and a flash of red hair in my peripheral vision tells me that my intuition was right.

She's so easy to pick apart—*predictable.*

And I fucking love that an hour of ignoring her means I have her wrapped around my little finger.

3 ...

2 ...

1 ...

"I liked your scene."

I don't turn to face her, instead schooling my expression into something indifferent despite my pounding heart and my clammy hands.

"Thanks. Are you enjoying yourself?"

My voice is low and flat—emotionless.

I can feel her studying my face—wondering *why* I'm not grabbing her wrist and dragging her out onto the street. The thought of her trying to deconstruct me is appealing, so I keep my eyes forward.

"Yeah. I like it. I want to come back, actually. Maybe try out a scene."

I grind my teeth and hope she doesn't notice.

No one's touching you.

Not while I'm around.

"You should."

Several heavy seconds of silence pass before she laughs. "Do you have a fever or something?"

At this, I turn to face her with furrowed brows. "What do you mean?"

"Never mind," she says quickly, brows punching together in confusion.

"Tell me."

Her eyes lock onto mine, and I can see the way she *obeys* so well. One command, and she's putty in my hands.

I am so fucked.

"I just thought you'd have a problem with me being here."

I do. I really fucking do. I want to scream it. I want to lock her up in the dungeon for being here and chafe that perfect ass until it's red and she's screaming my name.

But I don't.

Two years ago, I would've lost my shit. I would've acted on my impulses. But now that she's talking to me as Starboy? I have to play it cool. I have to think long term. There's no way in hell I'll let her walk out of my life again, so I have to figure out a way to keep her interested in both Starboy *and* Orion.

And it seems giving her a bit of the cold shoulder works at getting her interested in the latter.

"You're a big girl. You can do whatever you want."

I almost laugh at her shocked expression. Instead of letting me see it, she turns to face the scene, attempting to hide the flush on her cheeks and neck.

"What happened to my stepbrother, and where did you hide his body?" she asks drolly.

I let my lips quirk into a smile. "Funny."

"Really, though. You're freaking me out."

I slowly turn to face her, and she's already looking up at me with wide eyes.

You're going to regret pushing my buttons, Little Dancer.

Stepping closer, I place my hands on her shoulders and back her against the wall behind us. She lets out a tiny gasp when I step into her space so our bodies barely touch.

"A few weeks ago, you accused me of interfering in your life *too much*. And now that I've taken you at your word and backed off, you can't help but wonder why?"

Her cheeks flush even more pink, and *fuck,* she's beautiful when she's blushing. I want to see how much she'd blush if I asked her to join me in Purgatory. If I gave her no option but to bend over so that I could degrade her in front of everyone watching—edging her with my fingers until she was leaking down the insides of her legs, leaving bite marks along her delicate skin, filling her mouth with rope and using that ponytail to expose her throat so I could collar her once and for all...

One day, I'd make her mine. *Officially.*

I just had to get her to like me again first.

"You're right." Her hand comes to my chest, palm flat against my racing heart. The gold bracelet is visible, and I can't help but reach out to touch it. The fact that she's unknowingly letting herself be claimed by me only fuels my hunger.

Touching the bracelet must wake her from her stupor because she inhales sharply and drops her hand back down to her side.

"What do you want from me, Layla?" I ask her, studying her expression.

Getting lost in her darkened hazel eyes.

Wanting so badly to kiss those pouty lips again.

She opens her mouth to say something, and my eyes drop to where her tongue runs along her lower lip, wetting it. I can smell the sweet scent of the cosmo she was drinking, mixed with her cherry lip balm. Her eyes are usually makeup-less, but tonight, she's wearing winged liner and mascara.

I'm so hard that my whole body is pulsing, radiating outward from my core.

I'm worried my cock might bust through the fabric of my pants.

Everything about her is perfect. Like it was created for me. I want so badly to give in—to *force* her to concede to whatever this is.

Plus, I'm not sure if I can bear another fucking rejection from her. If I've learned anything from the past seven years, it's that I never want to be rejected by her again.

All of this is risky because, at the end of the day, if she still doesn't want me ...

I'm not sure I'll ever recover from that.

Taking a step back, I don't let her answer. Instead, I turn and walk away, taking the stairs down to the main floor and walking back into the office. Once there, I pull my burner phone out and send a text.

> I hope you're being a good girl and obeying my orders.

She doesn't answer, so I sit back and rub my face with my hands.

This is sick—that I just left her physical presence only to connect with her online. But I have to—I *need* her in a way that scares the fuck out of me.

If I can't be close to her in person, I need this connection online.

LITTLEDANCER

Aw, miss me? ;)

Relief fills me. She must be back in the bar area, as we don't allow phones on the floor.

> You have no idea.

LITTLEDANCER

I'm out, actually. No time to ... you know.

> Out where?

LITTLEDANCER

If I tell you, will you show up?

I smile. She'd love that, wouldn't she? Showing up here in my mask. Perhaps dragging her down into Purgatory with me.

I palm my erection.

> Not tonight. But if I did, what would we do?

Three dots appear and disappear.

LITTLEDANCER

Whatever you wanted.

I stroke my cock through the fabric of my pants. I'm aching for her, and I need to know she wants it just as badly as me.

> You have no idea what you're asking, Little Dancer.

LITTLEDANCER

I want to meet you.

Fuck.

> I want to meet you, too.

LITTLEDANCER

I'm wearing your bracelet, and it reminds me of you.

> How so?

LITTLEDANCER

It makes me feel like I belong to you.

I stare at her message, palming my cock and thrusting my hips up into my hand.

Do you want to belong to me?

LITTLEDANCER

Yes.

Show me.

I know I shouldn't ask. I know I should tell her good night and leave her be. But a small part of me wants to see how far she'll go.

LITTLEDANCER

How?

Send me a picture as proof. Remember, you're not allowed to touch yourself.

Three more dots appear and disappear before a message comes through.

LITTLEDANCER

Okay, give me a minute.

I set my phone down and stand, walking over to the office door and locking it. As I sit back down at my desk, I unzip my pants and pull my cock out as I wait.

Somewhere in this club, Layla is by herself and willing to prove that she belongs to me.

I wrap my palm around my cock and slowly move it

up and down, circling the head and using my precum as lube. A shaky breath escapes my lips, and I roll my hips up into my tightened fist. I'm already close—with her, it never takes long.

Is it fucked up that I think of her every single time I come?

I edge myself as I wait for Layla's evidence.

Is she in the bathroom?

Or did she find some unoccupied, dark corner?

God, what I'd give to spy on her.

Groaning, I feel my orgasm sneak closer. Releasing my grip on my cock, I pant heavily as I wait.

My phone pings, and it's a picture.

It's a mirror reflection photo. Layla is standing in the bathroom—the black and white checkered tiles are a dead giveaway. She's holding the phone up to the mirror, and she's leaning forward slightly to show off her dress, which is pulled down past her perfect tits.

Fuck. Me.

They're fucking perfect—pink nipples, perky, and just big enough to fit in my hands. I can't see her face, but the hand with the bracelet is around her throat.

Fuuuck.

I stare at the picture as my heart races. Seeing her like this … it hits me hard.

I pull my shirt up and wrap my hand around my cock, stroking myself. My balls pull up and I can't hold back anymore. Now that I can visualize how my cum would look painted all over her chest, there's no turning back.

My cock swells and pleasure claws to the base of my spine
before I explode all over my hand. Large ropes of cum
land on my bare stomach, abs violently clenching with
each wave as I imagine how it would feel to fill her with
my cum—to pump her so deep that she leaks for days.

More cum dribbles out of my still convulsing shaft.

I drop my phone onto the desk and lean all the way
back in my chair as I come down.

Fuck.

She's mine.

No one else gets to see her like this, not in this way.
The thought of anyone else laying eyes on her, appreci-
ating what's meant for me alone, stirs something possessive deep inside me.

She's mine, and I won't let anyone forget it.

Least of all her.

I sit there in stunned silence until I hear my phone
chime with a text. I pick the burner phone up with my
clean hand and read her text.

LITTLEDANCER

Does that prove it enough?

> That picture is for my eyes only.

> And, yes. Well done. But you can still
> send me another photo for research, just
> to confirm.

LITTLEDANCER

For *research*

I assume you enjoyed the photo…?

Trust me. I enjoyed it.

LITTLEDANCER
Prove it.

You want a dick pic?

LITTLEDANCER
Don't make me beg. At least not yet.

She's going to be the death of me.

I spontaneously snap a picture of the mess all over my hand and still-hard cock, sending it and grinning when she doesn't respond right away. I angled it so that it's only my bare stomach and my non-tattooed arm, and hardly shows the jeans I was wearing just a few minutes ago with her.

Bet she didn't expect to get a raunchy picture while out with her friends.

LITTLEDANCER
Holy ... *hot face emoji*

Just imagine how much of a mess I'll make on your pretty face one day.

LITTLEDANCER
And when will that be?

You've been so good. Perhaps I should reward you.

LITTLEDANCER
I like rewards.

Such a good, little slut.

LITTLEDANCER

Okay. I need to rejoin the real world now
so that I don't melt.

Color?

LITTLEDANCER

Bright freaking green.

I'm grinning like an idiot at her response because I know how sassy Layla can be, and I can picture her saying exactly this. People think she's so pure, so wholesome, but she has a delinquent side to her as well. I got glimpses of it growing up. For example, she got a tattoo the day she turned eighteen—a small heart on her left rib cage. She hardly ever swears—but every once in a while, she says the F-word, and it sounds extra dirty coming from her. And despite the ballet dancer persona, I've seen her kickbox and throw the kind of punches that could kill a person.

LITTLEDANCER

Are we still scheduled to talk tomorrow
at 10a.m.?

Yes. Good night, Layla.

LITTLEDANCER

Good night, Master.

After cleaning myself, I walk out onto the floor, only to see Liam and Kai leaning against the bar while sipping their sodas. Smirking, I school my expression into something I hope comes across as casual and easygoing

despite feeling anything but. My eyes flick around the
bar for Layla, but I don't see her.

"They left," Liam tells me with a knowing expression.
"Off to the next place."

I nod once. "How are you?"

He looks around. "Nice place you have here."

"Thanks." Looking over at Kai, I arch my brows. "And
you?"

Kai shrugs. "Busy."

I swipe his soda from his hand and take a sip. "Doing
what? Praying?"

He smirks. "Funny. But no, I'm helping a friend with
some renovations."

"You have friends?" I tease.

He huffs a laugh. "Julian. He just moved back to
Crestwood from London."

My brows shoot up as I look at Liam—and my oldest
brother just sips his drink and looks away as if he doesn't
want to get involved.

"Julian, as in your best friend growing up?" I hedge.

Kai shrugs. "We reconnected recently. They don't
know anyone here, so I offered to help around the house
with some small repairs."

"They?"

Kai looks away. "Julian and his wife, Sophie."

I steal another sip of his drink. Malakai and Julian
were ... close. I always wonderered if they were more
than friends. As far as I know, nothing ever happened
between them, but one day they stopped talking, and a
few weeks later, Kai went off to seminary school, and

Julian moved back to London, where he'd spent his childhood. And despite Kai dating around here and there —he's not celibate like a priest, after all—nothing serious ever panned out. Now that he's headmaster, he waxes poetic about being too busy to date, but sometimes I wonder if he'll ever find someone to settle down with.

"Miles is meeting us at the pub down the street," Liam tells us, pocketing his phone. "Shall we?"

"Yeah. Give me a second to make sure everyone's good here before I take off for the night. Meet you there?"

Kai gives me a high five as Liam waves over his shoulder. Once they're gone, I take a deep breath and walk over to the bar, hands still shaking from my conversation with Layla.

I check in with the bartenders, and then I walk back to the employee room to grab my jacket, slowly pulling my arms through the sleeves and mentally preparing myself for an onslaught of questions from four of my brothers.

It's only luck that Chase and his wife, Juliet, don't live in Crestwood anymore. There's no way in hell my next oldest brother wouldn't be able to see through the facade I'm attempting to project.

My regular phone pings, and I check my notifications. The only person I get notifications for is my stepsister, but the image and caption that comes through on her social media nearly knocks me over.

She's laughing and holding up a bottle of beer with her right hand—the hand bearing the gold bracelet I gave her. It's slightly blurry, but of course she's fucking gorgeous.

And the caption ...

Yours.

I realize then that I'll do whatever it takes to make Layla truly mine.

Not just Starboy's.

Mine.

CHAPTER TWELVE
THE PHANTOM

Layla

Taking a deep breath, I stare at my reflection in the floor-length mirror. I'd rented the dress for the night—the actual cost of it was three times my mortgage—and I could tell the dress was exquisite from the way the fabric hugged my body, clinging in all the right places. Stella, Mile's wife, had helped me pick it out last week.

The shoulder held its shape perfectly on one side, while the bodice offered full support and a slight stretch for comfort. The dress is a floor-length black gown with an A-line silhouette, featuring a high slit along my right thigh. One half is sleeveless, while the other drapes elegantly over my shoulder, the black material clinging to my arm down to my wrist.

It's classic and modest on the sleeved side but shows off a lot of my chest and collarbone on the other side.

I'd paired it with clear pumps that had flowers embedded into the synthetic material. They're gorgeous, but they're not the most comfortable—still, I hardly ever get dressed up outside of performances, so I liked having an excuse to wear them.

Besides, my feet knew how to take a beating.

I'd pulled my hair back into a low ponytail and kept my makeup and jewelry minimal, aside from some cream blush, mascara, and nude lipstick.

And of course, Starboy's bracelet.

It wasn't a requirement to dress up, but the four of us agreed it would be fun, and since we were going for Zoe's birthday next week, we used it as an excuse to get gussied up.

When I emerge from the bedroom, Sparrow looks at me warily from his position on one of his many cat beds around the house.

"I know, I know. I hardly ever go out."

He lets out a soft meow.

"I won't be back too late, okay?"

I'd fed him earlier and set the air-conditioning to keep him cool. We're supposed to have a heatwave tomorrow, and I can feel the warmth emanating from the front door. It's not unusual to get heat waves in April here, but the temperatures are still supposed to be record-breaking tomorrow. As a native Los Angelean, I know all too well how important it is to cool the house beforehand.

Sparrow stretches on his bed, yawning. I grab my sparkly clutch purse and check my phone. We'll be going to Hollywood for the show, and since I'm on the way to Hollywood from Crestwood, they offered to pick me up. My phone chimes with a text from Zoe letting me know she's outside.

"Okay, be good," I tell Sparrow, blowing him a kiss.

I open my door, and the warmth hits me all at once. It's dry and windy out, and as I close and lock my door, Liam's Jeep Wrangler sits idling by the curb—and Orion is walking around to hold the back door open for me.

Didn't realize he'd be hitching a ride, too.

The instant he turns around, his hand stills on the door handle as his eyes sweep over my dress. His gaze lingers on the slit, and I smile as I walk closer. When he looks back up at me and manages to open the back door, there's a spark of admiration and a hint of vulnerability in his expression. His mouth parts slightly as if he's about to speak but is momentarily lost for words before a slow, genuine smile spreads across his face, softening his features.

My heart skips a beat.

He looks good—*really* good.

His suit is a deep midnight blue. It has a subtle sheen that catches the light of the setting sun. The jacket is open and perfectly tailored, hugging his broad shoulders and tapering down to a narrow waist, with slim lapels edged in black satin. The trousers are slim-fit, with a slight break at the ankle to reveal polished black leather oxfords. Underneath, he's wearing a crisp white dress shirt.

Instead of a traditional tie, the collar of his shirt is

unbuttoned. His pocket square is a dark, intricate paisley pattern, matching the jacket's lining. Finishing the look is a custom waistcoat in a textured black fabric with subtle embroidery.

My stomach flips over as I walk up to him. There's a mix of awe and warmth in his expression, his gaze lingering on my lips for a second too long.

"Hi," he says, gesturing for me to climb in.

"Hi," I say breathlessly. He holds his hand out for me, and I take it—electricity zapping up my arm as I climb into the back seat.

Once he closes the door, I momentarily forget that Zoe and Liam are in the front seats.

"Oh my God," she says, eyes widening. "You are so smitten—"

The other back door opens, and she makes the lips-sealed motion before she turns to Liam, her husband.

His eyes meet mine in the rearview mirror, and he winks once as if to say, *your secret is safe with me.*

My face flushes as Orion climbs into the other back seat, and I keep my eyes ahead as I buckle myself in.

"You're a smokeshow, Lay. Isn't she a smokeshow, Orion?" Zoe asks, stirring the pot as always.

I don't look over at him, but I hear him mumble something in agreement before he turns away and faces out his window.

Zoe and Liam look great, too—Zoe in a strappy, bright red silk dress, and Liam in a black three-piece suit.

We all make small talk, and Zoe talks about the book she just finished up. She writes fantasy books, and her second book is releasing in a couple of months. I can't wait to read it—she's very talented. As one of her best friends, I get early reader priority.

I see Liam pull her hand to his mouth, kissing it once. He looks at her with pure adoration, and I have to look away because it feels like I'm witnessing a very private moment.

"How's intensive going?" Orion asks me.

I shrug. I'd done a two-hour intensive earlier today, and Orion's question reminds me that Bradleigh hadn't been present at the classes all week, nor had she called in sick, which was the first in over three years. I'd spent the majority of the class gnawing my nails down with worry and was waiting for an email back from her mom, but she hadn't responded.

"Good."

"They're lucky to have you," he says, eyes boring into mine. "I still remember taking you to yours. Remember? I'd just gotten my license, and I then spent most of my free time driving you around to various classes all over the city."

I laugh. "I remember, and I'm grateful for you."

His expression softens. He reaches for the black box between us—something I hadn't noticed until just now.

"Belated birthday present," he tells me, handing the box to me. "Don't open it until later, okay?"

My mouth opens and closes. "My birthday was in December."

He smiles, but he doesn't look at me. "That's why I said it was belated," he says playfully.

"My birthday is next week, and this is *literally* my birthday celebration, but okay," Zoe chides from the front seat as she crosses her arms.

I laugh, but there's a tightness in my throat, a mix of surprise and emotion making it hard to speak. The warmth of his thoughtfulness is almost too much to bear, and even though I don't know what it is, a small part of me is grateful that we've gone from hating each other to exchanging gifts.

"Yeah, yeah. You already know what I got you," Orion teases.

"What'd he get you?" I ask her.

"A weekend of watching Captain so we can go on a little getaway," Zoe says glumly. "And while it's very thoughtful, I'm not sure Captain is ever going to willingly go back to your apartment with that demon spawn of a bird who terrorizes him."

We all laugh, and my fingers trace the silky ribbon of the box. I need to know where people are getting these fancy gift boxes because it reminds me of the one Starboy got for me.

"Thank you," I tell Orion earnestly.

The rest of the drive into Hollywood is relatively quiet, and by the time we get to the Pantages, it's fifteen minutes until showtime. We park in one of the premium spots that I'm sure Liam reserved. As we enter the packed threater, we're giggling and drawing attention to ourselves because we're all overdressed.

We're ushered to our private box, where we're lavished with hors d'oeuvres and champagne. Orion asks for sparkling water, and I have one too many glasses in the seven minutes we have to drink before the show starts. I'm giddy and buzzing with excitement, and once the lights go out, I do a little dance.

It doesn't even matter that I'm seated next to Orion.

He just smiles and looks ahead, his hand resting on our shared armrest.

The music by Andrew Lloyd Webber begins, and I'm grinning. I can never get enough of the mysterious Phantom, a musical genius who lives beneath the Paris Opera House, and his obsession with Christine Daaé, a young and talented soprano.

One day, I'll see the show in Paris.

I watch as the musical moves through the parts I have memorized. The eerie, haunting music gives me goose bumps, and when I look over at Orion, he's watching me.

"What?" I whisper, suddenly embarrassed for having such visceral reactions to the show.

He shakes his head and smiles before looking away.

I watch as *"Music of the Night"* plays, revealing the Phantom's inner torment. My heart wrenches at his longing for connection. The next part of the play has me anticipating what comes next as the Phantom's presence looms over the festivities. And then my favorite scene— the one where Christine unmasks the Phantom—starts. I lean forward in my seat, resting my arms on the railing as my eyes water.

"You okay?" Orion's hand comes to the small of my back, and I turn to face him.

"She's horrified it's him. You can see it in her face. I never understood that. They shared such a connection," I whisper passionately. "It's a vulnerable moment for him, and she acts revolted by him."

Orion's face, while masked in darkness, tenses slightly. A crease forms between his brows, and his eyes dip to my lips before looking forward. I follow his gaze to the stage.

"Loving her so deeply, and knowing she can't look at him without fear ... I guess it's hard to hide your feelings when they're that strong," he whispers. "I can understand that." His tone conveys a hint of something personal like he's revealing more than just his thoughts on the Phantom.

When I look back at Orion, he's watching the stage intently.

I want to ask him if he's referring to the woman he's dating, but instead, he looks at me and holds a finger up to his lips.

"Watch. I know you want to."

The rest of the play goes by quickly. I cry during "*All I Ask of You*," naturally, and I swear I see Orion avert his gaze whenever I turn to face him.

And of course, the end has me nearly sobbing. It's his final farewell, the antithesis of a happy ending.

"What the hell was that?" Zoe asks, eyes shimmering with unshed tears as the lights come back on after the curtain call.

I swipe my cheeks. "I know."

She shakes her head. "I'm *so* going to write some

angry fan fiction where Christine and the Phantom get a happy ending between projects."

I laugh.

We're all quiet and introspective as we walk back to the car.

Stopping for burgers before we drive home, we all talk about the other brothers—namely Miles and Stella, and their adorable daughter, Beatrix. I laugh when Zoe spills her soda down the front of her dress, and my chest aches every time she touches Liam tenderly. Orion and I joke like old times, and every so often, I catch him looking at me.

Just as we pull off the freeway to get to my house, I let myself imagine this life. Just for a second. A double date to see a show, a casual dinner, a brooding Liam and a playful Orion who couldn't stop looking at me ...

What if?

Is that even something he would want now that he's seeing someone? It could be kind of great—a mix of familiarity with a dash of intrigue and hot sex. I mean, I assume it would be hot—with the kinds of things he's into, at least, and how just kissing him left me aching for more.

As we pull up to my house, I lean forward and hug Zoe before kissing Liam on the cheek.

"Thanks for being the designated driver, old guy," I tease.

"Get out of here," he jokes, but his smile is all warmth.

"I'll walk you to your door," Orion offers.

He comes around to the side of my car and opens the door. I grab the giftbox and my purse, and we walk up to my door together.

The night air is warm and dry as the wind swirls around us. The street is quiet, save for the soft rustle of leaves in the breeze and the distant hum of the 5 freeway. He walks beside me, his stride matching mine, every step measured, almost deliberate. I can feel the tension between us, thick like the shadows stretching across the pavement.

As we approach my door, his presence feels larger somehow, like he's holding something back, something he's not saying. I glance at him out of the corner of my eye—his jaw is set, his eyes fixed straight ahead, but there's a tightness there, a weight that pulls my attention.

We reach the steps, and he hesitates, just for a fraction of a second, but enough for me to notice. He's close now, close enough that I can feel the warmth radiating from him and hear the steady staccato of his breathing. My heart rate spikes. His eyes finally meet mine, and there's something there, something deep and intense that sends a shiver down my spine.

He opens his mouth as if to say something, but the words don't come. Instead, he just watches me, his gaze searching mine like he's looking for something. The air between us feels charged, heavy with everything he's not saying. And at that moment, I realize there's something here I hadn't noticed before, or at least something I tried *so hard* to push away.

Something simmering beneath the surface.

His hand hovers near mine as though he's debating whether to reach out, to close the space between us.

Do it.

Don't do it.

Do it.

I take a step back, almost instinctively, and his eyes flicker with something—disappointment, maybe, or regret. But he doesn't push. He just gives me a small, tight-lipped smile.

"Good night," he says, his voice low, almost hushed, like it's taking everything in him to let me go.

"Good night," I whisper.

As I turn to unlock the door, I can feel his eyes on me, the weight of his presence lingering long after I've stepped inside. The door clicks shut, and I lean against it, my heart racing, replaying every moment, every look, every unspoken word. Setting the black box down on the small table near the door, I kick my shoes off and take a deep breath.

It feels like I've just missed something, and that thought leaves me breathless.

CHAPTER THIRTEEN

THE SOLACE

LAYLA

I wake up two days later to a text from my dad.

> DAD
>
> I'm not feeling well, so let's rain check our breakfast. Sorry, La-La.

My adrenaline spikes as I press the Call button. We were supposed to go out to our favorite breakfast place in Malibu today since I didn't have intensive until later this afternoon. My dad picks up on the third ring.

"I'm fine," he tells me, but his voice is hoarse. "I have an appointment with my doctor today."

"What's wrong? I can be there in two minutes," I tell him, placing him on speaker and jumping out of bed.

"Nothing, really. My left arm is a bit numb again."

I break out into a cold sweat. Two years ago, he was

hospitalized for a suspected stroke because his left arm went numb, coupled with a headache. It ended up being an early sign of his prediabetes and uncontrolled blood sugar levels, but I've remained vigilant ever since.

"I think we should go to the hospital. I'll be right over, okay?"

"La-La, it's really nothing. You should go."

"Better safe than sorry. I'll see you soon."

Hanging up, I quickly dial Orion's number. He picks up almost immediately.

"Already talked to him. I'm on my way."

Relief washes over me, and my lip trembles as I nod to no one in particular. "Okay. Thanks. I don't think we should wait for his appointment. I'm going to drive him to the h-hospital—" My voice breaks, but I manage to compose myself.

"I'm ten minutes away. I'll drive all of us."

I squeeze my eyes shut. Orion can be an asshole sometimes, but he's always been reliable. No matter what, he was there for me—for us. That never wavered, even back when we weren't on speaking terms.

"Thanks, Orion."

"Take a deep breath, okay?" I inhale deeply, exhaling audibly. "That's it. Again."

I do as he says, and to my chagrin, it helps quell the panic starting to rise. The scare two years ago had given me a bit of post-traumatic stress disorder, and despite getting the all clear from Dad's doctors, I still dreaded the day there'd be another instance of having to rush him to the hospital. I know as parents age, it's inevitable.

But seeing as I don't even remember my mom, he's all I have.

I can't lose him.

I don't think I'd ever recover from that.

"Thank you. I'll see you in a few minutes."

I don't bother showering. Instead, I brush my teeth and pull on leggings and a cropped tank top, seeing as the temperature outside is already in the low nineties—at eight in the morning.

It's going to be sweltering today.

Quickly feeding Sparrow, I don't bother cleaning him up as I check the air-conditioning is set, grab my bag, and close the door a little too loudly behind me.

Jogging to Dad's house, I walk up just as a sleek black sports car pulls into the driveway. I'm so used to Orion's bike that it's strange to see him drive an actual car.

A few minutes later, we're loading my dad—who protests the entire way—into the passenger seat of Orion's car. Orion pushes his seat forward, and I climb into the back.

It's twenty minutes to the hospital, and I pepper my dad with more questions to rule out a possible stroke or heart attack. The numbness is the only symptom, thankfully. Once we get to the emergency room, my dad is seen almost right away.

We're asked to wait in the waiting room, and he tells us he'll be fine as they put him in a wheelchair and lead him through double doors.

I turn around and see Orion standing right behind me, arms at his sides.

"Hey," he says, opening his arms.

I don't even think—I just fall into them and let him hold me. I'm sweaty from running to my dad's house and also the fact that it feels like the inside of an oven outside. But Orion smells *so* good—that familiar smoky, leather scent. Closing my eyes, I feel him squeeze me tighter, and my throat clogs with unshed tears. One of Orion's arms comes to the back of my head, and he slowly strokes my hair.

"He'll be okay," he says, resting his chin on the top of my head.

Memories of the last time we were here together flood through my mind—how we hardly spoke, let alone touched. We were cordial, but I left the room whenever we were alone so I didn't have to talk to him.

What a difference two years makes.

And then before that ... when his mom died.

I remember holding him just like this—his head in my lap as he cried. As the coroner came to the house to take Felicity's body after she took her last breath and we'd all had a chance to say goodbye. His hands had clung to my shirt for hours as he napped next to me—as my dad sat in the living room staring at the wall.

Going through something like that—watching someone you love die—changes you.

And I've learned that in times like that, you need someone to lean on.

I pull out of Orion's grasp and give him a watery smile. "Should we go sit down?"

"Yeah."

The waiting room is packed full of people—as it always is with a heat wave. Lots of people get heatstroke, especially with temperatures like we're currently experiencing. We find a bench meant for one person and manage to squeeze onto it. Orion is huge, and his whole body presses against mine. As subtly as I can, I scoot closer to the end to give him more space.

"I don't bite," he murmurs. "In fact, I remember a time when you used to want to sit on my lap."

My cheeks burn as I look away. "It's different when you're nine versus twenty-six," I grumble.

Orion looks down at me, and his eyes land on my lips briefly before he looks away.

Neither of us has spoken since the night at *Phantom of the Opera* two days ago. I'd forgotten to open his birthday present, having gone right to bed after getting home from the show. The truth is, I was scared to see what he'd gotten me. Most of the past two days were spent oscillating between thinking about Starboy and trying not to think about Orion. And despite checking in with Starboy twice a day, we haven't had the opportunity to do a video call again. We talk all day—texting and sending funny memes to each other. I snap selfies of doing barre, and he takes pictures of his smoothies and rumpled sheets.

Last night, Starboy had sent a picture of himself wearing the mask while lying down on a bed. I couldn't see below his neck, but just the sliver of skin across his throat was enough for me.

Wish you were here.

Four simple words, and I'd been so tempted to break the no-touching-myself rule—especially knowing what he looked like *down there* and what he'd said afterward.

Just imagine how much of a mess I'll make on your pretty face one day.

I'd memorized the image of his cock and the mess he'd made because of me.

I snap out of my dirty thoughts as Orion shifts next to me. I bounce my knee nervously as doctors, patients, and family members walk by us in the crowded emergency room.

"You okay?" Orion asks, leaning an inch closer to me. The smell of leather and tobacco fills the space between us, and despite knowing he doesn't smoke, his musky, smoky scent is damn near intoxicating.

"Fine," I lie absentmindedly. I'm anxious to get the all clear for my dad.

"I'm going to get a coffee. Want one?" he asks, standing.

"Sure."

"We might be here for a while," Orion says, looking down at me. When I meet his eyes, I know he's remembering the last time, when we had to wait over fifteen hours to take Dad home. "Did you bring something to do? A book or something? If not, I can run to your house and grab you something."

I'm not really in the mood to read, but I know he's right. Doing something will take my mind off it.

"My Kindle is in my bag."

"Good. I'll be back in a minute."

I lean against the wall and push my glasses up on my nose before taking a deep breath.

My dad is in the best place he can be.

Everything is fine.

He'll be okay.

Orion comes back a minute later with his arms full.

"Here," he says, handing me a coffee. "I got snacks." I try not to stare at how well his ripped jeans fit his narrow hips and muscular thighs or the way the white T-shirt clings to every one of his muscles.

He sits back down next to me. If possible, the bench seems even more cramped now than it did before. Orion's thigh presses against mine, and my whole body buzzes with energy.

When I'm done with my coffee and after I've gone through a granola bar and a bag of chips, Orion throws our trash out and reaches into my purse, handing me my Kindle.

I glance down at the Kindle on my lap and try to flip it quickly so that he doesn't see the stickers I've decorated it with.

You had me at trigger warning.

Villains do it for me.

My favorite necklaces are hand necklaces.

Call me a good girl.

"What are you reading?" he asks, lips twitching with an almost smile.

My cheeks heat. "*Pride and Prejudice*," I tell him quickly. That, *The Hobbit*, and *Dracula* are my go-tos whenever someone in the non-romance community asks me what I'm reading.

His eyes sparkle with mischief, like he knows I'm lying. How could he? There's no way.

"Which part are you on?"

My mind goes completely blank. Despite having read all of Jane Austen's novels multiple times, being put on the spot like this causes me to panic.

"The part with ... Mr. Darcy's wet shirt."

He huffs a laugh and looks away. "I didn't realize that was in the book. I thought it was only the movie."

If it were possible to blush harder, I would.

"The person I'm seeing reads fan fiction," he says quickly. "Have you read any of that?"

My mind spins with the information he just dropped onto my head. I can't compute it. The woman he's seeing reads *fan fiction*? It's an entirely different betrayal because I mostly read fan fiction. I wonder if I know her from the groups I'm in? Does she enjoy it when Orion drops wax on the backs of her thighs, or are their scenes more intense? How did they meet, and what did they talk about? My core flutters with jealousy and intrigue—but mostly jealousy.

"Oh? What's her favorite fandom?" I ask, knowing his answer will hurt me if it's the same as mine.

He shrugs. "I think she reads it all. She mentioned a *Twilight* story the other day."

My chest aches, and my eyes feel prickly. *Why* am I having this reaction? Orion is free to date whoever he wants. He's not beholden to me just because we shared a drunken kiss a few months ago and a "moment" the other night.

"What's she like?" I ask, hurt lancing through me like I've been shot by an arrow.

Orion looks over at me, studying my face intently. "Beautiful. Smart. Accomplished."

Ouch, ouch, triple ouch.

"I'm really happy for you," I squeak out.

"Are you seeing anyone?" he asks casually.

I open and close my mouth. Am I? It suddenly occurs to me that I could tell him a little about Starboy. The idea of making him jealous appeals to me, especially since my stomach is still roiling with how he described the person he's seeing and how affectionately he spoke of her.

"Sort of," I admit. "It's new. We met online," I say slowly, watching Orion for his reaction as I distractedly play with the bracelet Starboy gave me.

However, instead of jealousy and anger, his face softens. "I'm happy for you, sis."

His words crash through me, and I feel sick. *Sis?* He's never called me that—not once. But he is my stepbrother. That line was drawn in the sand the second his mother married my father. Still, it doesn't sit right.

I don't like it at all, but I don't have a valid reason. Between that and the comment about the woman he's seeing, I feel petulant.

Like I want to argue.

Like I want to throw him off his game, too.

"Sis?" I ask, arching a brow. "That's a new one."

He smiles, but it's warm and friendly. It freaks me out

because a month ago, he would've brooded all day at finding out I was seeing someone. I mean, this is the same man who berated my date to within an inch of his life a few weeks ago.

But he doesn't seem to care about this new development of mine—and calling me *sis*?

What the hell is going on?

I attempt to distract myself with a stalker romance, but I see him pull his phone out every few minutes. After the third time, I can't help but ask the question I've been dying to know.

"Talking to her?" I ask, my voice just a tad too snippy.

He smirks before turning to face me. "If I'm not mistaken, you sound a little jealous, *sis*," he says, his voice low and almost sultry.

My mouth pops open. "I could never be jealous of you," I nearly whisper-hiss. "I'm just … curious. I don't think you've ever talked about dating anyone since I've known you."

"That you know about," he adds.

I dip my chin. "Touché." Drumming my fingers along the front of my Kindle, I practically word-vomit the next question. "What's her name?"

Orion smiles, and I fight against the knot of envy lodged in my chest. "Why? Are you worried you know her?"

I shake my head. "No. I mean, I doubt I do. If she's … you know," I add, whispering so that the people standing right in front of us don't overhear our conversation.

"A submissive?"

My cheeks burn. "Yeah."

"She's not. Not yet, anyway. But she's willing to learn. I think she's a natural," he adds, leaning an inch closer to me. The tobacco smell gets stronger as he gets closer. "You'd be surprised how many people naturally want to submit. To give over that control." He leans another inch closer. "No thinking. No deciding, except whether you want more of whatever your Dom is giving you. Some people find it to be a reprieve from daily life."

I'm barely breathing—barely *thinking*. He's so close to me, and all I can think of are his light blue eyes boring into mine and the way he so confidently led the scene at Inferno a few nights ago. How in command of himself he was—how domineering yet gentle he was to Haley.

I haven't done much with Starboy, but what I have done has already worked at grounding me. Knowing he was controlling me in a very small way yet seeing how *uncontrolled* I made him? It was really hot. I wanted more. And if Starboy took control like Orion did for Haley?

There'd be no going back for me.

"I suppose I can understand that," I answer thickly. "When did you ..." I trail off, unsure of how to ask another invasive question.

"Right around the time I stopped drinking," he tells me. "But control has always interested me. Caring for people. Being the youngest brother meant I couldn't flex those caretaker muscles often ... until I met you, at least."

Now I really do stop breathing as he continues. His brows scrunch together as he looks down at me.

"I sort of stumbled into it. I went to rehab—"

"You did?" I ask, guilt lodging inside me. "When?"

He shrugs. "Around the time Miles got married to Stella. It was mostly to mitigate any withdrawal symptoms, and let's be honest, half the places around here are glorified spas. But it was easy. I did my time and left. The problem is, it wasn't the alcohol I was drawn to. It was the control—the way I could wield my mind into numbness so I didn't have to feel anything." His eyes bore into mine. "Most people are out of control when they drink, but for me, it allowed me to focus on the task at hand and drown everything else out. That first night back from rehab, I walked into the local pub and talked to a woman there. She was there for a munch—which is a casual meetup for anyone in the kink lifestyle. She told me all about it, and I realized it was exactly what I'd been looking for. I joined a local munch shortly after that."

"Is that where you met Haley?" I ask, genuinely curious.

Orion nods. "Yes. Actually, her first munch was also Liam's first munch, and she tried to pick him up ... needless to say, she and Zoe are friends now, but it was funny to watch Zoe and Liam try to resist their feelings at first."

I smile, thinking of how Zoe and Liam got together. How she lured him out of his shell, and they both discovered his kinks together. They both resisted for a while because Liam is twenty years her senior, but I've never seen a couple more in love.

Well, maybe except for the other Ravage brothers— Chase and his wife, Juliet. And Miles and Stella, who live in Ravage Castle with their young daughter, Beatrix.

Despite being curious, I don't ask what his kinks are. It feels too personal, and it's none of my business. Plus, I'm not sure I want to know—it'll just make the whole idea of him as a Dominant way too real for me. I'd seen enough at Inferno, and I had an idea about his inclinations.

"It's weird learning stuff about someone you once knew everything about," I tell him, looking away so he can't see my pained expression. I can feel his eyes boring into the side of my head, though, and he sighs heavily.

"Trust me. I know the feeling."

I'm just about to look at him when a doctor calls out my dad's name from a few feet away.

"Family of Scott Rivers?"

Orion and I both shoot up from the bench. "I'm his daughter," I say, fumbling with my Kindle as I bend down to grab my purse without bursting into tears.

"Go. I'll get your things," Orion murmurs, placing a warm, reassuring hand on the back of my head.

I mutter a quick thanks as I walk over to the doctor.

"Your dad is fine," he says, smiling. Relief washes over me as Orion comes to stand next to me. "We're going to run a few more tests to rule out a stroke and heart attack, so he'll likely stay overnight until his blood sugar comes down, but it appears the tingling and numbness were casued by diabetic neuropathy and very common for someone with uncontrolled diabetes." He looks at Orion. "Is this your husband?"

I almost laugh out loud, but Orion speaks before I

have the chance. "What do you mean uncontrolled diabetes?"

The doctor looks back and forth between us. "He should be taking medication. His blood sugar numbers are extremely high."

My brows furrow. "He was diagnosed with prediabetes last year. You're saying it's progressed?"

The doctor nods. "Yes. When we discharge him, we'll prescribe medication, but I recommend that he see his regular doctor as soon as possible."

My eyes well with tears. "Thank you."

The doctor nods once. "Normally, we'd say you could visit him, but unless you absolutely need to see him, we recommend that you go home. We're swamped because of the heatwave."

"Of course, Doctor," Orion says, reaching a hand out. They shake hands, and a second later, the doctor walks away. "Come on," he says, placing an arm around my shoulders. "I'll drive you home."

CHAPTER FOURTEEN

THE CO-HABITATION

ORION

I'm not sure how it's possible, but the temperature has soared even more as we make our way back to my Bentley Continental—a car that Chase, my brother, sold to me a couple of years ago.

I still give him shit for charging me the market rate, but I needed a car in case I couldn't drive my bike.

Layla and I are quiet on the drive back to her house, and I don't bother making conversation. She needs space to process everything, so I play a Sleep Token album and let her zone out. When we pull up to her house, I jump out and open her door. The least I can do is make sure she gets inside okay. Despite not wanting to leave her alone today, I know she needs it.

When she unlocks the door, her cat Sparrow comes

running to the front door ... as does a wave of dry, stuffy heat.

"Crap," she mutters, leaning down and reaching for him and picking him up. "Did the AC go out again?" she asks him as if he can answer. "You must be so uncomfortable. I'm so sorry, love," she tells him, nuzzling her face into his.

Lucky fucking cat.

"Everything okay?" I ask.

She sighs and walks over to her thermostat after setting Sparrow down. "No. It's eighty-seven degrees in here—my AC has been on the brink of collapse for a while." She looks away as her cheeks heat. "I had some guy here a month ago, and he charged me four hundred dollars to tell me I needed a new unit, but I don't have eight thousand lying around for a new one. I was hoping it would last me through the summer ... it's an old house—"

"I have a guy. I'll have him come take a look." I already have my phone out, and I'm texting the contractor I use for household things.

"No, that's okay. I know there's financing available. I'm just not sure how soon he can get here." She looks at Sparrow with knitted brows.

I step forward and place my hands on her shoulders. "Layla, let me take care of this. Let me take this one thing off your plate."

She sighs and gives me a weak smile. "Fine. Thank you."

"Does he have a carrier?" I ask, squatting down and petting the cat that looks like it got electrocuted. Layla cocks her head, and I continue. "You're coming to stay with me."

She stands up taller and crosses her arms. "No, that's okay. I'll just go to Dad's—"

"I have a pool," I say smoothly, smirking. "Plus, Scott has the dog door that Sparrow climbed out of that one time." I refer to the time Layla stayed at her dad's for a couple of nights while she had her house painted. Sparrow had figured out how to climb through the dog door they'd put in for their old dog. Her dad hadn't ever closed it up, and the cover was nowhere to be found.

"Yeah, you're right. Are you sure it's okay?"

I shrug. "It's probably better if you stay with me, anyway. That way when Scott is ready to be picked up, we can go together."

"Okay. Yeah. Let me just grab a few things. Sparrow has a carrier in the closet over there," she says, pointing at the small door off the kitchen. I'll be back in a minute."

She disappears around a corner, and I look down at the fluffy white beast. "Hey," I say. "What do I need to do to get on your good side? Treats? Belly rubs? Or are you going to make this difficult?"

He meows loudly, rubbing against my leg.

I laugh as I pet him, and his back arches when I run my hand over his soft fur. I'm not really a cat person, but he's pretty cute.

"That was easy."

Walking to the closet, I pull it open. Everything here

smells like Layla. Aside from the pictures she's posted, I haven't ever seen what she's done with the house. It's very *her*. Every single thing is intentionally placed—from the delicate art hung on the walls to the warm colors of the paint and furniture. The kitchen is tiny, but she somehow makes it feel cozy and homey. Plants fill every crevice and corner, blankets everywhere, string lights, and candles galore. The feminine energy is strong, and I fucking love it. It's like she somehow created an English country cottage for herself in the middle of Los Angeles.

I peek into the other room, and there's a reading nook in one section of her living room. A rumpled blanket has been discarded on a large reading chair, and there's a book on the windowsill. It's too far away to see the title, but I can almost guarantee it's a dark romance book.

I bet she spends 90 percent of her time here, I think, smiling.

When I walk down the short hallway, I hear her shuffling around in the back bedroom, so I quickly go into the other room.

Of fucking course it's a library—a very disorganized, work-in-progress one. Stacks of books as tall as her are against one wall, and half the room is painted a light blue color. It's like she started to paint but lost track of time. The floor-to-ceiling, built-in shelves are bare, sanded down to the raw wood that probably came with the house. I walk in farther and see the instructions for the can of dark wood stain sitting on a stool, along with a foam brush.

Once I'm done snooping, I walk back into the hall-way, looking up for the attic hatch. When I see the square, I stand on my tiptoes and push on it. It pops open, and I slide it over a couple of inches to let the hot air up while she's away. Then I walk back into the main room and grab the plastic carrier from the closet. To my surprise, Sparrow meows and runs right into it.

"Thanks, dude," I tell him, placing him on the counter gently as I look for his food.

Sneaking him some treats, I pack up a couple of cans of cat food and throw his water and food dish into a bag. Since Layla is still packing, I grab a glass of water and walk over to all of her plants, watering them with cold water to ensure they don't die from the heat. Just as I'm reaching up to the plant on top of her kitchen cabinet, I hear her clear her throat from behind me.

When I turn around, her cheeks are pink, and she looks ... amused? Aroused? Maybe a little bit of both. Or maybe she's flushed because it's stifling inside this house.

"Thanks for doing that," she says, gesturing to the plants. "I'm ready."

My eyes dart down to the backpack in her hands, as well as a rectangular box I realize is Sparrow's litter box.

"Let's go. By the way, I popped the hatch open," I tell her, gesturing to the hallway. "It'll help move the hot air into the attic."

"Oh. I didn't even know I had an attic." She laughs.

I smile as I take Sparrow's carrier, the litter box, and her backpack, and she locks up as I load my car. Everything goes in the trunk except Sparrow, who I buckle into one of the small back seats. When I turn to Layla to let her into the passenger side, she's watching me with that funny expression again.

Smiling, I turn the music from earlier back on, and we drive to my penthouse in downtown Crestwood. There's a lot of traffic, so it takes almost forty-five minutes. By the time we park my car, wave to security, and walk to the elevator, it's over a hundred degrees out.

Layla looks a bit pale, so I quickly press the P button for the sixteenth floor, a.k.a. the penthouse.

When I walk into my apartment, the cool air is a total relief.

I let Sparrow out of his carrier immediately, and Layla sets his litter box up in the corner of the utility room. Refilling his water dish, I put it near the kitchen island.

Layla slowly follows me, her eyes taking in everything. Since I hardly changed anything after buying the place from Chase, it still feels like it's not actually my place. As her gaze flicks over the fur rug and leather couch, I let my eyes wander over her face and neck. She'd pulled her hair up into a bun at her house, and wavy tendrils cling to her forehead and the back of her neck. She's wearing a white sports bra and black hi-rise leggings, and my mouth goes dry as I unabashedly skim over her narrow waist and muscular legs. And with her round glasses? She reminds me of Evelyn Carnahan from *The Mummy*.

I shift my body slightly to accommodate my growing erection.

"Drink," I tell her, grabbing a glass and filling it with cold water.

Arching one brow, she takes the glass from me. "Bossy."

I can't help it. Leaning forward, I let myself get within a couple of inches of her face. Her eyes go wide, and she sucks in a sharp breath.

"You think that's bossy?" I chuckle, leaning back.

She blushes and takes a few large gulps of water. "Of course my air-conditioning crapped out during a heatwave."

I grab a glass for myself and smile as I take a few sips. "Naturally."

"Thanks again for letting me stay over. Your place is nice."

"I left everything as is when Chase moved out. Most of it is his."

"It's big," she adds, looking around.

I smirk. "It is."

"Open."

"Yeah."

"I don't want to interfere with any potential hot dates you bring home," she admits, finishing her water. "You know, like the girl you're seeing."

I watch her throat bob as she swallows, mesmerized. "Trust me. You won't," I tell her, my voice an octave too low.

"Master!"

Layla and I both crane our necks to see Earl flying through the penthouse. He lands on one of his many perches around the house, and Layla laughs.

"Oh my God, your bird! I completely forgot."

"Pretty girl," Earl states, walking closer to the edge of his perch and, therefore, closer to Layla. "Earl missed pretty girl."

Layla looks at me, and I shrug. "No idea who he's referring to."

"Master loves his pretty girl and wants to fill her tight, little f—"

"That's enough," I say quickly, reaching out for him. "Let's get you back into your aviary, old man."

Just then, Sparrow comes around the corner, and Earl begins to growl. Because yes, apparently, I have a bird who growls.

A minute later, after putting Earl back in his aviary, I walk back into the kitchen to find Layla on her phone. "Everything okay?"

She nearly drops her phone, quickly placing it back in the pocket of her leggings. "Yeah, just texting someone."

"I was going to go for a swim. Care to join me?"

Her eyes go wide. "Right. The pool." She looks around and laughs. "Sorry, this is just so weird for me. You, me, *us*. Being cordial. Until the other night, I don't think we've spoken this much in …"

"Seven years?" I offer, trying to school my face into something other than veiled pain. "But yeah, it's weird for me, too."

She shakes her head. "I'm just trying to wrap my mind around it, that's all."

"Go change. There are several guest rooms—pick one. We'll cool off in the water, and maybe we can get reacquainted with each other."

Her hazel eyes bloom a bit darker, but she nods once. It looks like she wants to say something, but she grabs her backpack and walks off instead. Once she's out of sight, I lean over the island on my elbows and rest my head in my hands.

"Fuck," I mutter.

My phone vibrates, and Kai's name pops up on my caller ID before I press the answer button.

"What's up?"

"Just wanted to check on you. How are things?"

"Uh," I look over my shoulder in the direction Layla went. "Layla is here," I tell him, my voice low in case she comes back.

"Oh? That's a new development."

"Yeah, Scott had a health scare this morning."

"Oh fuck. Is he okay?"

"He's fine. How many times do you have to self-flagellate when you swear?" I tease.

"Fuck off."

I laugh. "You can come over if you want. We're about to go swimming."

"And subject myself to the thick, sexual tension? I think not."

"How are you doing?" I ask, leaning against the counter.

"Fine."

I wait a few seconds for him to elaborate, but he doesn't. "Fine? How's Julian? And his wife?"

I'm grinning as I say it, and I'm sure Kai can tell. "They're fine."

"So wordy today, brother."

"Be careful. I'll come over there just to fuck with you."

"I dare you."

"In all seriousness, have you told her how you feel?"

I run a hand through my hair. "I'm working on it."

No one knows about Starboy, and I'd prefer to keep it that way for now. I want to ask him more about Julian, but he speaks before I have the chance.

"Tell me you have a plan."

"A plan for what?"

"To win her over. For the love of all things holy, make your move."

I wince. "It's not that simple."

"How is it not simple? I've never seen you have problems picking women up."

Running a hand through my hair, I groan. "Yeah, but she's different. Plus, I don't know what she wants."

Malakai sighs on the other end. "Okay, here's what you do. What's her favorite thing in the world?"

I open and close my mouth. "I don't know ... she likes books."

"Okay, great. Books. Make yourself a part of those things, but don't be too obvious. Show her you're genuinely interested and care for her."

I rub the back of my neck. "How?"

"Where does she read? Make it so that she has to think of you whenever she's there."

I'm quiet as an idea begins to form in my mind.

"And for the love of God, don't rush it. Be patient. I know you're spontaneous, and patience isn't your strong suit, but let her see the real you and give her reasons to want more. It's about connection, not just chemistry. I mean, a little bit is chemistry, so it wouldn't hurt to turn on the charm."

"Who would've thought the brother who's a pastor would give me the best dating advice?"

"Very funny. I'll leave you to it. Good luck."

He hangs up before I can protest, and I heave a heavy sigh before walking to my bedroom and changing into my swim trunks. I open my bedside drawer and pull out my burner phone, delighted to see a text from LittleDancer.

> **LITTLEDANCER**
>
> I might be offline a bit today. At my stepbrother's place. My dad had a health scare, and my AC went out. I'll update you when I can. :)

I quickly text back so that *Starboy* doesn't leave her hanging.

> I'm sorry to hear that. I'm here if you need to talk. Also, you have a stepbrother? I didn't know that.

She responds almost immediately.

LITTLEDANCER

Yeah … he's a pain in the ass most days.

I laugh.

You guys are close?

Three dots appear and disappear several times.

LITTLEDANCER

Not really.

My smile disappears. *Fuck.*

I'm always here if you need me.

I put the phone back in my pocket and sit down on my bed. She doesn't think we're close—why is that? I mean, we're not best friends, but we're definitely not strangers anymore. Not after the last couple of weeks.

He's a pain in the ass most days.

I've been playing it safe. Being the nice guy—making sure she's safe, looked after, cared for. But maybe I needed to turn it up a notch. She seems to hate whenever I talk about the supposed woman I'm dating. And I know she finds me attractive.

I also happen to know that she's not allowed to relieve herself until I tell her that she can.

I also know she loves books … and my idea is too good to ignore.

Those are all things I can capitalize on.

Walking out of my bedroom, I decide to make her see what she's missing—and perhaps make her fall for her dear stepbrother.

It's a dangerous game to play, and I might lose everything.

She might think she's immune to my charms, but I'll prove her wrong.

She wants a villain?

Well, I'm the one who can give it to her—the guy who buys her flowers *and* burns the world for her.

CHAPTER FIFTEEN

THE SWIM

LAYLA

I waver in front of the mirror as I stare at my reflection. I'd grabbed a swimsuit without thinking, and it just so happened to be the one I'd worn to the beach with Zoe three weeks ago. The one I'd gotten a size too small because it was half off. It's not my body that's the problem, and it's taken me years to heal from my adolescence of hating myself to be able to say that. I know that my workout routine means that I have abs and sculpted muscles shaping my legs. I'm not overweight, but I am curvy. I'm *strong* and I'm proud of how hard I work.

No, it's not that.

It's the skimpy blue swimsuit that barely contains my breasts and barely covers my ass crack. I'd laughed when Zoe made me buy it, and it worked for sunbathing, but to wear it around Orion? I had major underboob, and

I now regret taking the pads out of the top cups because my nipples are *very* obviously ready to play.

Wonderful.

I pull my hair back into a loose bun, and then I mutter *screw it* several times before pulling the door of the beautiful guest room open.

The whole apartment is beautiful. Marble floors that are so shiny I could eat off them, gorgeous, colorful art pieces, leather furniture, and things I would never really associate with Orion, like fresh flowers. *Peonies,* as a matter of fact.

Interesting choice. Maybe his housekeeper likes them.

Or his girlfriend, I think glumly.

Orion isn't in the kitchen anymore, but I refill my water and walk over to the patio door, and when my eyes land on my stepbrother ...

Holy—

He's standing a few feet away from me, wearing tight swim shorts that cling to his ass muscles. His back is wide and strong, his large muscles knitting together with every movement. A black tattoo snakes down his right arm and all down the right side of his back.

My hand involuntarily reaches for the handle of the patio door. It clicks open, and I step out just as he turns to face me.

Fortunately, I don't seem to be the only one left speechless.

His mouth drops open slightly as he takes me in, but

then his face drops into his usual cocky smirk. He begins walking to the pool.

"I'm going to do some laps," he says brusquely.

"Me too."

I don't swim often, but moving in the cool water feels nice. And the view? Incredible. All of Crestwood and Los Angeles is open before me, and it feels like I'm swimming in some exclusive club rather than my stepbrother's apartment. The pool has no edge—the water falls off the side into an infinity-type design, and there's a glass railing that overlooks the city. A few deck chairs are on the opposite side of the pool with what looks to be a state-of-the-art outdoor kitchen.

It's very fancy, but it doesn't scream Orion. Then again, how would I know that?

I submerge myself and dip my head, taking my scrunchie out and letting my hair fall down my back before leaning against the wall of the shallow end. Orion swims closer, popping up right in front of me. I try to scoot back but I'm pressed against the wall and too surprised to do anything.

He lifts a hand and runs his index finger over the strap of my bikini before I even have a chance to react. "Pretty swimsuit," he murmurs, smiling. "Did you wear it just for me?"

My skin pebbles as my mouth drops open, and I just *know* he can see the way my nipples harden at his touch. I can't breath—and he only moves an inch closer as if he's going to say something else.

But then he pushes away, swimming freestyle away from me.

God. He's such an arrogant jerk sometimes.

I continue standing against the opposite wall and watch as he moves fluidly through the water, attempting to catch my breath.

He must swim a lot. He's not even out of breath when he stops right in front of me and pops up from the water, wiping his face and flicking his hair to the side.

"You know, it's rude to stare."

My chest burns with embarrassment. My skin is still tingling from where he touched me a minute ago.

"I was just admiring your cardiovascular health. You're not even out of breath. How many laps do you do every day?"

He smirks and moves closer again so he's only a few inches away, but this time I'm more prepared. We're standing in the shallow end, so the water only comes up to my waist. I don't let my eyes wander down to his chest as he gets closer, but I can see how the water collects and drips off his perfectly hewn pectoral muscles.

"A lot," he says, his voice husky. "There are certain ... extracurricular activities that require peak *cardiovascular health*," he adds, his lips pulling into a lopsided smile.

I'm panting from the heat. That's all. It's over a hundred degrees out, and despite the pool being cold, I'm sweating and not breathing from the *heat*.

"That's good. Your girlfriend must be pleased," I retort, instantly regretting it when a large smile breaks out on his face.

"Oh, she is."

I clench my jaw and cross my arms, trying to think of something to say to change the subject and *not* imagine what it would be like to sleep with Orion.

"I like your tattoo," I tell him, pointing at the pointe shoes visible on his left pectoral.

His lips twitch. "Thank you."

"Did you get it for your mom?" I ask, my voice soft as I wipe the water off my cheeks.

Orion's eyes twinkle like he's keeping a secret—but before I can ask why he's not answering, he turns around and swims away from me.

When he's on the other side of the pool, I start to do the breaststroke. My nipples are hard from the cool water, and that only enhances the arousal pulsing through me. My mind wanders to the image Starboy sent the other night, and as I swim, my arousal gets more potent. It doesn't help that Orion swims beside me, his muscles flexing with each fluid movement through the water. I lick my lips, and when I get to the middle of the pool, I turn over onto my back and begin to float.

How is it that *both* men make me feel so alive? It should be easy—I should be able to turn it off for Orion. After all, we grew up together. He's always been my stepbrother in my mind. Except that's not true, either. Before we stopped talking, something *had* shifted between us. I remember my eighteenth birthday, specifically, and the way it somehow felt *different* when he placed his arm around my shoulders during dinner. He'd dropped his arm and never touched me like that again—like he could sense when things had shifted, like me.

Neither of us would ever admit it, but I remember, even now, the way his eyes would linger. The way I'd stare at his neck while he chewed his food and swallowed, the way he gripped utensils with his large hands, and the way he'd do pull-ups while I did barre.

The air around me changed whenever he was around, and I'd be stupid if I couldn't admit that it had *always* been that way.

Even when I said I hated him.

Especially when I said I hated him.

And that kiss a few months ago? It *smoldered*. I'd never been kissed like that—never been held like that or touched like that.

It was like he revered me at that moment.

And the look in his eyes ...

I squeeze my eyes shut tighter as my chest aches.

Starboy, on the other hand, isn't my stepbrother. It should be an easy choice.

The sun beats down on my stomach and chest, and when I open my eyes, Orion stands above me on the side of the pool—darkened eyes on *me*.

I quickly stand upright and dunk underneath the water.

How did this all get so confusing so quickly? How did my feelings with Orion become so muddled with my feelings for Starboy?

It would be great if the universe could space things

out. Nearly three years of celibacy and then *bam!* Here are two hot guys, and you can only choose one of them.

Talk about not fair.

I walk to the stairs of the pool and climb out, reaching for my towel. I dry off, and when I look over at Orion, he's walking away.

I head into the cool apartment, and Sparrow comes running over to me, sliding between my legs.

"This place is nice, huh?" I ask, squatting down and petting him along his spine. He arches his back and lets out a loud meow. "I know. I like it here, too."

Wrapping the towel around my waist, I walk into the kitchen and see Orion scooping out some of Sparrow's wet food.

"I figured he was hungry," he says, placing the food bowl on the floor.

I lean against the counter as the cold water from my hair drips down between my breasts. Orion glances up at me, and I swear I see something shutter behind his eyes before they flick down to my chest and back up in half a second.

His right hand twitches at his side.

"I'm going to shower," he says, his voice low.

As he brushes past me, his arm briefly touches my shoulder, and it feels like a million fireworks go off inside me all at once as a full-body shiver works through me.

The pulsing between my legs gets worse, and I bite my lower lip.

I should not be thinking things like this about him.

Not only is he completely off-limits, but he's dating someone.

And there's Starboy, too.

I hang around for a few minutes, inspecting his kitchen. The fully stocked fridge and pantry are filled with healthy stuff, albeit there are a few treats here and there. Professional-looking pots and pans. Enough sparkling water to last a lifetime—strawberry flavored. The living room is basic with almost nothing personal, except a couple of pictures in frames on the fireplace mantel. I walk closer, smiling when I see an old picture of Orion with his brothers. He can't be older than eight or nine—he's tall and lanky with floppy, dark hair. Chase stands next to him, a knuckle in his hair, causing Orion to laugh in the photo. Liam and Miles look like they don't want to be there, and Kai is smirking at Orion and Chase —ever the middle child.

My eyes wander to the other photo, and my heart nearly stops.

It's me—the morning of my audition with the Paris School of Ballet.

It's the selfie I sent him. *The last one.*

Before everything changed.

Before he ruined my future.

Swallowing the lump in my throat, I back away slowly and walk down the hallway to my guest room.

The sound of running water catches my attention from the open door at the end of the hallway. I stop walking and listen closer, realizing that it's likely Orion's room and attached bathroom.

Tiptoeing closer, I hold my breath as I step inside the bedroom, and his room comes into view. I know I should turn around and mind my own business. I *know* this is wrong, yet I can't help but be mesmerized with the layout of his room. The walls are white, and most of the furniture is dark wood. The bedspread on the massive bed is a dark gray linen, and I run my hand over the soft material. Two dark wood nightstands frame the bed, as does a matching dark wood bed frame. It's tidier than I expected.

His closet is open, and I take a peek inside. It's large —almost as big as my bedroom at my house. The smell of leather and smoke permeates the air, and I inhale discreetly. Closing the door quickly, I realize that inhaling his scent like a creep won't be the worst thing I'll be caught doing if I don't get out of here quickly—

A low, guttural groan cuts through the silence.

I stop moving and listen, wondering if I'm hearing things or if it's coming from Orion's bathroom. I look over my shoulder to see the bathroom door cracked, and amid the sound of the shower, I hear another sound.

"Fuck," Orion rasps from inside.

Everything inside me pulls tight as I inch closer to the cracked bathroom door while my subconscious screams to walk away. But I'm entranced now, and I can't help but want to hear more. When I get within a few inches of the door, I slowly shift my head to look inside the bathroom and—

I jerk back and close my eyes because Orion's naked

body is *right there* and visible through the glass shower door. And ... he's masturbating.

My pulse spikes as heat flares through my veins, and a shudder passes through me at the sight of my stepbrother with his ... *thing* ... in his hand.

I lean forward again, suddenly addicted to the erotic visual of Orion masturbating. He's so large that he fills the shower, and the water falls over his face and chest as he slowly strokes up and down his thick shaft. And it's— *thick*. Swallowing, I stare at the dark pink head, at the way it seems to be straining, veiny and taut and *hard*. His head is dropped backward, eyes facing the ceiling, and his legs are spread slightly. He's facing me, and my mouth goes dry as I watch him slowly move his hand in an up and down, fluid motion.

I pull back again, closing my eyes and pressing my legs together as I breathe through my nose. I'm spying on him, and it's screwed up. I shouldn't be here. But I can hear the water splash off his hand—can hear the way he slides his hand quicker now, the low rumble emanating from the shower, the hiss of pleasure coming from his lips.

A cloud of steam barrels out of the bathroom, and I'm suddenly lost in a sea of Orion—musky, with a hint of tobacco, leather, and smoke.

It's his body wash—that's what he's using that makes him smell so good.

I look through the crack again, and instead of going slow, he's now actively thrusting into his hand— barreling closer to his climax with the sort of desperate fervor you'd expect a starved man to exhibit while eating. Everything inside me turns to liquid as I watch him come undone, and I no longer feel regret for stumbling into this.

It's the hottest thing I've ever seen.

I *want* to touch myself. *Need* to. But I curl my fists and stare entrenched as my stepbrother bites his lower lip and rolls his hips into his fist. I imagine that he has me pressed against the wall, and he's entering me from behind—one hand grabbing my hair, and the other one pulling my hips onto his cock.

I imagine the filthy words he'd say, thinking of how commanding he was with Haley. Would he say those kinds of things to me, too?

You can take more.

He'd growl it. How would that growl sound echoing off the marble walls of the shower?

How would it feel for him to say those words to *me*?

The veins in his arms strain, running down to his hand as he squeezes tighter, that same low rumble escaping his lips again. His breathing is sharp and ragged, and he's still facing his face up with his eyes closed.

The space between my legs pulses, and I squirm as I watch his hips begin to jerk erratically. My lips part as I observe everything happening, and just as I'm about to walk away—for good this time—he drops his head and opens his eyes.

Looking straight at me.

Neither of us has time to react before his mouth

drops open, and large, thick ropes of cum shoot out from his cock and onto the floor as he groans. His eyes never leave mine as his face goes slack, and his whole body shudders and shakes. His eyes shut briefly as he moans again, the aftershocks rolling through him.

I turn and stumble away.

CHAPTER SIXTEEN

THE ENTICEMENT

ORION

I'm still smiling as I throw a black T-shirt over my head and run my hands through my wet hair. The gray sweatpants sit low on my hips, and my situation is very obvious because I didn't bother wearing boxer briefs. Layla retweeted a picture of gray sweatpants last year that had this caption: *Have you been harassed during gray sweatpants season? You might be entitled to some compensation.*

So I went out and bought five pairs.

I thought messing with her as Starboy was fun, but this? Tempting her as Orion? Making her realize what she's missing, what's right in front of her? She has no idea what or who she's dealing with. Online, she thinks she's getting close to someone she can trust, someone who understands her. As Starboy, I've become her confidant, her secret *obsession*. She spills her heart out, thinking she's safe behind the screen, completely unaware that I'm the same person standing in front of her now.

Layla's always had this naive charm, thinking she can handle anything and anyone. But I'm a storm she can't outrun, a shadow she can't escape. Not seven years ago, and not now. Her composure is bound to shatter. What happened in my bathroom a few minutes ago is proof that I—*Orion, her stepbrother*—is her one weakness.

The jealousy.

The lingering gazes.

How long has she had feelings for me? Has she always denied them to herself, tucking them away somewhere in the back of her mind?

And why did I want to use those feelings to my advantage?

I read dark romance because I always fall for the villains. I want someone whose intentions are good, but instead of buying me flowers, he cuts off my ex's hands. Nice guys are just that—they're nice. *But I want someone who will be all-consumed by me no matter what.*

You don't become a sadistic Dominant without learning the art of manipulation, turning hearts and minds into my playthings. Layla is no different. The question is, am I willing to do this? Am I willing to draw her into my life like this? The allure, the danger, the promise of something she can't quite grasp?

And when she realizes she's in too deep, when she

understands she's fallen into a trap she can't claw her way out of, it'll be too late.

Just like my father.

I feel a twinge of guilt at that thought, but not enough to stop.

There are so many boundaries I'm willing to cross when it comes to her.

I want someone who will be all-consumed by me no matter what.

Well, Little Dancer ... you got your wish.

Walking out of my bedroom, I glance at the closed door of one of my guest rooms, jaw grinding when I think of how she's probably in the shower.

Is she obeying Starboy's orders?

Or is she being a bad girl and touching herself?

I decide to find out.

Once I'm in the kitchen, I pull my burner phone out of my pocket and text her.

> The rules still apply, even now.
> Remember, I'm here for you, but I need you to keep me informed if anything changes.

She doesn't answer right away, so I start pulling ingredients out to make us a late breakfast. I assume she still loves waffles, so I pull out the waffle maker to warm up while I mix the batter. Just as I crack an egg into the bowl, a text comes through on my phone.

LITTLEDANCER

Don't worry. As hard as it's been these
last few days, I'm being a good girl.

I smile as I lock and pocket my phone. She'll obey me, and it'll just make it more entertaining for me as Orion to try to break her. Who knew I'd ever be in competition with myself in this way? Certainly not me.

I finish the batter and begin ladling it into the waffle maker. While it cooks, I pull the fresh strawberries out of my fridge and macerate them in sugar while I wait for the waffles to brown.

I'm distracted, whistling a Sleep Token song as I finish washing my hands, when I catch movement behind me.

Layla leans against the back wall of the kitchen, watching me with an open expression. A pensive shimmer passes behind her eyes, and I drink in her outfit —black yoga shorts and a brick-red tank top that matches the shade of her hair. Her glasses are perched on her nose, and her long hair is thrown up into a loose bun.

She becomes increasingly uneasy under my scrutiny, awkwardly clearing her throat before pushing off the wall.

"S-sorry about earlier," she says while looking at the floor.

I finish drying my hands on the towel before slowly walking over to where she's standing. She squirms— visibly—and my eyes clock the way her throat bobs, the way she shifts her weight from one foot to the other. I keep my expression neutral as I get closer, as I *relish* in the way she begins to blush after her eyes flick to my sweatpants.

I'm fucking addicted to this version of her—of the stammering, unsure, shy, *aroused* version of her.

I am so fucked.

"I got turned around, and I didn't realize I'd stumbled into your room until—until—"

Her voice is small, almost feeble. The corners of my mouth quirk up as I stop a foot away from her, arms crossed.

"Until what?" I ask, fully smirking now.

"I didn't—I mean, I wasn't—"

I reach out and place a finger under her chin. "Are you saying it was an accident?" I ask, my voice a low purr.

She swallows as her eyes flick between mine, trying to ascertain my mood.

Tell me it was an accident, I want to tell her. *Tell me you didn't mean to watch me. Tell me you didn't take a cold shower or wish you could have been in that shower with me as I pumped into your cunt.*

I dare you.

"Layla?" I ask, eyes on her lips as she opens and closes her mouth.

She has such a pretty fucking mouth.

"Of course it was an accident," she rushes out, cheeks red. "Anyway, I'm sorry, and it will never happen again."

My ears ring, and I can't help but think back to the day of her audition. For some reason, her eyes have that same cloud of resolve around them, and it terrifies me.

I don't ever want to see you again.

I shut down.

I have to.

This was a terrible idea. How did I ever think I could face rejection from her again after what happened? After she rejected me twice before?

I drop my hand as disappointment fills me. "Of course," I answer, my voice cold. "Breakfast is ready. Take a seat."

"I'm not—"

"Sit down now," I practically growl. Her eyes go wide, and I pull my emotions close, feeling guilty for lashing out. "You're hungry. So eat."

Her eyes flash briefly before they flick downward. "Okay."

I walk back over to my kitchen island and pull a stool out for her to sit on, and she sits without saying anything else. I slide a plate of waffles over to her, topped with strawberries, syrup, and powdered sugar. Once she realizes what's in front of her, those gorgeous hazel eyes snap back to mine.

"You made waffles."

I dip my chin and walk my plate over to the chair next to her. "I remembered that you used to like them." Sitting down, I begin to eat, and Layla stabs a strawberry with her fork before looking up at me.

"They're my favorite," she says, chewing.

"I know."

We eat in silence, and I talk myself down from the ledge.

I'm sorry, and it will never happen again.

Those words out of her mouth triggered the same knee-jerk panic I experienced seven years ago, and even though we were talking about something entirely different today, hearing Layla make forever promises still scares the fucking crap out of me. Hearing her declare that she could *never* let herself be curious about me, how she could *never* allow herself to be turned on by something I do is hard.

An idea strikes me.

Maybe I'm not being obvious enough.

Maybe I'm not getting enough of a rise out of her, and she has no problem constructing and reconstructing that wall between us.

I need to do something that will throw her completely off kilter.

Something she won't be able to stop thinking about.

Maybe I'd have to dangle the possibility of *losing me* in front of her.

And I had just the thing for that.

When she finishes her breakfast, I hand her a strawberry-flavored sparkling water.

"I need to make some phone calls for Inferno. I'll be in my office. Help yourself to anything," I tell her brusquely.

"I'll clean up," she offers, hopping off her stool and gesturing to the dishes.

"Sure. Thank you."

I turn and walk away, knowing that Layla is now

intensely curious about me and my life despite telling herself she can't feel this way about me.

On my way to my office, I stop by my bedroom and hide my burner phone in a drawer on my bedside table. And then, with a heavy sigh, I pull a turquoise bag down from the top of my closet, setting it on a shelf at about eye level.

It's all coming together.

Smiling, I walk out of my room and down the hallway to my office, anticipation rushing through my veins.

The bait is set, and now all I have to do is wait for Layla to take it.

CHAPTER SEVENTEEN

THE JEALOUSY

Layla

I amuse myself with my Kindle for an hour, but being in Orion's house has me feeling restless and inquisitive. I don't have to teach ballet intensive for three more hours, so after reading the same page several times, I set my Kindle on the coffee table before reaching down and petting Sparrow. He's oddly comfortable here, purring contentedly as he dozes at my feet. When I stand, he looks up at me for a second before setting his head back down and rolling over onto his back, stretching.

"Yeah, yeah, I get it," I mumble resignedly. "You're enjoying this life of luxury, aren't you?"

He meows in response, yawning and closing his eyes, completely blissed out.

I chuckle as I stand and stretch. Slowly walking

around the living room, I take in all the details to get a better picture of my stepbrother, but there's almost nothing personable in here. I'd visited once or twice when Chase lived here, and it looks like Orion didn't make *any* changes when he took over the deed to the apartment. Aside from the pool and massive aviary, of course. Walking into the kitchen, I open the pantry and glance at his food again. There are a lot of ingredients I overlooked earlier, which means he probably cooks a lot. That makes sense, seeing as he made me waffles from scratch.

You can tell a lot about someone based on their food, and Orion seems to prioritize cooking. I think back to when we lived under the same roof. I suppose he used to cook a lot back then, too. He'd oftentimes make food for the four of us, and it was only when he started drinking more that he stopped.

Swallowing, I walk into the dining room next. It's beautiful, looking over the Los Angeles basin and the ocean a few miles past that. There's a table with his mail, but it looks like it's all utility bills and spam.

I walk back out into the living area and down the hallway to the wide stairway. I hadn't realized there was a second story, so I walk upstairs where I'm surprised to see another small kitchen, a home theater, a game room, and a gym. None of them have anything personal, so I'm in and out in a minute. I don't even know what I'm searching for—something to show me who he is, I guess. Something tangible.

I walk back down to the first story, tiptoeing down the main hallway. There's a closed door, and I can hear Orion speaking to someone on the phone. Must be the office. I keep walking down the hallway, peeking into one of the other guest bathrooms. For an apartment, there are a lot of rooms between the two floors.

And none of them gives me a better picture of my stepbrother.

I look to my right and glance into what I now know is Orion's bedroom.

My cheeks flame when I think of what I saw earlier—of how he made eye contact with me as he came.

Goose bumps erupt along my skin when I think about it, and I chew on my lower lip as I debate snooping some more.

Making a split-second decision, I go right and walk into his bedroom.

Out of all the rooms, this one smells the most like him. There's a fancy phone charging station, and next to it are his wallet, keys, and some loose change. There's also a black-and-silver Hermès watch. I walk over and pick it up, brows furrowed when I realize it's the same watch his mom had gotten him for his high school graduation years ago. Something catches in my throat when I set it back down.

I miss Felicity every day, but my birthday is always the hardest. I had just turned eighteen when cancer took her, I wish I'd had more than ten years with her. For all intents and purposes, she's the only mother I've ever had because I don't remember my birth mother. Felicity loved me, and I loved her—but Orion was her pride and joy. They had a special connection—the sort of affinity that almost hurt to look at because it was so pure. When she died, Orion took it *so* hard.

And then I pushed him away completely.

I take a deep breath and walk over to his closet. The door is open, and I step inside the large walk-in dressing room. As my eyes wander over the leather and black, gray, and white, I'm suddenly nostalgic for what we missed out on over the past seven years. The friendship, the closeness ... he was *everything* to me at one point. One day, he was there, and the next, he wasn't.

I pick up a black hoodie and bring it to my face, inhaling his familiar smell. It's just like Starboy's hoodie ...

I chuckle to myself at the idea of mixing Starboy and Orion into the same person.

It's impossible.

My eyes catch on a small turquoise bag sitting atop some folded sweaters. Checking behind me, I confirm that I'm still alone as I pull it from the shelf. My heart hammers inside of my chest. As I glance inside, I gasp as a small leather ring box comes into view. Reaching inside with my free hand, I let the bag drop onto the floor as I pull the box open, already suspecting what it is.

My breathing hitches when I see a classic Tiffany engagement ring. The diamond is massive—this must've cost a fortune. And the band is rose gold, something I happen to love in jewelry.

He bought a ring for *her*—for whoever he's dating.

Ice spreads through me, turning my food to lead in my stomach. An acute sense of loss rushes through me, as does betrayal. *But why?* We're not dating—not even close. He's allowed to be in love, to envision a life with someone else. My eyes sting as I reach down for the bag and drop the box into it a little too roughly, shoving it back onto a random shelf.

My breathing quickens as I exit Orion's closet and then his room.

Why do I even care? Why does the misery feel so acute, almost like it's a physical pain? Swallowing the despair lodged in my throat, I walk into the guest bedroom where my things are and slam my door closed before I begin packing everything up.

Screw this.

I can't be around him and think of how he'll plan it. Of how he's going to be someone's fiancé soon, and then have a wedding …

God, what is my problem? Why am I so jealous, and why am I having this reaction?

Sparrow meows loudly outside my door, and when I pull it open, Orion is standing there with his arms crossed.

"Everything okay?" he asks.

A raw and primitive grief washes through me, and I can't understand why. He's *Orion*. My stepbrother— someone I've known since I was eight. Yet all I can think about is how he belongs to someone else now.

I shrug, feeling resigned as I look down at my bare

feet. "Fine. I think I should go and check on my dad, make sure he's doing okay—"

"Layla."

His voice is low, and when I look back up at him, something tortured passes over his expression before his jaw hardens.

"I told you before, you're welcome to stay here. It's nearly one hundred ten degrees out right now."

I clench my teeth as I look down again. My throat aches, and when he takes a step closer, I close my eyes, feeling utterly miserable.

"What's wrong?" he asks, and I can smell the strawberry flavor of the sparkling water he drinks.

The pain inside me becomes a sick and fiery gnawing, and I feel sick to my stomach.

He chose a ring for someone else. He's going to ask *someone else* to marry him. And the worst part is, I've pushed him away time and time again, so why am I surprised? Why would someone like him, someone charming, handsome, charismatic, funny, bossy, and kind, stay single?

I may have feelings for him—feelings I don't want to acknowledge—but I have no claim over him.

And maybe I never did.

"Tell me what's wrong," he says, his voice low and pleading. "I can't help you if you don't tell me what's wrong."

I squeeze my eyes tighter as a tear escapes. He can never know—he can never know I found the ring or that

I'm so bitterly jealous that I feel like I might be sick at his feet.

When I open my eyes, his shoulders are heaving as he breathes, as his eyes lock onto mine. And there—in his darkened pupils, in the way his lids droop a bit lower as his eyes dart around my face—I see it.

A flicker of *something* behind his intense expression.

Without thinking, I stand on my tiptoes, reach for his neck, and pull him down for a kiss.

He stumbles, completely taken off guard. One of his hands land on my waist and the other comes to my face to drag me in closer. And just when I expect him to push me away, the hand on my waist pulls me roughly— almost *violently*—against his body as he kisses me back.

In the same breath, my mouth opens as my hands tremble, as my knees shake, and his tongue darts inside my mouth. He inhales sharply, and I moan. The shock of him—of kissing him and how *right* it feels is utterly intoxicating. *Just like last time.* His lips are soft, and he smells a little minty and a bit like strawberry. My hands come to his arms, and I trail them down his corded muscles. He groans against my mouth as a full-body shudder works through him, and I suddenly can't get enough. He pulls back slightly, but he doesn't let me go.

"Layla," he whispers, his breath hot against my ear.

"Don't stop," I whimper, pulling his face back to mine and kissing him again. He doesn't stop me, instead letting his lips recapture mine—more demanding this time. *Punishing.* Almost bruising.

He walks me back to the bed, and I place a hand on his chest, feeling the way his heart is quickly pounding against his ribs. Touching me with demanding mastery, he scrapes my sensitive skin with his calloused fingertips, running down my arms and then back to my waist. I gasp and pull away as his other hand comes to one of my breasts, cupping it as he lets out a low, possessive growl. My body turns to jelly as one of his hands comes underneath my top, and when he presses his hips against my pelvis, I'm shocked to feel the rigid length pressing against my stomach.

This is normal, completely normal. I'm kissing my step-brother—

A heavy, guilty thought enters my mind as Orion groans again, placing both hands around my waist and squeezing.

I expect full monogamy while we're doing this. I will abide by the same rules.

Just as I think it, Orion pulls away and takes a step back. Shivers of delight—or perhaps adrenaline—cause me to tremble and touch my fingers to my lips. My eyes find Orion's. He's breathing heavily, and his eyes are nearly black with arousal. Blood pounds in my brain as I try to catch my breath, and if his wild expression is any indication, he's doing the same.

"I'm sorry. I didn't—we shouldn't—"

"And why is that?" he asks, almost pained.

I tilt my head in confusion. "Because you're dating someone else, and so am I."

His eyes narrow ever so slightly. "Then why did you kiss me?"

I cross my arms as my eyes begin to sting with more tears. "I don't know. Why did you kiss me at Zoe and Liam's wedding rehearsal dinner?"

A hurt expression rolls over his face, and he runs a hand through his hair. He laughs, but it's not kind. Instead, it feels like he's angry.

Like I should know the answer, somehow.

"Stay as long as you want," he says. "But I can't be in the same room as you right now." He quickly turns around and walks out of my room.

He walked away last time, too.

I stand there in stunned silence for several minutes, only coming out of my stupor when Sparrow begins to meow and weave between my legs.

What the hell is wrong with me?

I find an engagement ring and lose my shit, and then I decide to solve things by *kissing* Orion?

I grab my purse and keys, walking into the hallway and stepping into the sandals from earlier. Just as I press the button for the elevator, Orion comes around the corner and stops when he sees me.

"I need some fresh air," I tell him, jamming the button harder.

"In this weather?" he asks, crossing his arms and frowning.

I ignore his question. "I'll be back soon."

"Fine. See you later," he says, eyes on mine. His voice

is cold. Unfriendly. But there's something behind his eyes, some kind of hurt or betrayal or—

With a pang, I recognize the look on his face.

Fear.

Stark and vivid *fear* glitters in his eyes.

The elevator chimes, and the doors slide apart. "Yeah. See you later," I mutter, keeping eye contact until the doors slide shut.

CHAPTER EIGHTEEN

THE DROP

Orion

Six Months Ago

Everyone claps as I finish my best man speech. Liam pats my back, raising his champagne to my water, and we drink to his impending wedding with the delightful Zoe —who is watching me with misty eyes.

Thank you, she mouths, smiling and holding her glass up from where she's seated next to Liam. The wedding is tomorrow, and as I look around at my brothers and their spouses—except Kai, who will probably belong to God forever—something empty and unfulfilling slithers through me. It's not that I want to be married tomorrow, but I'd like to do this whole song and dance with someone one day. I'd like to have a rehearsal dinner where everyone is laughing, and we can joke and be a family.

I sit down next to Liam and force myself not to look across the table, but it doesn't matter. Regarding my stepsister, it never matters how much I try to stay away.

It never works.

I take her in and let my eyes soak everything up. She's talking to Juliet, sitting next to Chase, her husband and my brother. Stella, Miles's wife, is on the other side of her, and the three of them gab like they're all best friends. Layla throws her head back and laughs, and it takes me a second to realize the three of them are holding tequila shots. A smile plays on my lips as I watch Layla lick the salt off her hand. She brings the small glass of amber liquid to her mouth and throws it back without making a face, even as she sucks on the lime.

"Layla is a fucking superstar," Stella says, her British accent slightly slurred.

Layla smirks. "I can hold my alcohol ... unlike you, it seems."

Stella swats her shoulder before all three of them laugh together.

"Another," Juliet says, holding another shot up.

"It's a good thing you live so far away. You're a bad influence," Stella says, and the three of them throw back another shot.

"Something interesting catch your eye?" Chase asks, having grabbed a chair and moved over between Liam and me sometime in the last twenty seconds.

"Fuck off," I mutter, sipping my water.

"It's nice to see them all together, you know?"

We watch as Zoe walks over to Layla, Stella, and

Juliet. The four of them do another shot, and I can't help but envision a future where all four are sisters-in-law.

Except that'll never happen.

It doesn't matter how much I want it to happen or how often I dream of the day when Layla looks at me with anything other than contempt.

She'll never want me like that.

What keeps me up at night is knowing that she has no idea why—the real reason I interrupted her audition for the Paris School of Ballet. If she hates me forever, then so be it. At least she'll never have to know what those vile judges said about her. She can and has directed all of her rage at me, and it's preferable than to see her questioning her talent or value.

I'd take the bullet for her if it meant those words never caused her to have harmful thoughts about food again.

"Yeah. It's nice to see them all together."

"Best man and maid of honor." Chase leans back in his chair.

"What are you insinuating, Chase?"

He shakes his head and looks away. He's the most playful out of all of us, but he and I are a lot alike. He obsessed over Juliet for a long time before they got together since she was his best friend's sister.

"Nothing. Just that … Liam seems to think you have a thing for your stepsister."

"What the fuck, man?" Liam leans in closer to the two of us. He glares at Chase. "So much for keeping secrets," he growls.

"It doesn't matter," I tell them, standing up. "It's never going to happen. I need some fresh air."

I walk away from the rehearsal dinner table and down a random hallway of The Black Rose, passing an office and a storage closet.

"Orion."

I turn around to see Miles jogging after me.

"What's up?" I ask, shoving my hands into the pocket of my dress pants.

"I just wanted to make sure … you know …" He winces. "Chase told me."

I roll my eyes. "Wonderful."

He takes a step forward and claps my shoulder. "I remember how close you and Layla used to be. And though I don't know exactly what happened, I do know one thing."

"Is this where you give me unsolicited, older brother advice?" I ask, a hint of sarcasm in my voice. Out of all of my brothers, Miles is the most serious. *And* the grumpiest. It still astounds me that he and Stella work so well together since she's so bubbly and effervescent.

His lips twitch. "Perhaps." He looks down and begins to speak. "I think the two of us are the most alike," he says slowly. "We're softies underneath our hard shells. We put up armor so that no one can hurt us. Whatever happened between you and Layla …"

He pauses, searching for the right words. "Look, we both have darker interests. We both find solace in the shadows and the complexities of the world, things that people like Chase and Liam wear proudly on their sleeves. It's so easy to descend into that darkness, to let it consume us. But sometimes, if we're lucky, we're shown a light. My life wasn't easy before I met Estelle. I never expected *anyone* to love me like she does. But ... she does."

He looks over at me, his expression sincere. "It's rare, brother. But it's also scary as fuck."

I swallow before I answer. "That's all good and well, Miles. But she hates me. And it seems like she always will."

Miles huffs a laugh. "Trust me. She doesn't hate you. You should tell her."

I look down at the ground. "It's not that simple."

"I never said it would be simple," he replies. "But it'll be worth it. One day ... maybe a week, or a month, or a year from now, I want you to remember this conversation. When you finally pull your head out of your own personal pity party, you might find that she doesn't hate you as much as she says she does. And when that day comes, I expect a thank you."

Did I mention he's also the brother most prone to gossip and nosiness? If there's drama, there's a good chance he's the culprit. He loves to meddle.

I smile. "You're a fucking bastard."

He laughs and claps me on the back. For a moment, we stand there in silence, the weight of his words settling between us.

"Thank you," I tell him.

"Anytime, little bro. Don't forget to get your light."

He turns and walks away, and I continue walking

down the hallway. Shoving the back door open, I take a few calming breaths and suck in some cool air. It's unseasonably cold tonight—almost freezing out—and I begin to shiver almost immediately. Leaning against the back wall, I run my hands down my face. Only another hour, and then I can go somewhere to take my mind off this whole fucking wedding, and the fact that Layla and I, as the best man and maid of honor, have to walk down the aisle together tomorrow.

My fingers begin to ache with the cold, so I turn to open the door, but it's locked.

Fucking wonderful.

I feel for my phone, groaning when I realize I left it on the table when Zoe and Liam wanted a selfie with the three of us. I walk around the side of the building, but it's gated off and doesn't connect to the main street of Crestwood.

Guess I'll freeze to death.

Just as I'm considering hopping the fence, the back door squeaks open, and Layla walks out. She doesn't see me at first—she just stares straight ahead, unsure of if she's going to chance freezing to death or take a step back into the warm building.

She chooses the former, stepping into the cold.

"Wait, don't let it close—"

The door slams shut, and she whirls around to face me. "What the hell are you doing here?" She turns around to try to go back inside, but the door doesn't budge when she tries it.

"I warned you," I murmur, walking up to her.

"Whatever, Orion," she says, her words slightly slurred. "It's really freaking cold out here."

"Do you have your phone?" I ask, shrugging my coat off.

"No," she says glumly, turning to face me just as I hand her my jacket. "No thanks. I'm fine." She lifts her chin and crosses her arms.

"Wear the fucking jacket, Layla. You're wearing less clothes than I am."

She grinds her jaw as she drinks me in with an unfocused gaze. I let my eyes roam over her gold silk dress, which brings out the gold flecks in her hazel eyes. Snatching the jacket from my hands, she throws it on and pulls it around her slim body.

Fuck. She looks really good in my jacket.

"Have you checked to see if there's another way back inside?" she asks.

My lips tug into a lopsided smile. "I have. We're stuck here unless you feel like scaling a wall in those shoes," I add, glancing down at the black pumps. When I lock eyes with her again, she's watching me with furrowed brows.

"Why *are* you out here in the freezing cold?" she asks, teeth chattering.

I shrug. "I just needed some air."

"Right."

We're quiet for several seconds, the sound of her chattering teeth the only thing I can hear besides my breathing.

"Remember that time Dad caught you smoking when you were twenty?" she asks suddenly.

I huff a laugh. "I do. My mom didn't talk to me for days after that."

Her lips twitch. "I've never told anyone this, but after that, I asked one of my friends for a cigarette, just to try it."

I'm grinning, hanging on her every word. "Really?"

She laughs. "I wanted to be like you so badly. When I was fourteen, you were my favorite person." I swallow thickly, trying to push down the anguish that fills me when I remember how close we used to be. Her eyes darken with pain as she takes a shuddering breath. "I miss it sometimes." She looks up at me through her lashes. "I miss you."

Her words are thick. She's drunk—perhaps more than she's letting on. Somehow, she's always been able to handle her alcohol. Not that she drinks a lot. I can count the number of times I've seen her drunk on one hand. But it's quite impressive how much she can drink.

"I miss you too," I tell her, stepping closer. I swallow the nerves working through me, the way my hands begin to shake—though perhaps it's the cold.

Trust me. She doesn't hate you. You should tell her.

I want to tell her everything from the time we were apart. I want to confess my sins, drop to my knees, *beg* her to look at me with something other than hatred. I'd do fucking anything to be in her life again—even if just as her stepbrother.

My heart broke that day, and life hasn't been the same since.

I miss her, sure.

But I also *need* her.

And that scares me so fucking much.

She's watching me with careful concern—a crease between her brows as she studies my face. I've never really been able to hide my emotions, so maybe she can see exactly what I'm thinking. Maybe she can feel the torture it causes me to stand so close to her.

"How drunk are you?" I ask, my voice low.

"Very," she answers, eyes piercing into mine.

"I should get you inside," I tell her, stepping closer so that I back her up against the back wall of the restaurant.

"You should," she agrees.

I place a hand on the wall above her head, and she sucks in a sharp breath. My heart is pounding inside my chest, and my nerves are frazzled and electric with every second that passes between us.

I'm entranced by the silent sadness of her face, and being near her makes me want to hold her and never let go.

I'm sorry, I think.

Reaching up, I place my other hand against the side of her face. "Layla," I say, eyes tracking down to her lips.

"Orion," she breathes, chest rising and falling. She smells like a mixture of strawberries, tequila, and smoke —our scents combining and reforming into something that compels me to dip my head lower.

"Tell me not to kiss you," I say, breathing her in.

"Don't kiss me," she whispers, her pupils dark as she scans my face.

I don't listen.

Instead, I gently press my lips against hers. Layla immediately opens her mouth and wraps her arms around my neck, pulling me closer.

I am so fucked.

My tongue traces the soft fullness of her lips, though I want to lick and devour every inch of her.

One time, in college, I did ecstasy. It felt like my whole body was on fucking fire—like just touching someone would make me come.

This is a hundred times better.

She moves against me with a hunger that contradicts everything I thought I knew about her, about how she felt about me. It's hungry, crazed ... demanding.

I move my hands behind her head, fisting her long, wavy hair with one hand as the other skims down her back. Gripping her waist, I pull her into me, and she gasps into my mouth when she feels how fucking hard I am.

This is how much I want you, I want to whisper against her neck.

But I don't say anything—too dazed by the fact that I'm finally kissing her to do anything other than to savor it completely.

Savor *her* completely.

This might be my only chance.

She quivers in my arms as I kiss her jaw, her neck, her collarbone... I want her. I've always wanted her. There has never been anyone else *but* her, and it's very fucking evident by the way my heart is beating a thousand beats per second, as my hands shake as I touch her, as my hips rut against her. I plant kisses on her bare shoulders, letting my jacket fall to the ground. She moans and runs a hand through my hair as I come back up to her face, recapturing her lips with mine.

"Oh God, Orion," she whimpers, her hands exploring the muscles on my chest.

"Tell me what you want," I say, my voice breaking as I press myself against her and grip her dress with both hands.

She inhales sharply, pulling my mouth back to hers.

Suddenly the back door slams open, and Layla pulls away, panting.

"There you—" I pull away from Layla to face Liam, and my brother's grin is wide and conspiratorial. "Sorry, I didn't mean to interrupt anything," he says, propping the door open and walking back into the building without saying anything else.

Layla and I both stare at the open door, and as her hand comes to her lips, something light and hopeful sparks inside of my chest.

Maybe ... just maybe ...

I step closer. "Layla, there's something I should tell—"

"I told you not to kiss me," she whispers.

At first, I think I mishear her. "What?"

Her eyes shine with tears, and suddenly, I'm reminded of the audition. She has the same accusatory look in her eyes, and I know she's going to reject me again.

I take a step back as hurt lances through me. "Go back inside."

She doesn't move. "You can't just keep doing whatever you want." Her voice thick with unshed tears.

She felt it, too. Whatever the fuck is between us, she felt it. I *know* she did.

Bending down, I grab my jacket and straighten, looking down at her.

"Trust me, *sis*. You've made your point very clear," I practically snarl. "It was a mistake."

Her mouth drops open, and I recognize the hurt splayed over her face. *Good.* If I hurt her, she can't hurt me.

Her hands shove my chest, and her eyes well up. "I don't want to see you ever again."

There's no conviction in her words, but they still fucking hurt, nonetheless.

"You know," I say, my voice sharp with cruelty as I step back from her, "I should know better than to think you would ever admit how you really feel about me. No, that would require letting someone in."

She flinches as a tear rolls down her left cheek, and my heart squeezes at the pain marring her expression.

That's what I do, right? I hurt people.

The sting of my own words hangs in the air. Layla takes a shaky breath, but I can't bear to hear her push me away again.

I'm not sure I'd survive.

So I walk away from her.

I can't focus.

My emotions are running ragged, and as I bring the riding crop down on my submissive, I feel nothing. Usually, hearing them whimper and squirm is enough to get me hard, but nothing is working. I feel numb, like there's a cage around my emotions, and I'm just going through the motions.

"Yellow," she says, turning around to face me.

Her name is Nadine, and her long, red hair is damp with sweat. We've always had a good time together, but I can't separate myself from the other person with long red hair who occupies my thoughts.

"Talk to me," I say, crouching down. *Going through the motions.*

"I need a break," she says, sitting up and grabbing some water. I watch her as she takes a sip from the glass on my bedside table. I called Nadine because she's the sub with the least number of limits—someone who lets me indulge in my sadistic tendencies without having to stop. She knows her limits—as do I.

But she's not who I want right now. And that makes me want to punish her for it.

"Ready?" I ask her.

"Yes. Harder this time, Master," she tells me, bending over and exposing her bare ass. "Use the paddle, please."

I throw the riding crop off to the side as I reach for the paddle. "Good girl."

I bring it down with a heavy thwack, and she cries

out. There's no recovery time—as soon as I lift my hand, I bring it back down against the globe of her ass.

"Color?" I ask, practically growling as sweat clings to my hairline.

"Green, Master," she sobs.

"That's it. You're so good at taking pain, love."

I bring the paddle down again—and again, and again, and again.

Her ass cheek blooms bright red, and when I'm one whack away from breaking skin, I switch to the other cheek. I check in with her color-wise, too entranced to *look* at her. To get a visual of her face, to gaze into her eyes to make sure she's not in a frenzy like I know she's prone to be.

"Please, Master," she sobs. "More. Harder."

My brows furrow, and I keep going—down her legs, one at a time. My cock doesn't respond at all, but it still feels good—so much so that I lose myself and go into autopilot.

I think of Layla's words.

I told you not to kiss me.

My lips curl away from my teeth as sweat beads down the sides of my face.

You can't just keep doing whatever you want.

Like fuck I can.

I grip the paddle, my fingers curling around the slippery leather as I bring it down hard and fast against Nadine.

I don't want to see you ever again.

The smack of the paddle breaks me out of my stupor.

"Color?" I ask, my voice monotone.

"Green."

She sounds weak and feeble, so I set the paddle down and walk around to face her.

Her pupils are nearly black, and her cheeks are black from her mascara. Layla's face comes into view for a second, and I crouch down to take her face in my hands.

"Look at me."

She doesn't. Instead, when I move closer, her whole body goes limp as she falls onto her stomach.

"Nadine?" Turning her over, I brush a hand along her hairline. It's wet, and she looks pale. "Color?" I ask, guilt threading through me.

"Green," she whispers, lips dry.

Fuck.

"We're going to take a break," I tell her, rolling her back onto her stomach and walking over to my side table for the soothing balm I use during aftercare.

She doesn't move as I rub it into her sore spots, and the guilt gets heavier as bruises begin to bloom along the entire backside of her legs.

This is my fault.

She's been giving me her colors, but I haven't been doing my duty as a Dominant and visually confirming that she's okay. Nadine tends to go hard, always to her detriment, and I should've been more careful with her.

Instead, I got lost in my own intrusive thoughts, not checking that she'd gone into a submissive frenzy. She knows her limits—but only when she's of sound mind.

She would've kept saying green until she passed out or worse.

I gently rub the cream into her skin, out of view, so she doesn't see me and beg me to keep going.

She can't.

I can't.

My chest aches as she eventually falls asleep, and I do everything I can to make her comfortable. Setting out some ibuprofen and water for when she wakes up, I let out a heavy sigh and run a hand over my face.

I try so fucking hard to keep my fragile control, but I lost it tonight. And now Nadine will face the consequences.

Walking out of my bedroom, I hear Earl squawking from the kitchen. When I enter, he's sitting on the island with a rubber band stuck around his feet.

"Earl stuck," he says, his voice frantic.

"Shit, sorry, buddy," I say, walking over as he lifts his leg out. An old rubber band is wrapped around his twiggy leg and handle of a drawer, and more guilt washes through me. It's an easy fix for me, but it makes me wonder how long he's been calling out for me. Once I'm done, I carry him over to his aviary, shutting him inside and ensuring he has enough food and water.

"Pretty girl?" Earl asks, his voice warbling and unsure.

"No. Not tonight."

"Earl sad," he croaks.

I swallow as I walk away. It's well past midnight, but I need to do something to clear my head. Stripping down to my boxer briefs as I walk to the pool, the icy cold bites down to my bones.

"Fuck," I hiss, jumping in and swimming.

I swim until I'm gasping, until my arms feel like jelly, until my whole body trembles. While I sit in the water, my breathing turns shallow, and I can't stop shivering.

Top drop.

The realization hits me as I get out of the water. Of course because I didn't plan on swimming for two hours, I don't have a towel. My teeth chatter as I grab the clothes I tore off earlier, feeling lightheaded, cold, and really fucking shitty. Just as I'm about to walk inside, it begins to snow.

In fucking Crestwood, California.

I stop walking and turn around as the snow begins to fall in earnest, soft drifts clinging to my patio furniture and the concrete. I'm too shocked to move.

I was a young kid the last time it snowed in this part of California.

It's so easy to descend into that darkness, to let it consume us. But sometimes if we're lucky, we're shown a light.

One day ... maybe a week, or a month, or a year from now, I want you to remember this conversation. When you finally pull your head out of your own personal pity party, you might find that she doesn't hate you as much as she says she does.

One day.

Despite feeling emotionally depleted and on the brink of hypothermia, I smile. It's cathartic. Everything about tonight feels cathartic.

I could choose to let the guilt eat me alive, or I could keep trying.

I know in an instant that I'll never stop trying.

I'll never stop loving her. My obsession might be unhealthy, but I can't imagine my life without Layla.

She pushed me away tonight, but one day, she'll kiss me first.

One day.

CHAPTER NINETEEN

THE PREDICAMENT

LAYLA

Present

My heart continues to race in my chest when the elevator doors open to the parking garage of Orion's building. I'm just about to walk to the sidewalk outside, heading for a nearby café or anywhere that's not his apartment when I see a man exit a white Audi in the parking spot closest to me.

Malakai Ravage. *Technically* one of my five step-brothers.

He closes his door and locks his car, walking over to where I'm standing.

"Hey, Layla," he says, bending down and pulling me into a friendly hug. "You okay?" he asks when he pulls away.

I open and close my mouth. "Uhh ..."

His gray eyes bore into mine, flicking between them as he slowly realizes that I'm most definitely *not* okay.

"I was just about to get a coffee down the street," he says gently. "Care to join me?"

I nod. "Sure."

We walk in tandem, and the blistering heat makes me feel even more nauseous than I was feeling before.

Before—when I found an engagement ring in Orion's closet, and then kissed him.

Fortunately, there's a coffee shop in the next building over, and the small space is cool and blasting the AC.

"What's your order?" he asks, pulling his wallet out.

I shrug. "Something decaf. I've had way too much coffee already today."

Malakai smirks as he walks over to the counter to place our order. I zone out until he walks back with two smoothies and what looks like two blueberry muffins.

"Got this, too," he says, sliding one of the muffins over to me.

"Thanks." I take a sip of the smoothie, and just as I ask what flavor it is, a child's voice cuts through the ambient noise of the café.

"Miss Rivers?"

I turn my head to see Bradleigh grinning at me from a nearby table. Before I can react, she jumps up from her seat and runs over to me, wrapping her arms around me.

"Hey, you," I say, my voice cracking with emotion as she pulls away. I'm reminded of the fact that she hasn't attended ballet intensive all week, but before I can ask her about it, her eyes catch on Malakai, and she smiles even wider.

"Wow! You know Headmaster Ravage?" she asks, rushing over to Malakai.

I laugh. "He's actually my stepbrother. My dad married his mom."

Bradleigh beams up at Malakai. "Wow. That's cool."

I wave at Bradleigh's mom, who's watching us with a gentle smile. It takes me a second to realize that Bradleigh must go to St. Helena Academy, where Malakai is the headmaster.

"How are you doing? Are you practicing your pirouettes?" I ask, opting not to bring up her absence in case she doesn't want to talk about it.

Her face falls. "Not really."

I swallow and look over at her mom. She shrugs, nodding toward the corner of the coffee shop.

"I'm sorry to hear that. Hey, I'm going to talk to your mom really quick, okay?"

Malakai jumps in and offers Bradleigh his muffin. "Go nuts, kid. Let's get you all sugared up for your mom."

I walk over to Bradleigh's mom, and we go to the other side of the room. "Everything okay?"

Her mom is young and pretty. From what I know, she's a single mom who works hard to make sure Bradleigh has everything she needs.

"Bradleigh is being bullied in school, and she hasn't really been up for ballet intensive," she begins. "And I'm sorry, I meant to email you, but work is really busy. I haven't had a moment to breathe, and—"

I reach a hand out, taking her hand in mine. "How can I help?" Her lower lip wobbles, and that's when I see the dark bags under her eyes. The sweatpants. The messy hair. She's barely hanging on, and I'm sure Bradleigh's predicament isn't helping. "What if I took Bradleigh out for a bit this weekend? We could go to the dance store, or maybe we could go get our nails done. Or we could go shopping?" I offer.

Relief washes over her. "That would be amazing, but you really don't have to—"

"Does this weekend work? I have a performance on Friday and Saturday night, but maybe I can take her out on Saturday morning?"

Bradleigh's mom's eyes glisten with tears. "Oh my God, that would be great. I just need some extra sleep, to be honest. It's hard doing this alone sometimes."

I give her a gentle smile, reaching into my pocket for my phone. "I can't even imagine. What's your number? I'll call you on Friday, and we can coordinate."

We exchange numbers, and then walk back to the table, where Malakai and Bradleigh are playing rock, paper, scissors.

"Come on, sweetie. Time to go. If you get all of your homework done, I told Ms. Rivers that the two of you could go to the mall this weekend."

Bradleigh's brown eyes light up. "Really?"

"Only if you finish your homework," I tell her.

She hugs me, and then they say goodbye. Bradleigh's mom mouths *thank you* over her shoulder before they walk out of the coffee shop. I sigh as I sit down across from Malakai, who clears his throat.

"She got bullied pretty badly last week," Malakai tells me. "Some of the girls in her class were calling her names."

I wince. "Of course."

"They were immediately suspended, and if there are any more incidents, they'll be expelled."

I snap my eyes to Malakai. "Good. I mean, I know they're kids, but—"

"St. Helena has a zero-tolerance policy for that kind of shit. You remember what Chase did for Jackson Parker, right?"

I squint at him as I take another sip. "Kind of. Didn't he join the board so Jackson wouldn't be discriminated against?"

Malakai nods. "Anyway, it's important to me that children learn that love is love, you know? Bradleigh adores you," he adds.

"She's my favorite," I whisper.

Malakai laughs. "She's lucky to have you."

We eat our muffins in silence for several minutes— after Malakai gets another one, that is.

"So," Malakai says, rubbing his hands together and sitting back.

"So," I mimic, giving him an angelic smile.

Before Orion and I stopped talking, I wasn't very close to my other stepbrothers. In fact, I hardly knew them since they didn't need to live at home. But of course they came to visit Felicity often, and despite being the closest to Orion, I still considered them family. And then when Orion and I stopped talking, I got really close to Zoe and sort of latched onto her, and by proxy, Liam Ravage. They all treated me like their little sister—coming to my ballets, taking care of my dad after Felicity died, and checking in with me.

So while Malakai and I aren't the best of friends, I'm comfortable around him.

They all sort of feel like uncles more than step-brothers.

"Are you going to tell me what's wrong, or am I going to have to guess?"

"I'd love to hear your guesses," I reply, smiling as I take another sip of my smoothie. "But if you must know."

I brace myself.

If Liam told Zoe about the kiss he saw between Orion and me at their rehearsal dinner, there's a good chance he told his other brothers.

"I kissed Orion."

Malakai arches a brow as he takes a long, deep sip of his smoothie. "Oh?" he asks several seconds later.

I narrow my eyes. "Did Liam tell you?"

Malakai chuckles. "No, but what does Liam know that I don't?"

My cheeks burn. "Orion kissed me at their rehearsal dinner. And today, I kissed him."

Malakai nods. "Oh, yeah, I did know about that," he teases. I kick him under the table, and he laughs. "Sorry, couldn't help it. And how are you feeling about the kiss?"

I push my glasses higher on my nose. "I liked it?"

Malakai snorts. "Well, I gathered that. Considering the way you act around each other, that doesn't surprise me."

"What do you mean?"

Malakai leans forward, and I glance down at his clasped hands. He has a cross tattoo on his right, middle finger, and it always struck me as odd for a pastor to have a tattoo.

"Forgive me for saying this, Layla, but you and Orion have been obvious about your feelings for years. It's sort of a running joke between me and the other brothers. And Stella. And Zoe. And recently, Juliet."

My mouth drops open. "Obvious how?"

He grins. "Well, for one, you both look for the other whenever you enter a room. You mimic each other's body language. You fight like cats and dogs, but it's not malicious—it's like there's tension clouding your judgment. You know?"

I scoff. "I do now, thanks."

"Before, I asked you how you felt about it, not if you liked it. What does this mean for the two of you?"

That same anguish from earlier fills me. "It can't mean anything. Right before I kissed him, I found an engagement ring meant for the woman he's seeing."

Malakai has zero reaction, even when I study his expression for several seconds afterward.

"Are you sure it was meant for who he's seeing? It could be something passed down from our mom, or maybe he's holding it for a friend. I know Liam hid his ring for Zoe at my house so she wouldn't find it."

I hadn't considered that.

My mouth opens and closes, but it still doesn't make sense.

"Even if it's not meant for the woman he's seeing, he's still seeing someone. And so am I. I shouldn't have kissed him."

Malakai leans forward. "Seems like you need to make a choice. The guy you're seeing ... or Orion. I know who he'd choose."

I look down at the table, playing with the paper from the muffin. "He seems to really like her. I think you're giving me too much credit."

"Trust me, Layla. You'll always be Orion's first choice."

I should know better than to think you would ever admit how you really feel about me.

Those words had haunted me for months, as did his hurt expression. He knew I had feelings for him that night, even before I could admit it to myself.

And earlier ... the look on his face...

Malakai's words send butterflies skittering through me, and I can't help but feel my lips lift into a smile.

"Okay, so I have to choose. That will be *so* easy."

"Who's the other guy?" Malakai asks.

"He's someone I met online. We haven't actually met in person. But we—the connection is intense."

Malakai shrugs. "Then meet him in person and see which connection is stronger. Listen to your heart."

I smirk as I look back up at him. "Thanks. Yeah, I guess I shouldn't decide until I meet the other guy." Several seconds pass before I ask my next question. "What about you?"

Malakai instantly goes still. "What about me?"

"What's new with you? Are you seeing anyone?"

"Romantically?" he asks, narrowing his eyes.

"Yes?" I answer, laughing.

He shakes his head, but something secretive passes over his expression. "No. I've been too busy. Today's my first morning off in weeks."

"Doing what? At St. Helena?"

"No. I had a friend move back from London and buy a fixer-upper just outside of town. It needs a lot of work, so I'm helping him with some of the small stuff."

"Pastor, handyman, therapist. Is there anything you can't do?"

He shakes his head and looks down at the table. "There's a lot I can't do. But enough about me. What's the plan?"

I shrug. "I guess to meet with the online guy and make my choice after that."

He nods before standing. "I suppose my opinion doesn't matter?"

"No, it does."

We walk out into the blinding heat together, and when we get to the entrance to Orion's building, he turns to face me.

"You asked for it," he teases, crossing his arms. "My opinion? You have to look at compatibility, too. Shared interests, morals, where you see yourself in five or ten years. Because sometimes you can have all the chemistry but no future. And speaking from experience, nothing is more heartbreaking than forming a connection with someone physically while knowing it can never go further."

I digest his words as I begin to sweat, eager to get back into the air-conditioned building.

"Speaking from experience?" I ask him, smiling ruefully before looking down at my shoes.

"Trust me, Layla. It's the worst kind of torture to want someone you can't be with long term."

I swallow. "I can see that." Looking up at him, I take in his furrowed brows and crossed arms. A small part of me wonders who he's talking about—and what happened—but before I can ask, he pulls me into a quick brotherly hug.

"I'll see you soon, okay?"

I look at the door of the building. "Did you want to come up? I'm sure Orion would love to see you."

He grimaces. "Nah. I should get back to Julian and Sophie."

"Sophie?"

Something dark flashes behind Malakai's eyes. "Julian's wife."

"Oh, I didn't realize Julian was married," I say slowly, watching his reaction.

"Yep. It was sort of arranged from a young age, I guess. They both come from old money in England. Anyway, I should go. Good luck with everything, Layla."

"Yeah, you too."

I open the door to the building, and once inside, Malakai walks around to the parking garage to his car.

When I turn around, I come face-to-face with the security guard. *Shoot.* We'd entered through the garage earlier, bypassing security.

"Oh, hi. I'm here with Orion Ravage—"

"The infamous Layla Rivers," he says, smiling jovially.

My brows shoot up. "You know who I am?"

"You're famous around here."

"I am?"

"Yep. You're on the list of Mr. Ravage's pre-approved visitors."

"Oh—"

"The funny thing is, you're the *only* one on the list."

My mouth opens and closes as he walks over to the elevator, pressing some kind of badge against the keypad, which I assume gives him—and me—access to the penthouse.

"Have a nice day, Ms. Rivers."

CHAPTER TWENTY

THE ANTICIPATION

ORION

I look up from the sink in my primary bathroom, taking in my messed-up hair, wild eyes, and clenched jaw. It looks like I've been pacing the apartment for the past hour, which is exactly what I've been doing.

I need some fresh air.

I'll be back soon.

See you later.

I've been analyzing and overanalyzing Layla's words from earlier the entire time she's been gone. Kai had texted me that he was with her next door, and I know he'll help her come down from the shock of what just happened, but I still have no idea what she'll decide.

I rub the scruff on my jaw as I sigh heavily, hanging my head as I think about the look on Layla's face as the elevator doors closed.

Hurt, desperation, panic, arousal.

When we kissed at Liam and Zoe's rehearsal dinner, she was angry afterward. She pushed me away and shut me out. So why am I holding on to some tiny thread of hope that she might not do the same thing this time around?

She kissed me.

This isn't like last time. She saw the ring, panicked, and kissed me.

She has feelings for me, but in an ironic twist of fate, she also has feelings for Starboy.

Just as I walk out of my bathroom, the burner phone chimes from inside my bedside table.

A smile creeps across my face as I pull it out and open the text from Layla. She must be back—I didn't have the courage to wait for her in the front of the apartment.

> LITTLE DANCER
> I need to see you.

Dread and excitement spread through me, sending jolts of confusion to my brain.

> LITTLE DANCER
> And I'd like to see your face, if possible.

> We can meet in person, but I'll keep my mask on.

> LITTLE DANCER
> Fine.

> Are you going to explain this sudden urge to see me?

LITTLE DANCER

It's nothing.

> Don't lie to me, Layla.

LITTLE DANCER

I've just had a weird day, and I'd like to
see if our chemistry is physical.

> Physical, how?

LITTLE DANCER

Are you really going to make me spell
it out?

> Yes.

LITTLE DANCER

I want to try doing a scene with you.

> You're going to need to be more explicit.

LITTLEDANCER

I just need to see you, okay? So we can
do … whatever you want to do.

Fuck.

Her blanket statement is tempting. The open-endedness … the possibilities.

Except she needs me.

She needs someone to guide her, to *show* her.

To *dominate* her.

> I can send you my in-person submissive
> contract. I need you to fill it out
> thoroughly. If you have any questions,
> text me.

LITTLEDANCER

Okay.

> I need you to be sure about this.

LITTLEDANCER

I am.

> I'll think of a public place we can meet tonight.

LITTLEDANCER

What about Inferno?

I shake my head and sigh.

> What about it?

I want her to spell it out. I *need* her to understand what she's getting herself into.

LITTLEDANCER

Could we meet there?

> I'll reserve a private room. When you arrive, tell them you're there to see me. 9:00p.m. Bring the contract, and do not be late.

LITTLEDANCER

Yes, Master.

What should I wear?

I consider her words. It hasn't ever mattered to me what my submissives wear. Inflicting pain happens whether or not my submissive is wearing clothes.

Lately, my scenes haven't been sexual in nature—
though I can't make the same promise with Layla. The
thought of laying her across my lap with a paddle ... or
watching the blooming redness spread across her fair
skin.

> It doesn't matter to me. Something
> comfortable.

LITTLEDANCER

Okay. See you soon. :)

I quickly send off my regular (anonymized) submissive contract. It's forty-eight pages of clauses, rules,
experience, and checkboxes for any potential limits, as
well as *my* limits.

I'd adopted the contract Chase used for his submissives and made it my own by adding several additional
pages about what it means to be with a sadistic Dominant, as well as any degrading words or phrases I should
avoid.

> I've sent the contract. Please look it over
> and be thorough with your answers. Like
> I said, I'm around if you have any
> questions.

LITTLEDANCER

Thank you, Master.

I pocket the burner phone and run my hands over my
face.

Tonight, I'll get to do my first scene with Layla.

Except it won't be *me*, will it?

A dull ache pierces through me when I think of if she'd still want to do this with me if I wasn't Starboy.

The doom spiral continues when I think of how I need to approach tonight. If we connect, she'll push me —*Orion*—away.

And then I realize, how the fuck am I going to keep her from finding out it's me? We'll have to resort to sign language, and I'll have to hope she doesn't realize it's my body underneath the black hoodie.

Fuck.

I'll have to tell her tonight. I'll have to come clean.

I pull on a T-shirt and boots before turning the corner and walking down the hallway. I ignore Layla's closed bedroom door with classical music playing on the other side. I stop for a second, suddenly nostalgic for when we lived together under one roof. She'd hole herself in her room with her books and her Beethoven, and knowing she's probably doing the same thing now, almost a decade later...

I can't fuck this up.

I know she's teaching ballet intensive later today, so I walk through my apartment to the kitchen, jotting down a note for her.

BE BACK LATER. HELP YOURSELF TO ANYTHING.

Grabbing my keys, I take the elevator back to the parking garage and unlock the Bentley. I wish I could take my bike, but it's too hot out.

I head out of downtown Crestwood, hopping onto the 405.

I have to clear my head before tonight, or I'll risk ruining everything. Luckily, I know exactly how to distract my busy mind.

I have to play this perfectly, or I could lose her forever —as both Orion and Starboy.

CHAPTER TWENTY-ONE

THE REALIZATION

Layla

When I return from my intensive, Orion is still gone. He left a note, but I figured he'd be back by now.

Unless he's with her.

The thought of spending the night alone in his apartment when he was with *her* ... I'd rather go back to my stifling house than stay here alone.

In order to distract myself, I contemplate my outfit choices that I have with me at Orion's apartment. I wasn't expecting to meet with Starboy, and I only have hot weather lounge clothes with me, as well as things to teach intensive. In a moment of panic, I invite Zoe over— and ask her to bring things for me to wear. She and Liam have a date tonight, so she quickly drops off a suitcase full of clothes, kisses me on the cheek, and wishes me luck.

"Remember, just because he's famous doesn't mean he doesn't have red flags."

"I know," I tell her, smiling. "Trust me, I'm taking every precaution I can."

Zoe twists her lips to the side. "Public space. Safe word. Condoms—"

"What? You think we're going to—"

Her eyes sparkle as she shrugs. "Always better to be prepared, you know? Don't worry, I packed some for you in the suitcase. Remember, don't let him push you into anything you're not comfortable with. He'll appreciate— and expect—you to use your safe word for *anything* you're not comfortable with. Just because someone is experienced doesn't mean they know what they're doing or will implement their safety measures during a scene. Trust your gut. Use common sense. I know where you are, so I'll have Orion's guys ensure everything is legitimate."

"But don't let Orion know," I tell her. "The last thing I need is for him to find out."

"My lips are sealed, babe." She blows me a kiss. "Most importantly, have fun. I wish I could stay and hang out."

"No, it's okay. Have fun on your date, and thanks for the clothes. I owe you."

Her smile falls a bit as she steps into the elevator. "Are you sure you want to do this? I mean, considering everything with Orion."

I take a deep breath. "I need to make a decision, and I

need to know if this thing with Starboy is going to lead anywhere serious or not."

I hadn't told Zoe about the kiss yet. Truthfully, I'm still processing it.

"I get it." She presses the button for the ground floor. "Good luck. Tell me everything."

"I will," I say quickly as the doors shut, leaving me alone in Orion's apartment.

Dragging the suitcase into the guest bedroom, I texted my dad to make sure he's okay, which he is. He sends a selfie of himself next to the television, holding up a carton of milk. I tell him to keep me updated. The doctors ruled out a heart attack and a stroke, but the blood sugar issues would have to be dealt with. I chew on the inside of my cheek as we chat for a few more minutes. He's supposed to be discharged tomorrow morning, so I tell him that Orion and I will be there to pick him up when he's ready.

With my dad sorted, I focus on the task at hand.

What the hell do I wear to meet a Dominant for the first time?

He said he didn't care and to be comfortable.

I rummage through Zoe's clothes for something that could work on me. She's shorter and curvier than me, and it's still a thousand degrees out, but when I pull on an innocent-looking, white eyelet dress with a sweetheart neckline and buttons going down the front, I immediately know it's the outfit. Paired with my white sneakers, it's my style completely—even if it's more revealing and the neckline slightly more plunging than normal.

I have a few hours until I'm supposed to meet Starboy, so I cuddle up on the couch with Sparrow for a few minutes before tackling the contract he sent. Earl flies into the living room at one point, squawking, "Master loves pretty girl! Master loves pretty girl … such a good little fuckhole," before flying off.

I chuckle. Sparrow doesn't even bat an eye at the flying bird—he's the laziest cat in existence.

I make myself dinner.

Orion doesn't return.

Walking back to the guest bedroom, I send the file to Orion's printer. Quickly going upstairs, I grab the document and a pen, flipping through the dense document.

It's *forty-eight* pages.

Orion's office is dark and moody, with dark wood paneling and an old oak desk in the middle of the room. I peruse the books he has scattered around the shelves—things about BDSM, consent, and some books that look like college textbooks on things like sexuality and philosophy.

It strikes me how similar Starboy and Orion are. How they both seem to approach the lifestyle from a place of open communication and education.

Maybe they know each other?

Closing his office door, I walk back to the guest bedroom and sit at the small desk, flipping through Starboy's contract.

I check the relevant things: submissive, beginner,

straight, monogamous. Just the idea of sharing him makes me feel nauseous. His limits are underneath that, and as my eyes scan the list, my hand comes to my throat.

Hard limits: Chastity, scat play, age play, pet play, swinging, swapping, sharing.

Soft limits: Penetration.

My eyes go wide at that last part, and I keep reading.

For me, this dynamic is about power more than sex. Occasionally sexual intercourse may occur, in which case I will ensure all parties are safe and tested regularly. But it shouldn't be expected. There are a lot of things between a Dominant and submissive that can trend sexual, but it's up to my discretion. A verbal and nonverbal safe word is required before any play occurs.

The next section is a list of his preferences.

Spanking

Paddling

Caning

Flogging

Wax play

Nipple clamps

Electric wands

Mental bondage

Orgasm control

Hypnosis

Forced orgasms

Orgasm denial/edging

Humiliation

Degradation

It then goes into the types of things he's had his submissives do before pertaining to those last two notes.

Eating on the floor

Kneeling on rice

Scolding

Writing lines

By the time I finish reviewing his limits and checking off my hard limits—which entail almost all of Starboy's limits, plus anything involving bodily fluids—I'm antsy and anxious about tonight.

By the time I get to the soft limits, I'm a little bit less sure of things.

I mark "no" next to anything having to do with food —including eating off the floor.

I also mark "no" to any degrading terms about my body. I'm not sure I'll ever recover enough to hear anything like that.

I've only recently learned about some things—like infant play and pegging, both of which I mark as soft limits.

I mark no for 24/7 … though the idea is intriguing. To be his submissive 24/7? It could be fun, but I don't think it's for me.

Only in the bedroom, then.

By the time I get to the end of my limits, there's more information about our dynamic and a nondisclosure agreement.

You will address me by our predetermined honorific.

You will thank me for pleasure *and* discipline.

You will not come without my permission, even when we are apart.

Know your limits. Memorize them.

Communication is key. This will be tested before we begin.

Never assume you know what I want.

I will respect you wholly and completely, and I expect the same respect from you.

You will be on time for any play—*always*.

You will kneel for me before every scene.

There are three more pages of rules—and my head begins to spin. He's nothing if not thorough.

I sign and date it after that, folding the papers once so that they fit into my purse.

After taking a quick shower, I pull the dress on and move the top half of my long hair away from my face. I forgo most makeup, instead putting my contacts in and adding cream blush to my cheeks, a quick swipe of mascara, and cherry-red lip gloss.

It's only eight o'clock, so I decide to leave for Inferno early. Taking advantage of their one-drink rule seems like a good way to calm my nerves. When I exit my bedroom and walk through the apartment, I realize Orion still isn't back.

It doesn't matter. You're not trying to impress him tonight.

I quickly pull my phone out and send him a text.

Going out tonight. I'll be back later. Don't wait up.

I glance down at the screen as I take the elevator down to the ground floor, but he hasn't even read it by the time I get to street level.

I'd debated opening the belated birthday present he'd gotten me, but something told me to wait. I'd brought it with me to his apartment, so I had it with me just in case.

Turning my phone on silent, I walk the three blocks to Inferno. It's still hot, but since it's dark out now, it's cooled down significantly. The warm air tickles my skin, but it doesn't feel oppressive like it did before. When I arrive at the front door, I take a deep breath and walk inside.

Like last time, a woman sits behind a desk, wearing a business casual outfit and typing on a computer. I pause by the door, my heart pounding in my chest, but she looks up at me and smiles.

"Hello, Ms. Rivers."

I open and close my mouth. "I'm here to see ..." I'm unsure of what to call him. *Starboy? The masked man?* I don't know his name, so I rack my brain.

"I know. He's already here and waiting for you in the hypnosis room. Please feel free to grab a drink beforehand." She stands and opens the wardrobe doors. "Have fun," she adds, smiling.

Hypnosis room?

"Thank you."

I step between the coats, walking through a doorway and into the bar area of Inferno.

He's here. He's already waiting for me.

My skin pebbles as I walk up to the bar. A bartender is making drinks, and I give him a small smile.

"Can I get some tequila, please?"

"Of course you can," he says, eyes friendly and sparkling as he pours someone else a fancy-looking drink. "How's your night been so far?"

I blow out an anxious breath of air. "Oh, that's a loaded question."

He laughs. "I'm Mark."

"I'm Layla," I tell him, shaking his warm hand.

His eyes go wide. "Chase Ravage's stepsister, Layla?"

"You know Chase?" I ask, leaning forward.

He huffs a laugh. "Unfortunately for me. The guy's a pain in my ass, but he is my brother-in-law. I'm Juliet's brother's husband."

Realization dawns. *Of course.* "Right, I remember you now. I think we met at one of the various weddings. Maybe Miles's?"

He pours my drink and hands me a wristband so that they know I've gotten my one allotted drink. "I think it was Liam and Zoe's rehearsal dinner. But honestly, I don't remember most of that night. The alcohol was floooowing," he says, smirking.

My cheeks heat when I think of that night. The kiss with Orion.

Guilt swirls inside me when I think of what I'm about to do. When I think of betraying Orion in a weird way, maybe I should call this whole thing off until my feelings for him settle down.

If I don't meet Starboy, I'll never know …

"Yeah, it was a wild night for sure."

"What brings you to Inferno?"

I add the fancy salt to my hand, shoot the tequila shot, and then bite into the lime.

"Damn," Mark mutters, shaking his head. "You're a pro."

"I can assure you that I am not," I reply, laughing. "I'm meeting someone here."

He swirls his finger in front of him as he gives me a conspiratorial smile. "Ooooh? Well, have a great time. Orion is around here somewhere. I saw him earlier."

His words roll through me slowly, sending a shock wave skittering down my spine.

"H-he is?"

Mark shrugs. "I think so. Unless he snuck out the back door."

Dread fills me. *Of course* Orion is here. I can't run into him—can't let him see what I'm about to do and who I'm about to do a scene with.

"I should get going," I tell Mark, slinging my purse over my shoulder. "Thank you for the drink."

Mark studies me with narrowed eyes. "Be safe."

"Yeah, I will, thanks," I say absentmindedly, waving goodbye as I walk upstairs to the private rooms.

Unless he's here with the woman he's seeing?

That thought has me curling my fists at my side. What if he's here with her?

The tequila I just drank threatens to come back up, and I place a hand over my throat.

Here I am, getting jealous that Orion might be with the person he's seeing, just before meeting the guy *I'm* seeing.

This is so screwed up.

It's his club. He's allowed to be here. But I *hate* the idea of him coming here right after our kiss—like he needed to see *her*. Like he had no desire to be near me.

I'm such a hypocrite.

Continuing my walk down the hallway, I try not to imagine my stepbrother in one of these rooms. Instead, I get to a nondescript door at the end of the hallway labeled "Hypnosis." Taking a deep breath, I smooth my hair down before pushing the door open.

It's empty, but there's a door in the back between two large bookshelves.

Closing the door behind me, I look around the room —which is set up to look like some sort of office. There's a desk with a couple of fake prescription pads. There are legitimate books on psychology lining the shelves, and it reminds me slightly of Orion's office.

Stop thinking about him.

There's a large, cozy-looking couch made of white leather, and though the lighting is low and ambient, it feels warm and comforting. My heart gallops a mile a minute inside of my chest, so I take a seat on the couch as I wait.

Checking my phone, I realize I have a text from Starboy.

MASTER

Please make yourself comfortable. I'll be
in shortly.

I sit down, crossing my legs and pulling the contract out of my purse. I place it on my lap and attempt to smooth it out. My eyes skim over the things I previously circled, and my foot taps my shin nervously as I wait for Starboy.

Is he tall?

Being nearly 5'9" means it's definitely something that worries me—I like to wear heels, and I like the people I date to be taller than me when I do, and unfortunately finding men taller than 6'2" is rare. I tell myself that even if he is shorter than me, it doesn't matter.

We've formed a real connection. His height wouldn't change that.

I'm just turning over page forty where I've circled the term "nipple clamps" when the door behind the desk clicks open.

I don't breathe—I *can't.*

My pulse spikes, and my heart thumps heavily in my chest as a man walks into the room.

It's Starboy—he's wearing the hoodie, dark pants, and the mask.

And he's *tall.*

I can tell by the way he nearly has to duck under the doorframe.

He stands there for a second, almost like he's surprised to see me.

I'm sure I look like a deer in headlights ...

The door closes behind him, and he takes a seat at the desk.

"Hi," I say, immediately regretting that I spoke first.

He leans back, and it's unnerving not knowing what he's looking at. The lighting is too low to see his eyes clearly.

"Come here," he signs, his veiny, golden hands forming the words.

"Should I bring the contract?"

He nods, and I stand, leaving my purse on the couch as I walk the contract over.

What does he think of me? Am I what he was expecting?

As I get closer, his eyes get clearer behind the mask— and the familiar blue color pierces straight down to my soul.

The same blue eyes that stared at me this morning.

It can't be.

I walk slower, my mind racing.

No, this isn't possible. It couldn't be him. Could it?

One of his hands goes to the back of his neck, and the slightest hint of a black tattoo peeks out of the sleeve of his hoodie. He spreads his legs slightly, waiting for me to reach him.

The closer I get, the stronger the smoky tobacco smell becomes, anchoring me in a reality I'm not sure I'm ready to face.

There's no way ...

My hands begin to shake when I reach the edge of the desk, and when he looks up at me, I see it in the way he carries himself. I'd know Orion from a mile away—the tapered waist, the thighs, the boots, the hands with perfectly manicured fingernails despite never going to a salon ...

The man behind the mask ...

It's Orion.

The realization slams into me, and my breathing hitches in my throat. Once the surprise flows over me, everything begins to click into place.

Mark saying Orion was here tonight.

The fact that Orion never answered my text earlier.

Disguising his voice by doing sign language.

Not telling me his first name—*Orion is a unique name, just like he explained.*

He'd read my favorite book. He'd listened to me explain my deepest, darkest fantasies. I'd trusted him, and he knew who I was all along.

Just doing a little research for someone special.

You're beautiful. I hope someone tells you that often.

If I knew you in real life, I'd ask you to be my submissive. Full stop. I'm holding back. So let me do this. For you, but also for me.

The picture Starboy sent me ... it was Orion.

Orion making a mess over a raunchy picture of *me*.

A white-hot bolt of arousal works through me, but a wave of uncertainty quickly follows it.

How could he do this? How could he hide this from me? My thoughts spiral, tugging at the threads of my trust in him. He knew it was me the whole time and didn't say anything. The hurt swells within me, battling against the relief that's beginning to form.

I could back away and call him a bastard, a liar. I could tell him that what he did was screwed up. That he took advantage of the situation, of my vulnerability.

But then again, haven't I always been drawn to him? Haven't I always felt a connection, even before I knew?

Is this betrayal, or is it fate?

The truth is, I'm relieved—relieved that they're the same person, and I no longer have to make an impossible choice. It's why I felt so connected to Starboy—why I was drawn to him right off the bat.

It was Orion the entire time.

But should I accept this so easily? Should I trust him after everything?

The question lingers, heavy and unresolved.

Trust your gut. Use common sense.

Zoe's words from earlier flit through my mind, and when I really dig down and listen, my intuition is screaming at me.

Yes.

Yes.

Yes.

I school my face into neutrality. "It's nice to meet you, Master."

And then I drop to my knees.

CHAPTER TWENTY-TWO

THE TRANCE

Orion

Watching Layla place her palms on her thighs and look down demurely, all while wearing that *fucking* dress. The virginal white, with its innocent eyelet pattern, and the way it shows off just enough to drive me crazy, but not enough to be vulgar.

I am so, so fucked.

Leaning forward, I pull her contract closer as I attempt to disguise my shaking hands. I was *so* sure she'd figure out who I was as soon as I walked into the room. She slowed down a bit when she was walking over, and I braced myself for it—for her reaction.

Instead, her eyes roved over my body before she kneeled before me. I know Layla is good at hiding how she's feeling, but if she knew it was me, she would've said something. *Right?*

I flick through the pages as Layla sits completely still in front of the desk. It's quiet except when I turn over the pages. Her answers surprise me. She's open to a lot more than I expected.

Never would've guessed my stepsister would circle anal play as a possibility, but here we are.

I'm already hard. Once I see that she's signed and dated it, I set it down, crack my knuckles, and stand. Walking around the table, I stop when I'm next to her, and place a hand on her shoulder, tapping her soft skin twice.

"Eyes on me tonight, Layla. For the sake of being able to sign," I tell her with my hands.

Her pupils are darker now. She nods once, and when her eyes meet mine, there's something fiery and anticipatory in her expression.

"I noticed you marked no for food play, as well as no on any terminology having to do with your body. Can you please elaborate?"

This must surprise her because her teeth drag her lower lip into her mouth as her eyes widen.

"Um ..."

I crouch down so that we're eye level. *"This is where my communication clause comes into play for a scene. You don't need to tell me more than you're comfortable with, but I'd like to get an idea of your firm boundaries before we begin, and with things like this, it's important for me to understand your medical history."*

She looks down at the ground, so I reach out and tap her twice on the shoulder.

"Eyes on me."

"I'm in recovery for an eating disorder," she admits, eyes clear and resolute.

Even though I know this, hearing her say it still makes my chest ache.

"It started about ten years ago when I began dancing professionally as a ballet dancer. I'd been dancing for nearly a decade at that point, but I auditioned for a children's ballet and was told I was too curvy to be cast in the ballet repertoire they were running. From there, it grew—I began restricting. Printing pictures of Audrey Hepburn and other women as 'thinspo,' and taping them on my bedroom wall."

She swallows, and I'm riveted. I never knew any of this.

I wish I did.

I wish I'd noticed.

"Thanks to my stepmother, I started seeing a therapist. She noticed my habits. I stopped restricting myself to six hundred calories a day. And it's taken time, but I've mostly recovered from body dysmorphia. I don't own a scale, and I practice intuitive eating. I haven't restricted in years. But I don't think I'd be very receptive to any degrading terms about my body."

"That's more than enough information. Thank you for telling me." Trailing a hand down her bare shoulder, I smile behind my mask when her skin pebbles. *"You are perfect. Your body is ..."* I shift my weight. *"Let's just say, everything about you is everything I could ever want in a submissive."*

She swallows.

"*I thought we could try erotic hypnosis today,*" I sign. "*You might have gathered that from the name of the room*".

"I did," she says softly.

"*It'll be easier if I use my voice.*"

"That's fine," she whispers.

I take a deep breath. Here goes nothing.

"Please stand and walk to the couch."

I make my voice lower than normal—slower.

I watch her face for a reaction, but there's nothing. She just flicks her eyes up to mine as she pushes into a standing position before walking to the couch. Moving her purse to one of the side tables, she sits down all prim and proper.

Fuck.

I'd give anything to corrupt her while she wears that dress and those sneakers. She's so pure.

Or at least she wants everyone to think that.

"Lie down and get comfortable," I tell her, keeping my voice an octave lower than I'm used to.

She kicks her shoes off and lies down, resting her hands on her stomach and crossing her legs like she's in an actual therapy session.

"Before we begin, we have to establish trust. As for a safe word, I think we should continue with the traffic light system. Can you tell me what they mean?"

"Red means stop the scene, yellow means pause and talk, and green means keep going."

I smile. "In more or less words, yes." I walk over to

where she's lying down. "Another part of this is trust. Do you trust me, Layla?"

"Yes."

I want to ask her why she trusts a stranger, but I don't. "You need to trust me. You need to know my voice. Is that clear?"

"Yes, Master."

"The main idea of erotic hypnosis is to dominate. Most Dominants are interested in physical domination. I am interested in mental domination."

Her eyes flick up to mine. "So we're not going to—" Her throat bobs as she swallows, and I smile underneath my mask.

"I never said this session wouldn't get physical."

"But your soft limit ... it said no penetration."

I crouch down next to the couch. "It's a soft limit for a reason. I don't want to rule it out, but it's not my default." Her eyes rake between my eyes in search of more information. When I lean closer, it's hard not to touch her—hard not to think of making her pliant and willing beneath me as I pound into her. "With you? I don't think I can stay away."

I run one of my hands along her bare leg, and we both shudder at the contact.

"I'm going to take control of your thoughts. I'm going to make you do whatever I want you to, so I'm going to ask one last time, do you trust me, Layla?"

Her eyes widen, and she turns to face me. "Is that possible? To make me do whatever you want?"

"Yes, it's possible. You will become powerless against my dominance. Do you understand?"

She swallows. "Yes, Master."

"Good. Close your eyes."

She does, and I sit back on my heels. "Today, just listen to my voice. Do as I say. And you will be rewarded. If you don't listen, you will be punished."

A visible shiver goes through her.

"Are you ready?"

"Yes, Master."

I crack my knuckles again and begin speaking.

"Start by taking a long, slow, deep breath."

She does, her chest rising and falling slowly.

"Another one."

I can see the tension leaving her body.

"You feel so good. It feels so good when you breathe in, pushing the stress out with each exhale. You're sinking deeper and deeper. Follow my voice and let go of everything. It feels so good to let go of everything. Let my voice sink into the deepest, darkest places of your mind. Your air is my air. I own every single sensation within your body. You like playing with me, don't you? Take another deep breath. Surrender to me completely, Layla."

I repeat the same sorts of lines over and over, watching her body sink into the couch, watching the crease between her eyebrows relax completely.

Her hands unfurl, slacking at her side, and her legs go from tightly crossed to loosened, opening slightly.

"Imagine that with every inhale, you're drawing pleasure in, and with each exhale, you're letting go of everything around you. Each wave of pleasure feels better than the last. Focus on my voice, Layla. Don't think about anything else. Your body feels warm. You have no desire to move. You're doing so good. Keep listening to my voice. Feel the heat puddling around your hips, down your legs, and now your entire body fills with pleasure. You want to let me into your mind, infusing you with my control. You have one purpose—to serve me, and to serve my needs. Such a good fucking girl."

Her breathing hitches, and my cock thickens inside my pants as she rolls her hips once. What I wouldn't give to sink into her tight heat right now.

"You're such a good little slut. I can see you starting to writhe on the couch. Doesn't it feel so good to be used by me? To please me? You want to be a good girl. More importantly, you need to be a good girl for your Master."

I stand and walk around to the foot of the couch.

"You're going to obey and let me sink into your subconscious. You're warm now, and your cunt is starting to seep, isn't it? You're so good at serving me. You feel your body sinking into the couch. You're happy here. Your pleasure is completely under my control. And when I'm in control of you, you are free to relax, but you will not come unless I tell you to. You like it when I talk to you like my dirty little cumslut, don't you?"

She whimpers, and I ignore the way my cock pulses, the blood rushing to my erection. It's hard to think— hard to do anything other than watch my stepsister start to pant.

"I want you to put your hand between your thighs. Can you feel your pulse there?"

Her hand moves between her legs.

"Imagine how good it would feel if I let you pleasure yourself. Gliding your fingers across every sensitive nerve ending. If I told you to do it, you would. Not yet, Little Dancer. You're here for me. Keep your fingers against your throbbing clit. Do not move them. Wait for my command. I want you to think of how the rest of your body feels. How your nipples tighten. How your legs ache because you're trying to hold them together like a good girl. How your cunt aches with arousal. How you can feel it between your thighs. Even without moving your hand, I can see how responsive you are to me. Do not move."

She gasps, and her hand between her legs twitches as she arches her back, but she doesn't move her hand.

"Good girl."

She lets out a low moan, and I chuckle as I look down at my stepsister losing her mind on the couch right in front of me.

I learned about erotic hypnosis a few months ago. The concept of putting someone in a trance, making them come on command, or extending an orgasm all appealed to me as a sadistic Dominant. It's like magic—being able to control their nervous system and watch as they lose control completely.

In a way, it feels like brainwashing, and I shouldn't enjoy it as much as I do. But I do. I enjoy it very much. Exploring someone's limits—exploring *my* limits—is fascinating.

Even with enthusiastic consent, women still put their trust in me completely. Little do they know, with hypnosis, I can hack and modify their desires. I can interpret something they say as entirely different. I won't cross the boundaries of a hard limit, but everything else is on the table during a session.

I enjoy the control.

Overriding someone's will, watching as they resist, watching their face as I push past it—in a consensual way, of course. It's a lot of fucking fun watching them mentally wrestle with my commands.

I walk to the head of the couch.

"Focus on the heavy sensation of your hand on your clit. You can push down now, but no other touching. You can feel the arousal building, can't you? Getting wet for your Master."

She twitches at that.

"You'd like that, wouldn't you? Or maybe you'd prefer to drop to your knees and serve me like the perfect little fucktoy that you are? You love worshipping me as you take me into your mouth. Sucking every last drop. My greedy girl," I purr.

Layla arches her back again, but her hand stays still.

"You're being such a good girl. Focus on my voice. Relax. Imagine sinking even deeper into the couch. Feel the pleasure coil deeper. Feel the way your body throbs, the way you need the friction of my cock. You're under my power, unable to move."

She moans, and her head rolls back slightly.

"You're such a good girl. Such a good whore. Purely for my pleasure. You can feel the pleasure pulling you closer to the edge. Shock waves of pleasure, over, and over, and over."

Layla shudders, moaning again as she squeezes her eyes closed tighter.

"My own personal sex toy. It's overwhelming, isn't it? Focus on that pleasure. I want you to feel it. Your skin, your lips, your nipples, your clit, your toes ... do you feel the desire flowing through you? It's overwhelming. But I want you to remove your hand from your clit and hold it six inches above your body."

She whimpers, a crease forming between her brows as she removes her hand from between her thighs, holding it up. Her hips roll once in search of friction. I memorize the way her nipples are hard and taut against the white eyelet material, the way she swallows, the way her lips part in ecstasy.

"That's it. Just out of reach. Can you feel the warmth? The heat coming from your cunt? I want you to imagine your hand pushing that pleasure from the palm of your hand to the spot where you need it most. Sink deeper into the couch. Allow your body to feel how wet you are, how engorged your clit is, how needy you are for your Master. Every cell inside your body is screaming for a release, isn't it? You crave it. You want it, more than air. But you're a good girl, aren't you? You won't touch yourself unless I give you permission."

She whines.

"I love it when you obey me, Layla." I drop to my knees next to her face, letting my eyes take in the sweat gathering on her brow, the way her chest heaves like she's running a marathon. The small crease between her eyes—the way she looks like she's being tortured.

Her arm shakes—the task of holding it up isn't easy.

"You're such a good girl. The perfect vessel for me, for my commands, a willing recipient of my dominance. Such a perfect submissive. So subservient. You're blossoming before me, like a flower—you crave my voice, my commands. Your submission grows deeper with each inhale. Your arousal grows with each exhale—*my* arousal. You are mine, and your submission is my greatest pleasure. Every time you hear these words, your body will respond. And your mind will surrender. Let these words resonate with you. You are mine. You will always be mine."

I clasp my hands behind my back to keep from touching her.

To keep from sliding a finger through her folds to see how wet she is.

If I touch her, I won't be able to stop.

"You're such a good fucking sex toy. You want me to use you. You are under my control. You've done so well. So obedient. So dedicated. You're perfect. I'm going to bring you out of the trance now. You can keep any of my suggestions or let them fade away. Come back. Come back to me, Little Dancer. Wake up. *Now.*"

Her eyes fly open, and I'm inches away from her

flushed face. She gasps, and her eyes are nearly black. Blinking rapidly, she searches my mask and then utters the one word that makes my heart stop.

"*Orion.*"

CHAPTER TWENTY-THREE

THE AWAKENING

LAYLA

The minute the word leaves my lips, Orion goes still. His eyes go wide behind his mask, and he braces himself like he's waiting for me to yell or punch him—like I have so many other times in my life.

I've spent over seven years pushing him away—telling him I never wanted to see him again. He obeyed me each time.

But he was here the whole time.

The past seven years flash through my mind like a rapid-fire movie.

The cocky smirks. The arrogance. But there was also vulnerability—trepidation every time he would look at me from across the room.

And his eyes always found me first, no matter where

we were or who we were with. He never wavered—never gave up.

The bracelet—

I've been his for so much longer than I realized.

"Layla," he murmurs, and it takes me a second to realize his hands are shaking at his sides.

I haven't given him any indication that I want this with him—with my stepbrother. Aside from the kiss earlier today, as far as he knows, I'm about to walk out of Inferno.

But that's the last thing I want to do.

Instead of sitting up, I reach for his hand, placing my palm against the back of his hand.

His hand. Orion's.

He spasms at the contact, and when I drag his hand to the space between my thighs, his eyes flutter briefly. I drag the hem of my dress up my hips and place his hand against my core—against the silk panties I know are currently soaking wet.

Something low and primal escapes his lips.

I use my other hand and reach forward, pulling his mask off, and his face comes into view.

He should be a painting. He should be studied and worshipped for centuries to come. His scythe-shaped eyebrows. His full lips. His deep, blue, *genuine* eyes—the way the blue bled into the black of his pupils, like a kaleidoscope. Every single emotion he's feeling plays across his features. Shock. Arousal. Adoration. Supplication. He's never been able to hide how he feels, ever the Scorpio.

How have I gone this long without realizing it?

"Layla—"

His voice breaks on my name.

"I need more," I tell him, moving my hips up into his waiting hand. "*Please.*"

Everything inside me feels like it's on fire. I've never been this turned on—never been this wanton and needy. I'd hump his hand if he'd let me. The friction I need feels so close, yet impossibly far away.

It feels like he's already embedded in my mind, and maybe that's because of the hypnosis, or maybe it's because it's *Orion*.

The gangly teenager who showed up on my doorstep one day, giving my eight-year-old self her first crush.

The cool high schooler who helped me with the bullies in middle school.

The stepbrother who helped me with my math homework, and Spanish tests, and watched my audition dances hundreds of times.

"Layla," he says again, his voice frayed.

He looks down at me, his expression unsure. Just moments ago, he was commanding me so beautifully, but right now, exposed and laid bare for me...

He can't hide behind the mask anymore.

He can't hide *anything* anymore.

And neither can I.

The feelings are too raw. Too *real*. Too much.

"Please, Orion. I need *you*. Touch me."

I see the resistance snap behind his eyes. His pupils bloom, and his expression grows hard and resolute as he moves one of his fingers underneath the band of my silk underwear. A burning sensation sears through my veins, scorching every nerve ending, every trace of his fingertips against my delicate skin. One of his fingers swipes through me, and then—

He stiffens, and his eyes flick to mine with a sharpened, dark expression. Slowly, he scoots away from my face down to my hips, and when he pulls my panties to the side, he sits back on his heels and uses his free hand to cover his mouth.

"Oh fuck," he growls, looking at me with black eyes. "You've got to be kidding me, Layla."

His voice sounds so *tortured*.

"Do you like it?" I ask, lifting my hips to show off my VCH piercing. "No one's ever seen it before. Well, except for the guy who did it—"

He snaps.

Using brute force, he spreads my legs with both hands, flattening my knees against the leather.

"You are *mine*," he snarls, nostrils flaring.

His words flood me with pleasure—with something warm and addictive and sweet like honey. I open my legs wider, and his eyes flare with intensity before he looks down at me.

I don't even feel embarrassed. He already knows the worst parts of me, and despite it all, he still wanted me enough to come here tonight.

"I don't share, Layla. This beautiful, decorated cunt? It's mine."

"Yes," I whisper, working my hips higher. "Please, I need you, Orion—"

"Call me Orion again, and we're going to have a problem."

I gasp, and everything becomes hazy with lust. I've been reduced to a body that desperately needs release—like a taut cord waiting to snap. I can't take much more.

Especially when he talks to me in *that* voice—the one I've only heard a handful of times.

His Dom voice.

"Please, Master. I need you inside me."

"That's nice. I couldn't give a fuck what you want," he says. His voice isn't cruel. In fact, his lips pull into a lopsided smile as he runs another finger through my folds. "I plan to savor you, Little Dancer. Every inch. Every lick. Every breathy word that leaves your lips. At *my* leisure."

Panic and elation rush through me. I don't want to wait—but I also know he'll make it worth my while.

"Color?"

"Green," I practically wheeze as his thumb brushes against the metal of my piercing.

"Good. I'm going to ask you some questions now," he says, his voice a low purr. "If you're a good girl and answer honestly, I'll reward you and let you ask a question."

He flicks the curved barbell, and I keen. I see stars, and my hands curl at my sides as my hips begin to circle, chasing some kind of friction. A smattering of pleasure skitters down my spine, giving me a taste of the reward he's willing to give me.

"*God*," I rasp.

"When did you get this?"

"A year ago. I didn't tell anyone. It was just something for me."

"Your turn," he says. "I'm sure you have questions for me."

"What else are you planning on doing to me tonight? Are you going to hurt me?"

He looks down at me as his brows furrow. One of his fingers teases the entrance of my core, trailing a slow circle around the hyper-sensitive area.

"Yes." His quick answer causes my whole body to tense with fear. "I will hurt you, but I will never harm you. And that was two questions," he adds, pinching my clit. *Hard.*

I let out a sharp gasp. "Oh God," I mutter, a full-body shudder working through me—down my legs, all the way to my toes. Everything begins to tingle with awareness.

He laughs. "So you are a masochist. I suspected that might be the case," he purrs, trailing his other hand up my bare leg. "Why are you here, Layla?"

His question catches me off guard. I'm not sure if he means literally or if he means how I practically *begged* Starboy to meet me tonight.

I suspect it's the latter, but it feels too personal. Too intimate. Despite having his index finger running down the slippery seam of my vulva, telling him about how conflicted I felt earlier feels like I'm sharing too much.

"I just wanted to meet the person I'd been talking to."

It's not *exactly* a lie. More like an omission. Besides, what does he expect? That I'll tell him I have feelings for him?

He doesn't speak. His finger stops its delicate intrusion, and his hand comes to rest on my inner thigh as the other one falls to his side.

Apprehension fills me.

"Turn over."

I swallow the dread climbing up my throat as I roll over onto my stomach. One of his hands pulls the hem of my dress up, exposing my thong and everything below my waist to him.

"I don't tolerate dishonesty," he says, his voice rough like gravel.

"I'm sorry," I whisper, voice trembling.

"And while we're at it," he continues, cutting me off, "spare me the apologies. They're meaningless unless they're genuine."

Anger and embarrassment flush through me at his reprimand. "It *was* genuine!"

He goes still, waiting. His eyes bore into mine, and silence fills the air. Embarrassment flashes through me, and the silence is deafening.

He is in control—something I need to remember.

He decides what he gives me and how much.

He decides the rules.

"Please, Master. I'm sorry. Truly."

He stands up without acknowledging my apology. I see him walk to the desk and pull something out.

"Because it's your first time, I'm going to be nice and let you choose. Paddle or flogger?"

My whole body continues to throb with arousal. I can't think—can't rationally acknowledge the implications of either fully, so I blurt out the first thing that comes to mind.

"Paddle."

"Mm. I hoped you'd say that."

He pulls out a long black paddle. As he brings it over, I admire the craftsmanship. It seems to be made of fine, dark wood. The handle is braided with black leather and gold, and the flattened end of the paddle ... has a raised R.

For *Ravage.*

"Choose a number. One through ten."

"One," I say immediately. It seems like the safest answer.

He uses one hand to lightly paddle the waiting palm of the other, and his tongue rolls against his cheek as he considers me. It's playful and threatening all at once. A cruel smile is splayed across his face.

"Great. We'll start with ten paddles. You only get *one* break."

Well, that's not the answer I was hoping for by choosing one ...

A cold sweat breaks out across my forehead, but I know arguing is futile. "Yes, Master."

He sets the paddle on my back, and then he bends down to lift my legs, positioning himself underneath me.

My ass is in his lap, and my cheeks heat as his hands slowly run up and down the backs of my thighs.

"We're still playing our game, Little Dancer. Ask me a question."

He reaches for the paddle, but I can't see what he's doing. I feel *so* exposed, so vulnerable.

I ask the first question that pops into my mind.

"What kind of paddle is that?"

He runs the wood down one leg, and I tremble with anticipation.

"It's custom-made. It was actually cut from a piece of furniture in Ravage Castle. When my father moved abroad, Miles donated a lot of his possessions. He had quite a collection of items. This one is made from a type of wood that's illegal now. I found it last year and repurposed it. I haven't used it on anyone, though."

I want to ask why.

I want to speak out of line and risk more punishment, but I bite my tongue.

He traces the smooth wood over the other leg, and I whimper when he nudges my legs apart slightly.

"I made it with you in mind, Layla. So that I could use it on you for the very first time. Rare, cherished, classic, timeless. Just like you. I told myself I'd be a good boy and wait, but patience isn't my strong suit."

He lifts a hand, and then he brings the paddle down on my left ass cheek.

I can't breathe. I'm—it's—too overwhelming. It's a

new kind of pain for me—sharp at first before it bleeds into a bone-deep ache. It gets worse before it gets better, and all I can do is internalize the pain. It expands outward until I can't get away from it until I'm writhing to get away from him.

"Give me a color, Layla."

"Green." My voice is shaky but resolute.

"If at any time that changes, I need you to tell me. I'll keep checking in with you, and I expect total honesty— not just what you think I want to hear. Is that understood?"

"Yes, Master," I rasp.

"Good. Now it's my turn to ask a question. When did you know Starboy was me?"

"When you walked in earlier," I tell him honestly.

"Before I hypnotized you?" he asks, his voice frayed. I wish I could see his expression—wish I could take in his layered emotions.

"Yes, Master."

"But you didn't have any qualms about me being Starboy?" he asks.

"That's your third question," I blurt. "But no. I'm surprised it took me this long to figure it out."

Thwack.

"Oh, f—"

Thwack.

The double hits stack the pain in a way that makes my eyes water. The heat of the blow builds gradually, but two in a row doubles the sensation, and my breath catches in my throat.

I can't say I hate it—like I told him before, I've been through worse things.

"Say it," he commands.

"Say what, Master?"

"Say *fuck*. You have no idea how long I've been waiting to hear you mutter the filthiest words imaginable."

I swallow as one of his hands soothes the burning on the skin of my right ass cheek. It's not that I mind swearing. I had a really strict ballet teacher one summer who would make us do two-hundred calf lifts if we swore. It was supposed to teach us decorum, but it just scared me from ever using a bad word. After that, it just always felt so foreign on my tongue. I have dirty thoughts and think bad words all the time, but when they leave my lips, I feel like an impostor.

No one expects the prim and proper ballet dancer to swear, and for so long, I let that persona take over everything. I hid my trashy books and my dark desires. I kept them from everyone I know, something only for me to know. I had lots of thoughts—lots of feelings, and emotions, and times I *wanted* to tell someone to fuck off.

It never occurred to me until recently that I could defy expectations and say whatever the hell I wanted to say.

"Fuck," I whisper.

Thwack.

My whole body goes taut. With each new swat, pain and pleasure blur together, and the sharpness dulls into a deep, throbbing ache in time with my racing pulse.

"Louder."

"Fuck," I say, my voice clipped with irritation.

"Color?"

"Green," I bite out.

Thwack.

Actual tears begin to squeeze out of my eyes. My body absorbs each hit, and the pain soon twists into a strange, perverse sort of pleasure. The heat from the paddle deepens, sinking into my bones and making the space between my legs slick with arousal.

It's strange. It hurt so much at first, but the gnawing sensation of my swollen clit and the touch of his calloused fingers against the backs of my thighs overrides the pain.

Enhances the pain.

"We're halfway done."

Thwack.

He hits the other ass cheek. Guess we're doing half and half. The pleasure shifts, its sweetness giving way to something more overwhelming, almost unbearable. The sensations boomerang back into full-blown pain, causing me to cry out. My muscles tensing involuntarily as the pain grows sharper, slicing through the haze of my arousal.

Thwack.

"Oh, fuck," I cry out, my back arching.

Orion holds me down, running a hand over the sore spots, but even that hurts against my sensitive skin.

"Color?"

"Green."

Thwack.

"Please," I sob, my body wracked with only pain. My breath comes faster, shallower, as if I'm running out of air, and the warmth that once radiated through my body now feels like a scorching fire.

"You can take two more," he growls.

Thwack, thwack.

I scream—two in a row sends me into a tailspin, and I can barely focus on anything other than the desperate, aching need for it to stop—and something that's slowly simmering underneath the surface of my skin.

"You did so well," he murmurs, running a hand over the backs of my thighs and down to the back of my knees. I hear the paddle clatter to the ground, but I don't have the will to look, or to move. I'm still reeling from the amount of pain I just experienced.

"Thank you, Master."

He chuckles, the sound low and deep. "You're catching on. Very good." His hand comes to my hairline, brushing the hair away from my face. The gesture is so gentle and sweet, and it catches me off guard completely. I feel drained in a way I've never experienced before, and despite the pain, I'm ... content. It feels like I'm floating. "You can ask a question now," he murmurs, running a hand under my dress and sending sparks of contentment through me.

"Why is penetration a soft limit?" I blurt. With the state I'm in, I can't dredge up my tact filter, but something tells me he doesn't care.

His hands stop for half a second, seemingly

surprised. Then he continues to stroke me—light, feather-light touches, dragging his finger down to my ankles.

Everything feels heavier like I'm about to be absorbed by the air around me.

"Because I wanted to wait for you."

I stiffen. "You mean, you've never—"

He laughs. The sound is loud, and it makes me smile.

"You think I'm a virgin? No, not even close." He leans down closer so that his breath is warm against my ear, his voice steady but laced with something deeper, something raw. "I added that soft limit after we kissed the first time. If it's not painfully obvious by now, I've never wanted anyone the way that I want you. It seemed pointless to pretend otherwise."

His words power through me, effectively rendering me speechless. Lifting my legs, he disentangles himself from underneath me and helps me to sit up. I pull my dress down as disappointment presses down on me. I'm still *so* turned on ... is the scene done?

Was this it?

Maybe tonight was just a taste of what's to come, but I hope not.

I hardly notice Orion standing in front of me until he places a warm hand on top of my head. I look up at him as my pulse begins to speed up.

His eyes lock onto mine with an intensity that makes me squirm. "And now that you're here, I'm not letting go."

"Yes, Master," I whisper, looking up into my step-brother's eyes. This doesn't feel weird—I'm able to stay in the moment, to think of all the ways I want to watch him unravel before me. I don't know what that says about our relationship, but I'm grateful there's no awkwardness.

I'll examine why later, when he isn't fisting my hair and looking down at me like *he* should be worshipping *me* instead of the other way around.

"Does it hurt?" he asks.

I know immediately what he's talking about.

"Yes. Still hurts. I probably won't be able to sit correctly for days."

Something deep rumbled out of his chest. "I bet my initials will look so pretty against your skin. A black and blue reminder."

"Yes, Master."

His presence consumes the space between us. "Don't worry. I'll make it worth your while. On your knees." His voice is firm, leaving no room for hesitation. The air between us is charged, heavy with anticipation, and I feel my body respond to the authority in his tone. "Look at me." When my eyes meet his, I see that spark, that unspoken connection. *His demand.* "You're mine," he whispers, his words sinking deep into me, carrying both a promise and a warning. "And tonight, I'll remind you exactly who you belong to."

CHAPTER TWENTY-FOUR
THE CONFESSION

Everything hits me all at once.

It's taking everything inside me to keep my emotions under control.

Everything.

All I've ever wanted, the only person who's ever made me feel a sliver of what I now understand to be love, is on her knees before me. And *fuck,* it's the most beautiful thing I've ever seen. I'm momentarily speechless. I swallow, my throat clicking, as I attempt to get back into the right headspace.

Layla.

Here.

Kneeling, waiting for my next command.

My fingers twitch in her hair, and when I run my hand to the back of her skull, she lets out a shaky breath.

That sound—the raspy, quiet, *raw* sound stirs something deep and primal inside me. Something I've tried to bury for years. I've been hard since she walked in, but my cock twitches once, heavy and thick as it presses against my pants.

"Let me, Master," she says softly. Lifting her hands, she stops before she touches me. "May I?"

I bite the insides of my cheek to keep from groaning. To keep from the low purr that wants to escape my throat.

She's asking for permission like the good little sub she is.

I can't concentrate. I've never been this unfocused—this unwilling to take control. *I* am the one who sets the scene. *I'm* the one who tells her what to do. But the Dominant part of my brain is still shocked into silence at the sight of my stepsister kneeling in front of me, all while she *knows* it's me.

I still can't believe she didn't walk right out that door.

"You may," I tell her, my voice gravelly.

Her darkened hazel eyes look up at me through her thick lashes, and I can't pull myself together enough to take control.

I can't take my eyes off her—I can hardly breathe.

As one of her hands comes to my belt buckle, I feel something I've never felt before—an overwhelming desire to allow her some power.

She's placed her trust in me, and that thought makes my chest tighten with something beyond desire.

I can't fathom how she can so easily trust me when I betrayed her so completely. When I pretended to be someone else. When I messed with her head. But here she is—willing to be vulnerable with me.

I'm powerless against it. Against *her*. I don't even want to resist. There's something so intoxicating about surrendering to her.

I've never felt more alive, more out of control, more completely *hers*.

The clinking of my belt buckle sounds through the room, and she pulls me closer unconsciously by lacing the leather through the buckle.

With deft fingers, she pulls the belt out from around my waist, letting it drop heavily onto the wooden floor. A determined expression on her pretty face looks up at me as she unbuttons my pants and then slowly drags the zipper down.

I should say something—move, pull her closer, *anything*—

In one swift movement, she pulls everything down, and my cock springs free.

It's not like she hasn't seen it. I'm pretty sure she memorized that dirty picture I sent her. And then there was the shower earlier.

Still, this is the first time she's seen my cock this up close as *me*. As her stepbrother.

As her Dominant.

That's what I am to her now, isn't it?

Though right now, I don't feel very dominant. I feel

like I'd give her anything as long as she never stopped touching my cock and looking at me like *that.*

Her eyes rake over me boldly like her heart is beating just as fast as mine.

And as she wraps one of her small hands around my aching shaft, my eyes roll into the back of my head.

"F-fuck." I bite my tongue to keep from groaning and seeming over eager. "Layla," I rasp.

Her thumb swipes over the drop of precum gathering along my slit, and then she does something unthinkable.

Something that practically has me coming instantly.

She brings her thumb to her mouth and sucks my precum off.

I couldn't look away even if aliens invaded the room.

"Do it again," I tell her.

She removes her thumb from her mouth and swirls it around my slit, gathering a string of precum.

"Oh shit," I mutter, my voice breaking as her tongue darts out and licks the head of my cock.

"Again, Master?"

"Y-yes."

Her head bobs forward, and just as her lips close around my aching length, one of her hands gently squeezes my balls.

A low, heady groan escapes my throat, and I close my eyes as pure, blinding pleasure shoots through me.

I'm not sure what kind of head I expected Layla to give me, but as she strokes one hand up and down my shaft, her other hand playing with my balls, and her tongue flattening against the taut head of my dick ... it wasn't *this*.

Everything she's doing feels euphoric, and I'm not sure if it's because of who's doing it or *what* she's doing with such expertise.

"Guess those dirty books paid off," I mutter, reaching my other hand out to grab onto her head with both hands.

"I guess so," she says, her words garbled because her mouth is full of *me*.

"You're so perfect," I tell her, guiding her mouth deeper onto my cock. "You like having your stepbrother's cock in your mouth?"

"Yes," she says, words muffled.

"You want everyone to think you're so innocent, but you're not, are you?"

She moans, looking up at me with doe eyes.

"Fuck, Layla, when you look at me like that, it makes me want to spill all of my cum down your throat."

She pulls off my cock with a soft *pop*. "So do it."

"Color?" I ask.

"Green." She gives me a bratty, little smile before her lips are back on my shaft.

I grip her hair and pull her onto my cock with a little bit more force.

"We never established a nonverbal safe word, so if you need me to stop, tap on my thigh three times, okay?"

"Okay, Master," she says, mouth full of cock.

Fuuuuuck.

The warm, wet feeling of her mouth on me, her soft

hands squeezing my balls gently, the slippery firmness of her tongue against the tip of my cock...

My balls start to tighten as Layla works me closer and closer to a climax.

I pull her farther down my cock, and her hands drop away so that it's just her mouth, and as I slowly slide her all the way over my length, she doesn't gag or attempt to pull away.

A low, guttural sound reverberates through my chest as she deepthroats me, as her mouth swallows me and sucks me farther into the back of her throat.

Instinctively, I start to fuck her throat, the sound making me hiss with pleasure. Her eyes are watery when she looks up at me, but resolute and single-minded.

"I know I told you that I'd make a mess of your pretty face one day," I tell her, my lips pulling away from my teeth as I jut my hips forward into her mouth farther, "But I think I'd rather come down your throat so a part of me can stay inside two places of you."

Her brow comes together in confusion, and I can't help but chuckle as my swollen cock pumps as far as I can go.

"Did you think we'd be done after this?"

Her head nods slightly, causing her teeth to graze the underside of my shaft. I wish I could say it deters my impending orgasm, but the sharpness only causes me to moan and fist her hair harder as my lashes flutter.

"God, you're so fucking good at this."

"I've had practice," she hums against my shaft, and I

instantly pull my hips back so that I pop out of her mouth.

"With whom."

It's not a question—not at all.

It's a *demand.*

"Kidding," she says sweetly, looking up at me with those hooded hazel eyes as one of her hands continues to pump me. "But you should see your face right now."

I grind my jaw as one of my hands trails down the side of her face.

"You think it's funny to make me imagine your mouth around another man's cock? You think I'd find that amusing?" She rolls her eyes, and my hand stills. "Roll your eyes again and I'll edge you for days before you're allowed to come."

Funny how the thought of another man's cock brings the Dominant right back up to the surface ...

"You wouldn't," she says, trailing her tongue along my shaft, tip to root and back up again.

Fisting her hair, I yank her neck back so that she has no option but to look me dead in the eye as I deliver my next line.

"I can, and I will. Don't think I won't. And don't mistake my reverence for weakness. I may have wanted you for years, but I still expect respect while we're doing a scene."

Her eyes widen slightly. "Yes, Master."

"Good girl. Now open wide." Her mouth drops open, and she lays her tongue flat—*waiting.* I can't help it. A heady groan leaves my lips as I thrust my hips forward, impaling her mouth with my pulsing shaft. Chills run through my body, and I have to close my eyes for a second to gather myself when she hollows her cheeks. "That's it. You suck my cock so well, pretty girl."

She stops moving, and I realize my mistake a second too late.

Fucking Earl.

Layla heard him earlier.

She pulls off my cock. "I guess that means your bird likes me," she mutters before continuing the world's best blow job.

"I like you, so naturally, he does, too."

Her eyes flash with something triumphant.

I could watch her here like this all day, every day.

She takes every secret and runs with it—first with Starboy, and now with Earl. Like nothing surprises her.

I keep expecting to say or do something to spook her.

But maybe it's time to lay it all out for her.

Maybe it's time to see if she's all in.

"And just for the record, I was watching you that night at The Angry Squirrel. I followed you from your performance."

She looks up at me, but she doesn't seem surprised. Instead, her free hand comes back to cup my swollen, aching balls.

"F-fuck," I stutter, rocking into her mouth. "That feels—"

I lose my train of thought when she sucks—actually *sucks* me into the back of her throat before running her tongue along the underside of my shaft and coming up for air.

"Jesus, Layla."

"You were saying, Master?" she asks, tilting her head innocently. "I believe you were in the middle of confessing all of your sins," she adds, stroking me with her hand.

I chuckle. "Just making sure you realize the depth of my obsession, *sis*."

She smirks before opening her mouth and waiting for me to drive between her perfect, pink lips.

"Tell me everything, Master. Please."

I jerk forward and fuck her mouth roughly, over and over and over until her eyes are watering.

"I've been to every single ballet performance. I bought fake pheromones for Sparrow so he'd feel at home in my apartment. When I first saw that you messaged me, I nearly had a heart attack. It was so fucking—fuck," I hiss as Layla gently bites down on my shaft. Her brow is creased as she looks up at me, and then she pulls off with a pop.

"Keep going, Master."

"Why'd you use your teeth?" I grit out.

She dots my shaft with kisses. "Because I never said I'd be happy about all of this," she says honestly. "And maybe you need a little punishment, too."

Fuck.

I never considered myself a masochist. Sadism is all I know—all I *want* to know. Same with being a Dominant.

Having someone put their trust in me completely, experiencing something so intimate with another person ... it's addicting. *Corrupting.*

But with Layla? I'd hand over everything I am on a platter if I knew she was the one doling it out.

She takes me back into her mouth.

"Clever," I mutter. "I'm the one you bought your house from."

This makes her pause, and when she looks up at me, her eyes are wide. She doesn't say anything, so I continue.

"You were looking for houses. I saw this one and bought it, thinking you'd like being close to your—"

I can't say Scott's name while we're doing *this.*

"Anyway, I listed it immediately for a little lower than I bought it for, and I had my guys fix it up. I didn't entertain any offers. It was always yours."

She pulls off me, looking perplexed. "Why didn't you just buy it for me outright?"

"Would you have taken it? I knew you'd never accept charity, so I had to get creative."

Her eyes glisten with emotion.

"Keep going," I tell her, running a hand down the back of her skull. "I'm close."

She moves back onto my cock, and I groan.

"My username. Did you ever notice the year?"

Again, she goes still—just now realizing how deep this fixation goes.

"My birth year," she whispers after pulling off. Her hands drop to her sides.

"Keep. Going," I say gently, grabbing her chin. "I want you to taste me. I want you to swallow every drop of my cum. Do you understand?" My voice isn't hard, but her spine stiffens obediently.

Submissives don't take kindly to being yelled at, and respect goes both ways.

She does as I ask, and a bolt of electricity rushes through me when she begins working my balls again and sucking me down into the back of her throat.

My eyes roll back as I begin to unconsciously rut into her mouth.

"My tattoo isn't for my mom. It's for you. I have peonies around my house because they remind me of you. I send flowers before every performance. The day you got stung by a bee when you were sixteen and went into anaphylaxis was the scariest fucking day of my life. I listen to all of the music playlists you make, and all of my videos use the classical works I know you listen to a lot. I—fuck," I groan, feeling my balls tighten as the base of my spine begins to tingle. "I'm really fucking close."

"Tell me more," Layla says, words muffled.

"Fuck, I—"

She bites—gently.

I hiss and fist her hair as I begin to pump into her mouth in earnest.

"You have no idea how completely—"

I groan, throwing my head back.

"How *fucking* completely you have me wrapped around your finger, Layla. You could want to slit my throat, and I'd happily hand you the knife because you'd be the one doing it—God—*fuck*—"

Layla moans as I fuck between her lips, my hips jerking unevenly. I see stars when she swallows her saliva, when her throat tightly squeezes me down farther.

She's going to suck my soul out.

Her fingers continue to play with my balls, and I'm suddenly on the brink of coming. Every muscle is tensed, every pleasure receptor pulling taut in anticipation of exploding inside her mouth.

"I'm going to come," I tell her, my voice hoarse. "Swallow every drop—"

I shatter, and my knees nearly give out as my orgasm rocks through me. Layla whimpers as my cock pulses into the back of her throat. I'm gripping her hair for dear life, rocking my hips as waves of pleasure flow through me. She sucks and swallows everything with each spurt, extending my orgasm. My fingernails dig into her scalp as I hiss and moan, and my mouth drops open when her tongue slides along the base of my shaft.

Like she's not wasting a single fucking drop.

My whole body convulses a couple of times and then Layla pulls off with one more long, audible swallow.

"I have questions," she says slowly, placing her palms flat and face down on her thighs.

"Give me a minute," I say, running a hand over my face. My whole body feels like it was just electrocuted, and everything tingles, like I'm about to black out.

Quickly tucking myself away, I hold a hand out to help her up. "Color?"

"Green," she says as she takes my hand. I help her into a standing position, grab her purse, and then I pull her behind me toward the desk.

"How did you feel about the scene?" I ask tentatively. "Where's your head, Little Dancer?"

She gives me a long, contemplative look. "I feel good. I enjoyed it."

"It wasn't too much? Be honest with me."

Her expression darkens, and one corner of her mouth tilts up. "It wasn't too much. I can take it."

She's going to cause me to spontaneously combust.

"Turn around," I order, and she does as I say. I drop to my knees and lift her dress, checking her over physically. She lets out a tiny gasp when I run a finger over one of the welted Rs. I'm filled with primal satisfaction at the thought of branding her as mine, of finally being able to use the paddle I bought for us. "Do you need anything? Maybe some soothing balm, or ice?"

"No, I'm okay," she says softly. I drop her dress and stand, taking her hand. "Where are we going?"

I don't release her as I pick the mask up and place it in the back pocket of my pants. "Back to my place. Don't forget your shoes."

"What—we're leaving?" she asks, bending down to grab her shoes. Once she has them, I tug her out the back door and through the discreet hallway. "I thought we would stay and—"

I stop walking and press her against the wall. It's dark—meant only for performers and employees to come and go without having to walk back through the club after a scene. I built it to connect to all of the private rooms.

"The first time I see you come will be in *my* bed."

CHAPTER TWENTY-FIVE

THE RECIPROCITY

LAYLA

That was, by far, the sexiest thing I've ever experienced.

I know I'm not very experienced. Being demisexual means that for the majority of my adolescence, I fell for my guy friends, and once in a while, I'd entertain the idea of doing stuff with them. But when everything happened freshman year of high school, I gave up trying. My formative years were spent in my room at home, reading and spending time with my family. I never dated—never wanted to. I'm not completely inexperienced, but it's harder for me to explore sex and relationships. I thought it was because of the assault.

Derek Nichols.

Star football player.

I'd been young and stupid. He set his sights on me, and I let him sweet-talk me into going on a walk around the field with him one night after a football game. Orion had driven me, and he was waiting in his car to drive me home. Derek took me out onto the field after everyone left. He showed me how to pass a football. He laughed with me, and I was smitten—or I thought I should be, at least. He was a popular senior, and I was a freshman.

He wanted to show me the locker room next, and I let him.

The next thing I knew, he'd flipped the lights off and his tongue was in my mouth. His hands felt so unwelcome, and I asked him to stop. Instead, he kept going.

I screamed.

He'd placed a hand over my mouth and had been using his fingers when Orion burst through the door.

I remember sobbing as Orion straddled Derek—punching him until his face was a bloodied pulp.

Derek was in a coma for three months, and he spent six months in the hospital. *And I lost trust in men.*

Until Starboy.

The connection happened so quickly.

I realize it's because Orion knew it was me and used that to his advantage.

As I look over at my stepbrother, I imagine what it was like to see my name pop up in his messages.

"I don't know if I ever thanked you," I tell him as we walk down the main street in Crestwood.

His apartment is only a couple of blocks away, and like earlier, it's still warm enough to be comfortable.

"For what?" he asks.

He's holding my hand—and hasn't let go since we

left Inferno. It should feel weird, but instead, it feels normal. Like we've been doing this in another version of this life somewhere, and those alternative versions of ourselves have somehow crossed over into this dimension.

"For what happened in high school. With Derek Nichols."

He huffs a laugh. "You were pretty mad at me back then."

I smile. "I know. But I felt ostracized from my friends. From the school. Everyone hated me. Back then, that's all that mattered. Plus, I remember getting over my anger at you pretty quickly."

Orion smiles as he remembers what he'd done for me the following week.

"I was a pretty great stepbrother," he says. It reminds me of the ice cream truck that sat parked in front of our house for weeks, serving only strawberry ice cream in cones with little Ls on them. At the time, I thought it was a sweet gesture.

I felt … cherished.

I look up at him, and he's staring straight ahead. Now … I see it in a different light.

I see a twenty-year-old struggling with trying to fit between a family with an emotionally absent father and his new family that was *so* different from how he was raised. My dad rode him really hard when he was younger. He used to say he was making up for lost time —insinuating that Charles wasn't doing a good job raising him.

I see a young man who had no idea what he wanted to do with his life. He floundered for so many years— bouncing between jobs and shirking his responsibilities.

I see the stepbrother he aspired to be—the one who took care of me and always made sure I was happy.

I see the need for control—always pleasing me, always making sure he was good for his four older brothers.

And now ... I see the man who's had feelings for me for years.

The audition ... he didn't ruin my audition because he was drunk.

He ruined it because he didn't want me to move to Paris.

Don't do this. Don't move to Paris.

I remember his voice cracking on the last word. I remember how anguished he'd looked.

I squeeze his hand. "Anyway, thank you. For kicking the shit out of him."

"Since we're being honest, I suppose I should tell you that I've spent far more time than is healthy ensuring all of his prospective employers know what he did so that he's unemployable."

I furrow my brows. "But didn't he end up playing for USC?"

Orion chuckles. "Nope. He was accepted and went for a week, but then the administrators got word of what he'd done. Plus, questionable videos may have been uploaded to his university account."

I stop walking. "You planted the videos?"

Orion shrugs. "I had nothing to do with it."

Narrowing my eyes, I focus on his mischievous expression. "You had someone else plant the videos, didn't you? What was it?"

"Let's just say it was an explicit video I paid one of his exes to send to my guy. And he *accidentally* sent it to his female professor."

I use my free hand to cover my mouth. "Oh my God, Orion."

"He's still living with his parents, and last I heard, he's in massive debt from some pyramid scheme."

I lower my hand, and I can't help but smile. "You ruined his life."

He tugs me closer, blue eyes blazing into mine. "You wanted a villain, baby. So you got one."

My breath catches. "You ruined his life ... for me?"

He places my hand around his waist so that I have no choice but to be pulled close to him.

"If it was legal to cut off the hands that hurt you, I would have. Trust me, I looked for a way."

I open and close my mouth. No one has ever ...

No one has ever done something like that for me.

In a sick, twisted way, I *like* that he ruined Derek's life. I like that he cared enough, that he *still* cares enough.

If he's a villain, what does that make me?

"Well, thank you."

We continue walking to his apartment, and when we arrive, I mull over his earlier declarations. It was an intense scene—if it was even a scene, I don't know. I'm still new to all of this. To the lifestyle. All I know is I *wanted* to be good for him. I *wanted* to please him. None of his confessions mattered at the end of the day because he did them all for me.

If I knew you in real life, I'd ask you to be my submissive. Full stop. I'm holding back. So let me do this.

For you, but also for me.

He knew. All that time, he knew it was me.

I'm still trying to wrap my mind around it, still processing his words and actions from the past week.

From the past *seven* years.

To be wanted like that ...

It's intoxicating.

We take the elevator up to the penthouse. Orion seems distracted, but I am, too. It's been a big night full of reveals and mental stimuli. As the doors slide open, something occurs to me. Orion walks out, but I don't follow him.

I've already worked it out that he's not seeing someone. He was referring to me the entire time. Which means ...

"The ring," I say slowly, eyes wide. "The one in your closet."

The doors start to shut, so I jump forward and into the penthouse.

For some reason, Orion looks relieved.

Like he thought I might let the doors close and go home.

I don't blame him for thinking that. I've been pushing him away.

But I'm not going anywhere now.

"What about it?" he asks, expression guarded.

It hits me then—how deep this runs for him. He's keeping it under wraps because he thinks it'll send me running.

"Is it ... did you buy it for me?" I ask, voice barely a whisper.

Something dark passes behind his eyes, and I see the resoluteness—the commanding, Dominant persona flare back to life.

It's a defense mechanism, of course.

Being the youngest brother.

Being berated by me, by society.

He got into the lifestyle for control. To be able to *exercise* control. And right now? He's not in control, so he's doing the one thing he *can* do to control the situation.

"I'm not ready to answer that," he says, voice clipped. *Another hard limit.*

"Okay," I tell him. My face is neutral, and he flicks his eyes between mine as if my answer is a trick somehow. It makes my throat clog with emotion. Stepping forward, I reach out for him. He looks so skeptical, and I have to show him that I'm not going anywhere. "Do you want to order some food? I'm famished."

His whole expression changes—softening, relaxing.

"Yeah. Me too."

———

Orion orders pizza. I change out of my dress and into something *sexy* yet cozy. In this instance, it's another pair of bike shorts and another sports bra. When I walk out, I relish in the way Orion's eyes lazily drag over every inch of my body. We sit down in his living room with the cardboard box between us. He gets me a beer, opening a can of sparkling water in lieu of a drink.

"Strawberry is an interesting choice of flavor."

He gives me a lazy smile as he leans back. "It reminds me of you."

My heart turns over inside my chest, and I take another bite of pizza.

"How come you never told me?"

He chews on his piece, and I watch his throat move as he swallows. I don't think he realizes just how sexy he is—especially right now, with mussed-up hair, an old white T-shirt, and black pants. His feet are bare, and his scruff is a couple of days overgrown. He looks unkempt, wild, and provocative.

"By the time I realized, it was too late. I don't think it truly hit me until the day of your audition. The threat of losing you spurred me into action."

"And then I told you I never wanted to see you again," I mumble, the pizza suddenly tasting like sawdust in my mouth.

He sets his pizza down and reaches out for my piece, placing it in the box next to his as he takes my hands.

"You had every right to say those things to me, Layla. I was a shitty person to ruin your audition, no matter how I felt about you leaving."

"I shouldn't have said I never wanted to see you

again. I wish—" My throat clogs with emotion. "I wish I'd had you in my life these past seven years."

His eyes find mine, darkening slightly. "Maybe it's a good thing I wasn't."

I tilt my head. "How so?"

"I just mean … it was hard to keep my feelings to myself from afar. I'm not sure I would've been able to had we still been close." He looks down at our joined hands, and his face clouds with uncertainty. "You know how my parents met, right?"

I shake my head.

"My dad was *obsessed* with my mom. So much so that he smothered her. Completely and irrevocably. He wasn't nice about it. To him, she was *his*. His possession …" He swallows. "I'm a lot like him, Layla."

My chest aches. "Orion, you're nothing like him."

"But I am. I'm possessive. I'm controlling. I might not drink anymore, but I came really damn close to going down that slippery slope, too—"

"No. You're not." I squeeze his hands firmly. "You're kind and generous. You bought my house so I could afford to buy it from you. You helped me with homework until I graduated. You're selfless and thoughtful, and you always make sure I'm eating enough—"

"Don't you see? I'm kind to *you*. I'm generous—to *you*. Everything I do is for you, Layla. Doesn't it bother you that I'd let the world burn to save you?"

His words send shivers down my spine. "You're nice to everyone. Stop pretending that you aren't." I scoot closer so that I'm right in front of him. "You are not your father. But more importantly, I am not your mother. Felicity was a wonderful woman. Beautiful. Kind. But she easily molded to your father's will and was easily folded into my father's life. You forget that not everyone is so easily controlled," I finish, letting my voice go a bit sultry at the end.

His eyes spark with something heated. "That's a shame. Here I was thinking you'd be easily coaxed into doing whatever I want you to do."

I pull my lower lip between my teeth as I lift one leg and place it over his hips, straddling him. I don't give him the option to protest. His rigid length pushes against me, and I shift to sit right on top of it. His lashes flutter, and in an instant, I'm leaning forward and smashing my lips against his.

He visibly shudders underneath me, and I don't think I'll ever get over his reaction to touching me. It's like he's being burned at the stake—like he's so used to holding back that touching me is a holy experience.

"Tell me this is real," he mumbles against my lips. His warm hands come to my waist, and his fingers dig into my flesh like he's holding me for dear life. "Tell me you're actually here."

"I'm here," I whisper. "And I'd like you to take me to bed."

CHAPTER TWENTY-SIX
THE RUINATION

ᴀʏʟᴀ

Orion stands, wrapping my legs around his waist. He groans into my mouth as he slowly walks us to his bedroom, and the world falls away. A swooping sensation starts in my core and expands outward, causing my whole body to tingle.

I always wondered about how female characters described their arousal—because it had never really happened to me with another person. I could live vicariously through my dark romance books, but I never thought I'd experience the sensation of my innards dropping down to the floor, the heavy ache between my legs, the way my skin has goose bumps from how warm his hands are, how *tightly* he's holding me.

My reaction to him was swift and violent, and I know

it's because my romantic feelings go much deeper than I realized.

He deposits me onto his bed a second later, and everything smells like him—even the dark gray linen duvet cover. A shiver wracks through my body, the absence of his body heat unwelcome, leaving me wanting him as close as possible.

My breathing is uneven as he stares down at me.

"You're so fucking beautiful."

His words clang through me, resonating with my insecurities and igniting the praise kink I suspected I had, like bright fireworks sparking in my brain.

"Thank you."

He rubs his mouth as his eyes skirt over my body, as if he's deciding how to proceed. The anticipation flares through me as dirty images flit through my brain—so many possibilities.

"Take off your clothes."

I cock my head. "Or you could do it," I suggest, propping myself up on my elbows and arching my back slightly.

He gives me a dark, layered look. "If I touch you right now, I won't be able to stop."

"Is that a problem?"

He sighs, taking a step back as he looks away. His jaw clenches before he looks back at me, and he seems frustrated.

"I plan to savor you, Layla. If I touch you right now, I'll fuck you into that bed and be done in seconds." His hand moves to the bulge in his pants, palming it, and my mouth goes dry. "I'm pretty sure my first taste of you is going to make me come in my pants, so let's ease off the other stimuli until I'm inside you, yeah?"

My lips pull into a rueful smile. "Oh really?" I slide one hand down between my thighs, and Orion stiffens as my fingers slide down my shorts. My middle finger begins to circle my clit over the material, and I let out a heady groan.

I know I'm not playing fair.

I know I'm teasing him and using his feelings for me to my advantage.

He steps forward, his hand dropping from the thick bulge in his pants. "Did I stutter?" he murmurs, reaching down for my feet and wrapping his hands around my ankles. He drags me to the edge of the bed, and a low growl rumbles through his chest. "I said, *take off your clothes.*" His command is assertive, his voice is low and guttural. "Don't make me tell you three times. Consider this your only warning. I won't be this lenient in the future."

"No? I dunno, I kind of like being punished."

His nostrils flare, but he doesn't say anything at first. He only crosses his arms and stares down at me with that commanding presence.

My blood runs cold at the look in his eyes.

"Sorry, Master—"

The instant the words are out of my mouth, he flips me over by my ankles so that I'm face down on his bed.

He climbs between my legs, and I gasp when he fists the thin material of my bike shorts—and rips them apart. The stinging welts are exposed, and I inhale a sharp breath when he lifts my ass and props my knees up, exposing me to him completely.

His hand runs down my sensitive, sore ass, and my cheeks heat with humiliation. In this position, I'm *so* exposed to him.

It's terrifying, but for whatever reason, it also turns me on. I shift my weight slightly, feeling the slick arousal between my legs catch on the ripped fabric of my shorts.

And then he spanks me—not too hard, but enough for my body to stiffen since he somehow managed to layer the sharp slap right over where he'd paddled me earlier.

"I said I was sorry," I cry out, my face pressed against the rough linen material of his bed.

"And I gave you ample warning." He smooths over the area with his warm palm, and it feels nice. "I'm going to make something crystal clear. If you do this with me, you *will* obey. I have no time for brats."

The word snags in my brain, and I think of what Zoe had told me once—that she's a brat, and that Liam loved to *tame* her. But that's not me ... I like submitting.

Right?

"I'm not a brat," I say, panting.

"Maybe not, but you're not exactly obedient, either, are you?"

I don't argue.

"Color?"

"Green," I say, my voice petulant.

He chuckles, but before I can ask why he's laughing, he brings another hand down on my other ass cheek.

My whole body goes taut, and the pain skitters along my nerve endings.

"In the bedroom, I'm in control unless we discuss alternative arrangements. You read my contract, so you understand the dynamic. Do you understand, or should I make you read the entire thing while I edge you to the brink of insanity?"

That sounds nice.

I don't know why I do it. Maybe I'm suddenly aware of the fact that if I am more of a brat, I will be punished. And perhaps he was right—maybe I *am* a masochist. Plus, a small part of me is still a little ticked off about everything that transpired with Starboy, and I want to shock him just as much as he shocked me.

I look over my shoulder at him and roll my eyes. "I understand, Master." His shocked expression is too good. I give him a coy little smile, and his hand comes up and down firmly on the back of my left thigh.

I yelp out loud. It's unexpected—the stinging sensation in an area I didn't expect is surprising. And not altogether unwelcome.

Why do I like this so much?

Why am I soaking through the front, intact part of my shorts with arousal?

My nipples poke through the thin sports bra, and the

rough material of the linen brushes against them with every movement.

"It's interesting. I didn't expect you to brat out on me during our first scene. Do you enjoy keeping your step-brother on his toes?" he purrs.

God, his voice when he's doing a scene ...

"Yes, Master," I whisper, trembling.

He quickly pulls my mangled shorts down my hips, and one leg at a time, pulls them off my legs, discarding them on the floor.

A warm hand pulls me up by the back of my bra, and he's holding my back against his chest as his hands explore my body.

He unconsciously ruts against me, the firmness in his pants pressing against the small of my back. With deft fingers, he slowly peels the sports bra up over my breasts. His hands cup them, and he groans as he plays with them unabashedly, fingers lightly kneading them, thumbs brushing over my tight nipples. It's a juxtaposition from the spanking punishment.

"Arms up," he murmurs into my right ear.

I lift my arms and he pulls my sports bra off, throwing it off to the side. My skin pebbles under his touch, and my ragged breathing pushes against his chest with every inhale and exhale.

"I know it feels natural to resist, to question, to fight back," he says, running a finger down the side of my body. "But true submission is beautiful. It's even more beautiful when someone resilient, capable, and strong—like you—submits completely. *That* turns me the fuck on more than anything else. That you would give me that power. It makes me feel omnipotent... and invincible. Do you remember what I said the first time we spoke over video?"

My brain can't focus on anything other than his finger trailing circles around my hip bone and the way his warm breath feathers against my ear.

"No, Master," I whisper.

"I said when I punish my submissive, it's only because she's letting me. It's all about consent—that's the core of sadism, of masochism, of any sort of dynamic. *I only have the power I'm given.* I don't take the power away. You hold all of it. Is that clear?"

I nod, but a low sound emerges from his mouth, skittering across the sensitive flesh between my ear and neck.

"Words, Layla."

"Yes, Master."

"Are you going to let me do this my way?"

"Yes, Master," I whisper, voice shaky as his thumbs dig into my waist. I drop my head back against his chest and close my eyes. I can feel his rapid heartbeat against my upper back. *God.* The way he's touching me feels so good, and I want him to keep touching me, to keep talking to me in that bossy tone.

"Lie down on your back."

He lets me go, and I do as he says, turning around and lying down in front of him. His eyes study me from head to toe, lazily taking in every inch. I nearly gasp at the way his eyes are perusing me, appraising me ...

On instinct, I bring my arms across my chest and start to cross my legs, but his hand jerks forward—forcefully spreading my legs.

"Don't hide yourself. Not in front of me."

I slowly remove my arms from my breasts, letting them fall to the side.

His eyes darken, two smoldering flames as he looks down at me. I take a deep, calming breath to settle my racing heart, but it doesn't help.

"Are you going to behave?" he asks, crawling between my legs.

"Y-yes, Master."

"Good." One of his hands comes to my inner thigh, and my whole body lights up. I circle my hips once, urging him to move his hand where I need it the most.

"Ah, ah, you said you'd behave," he growls.

The playful reprimand coming from him makes me whimper.

He's reduced me to a wanton sex machine.

"Stay still," he murmurs, a piece of hair falling over his forehead as he gives me a seductive smile.

"I—"

He slides his middle finger into me, curling it against my inner walls.

My eyes roll into the back of my head as I clench around his finger, needing more.

"Mm. You have such a greedy little cunt. I bet it tastes good, too."

"Fuck—"

"I love hearing filthy words come from your mouth."

He slides his finger out, and then drives it back into me so hard that the knuckles from his other fingers press against my pelvic bone and pull against my piercing *just* so. It's a sharp sensation, not quite painful, but *heavy* and unexpected. I contract around his finger three times. "In fact, I want you to tell me exactly what you want from me tonight using the filthiest words you can think of. Call it your first assignment as my submissive. If you're good, I'll do every single thing."

I see stars as he pulls his finger out and adds a second. Pleasure sizzles down my spine, causing my legs to tingle and my hands to go momentarily numb.

"I c-can't."

He removes his fingers, and a high-pitched whine escapes my lips. "Can't? Or won't? Come on, Layla. I know what kinds of books you read, remember?"

Shit.

He scissors his fingers inside me, and my body goes taut.

"You like that? Tell me what you want."

White-hot embarrassment flushes through me when I think of what I want from him. But I also know he's going to make me say it, one way or another.

I'm beginning to realize that a big part of sado-masochism is akin to torture.

"I want your mouth on me."

"On your what?"

I growl with frustration as his fingers slip out of me. He places them between his lips and ... sucks them clean.

"Fuck, Layla. I knew you'd taste good, but not this

good." He reaches forward and places those same two fingers against my lips. I can smell myself—a sweet and tangy scent that makes me rear my head back slightly. "Go on, taste yourself."

My mouth pops open, and I suck Orion's fingers into my mouth. Mixed with the taste of his skin ... it's not bad at all. Swirling my tongue, I watch as he goes slack-jawed.

"That's it," he says, voice hoarse. Removing his fingers, he places them against my opening, but he doesn't push them inside. "You want my mouth on what, Little Dancer? *Say. It.*"

"My pussy!" I shout, frustrated.

He laughs. "Very good. What else?"

My cheeks are burning. "I want you to make me come with your tongue while your fingers are inside me."

"Inside what?"

He's obnoxious.

"My slippery love channel. My sopping wet cunt. My slick canal. I read a *lot* of smutty books, and I can keep going. Take your pick, *Master*."

I'm panting by the time his eyes bore into mine, and two fingers slip back into me. "And then what?"

I chew on my lower lip. "And then I want to fuck you."

"You mean you want *me* to fuck *you*."

I close my eyes. "Yes."

He scoots down and lowers his head, and before I can protest, his mouth is on me, and his teeth nibble on my piercing, sucking it into his mouth and causing me to groan loudly. My whole body lights up when he does it a second time, his curved fingers slowly working in and out of me.

"You have no idea how much it drives me crazy that you have a clit piercing. I didn't think you could be more perfect," he adds, and his praise compliments what he's doing with his tongue and fingers.

My toes curl when he swipes up and down my slit with his tongue, groaning as he does. I start to jerk erratically, and pulses of pleasure rock through me, getting stronger, and stronger, and stronger.

"Such a pretty little cunt," he mutters. "Such a perfect fuckhole for me."

The praise-degradation combo sets me off, and my abdominal muscles squeeze tight as I try to stave it off.

"Oh fuck," I cry out, squeezing my eyes shut as my orgasm begins to crest—

He sits up and removes his fingers, and I let out a silent scream as everything dissipates, almost painfully. It feels like someone is stabbing me, and I clench around nothing a couple of times as I pant through the ruined orgasm.

I place my hands over my face as the tingling dissipates. "What the hell, Orion!"

When I lower my hands and open my eyes, he's looking down at me with flared nostrils. "You will not come without my permission, even when we are together." His jaw hardens. "Did you read the contract?"

It's an earnest question, but it only fuels my frustration. "Of course I did! You can't blame me for forgetting. I was a *bit* distracted, and I'm new to this, remember?"

His expression doesn't change, but his eyes have a distinct hardening. "Let's help you remember then."

He grabs my legs and pulls me closer, so that my pelvis is raised. Unbuttoning his pants, I watch as he pulls himself out of his pants. My vision goes a bit hazy as he begins to stroke himself.

"Birth control?"

"IUD," I tell him, excitement flaring through me at the prospect of actually doing this.

"I'm regularly tested. Have you been tested recently?"

My mouth drops open. "Are you seriously asking *me* if I—"

He places a hand over my mouth. "Yes. I'm asking if you've been tested recently because I suppose I haven't made it abundantly clear that I plan to fuck you bare and without a single barrier between us, and it would be irresponsible not to ask you these things as your Dominant."

After he removes his hand, I swallow once before answering. "I haven't been with anyone in over three years, and I've been tested since then."

"There. That clears things up, doesn't it?"

Warmth floods me when I digest his words—*fuck you bare* and *without a single barrier between us* float through my mind as Orion pulls his shirt off. He licks his hand and strokes his cock, gathering a bead of precum and spreading it around my opening.

"I've never"—I look to the side—"I've only ever used a condom with other people."

"Good. I want to be the first to fill you with my cum. I did say I'd fill you in two places tonight, right?" He gives me a wry smile. "Maybe we can try for three tomorrow."

My mouth drops open just as he hoists me up, fingers digging into the flesh of my hips, and lines himself up with my core.

And then he roughly impales me with his cock.

CHAPTER TWENTY-SEVEN
THE FIRST

ORION

My nails dig into Layla's hips as I let out a long, slow groan. Her warm cunt wraps around me, so fucking warm, so fucking tight.

Lashes fluttering, I pull back before pushing all the way into her, and her mouth drops open as I fill her completely, tip to root.

She moans, arching her back and shifting her hips to take me in deeper. Feeling her move on my cock is *heavenly*.

"Eyes on me."

Her hazel eyes meet my blue ones, and she doesn't look away as she begins rolling her hips underneath me, a breathy rasp leaving her lips.

"Fuck," I whisper, reaching down and holding her hips still. Letting out a low laugh, I grip her harder when she tries to fight against me. "Stop trying to top from the bottom, Layla. I've been waiting"—I pull out before slamming back into her, burying myself completely—"years for this. This is *mine*. Let me have this."

My voice is frayed with desperation, and she nods once.

"I promise," I tell her, eyes boring into hers. "I'll take care of you."

Her breathing grows shallow as I begin thrusting. She looks up at me with pure adoration and hunger, and I attempt to give that same look right back to her. My instincts tell me to look away, to take this for myself, but I can't look away from her. I can't help but want to give her everything I have, every vulnerability, every expression, every *second* of this.

With every snap of my hips, her lips part a bit more, and another raspy whimper escapes her pretty little mouth.

She squirms when I don't look away—but then I bring one of her knees up, opening her farther, and her mouth drops open.

"Oh God," she groans as I begin to drive deeper inside her, trying to claw my way as deep as I can, trying to fucking *bury* myself inside her so that she can never be rid of me.

I move one of my hands from her hip to her clit, and using two fingers, I slide them up and down either side of her piercing, causing her to contract around me.

"You feel so fucking good," I say on an exhale.

I hover a finger over her clit, and she shivers beneath

me, waiting. "You've been so good for me tonight. Waiting so patiently to come."

"Yes, Master," she says, her voice hoarse as I slowly drag my cock out.

"Look at me," I tell her. "Look how wet you are." I fist my cock, gliding her arousal along my shaft. My other hand moves between her legs, and when I tease her entrance with my fingers, it contracts. "That's it," I murmur, running a thumb up to her clit and swiping against it twice.

She shudders. "God, I'm so close—"

"Do you need to come?" I ask, swiping my thumb against her clit again. I don't stop—not even when her eyes roll back, and her body goes taut.

"Y-yes," she stutters, eyes squeezing shut. "Oh God, I'm going to—"

I pull back, removing my hand from her cunt. "That requires permission, remember?"

She releases a sob. "Please, Orion, I need to come—" I flick her piercing, and a low, heady groan escapes her lips. "S-sorry, M-master," she amends, hiccuping. Her whole body is shaking, wound up so tight like a coil ready to spring.

I'm leaking precum, so fucking eager to push back into her.

"How do you feel?" I ask, teasing her entrance with the head of my cock.

"G-good, s-so close—"

I slowly drive into her, and she cries out. "Fuck!"

A smattering of pleasure claws down my spine,

causing my aching balls to pull up slightly with the need to unload inside her.

"That's it. I like it when you're a good girl, but I think I like it more when you swear. Do it again."

"Fuck, Orion—"

"Who?" I ask, pulling out.

She groans as a tear slides down the side of her face. "I c-can't—p-please—"

"Give me a color, Layla."

"Green! Fucking green," she cries out.

I chuckle. "Well done. Do you want to come?"

Her eyes snap open. "God—yes—"

Gripping one leg, I spread her wider and spear back into her as my other hand moves back between her legs, pressing down against her clit. Her cunt pulses around me, a feathering sensation that has me hissing in pleasure.

"I'm going to—"

I roll myself on top of her in a languid movement, rolling my hips so that the head of my cock presses against her G-spot.

She explodes.

Her back arches, and the warm, contracting sensation courses from her pussy to my cock, drawing my orgasm up unexpectedly. Hungry, intense ecstasy spirals through me as she squeezes me. My balls pull closer as I continue pounding into her.

"Fuck, you're going to make me come."

My mouth drops open as I throw my head back, my body jerking as my cock curves, hardening and lengthening before a white-hot, searing sensation explodes through me.

I break apart completely as my face slackens.

My body jerks erratically, and then I'm pulsing into her.

Holy fuck.

I spill into her still convulsing core. It milks every last drop out of me, and I moan, eyes closed, for what seems like forever.

When I'm done, I open my eyes and drop down to my elbows, kissing her as I keep myself inside her. I stay that way for at least a minute. Her hands come to my arms, and she strokes me as our breathing steadies, both coming down from everything. My chest presses against hers, and when I pull back, she looks up at me with something that makes my throat catch.

My cock continues to throb every few seconds, and Layla wraps her legs around my hips, pulling me close.

"Fuck, Layla. That was ..." I kiss her, and she kisses me back.

"I know," she says against my lips. "I didn't know that sex could be like that."

"I'm only just getting started. How are you feeling about what just happened?"

"Good."

"As good as that was, I never gave you permission to come."

"That's convenient, because I want to do it again. All night. And maybe into tomorrow."

She smiles, rolling her hips once against my sensitive

cock. My hand shoots out, and I grip her firmly to keep her from moving, the sensation too intense. I stare down at her, eyes narrowed.

"Keep moving like that, and I'll chafe your ass even more."

She bites her lower lip. "I'd like that." Her eyes are glazed over, and she brings a hand to my face. "Please, *Master*."

I've turned my stepsister into a nymphomaniac.

"You didn't eat very much dinner," I say, lifting up and slowly pulling out of her.

"So? I could live on sex right now."

Chuckling, I spread her legs and watch as my seed drips out, shivering at the pleasure it brings me to see my cum dripping out of her perfect pussy. Taking my finger, I scoop the cum back into her, pushing it inside. She gasps.

"Mm, baby. You look so good pumped full of my cum."

Her hooded eyes watch me as I climb off the bed and walk to the bathroom. Wetting a washcloth with warm water, I walk back to where Layla is still sprawled on my bed. Placing it against her core, I clean her up, and then I help her off the bed.

"Go to the bathroom. I'll meet you in the kitchen."

She stands, and I take in her fully naked body. She's ... *fuck*.

I walk over to her, placing a hand on the back of her head and fisting her hair. I kiss her, yanking her neck back slightly and plunging my tongue inside her mouth. She moans, one of her hands coming to my chest.

I pull away. "We're not done. But you need energy. And I need a moment," I tell her, laughing.

"Orion," she whispers, one hand coming to my chin. Her eyes flit over my face, and something softens in her expression. "I'm glad it was you."

————

Thirty minutes later, I walk over to the kitchen island where Layla sits, carrying the meal I've made her— fettuccine Alfredo with a fresh tomato and basil salad on the side. She balks when I set her plates down, along with a glass of water. She'd changed into pajama shorts with a cat print and a plain black tank top. Her copper hair is clipped up on top of her head, and I can't help staring at her every chance I get.

"You just whipped up some fancy pasta, no big deal," she says, rolling her eyes as she digs in. "You like to cook. I remember that now, from before."

Cooking for her used to be my favorite thing.

"I do like to cook." Taking a seat next to her, she smiles at me as she eats.

Yeah, it still might be my favorite thing—cooking for her, watching her eat, watching her throat bob when she swallows.

"Have you ever thought about opening a restaurant? Maybe branching off from bars and kink clubs?"

I chew my pasta as I think about her question. After swallowing, I take a sip of my water.

"Maybe. I like the feeling of opening a new place. Of hiring people and being able to give people well-paying jobs. Nothing is like the satisfaction of seeing someone enjoy something you've created. Again, I think it comes down to control—to making decisions about a place, from the location to the aesthetic. A restaurant is something I've thought about."

"You're good at it," she says, and her praise means everything to me. "Your businesses. Most people can hardly get one off the ground, but you've managed three now."

"It helps to have money. I have privilege, and I recognize that. I don't take a salary at any of my places."

She cocks her head. "Really?"

I shrug. "I don't need the money."

Her expression softens, and she wipes her mouth with her napkin. "See? Charles Ravage would exploit his workers and pay himself a large salary." I look down at my plate as she continues. "Can I tell you something?" I look up at her, and she gives me a wry smile. "I think you're more like my dad than Charles. You know that saying? Nature versus nurture? Sure, Charles is your birth father, and you spent the first fourteen years under his roof. And who's to say how you would've turned out if your mom hadn't left him, taking you with her. But you also spent the second half of your life with my dad—one of the most selfless people I know. I watched the transition. Watched as you went from a shy fourteen-year-old to someone who helped Scott at the bar every weekend. Someone who learned the power of hard work. And look at you now."

I swallow as I stab a tomato with my fork, popping it into my mouth as I let her words roll over me. Every word she says, every look of pride, of *awe*, has me sinking deeper and deeper in love with her. It's like her words are a soothing balm for my fucked-up soul.

"You should be proud of yourself," she finishes.

I'm glad it was you.

Her words now and from earlier roll through my mind as I mull them over. I'm not sure what I expected tonight or how I foresaw our relationship progressing, but I suppose I shouldn't be surprised. Layla has never let her emotions get the better of her, and she's always level-headed. She trusts me, so I shouldn't be surprised that she didn't care or mind that Starboy was me the entire time.

But the part that leaves me reeling is that, after everything, she's giving me another chance. Seven years ago, I lost her trust—lost *her*. And for the longest time, I believed that was it, that the bridge had been burned beyond repair. I never imagined that I'd find my way back to her, much less that she'd look at me the way she looks at me now.

The last thing I expected was to earn my way back into her good graces. But here we are, sitting across from each other, and she's not just tolerating my presence— she's encouraging me, lifting me up in a way I don't deserve. Her support is something I thought I'd forfeited forever, but now that I have it, I can hardly believe it's real.

Layla's always been the kind of person who sees things clearly and doesn't let emotions cloud her judgment. That's who she was seven years ago, when she called me out at that audition, and it's who she is now. But I never thought I'd be on the receiving end of her trust again. I don't think I'll ever fully grasp the fact that she's willing to believe in me, to give me another shot.

Maybe I should've known that if anyone could see past the mistakes, past the years of silence, it would be her. We've always had a connection, even when everything else was chaos. And despite everything that happened, despite how I let her down, it turns out we're still compatible in ways I never imagined.

So here I am, sitting across from the woman I thought I'd lost forever, and she's looking at me like I'm worth something. Like I'm worth trusting again. And maybe that's the most unbelievable part of all—that after all these years, after all the damage I've done, she's still here, still willing to see the best in me.

I'm glad it was you.

"Fuck," I mutter, looking away.

"What?" she asks, eyes wide.

My lips tug into a smile as I set my fork and knife down, pushing our plates away. "I was hoping we could get through one meal before I fucked you again, but—"

I jump up, and she squeals with delight as I lift her onto the island in one fell swoop. Pushing her legs apart, she gasps when my hands land on her waist.

"Lie down."

Her eyes flick between my eyes, and her lips tug into a small smile. "Yes, Master."

I'm grateful that my housekeeper keeps the counters uncluttered—including the island. Layla lies back, and I pull her to the edge of the marble surface.

"I realize now that you've only come once, and I've come three times today," I murmur, peeling her pajama shorts down her hips and letting them fall to the floor. Standing, I step between her legs. "I suppose it's time to catch you up."

CHAPTER TWENTY-EIGHT

THE REVERENCE

Layla

Orion gazes down at me as one of his hands runs up my thigh. I squirm as the cool marble soothes the sore spots on my ass, and I realize with a start that I probably look ridiculous spread out on his kitchen island like this.

I squirm—and he doesn't look away.

I can't seem to get away from his heated gaze—not since we left Inferno. I can feel it wherever we go together, and I soon realized that his feelings for me go much deeper than I thought.

He grabs one of my ankles and moves it up so that my foot is flat on the edge of the island.

He repeats the motion with the other leg.

It's jarring to be this exposed and laid out like his own personal feast.

"Open wider," he commands, warm hands on the

insides of my thighs as he pushes them to the side, and then he runs both hands along the insides of my legs, getting close to my core but not close enough to expect any sort of relief.

I whimper and my half-hooded eyes flick across his face. Orion's thumb slips higher, grazing the area between my leg and vulva. I gasp, and he chuckles.

"Sometimes, the anticipation is better than the release," he says, blue eyes falling over my chest. "Take your shirt off. I want you naked."

I reach for the hem of my tank top, pulling it up and using my abdominal muscles to hold me up a couple of inches as I pull it over my head and throw it somewhere behind me.

His hand moves up to my stomach, and it lays flat against my lower belly—the rounder part I'm most self-conscious about.

I know realistically that it's normal for women not to have flat stomachs. Even me—who is considered a professional ballet dancer. I tense when he begins to massage my flesh, and his expression softens slightly.

"Relax," he says, voice low. "I need to know if talking about your body is okay."

His words startle me. "What do you mean?"

His brow wrinkles. "I did a lot of research on eating disorder recovery, and one of the things people in recovery consistently said was that comments about their bodies always set them off. Not just negative comments—all comments. So I want to be sure I don't threaten your recovery before I say something. I know I got carried away earlier and forgot to ask—"

"Orion." My throat catches, and I move my hand on top of his. *He did research?* That's really thoughtful. "It's okay. Like I said, as long as it's not degrading, you can say whatever you want about my body."

His eyes darken as his hand twitches underneath mine. Suddenly, he drops his head on my chest, placing a kiss along my collarbone. I get a whiff of tobacco and leather when his hair tickles my chin, and I inhale sharply when he does it again along the other collarbone.

"Good. Because I plan to worship you, Layla. Your body is perfect." His hand presses down against my lower stomach gently, and then he kisses my breasts— one after the other. The soft touches make my nipples harden, and I'm panting by the time he gets down to my stomach. "You're strong. You're beautiful. Every muscle, every curve, every freckle." He trails kisses to my hips, kissing each hip bone. "And not just because of how it looks. But because it's *you*. Because I can't get enough of your smell, of how soft your skin is, of your taste—fuck, I'd make a deal with the devil and sell my soul if it meant I only got to taste you for the rest of my life, Layla."

My breath hitches as one of his other hands works down to my seam.

I place a hand against his chest as my eyelashes flutter. His racing heart beats in tandem with mine.

My legs quiver as he inserts one finger inside me. I

gasp on an inhale, and he pulls his finger out, giving me a playful smile.

"What—"

Without warning, he plunges two fingers inside me. I see stars as he roughly pounds into me, and his thumb bumps my piercing. He doesn't relent, and my eyes roll into my head as my back arches off the table.

"Oh fuck—"

"That's it, Layla. No inhibitions. Not anymore. Tell me exactly what you want."

"That—doing what you're doing—"

My hands fly to the edge of the island, and I grip it for dear life. It only intensifies the aching, building pressure inside me, because it keeps me from sliding back—and allows him to go harder.

"Orion," I whimper.

"That's not my name," he says, tongue clicking. His fingers curl, dragging against the sensitive spot inside me.

"Fuck—yes, right there—*Master.*"

"Good girl. Do you have any idea how fucking hot it is to see you falling apart, to see you scream out those filthy words?"

"God—yes—"

"You have no idea what you do to me," he says, and when I look up at him, he's watching me with a tortured expression.

"Please, let me come," I say, tension building inside me.

My muscles contract, and he still doesn't relent.

Instead, he goes deeper, until he's inside me all the way to his first knuckle. The motion drags against the top of my opening, pulling at my piercing and sending a shock wave of pleasure searing through me.

"Fuck," I rasp, circling my hips.

"Louder," Orion commands.

"Fuck!"

He uses his other hand to flick my piercing, and something low and primal escapes me as sweet ecstasy spreads through me.

"I'm going to—Can I—"

"Can you what?" he asks, lips quirking into a roguish smile.

"Oh fuck, oh fuck, *pleaseMastercanIcome*—"

His free hand comes to my throat, squeezing just enough to add pressure and an extra element to my already convulsing body.

"Come."

The one-word command shatters some mental barrier I didn't realize I'd erected because I detonate a second later.

My hips jerk against his knuckles, opening wider as an intense flurry of pleasure skitters down my spine all the way to my fingers and toes.

All I see and feel is sweet, pulsing light.

"Fuck yes, you're gripping me so hard, Layla—"

His thumb swipes against my piercing, dragging pain into the exploding pleasure, and my body pulls even tighter. I can't think, can't speak.

"Give me one more," he says, gritting his teeth.

"Oh God—"

I squirm, trying to get away from the intensity. It feels like I'm about to pee or die, and my eyes pop open as he works his hand harder.

"Come on, Little Dancer." He does that scissor motion again, pressing against the inside of my inner walls, and it coaxes something agonizingly intense from inside me. My mouth drops open on a silent scream.

He adds a third finger, and my whole body goes as taut as a board. My legs quake as another orgasm crashes through me. It feels like I push him out as I groan, as something wet slides down my butt. This climax is brighter, pushing outward in wave after wave of the most intense orgasm of my life.

I vaguely register Orion groaning as I grip him fiercely, as my body jerks violently.

"Fuck yes," he whispers, coaxing the last of it out of me.

I'm breathless, and my heart begins to slow as something warm and comforting settles over me. I'm so, so tired—

Moving slightly, I feel the wetness beneath me. *That* wakes me up. I sit up and look down at Orion's wet shirt, the nearly black eyes—

"Oh God, did I pee?"

Orion's mouth is on mine, and I can taste the acidity of the tomatoes he was eating earlier on his tongue. He moans into my mouth with a frantic neediness I didn't realize was possible, especially since we just had sex. I pull him closer, running my fingers through his hair, and a whole-body shiver goes through him.

"No, you didn't pee," he says, smiling against my lips. "God, you're perfect."

"Did I—"

I can't say the word.

"Has that ever happened to you before?" he asks.

A bubble of laughter escapes my lips, and he pulls me up so that I'm sitting with him between my legs.

"No. Never. I thought it was a myth."

Low laughter rumbles in his chest. "I'm addicted to you. Everything about you."

I'm still shaking as his hands grip my hips, as he kisses me with everything he has, as he holds me like he never wants to let go. When he pulls away, he helps me up. I wince as I scoot off the marble onto my feet, feeling how wet the floor is.

"Turn around."

I do as he says, facing the island. I expect him to take me from behind, but I only feel his hand on my backside, smoothing over the sore spots from earlier.

"I branded you with my initial," he murmurs, hand smoothing over the skin of my hips, like he can't stop touching me.

"Good," I tell him, twisting around and placing both hands around his neck. "Because I've been yours for a very long time without even realizing it."

His throat bobs as he looks down at me, and I can't get enough of this man—of this sadistic, sweet, caring, teasing, *arrogant* man. It feels like I'm being shown paradise for the first time. How did I never know it could be like this between us? How did I never know it was possible to feel like this about another person? To adore them and also want them to touch you forever.

It's a brand-new feeling for me.

I've never been in love. Not even close. But this? I swallow as he kisses my forehead.

This is something close to love.

It has to be.

"Let's get you cleaned up," he says. "And then we have dessert."

I perk up. "Oh?"

"You'll never guess what kind of ice cream I got us."

I laugh as he drags us toward his bedroom, and then into his en suite bathroom. I stand there like a deer in the headlights as he turns the shower on. The glass steams up instantly, and then he tugs his T-shirt off.

I watch as he pulls his sweatpants down his legs, and just as I'm about to ask him if we're going to have sex again, he clicks his tongue.

"Just a shower, Layla. Come on. We have the rest of our lives to fuck. Let me wash your hair."

I take his hand and follow him into his shower, feeling like I'm stepping into something real and raw and uncharted.

His hands are gentle as he guides me under the spray, his fingers threading through my hair, massaging my scalp with a tenderness that takes me by surprise. There's an intimacy at this moment that feels deeper than anything we've shared before.

The rhythm of his movements is calming, almost hypnotic, as if he's washing away more than just the day's events.

It's like he's cleansing away all of our doubts, fears, and the walls I've built by telling myself I'd never have this with another person.

And the walls he built—telling himself that he'd never have *me.*

I close my eyes and lean into his touch, surrendering to the sensation. The water runs down my face, and it feels really good after the long day I've had. I relax into his touch fully.

This isn't just about washing my hair.

It's about trust, vulnerability, and letting someone else see the parts that are usually hidden from other people.

And Orion has seen every single part of me.

Somehow, he's managed to effortlessly carve out a space in my heart without me even realizing it.

Like he's always belonged there, quietly and patiently finding his way in.

Like he's been waiting for me to catch up.

CHAPTER TWENTY-NINE

THE CLOSURE

LAYLA

"Okay, so should we get our nails done first or wait until after we do a bit of shopping?" I ask, looking down at Bradleigh. We're at the mall for the morning, and then I'm going to my dad's house for lunch before my performance at seven.

He's doing well now that his diabetes is under control, thankfully.

Only took him a stern lecture from his regular doctor about his regimen, but he's okay now.

Bradleigh's eyes scan all of the stores, and she shifts her weight nervously. "What if they say something to me?" she asks.

I scrunch my brows. "Well, you're with me. And Orion will stand tall and get all scary if anyone says *anything* rude, okay?" I tell her, looking over her shoulder at Orion.

"Promise," he tells her, winking.

"Okay, maybe shopping first, then?" She looks up at me with an expectant smile.

"Sure. Let's go."

The three of us walk into the teen accessory store, and Bradleigh spends an exorbitant amount of time picking between two different pairs of earrings. She'd insisted that Malakai join us today, but since he was busy at Julian's house, I'd brought the second-best thing—his brother. We'd met Bradleigh at the mall, and her mom had gone back home to rest. Apparently, she was a nurse working overtime, and the whole bullying situation at school had taken a toll on Bradleigh, causing her to have nightmares.

Neither of them was sleeping very well.

She talks to us excitedly about ballet when we get pretzels and dip them in warm cheese sauce. I tell her about my performances at PCB, and she tells me about her dreams to dance for the Royal Ballet in London.

Orion is quiet for the most part, engaging with her genuinely but not wanting to interfere in the girls' trip. When we declare that it's time for nails, Orion winks and excuses himself to the bookstore.

Bradleigh and I decide to get matching yellow polish —her choice—and when her technician is still working on her nails, I walk to the outside of the store to get away from the strong fumes. A woman is sitting on the bench in front of the nail salon, and I have to do a double take.

Jean Fuller.

Also known as the judge from the Paris School of Ballet—the one who rejected me all those years ago.

You simply don't fit the image of a Parisian ballet dancer.

She's thinner now, if that's possible. *Older.* Her severe expression is fixated on something on her phone. As I take a step closer, I contemplate if I should say hello. I doubt she remembers me, but maybe it would be a good time to get some closure or something.

When I take another step closer, she snaps her head up to me, and I go still when I see the tears tracking down her face.

"Are you all right?" I ask, holding my hands out.

"I'm fine, *thank you,*" she snipes, her accented English bitter and cold.

I should just walk away. After all, she was rude to me —it almost seemed like she was holding a grudge against me that day, though I suppose I'll never know why.

"Are you sure?" I step closer, and it doesn't really seem like she's okay. Her hands are shaking, and her hair looks less polished than I remember.

Without asking, I sit down next to her.

She scoots away. "I told you, I'm *fine*—"

"You probably don't remember me," I say slowly, looking at her with what I hope is an open expression. "I auditioned for the Paris School of Ballet seven years ago, and my stepbrother interrupted the audition—"

"I remember," she says, sniffing. She reaches into her purse and pulls out a handkerchief, blowing her nose.

She doesn't say anything else, so I continue.

"I worked really hard for that audition, and I was devastated for a really long time that I never got to show you my repertoire."

"And?" she asks, looking annoyed.

I huff a laugh. I've thought a lot about this over the years. I held so much anger toward Orion, and at the time, it felt justified. But if I'm truly honest, I think the struggles I've had with my size and body shape probably would have been amplified had I lived in a foreign country away from my family and friends. Especially in a city as sophisticated as Paris.

"I realize now that it was never meant to be, and that's okay. Everything happens for a reason, you know? You told me I don't fit the image of a Parisian ballet dancer, and you're right. I never would've been happy there."

Jean's eyes flicker with a mix of confusion and curiosity, as if she's trying to decipher my intentions. I give her a small smile, genuinely hoping to convey what I'm trying to say.

"I ended up finding my own path. And it led me to places I never would have imagined. So, in a way, I'm grateful for what happened."

She blinks at me, her guard slipping slightly. "Grateful?"

"Yes. I don't know what you're going through right now, but I hope you find your own peace too. We all deserve that, don't we?"

Jean stares at me, her expression unreadable. For a

moment, I think she might snap back with another sharp retort, but instead, she just nods slowly, almost imperceptibly.

"Thank you," she murmurs, barely above a whisper, as if the words are foreign to her.

I stand, offering her one last smile. "Take care of yourself, Jean. I wish you well."

As I walk away, I can feel her eyes on me, her silence heavy with unspoken thoughts. Maybe she'll never fully understand my words, or perhaps she'll dismiss them entirely. But as I move away from the bench, I feel a weight lift off my shoulders.

I'm not that young girl anymore. I'm stronger, and I've moved on. And maybe, just maybe, Jean needed to hear that she can too.

I nearly walk into Orion. When I place my hands on his arms, I realize he's not looking at me.

He's looking at Jean.

"What did she say to you?" he asks, jaw feathering.

I huff a laugh. "Nothing. I wished her well. She seems to be having a bad day."

Orion sags with relief. "Good."

I arch a brow. "You can't avenge every person who hurts me, you know."

His darkened eyes look down at me, and for a second, it looks like he wants to say something else. Instead, he swallows.

"I heard she lost her job working for the Paris School of Ballet."

I cock my head as I narrow my eyes. "What a coincidence."

Before either of us can say anything else, Bradleigh comes running out of the salon, nearly colliding into us.

"Look! Banana nails." She shows off the cute little banana decals laid over her nails.

"Amazing. Who doesn't love bananas?" I ask, winking.

"Now maybe the girls won't make fun of me," she says under her breath.

I look at Orion, and his brows are furrowed in concern.

"Let's go take a walk," I tell her, my hand on her shoulder as I usher her out of the salon. I'd prepaid for our nails, so I wave goodbye to the technicians and head in the direction of the ice cream shop.

"I know things have been tough lately. I remember what it was like at your age, and it's not easy when people are mean. But I want you to know something really important: fitting in isn't everything."

Bradleigh crosses her arms, listening, so I continue.

"Sometimes, when others bully, it's because they're dealing with their own issues. That doesn't make it right, but it does mean that it's not about you—it's about them. You're unique, and that's a good thing. It might not feel like it now, but the qualities that make you different are the same ones that make you special."

"Sometimes I feel *so* different," she says, looking up at me with a crease between her brows.

"I know. And you know what? I realized that the people who matter the most are the ones who like you for who you are, not who they want you to be. It's okay if you don't fit into a certain group or if you feel like you stand out. Standing out is brave and strong. And I promise you, one day, you'll find people who love you just as you are. And when that happens, you'll be so glad you didn't try to change for anyone else. If you ever feel down or alone, remember that there's a whole world out there full of people who haven't even met you yet but will care about you so much. It gets better, and you'll find your people. For now, just keep being kind to yourself, because you deserve that."

"Thank you," she says. "Have you ever had someone be mean to you?"

I nod, thinking of Jean. Thinking of all the people in high school who called me a liar, or a slut. Thinking of anyone else who felt the need to be mean.

"Oh yeah. It's just a part of being humans. Only *we* can choose how we react to those mean people, you know?"

She nods, seeming lighter. "Yeah. All the mean people can fuck off."

I bark out a laugh, and Bradleigh joins in. As I look up at Orion, he's watching me expectantly.

"That's right. All the mean people can fuck off."

His eyes burn with something prideful—something *appreciative.*

"Ice cream?" he suggests.

"Yes, please. My favorite is strawberry."

He chuckles. "Hmm. I think I know someone else who loves strawberry ice cream."

Bradleigh peers up at me, eyes bright. "Ms. Rivers, are we twins?"

I pat her head. "I think we might be," I tell her, holding my nails up. "Yellow nails, strawberry ice cream, *and* not giving a fuck about mean people? That's more than a coincidence."

Bradleigh squeals with excitement, and as we walk up to the ice cream shop, Orion places his arm around my shoulders.

"I'm proud of you," he murmurs.

"Thank you."

His eyes are soft, almost as if he can see right through me. There's something in the way he's looking at me, something that makes me feel seen in a way I didn't expect from him, but I guess it shouldn't surprise me.

Maybe it's because his Starboy persona heard me when I was bearing my soul, or maybe because he's known me most of my life.

"You know," he says, a small smile tugging at the corners of his mouth, "you're like Odette in so many ways—kind, genuine, always true to your heart. But you've got Odile in you too. You stand up for yourself and for what you believe in. You can be quite intimidating. It's amazing to watch."

I could identify with both characters while up on stage. But it hadn't occurred to me that he saw both of those traits in me. It's a relief to be able to give him everything I have, and for him to see me how I'd always wanted to be seen by someone—without judgment or expectation. For so long, I had to tiptoe around my dates because of my demisexuality or my profession.

"Yes, well, you would know, seeing as you attend every single performance, you psycho."

He laughs. "I don't regret a single second."

I roll my eyes. "I'm sure you don't."

He leans down so that he's murmuring his next line into my ear. "Roll your eyes again. I dare you."

I don't stop smiling all morning.

CHAPTER THIRTY

THE RECKONING

ORION

The hospital calls me as soon as we get back to my apartment. Layla is still staying with me—my contractor is currently installing the new AC unit, so she won't be ready to move back into her house until later tonight at the earliest. After waiting for her for so many years, having her finally in my life feels almost unreal. The thought of her leaving, even if just to go back to her house, stirs an unexpected pang of anxiety in my chest. She must notice the tension in my shoulders because she kisses my shoulder before walking away to give me privacy.

"Hello?" I answer, though I'm pretty sure I know what they're going to say.

"Mr. Ravage?"

"Yep, that's me." My words feel silly—who else would they call? I'm his only point of contact.

"I'm sorry to be the one to call you, but your father was in a considerable amount of pain, and we had to give him pain medication. Unfortunately, we were unable to rouse him just now, and he appears to be in a coma. I've asked the doctor to assess him, and we've determined he doesn't have much time—maybe another couple of hours, if you'd like to come say goodbye."

I let out a long, slow breath. "Yeah. I'll be right there. Thank you."

I end the call and stare down at the screen, waiting for *some* kind of emotion to pass through me.

Nothing comes—I feel empty.

I feel nothing.

"Everything okay?" Layla asks, handing me a sparkling water.

"It's my dad. He's ... in a coma and they don't think he has much time left. They called me so I had time to say goodbye."

Her brows pull together, and one of her hands comes to the back of my neck. I nuzzle into her touch as I close my eyes.

"What do you need?" she asks.

The scent of fresh strawberries makes me relax into her touch even further, and I place a kiss against the inside of her wrist.

When I open my eyes, she's watching me with a worried expression.

"Nothing. I should go, though—so he's not alone."

Her brow relaxes, and she nods once. "Of course. My dad and I can always come stay with you, if needed."

I smile glumly. "It's okay. I think I need to do this myself."

"Okay. Let me make you a quick bite to eat before you go."

I watch her move to the kitchen, and something tightens in my chest. It's been so long since anyone has made me something to eat.

Not since my mom.

She's wrapping up an apple, stuffing crackers, beef jerky, and almonds into a bag, and I can't help but feel a mix of emotions I'm not even sure how to name.

I'm not used to this—someone thinking about me like this. It's such a small thing, really, making lunch, but it feels like *more*.

Like something I've been missing for a long time.

I stand at the island, silent and waiting. My hands twitch on the counter, and I crack my knuckles to give them something to do.

I don't want her to see how much this means to me, how much it hurts to realize what I've been missing, so I just stand there, taking it in, grateful and a little lost at the same time.

"Here you go," she says a minute later, placing a canvas, reusable bag into my arms. Standing on her tiptoes, she kisses me on the lips. "Check in with me when you can, okay?"

She pulls away, but I grab her waist and pull her close. One of my hands wraps around the back of her head, and she moans when I kiss her—when my tongue parts her lips, when I inhale sharply, when I don't let go.

After a minute, I pull away, taking the thoughtful lunch in my hands. "I will. Thank you for this. I'll see you later, okay?"

"Okay."

I walk toward the door, and Sparrow comes barreling around the corner of the hallway, meowing. He winds between my legs, so I crouch down to pet him.

"Take care of your mom," I murmur, running my hand over his soft fur.

He meows, and just then, Earl comes flying into the room, too.

"You too, Earl. I'll be back later."

"Cat family," he croaks.

I huff a laugh. "I guess."

"Pretty girl family."

His words send fire to something emotional in my brain, and I nod once. "One day."

———

I drop the packed lunch onto a chair as I walk into my dad's hospice room. It's a little nicer here—not as big as the suite, but there are at least plants and flowers.

A handmade quilt draped over the lower half of his body.

A humidifier going in the corner.

Swallowing, my feet stay planted. My hands curl at my sides, and I stare down at the man who was everything I wanted to be when I was younger, and everything I wanted to run away from more recently.

My life with him flashes through my mind.

Memories of following my older brothers around, with my mom chasing us all around Ravage Castle. There *were* happy times—I remember the camping trips, the family dinners, the family movie nights. But by the time I was four or five, my dad started drinking more. He pulled back, becoming obsessed with money. I spent my childhood making sure I didn't upset him, running to my mom when he yelled at us, and learning how to keep my mouth shut. The older I got, the more my brothers protected me from the chaos. Chase and Kai, especially, since once Liam and Miles moved out, they were no longer in the house to witness everything that happened.

He was so strong and intimidating, *terrifying* … and now?

I step closer. The machine next to his bed beeps rhythmically, but I don't miss the low resting heart rate or the low oxygen levels.

"Hi, Dad."

He doesn't move.

I've only ever watched my mother die, and I don't remember what I did while we waited for her to take her last breath. I had Layla and Scott—we all held hands for hours as we kept our eyes on Mom.

But this.

I swallow and sit down in the chair. Something heavy and unwelcome settles in my chest. The weight of the room presses down on me, like it's pulling me into the floor. The machine beeps on. I glance at the door, half expecting to see someone else walk through it, to share this burden with them, to fill the room with something other than the sound of this damn machine and the silence that hangs heavy between me and my father.

What the hell do you tell someone who's dying?

I grind my jaw as the minutes tick by. I'm restless, and uneasiness slithers through me.

I'm alone.

I'm alone.

I'm alone.

It feels like a betrayal, even though I know my brothers have their reasons for staying away. I wonder if they'll regret it later, if they'll wish they'd been here for this. Maybe they already do. Or maybe they're just too scared to face him like this, to see the man who once commanded rooms and shattered our nerves reduced to a frail figure bound by wires and tubes. I get that. I wish I didn't have to do this alone, either.

I wish someone else could take this moment from me so I wouldn't have to sit here and confront everything he was and everything he'll never be.

I regret not asking Layla to come with me because being the only person in a room while someone's actively dying is ... not fucking fun.

But I'm here. I'm the one who has to carry the weight of these last moments. The one who has to speak to him, even if he can't respond, because the words have to be said. It feels like whatever is between us is too big to resolve in these final moments, but I can't leave this room without trying. I can't walk away and pretend that it doesn't matter, that the last words spoken between us don't matter.

I'm just about to get up to grab some coffee when the door to the room opens ... and my four brothers walk in.

Miles is first, and his stoic expression takes in my father's frail figure. His jaw hardens, and he looks at me. Out of all of them, Dad's behavior affected him the most, and I'm truly surprised to see him here.

"Hey."

"Who told you?" I ask, propping my foot on one knee.

"Layla texted Estelle," he tells me, stepping farther into the room. Until a few years ago, he'd seen our father as regularly as I did. But then our dad had to fuck over Stella's family, and that was that for Miles.

Liam walks in next, and he nods at me before finding a place along the wall.

Kai steps in second to last, jaw tight as he walks over to Dad. And then he does something I never would've expected—he drops to his knees and takes our father's hands, starting to pray for him.

Chase walks in last. He comes to sit in the chair next to me. His hand claps my knee, and then we wait—we all watch as our father's heartbeat slows. At one point, he opens his eyes, turning his head to take in Kai, who's sitting on the edge of the bed and holding his hands.

Even the worst criminal doesn't deserve to die alone.

You're a better person than me.

I know.

It strikes me then—we're all better people than he

ever was. And maybe that's the point. Maybe all parents, even the bad ones, hope their offspring will be better off than they were.

And I know it took a lot for my brothers to be here.

Hospice nurses pop in a couple of times, and the afternoon wears on. I share my lunch with my brothers, and then Liam offers to get us more coffee—ever the caretaker as the oldest.

It feels strange to be here with them. To be sharing this moment. The instant he takes his last breath, we'll all be orphans. And it's that thought, I think, that hangs over us.

Around five, his breathing turns ragged.

At five thirty, the machine flatlines, and he lets out his final breath.

I always assumed the beeping would continue, but the nurses must turn the sound off at their station to give us privacy.

The silence is deafening, more overwhelming than the beeping that had filled the room just moments before. I feel the loss like a physical blow, but I force myself to stay steady, to stay present.

I don't have to endure the loss alone, though.

We all walk over to him, placing our hands on top of his.

"To being better," I say, my voice breaking on the last syllable. The words are heavy, but they carry a promise I hope we can keep.

"To being happier," Miles says. His voice is soft,

almost fragile, as if the weight of the moment could break him.

"To being kinder," Liam adds, placing an arm around my shoulder, his grip firm, grounding. I can feel the silent strength he offers, the way he's holding us all up.

Chase steps forward next, his jaw clenched, eyes wet but focused. "To being stronger," he says, his voice rough with emotion.

Not letting the Ravage name drag us down forever, I think.

Kai is the last to speak, his hand trembling slightly as he places it over Dad's. "To being braver," he whispers, his voice barely above a breath. His words linger in the air, a quiet vow to face the future without fear.

As we stand there, a quiet resolve forms between us, binding us together in a way that feels different from anything before.

A moment later, the nurse comes in and offers her condolences, and shortly after, Liam and Miles leave together, giving me a quick hug before exiting the hospital room.

Chase is next, and he hugs me for the longest before turning around and quickly walking out.

Kai turns to face me when I gather my things. "Did you drive here?"

I nod.

"Cool. I'll walk you out."

With one last glance over my shoulder, I walk out of the hospice room.

The two of us walk to the parking garage in silence. Once we get to my car, I give him a quick hug.

"You okay?" he asks, eyes studying me.

"Yeah. Surprisingly."

"Plans tonight?"

I crack a smile. "Yeah."

His lips twitch. "Let's get dinner tomorrow, yeah?"

I give him a handshake. "Sure. Drive safe."

I watch as he climbs into his car and drives away. Then I pull my phone out and text Layla.

> I'm on my way. Just have to make one stop first.

———

When I walk through the front door of Scott's house, it smells like home. Somehow, it always has. Closing the door behind me, I set my helmet down on the entryway table and walk through the living room to the kitchen, where I find Scott cooking what looks to be an omelette.

"Hey, Ri," he says, smiling as he turns around. "Everything okay? Your text sounded urgent."

I open and close my mouth a couple of times, and my stepdad must notice the hesitation, because he sets the dish towel down on the counter and turns the burner off.

"My dad died," I say slowly, trying the words out in my mouth for the first time.

Scott physically sags before taking a step forward. "Fuck. I'm so sorry, Orion. What can I do?" Without thinking, he opens his arms and pulls me in for a hug. I squeeze my eyes shut, but I don't cry. If anything, I'm relieved—and I don't feel like I'm missing out on having a father figure.

After all, I have Scott.

Pulling away, I sniff once, but that's all the emotion I show. "Nothing. It's over now."

"You sure? How are your brothers? Do they know?"

At this, I crack a smile. "Yeah. We all got to say goodbye."

Scott's face softens. "Your mom would be so proud of you all for that. She always worried you'd grow apart over the years, but it seems you've only gotten closer."

I nod. "It was good being able to say goodbye to our dad together. It seems to have healed something in all of us."

"Good. Well, I'm sorry for your loss."

I shrug as I look at him. "It doesn't feel like I've lost anything."

My stepdad's eyes go misty. "I'm glad. You know you'll always be my son, right? Blood relation doesn't matter. You're a part of this family, and you always will be."

I wince. I can't help it. Rubbing the back of my neck, I take a deep breath. His eyes soften as he watches me, but there's something else there too—a quiet understanding that settles between us, deep and unspoken. It presses on my chest, the heavy weight of guilt for keeping something so big from him. I swallow hard and take a breath.

"I, uh..." The nervous energy makes it hard to stand

still. "I actually wanted to ask you for something. Officially."

His eyebrows lift, curiosity replacing his usual fatherly sternness. "Go on."

I shift my weight, deciding to blurt everything out and rip the bandaid off. *Why the fuck not.*

"I love Layla. I've loved her for a long time now. And I want to make sure I do this right." My voice wavers for a second, but I steady myself, meeting his gaze head-on. "I want your blessing to ask her to marry me. When she's ready, of course. We only just started ... "

For a second, there's nothing but a distant hum of life going on around us. Scott doesn't move, his face unreadable, and I wonder if I've overstepped. But then, slowly, a smile creeps onto his face, warm and genuine.

"You already have my blessing," he says, his voice thick with emotion. He claps my shoulder, a little rougher this time, like he's holding back the flood of feelings rushing between us. "You'll be good for her. I know it."

Relief surges through me, and I blink back the sudden sting in my eyes. "Thank you, Scott. It means the world to me that you approve."

He clears his throat, pretending to be casual, but I can see the emotion tugging at the corners of his eyes. "Just make sure you don't screw it up, alright? She's my girl."

"I won't," I promise, my voice firm with conviction. "I'll take care of her. Always."

Scott nods again, his hand still gripping my shoulder

as if to cement the deal, then lets go with a sigh. "And if this recent health scare has taught me anything, it's that I wouldn't mind a couple of sprogget running around in the back yard someday soon—"

"One step at a time, big guy." I let out a relieved laugh.

"Don't make me wait too long."

I shrug and smile. "It's entirely up to her. I won't rush her."

"I know you won't."

After a quick goodbye, I linger for a moment outside the house that means so much to me, staring at the sky, feeling the weight of the future settle in, but this time it feels right. A life with Layla. The thought fills me with hope for the very first time in my life.

And maybe, just maybe, the future he hinted at—sproggets and all—doesn't seem so far away anymore.

CHAPTER THIRTY-ONE

THE LIBRARY

Layla

My eyes find Orion's the instant I lift my head from my curtsy. He's in the front row, clapping and hollering. My stomach flutters as he cups his mouth and whistles, pride showing on his face.

"Interesting development," Raphael says as we walk backstage a minute later. He turns to face me with a smirk. "I still don't forgive him for punching me, but I get it now."

"Get what?"

"He's in love with you."

He walks away whistling, and I'm too stunned to speak.

By the time I get to my dressing room, my heart is pounding in my chest. *In love with me?* I turn the handle, and I nearly gasp when I see Orion leaning against the vanity. He's wearing his leather jacket, black pants, and his boots.

His motorcycle helmet sits on my pink vanity.

"How'd you get back here?" I ask, breathless.

After closing the door, I bend down to untie my pointe shoes, but Orion takes a step forward.

"Don't. Leave them on."

I snap my head up, and he's right in front of me now.

"Orion—"

He tugs me forward in my full costume, his lips crashing against mine. I don't ask about his father as Stella told me Charles Ravage passed away earlier today, and that all five brothers were present.

But I don't know how he's feeling about it all. I don't know what he wants or needs, so I ask him.

"I need you," he rasps, scruff rough against my face. "And God, I've always wanted to rip your costume off."

"Then do it." His eyes darken, and as he takes a step closer, reality sets in. "Wait. Don't actually rip anything off," I tell him, laughing. "The seamstresses will kill you."

"Very well." Taking several steps closer, he backs me up against the door. "Then strip."

With shaking hands, I unclasp the bodice, removing it completely. My nipples tighten against the cool air. He runs his hand along my collarbone before roving down to my bare stomach, and then he helps me out of the tutu. I start to pull my trunks down my hips, but he reaches out and helps me step out of them. I'm now only wearing tights and pointe shoes—and it feels oddly intimate.

Orion cocks his head to the side. "Leave the shoes on."

"Yes, Master."

Groaning, his lashes flutter, and I can see the raw emotion in his eyes, the way his breath catches every time he looks at me. There's something almost tender in the way he watches me, like he's memorizing every detail, afraid I might disappear if he blinks. His vulnerability, the way his heart is so clearly on display, makes me want him even more.

I jump into his arms, and he pushes me against the dressing room door.

His hands grip my thighs, and they start their perusal up to the apex between my legs.

Everything inside of me is pulsing. When his hand gets to the seam, he quickly tears into the tights with a swift, determined motion, the fabric giving way under his fingers and making me gasp.

"Please," I pant, legs shaking from my performance.

He seems to sense my urgency because he hoists me up so I'm stable against the wall. The sound of a zipper sounds through the room, and then the thick head of his cock is pressing against me.

"Layla," he says, mouth on mine as he pushes into me.

We both groan, and my hands come to either side of his head, holding him close. He rolls his hips in soft circles, pulling out most of the way before pushing back in, and my mouth pops open at the feel of his thumb against my clit.

"Are you okay—"

He cuts me off with a deep kiss, and he groans when I run my fingers through his soft hair. The recessed light above us catches on the dainty gold bracelet around my wrist—the one I insisted had to stay on for the performance. The diamonds sparkle just so, highlighting the constellation pattern, and I gasp.

"Oh my God. It's Orion's belt."

He grunts, and a puff of air escapes his lips. "Took you long enough."

"You're so sneaky," I tell him, gasping when his nails dig into the flesh of my thigh.

"I know—"

I cut him off with a kiss, wanting his mouth on mine.

He continues to pound into me, continues to swirl his thumb over my swollen bud, and continues to destroy me with his kiss.

With his *need*.

"Orion—"

"Fuck," he says, breathless. "I'm never going to get enough of you."

His lips move down to my jaw before he kisses his way down my neck. My head drops back against the door roughly, and I groan as the tiara's band digs into my scalp. A sharp snapping sound follows as I feel it give slightly.

"My tiara," I rasp.

"You're going to have to tell the seamstresses the tiara broke because you fucked your boyfriend in your costume," he adds, smiling against my neck.

I should've removed it beforehand, but the fact that he *needed* to be inside me immediately sends shivers down my spine. It's only when my brain catches up to his words that I realize what he called himself.

"Boyfriend?" I rasp, circling my hips as he drives into me harder, making the door of the dressing room creak.

"For now."

His mouth brushes my collarbone—a place I've come to find is *very* sensitive, and my whole body goes taut.

"Oh God," I whimper, closing my eyes as my hands dig into his scalp.

He moves faster, groaning against my skin.

I move my hips down to meet him with every thrust, and his breathing changes before his lips are back on mine.

"I'm going to come—"

A low, supplicant noise escapes his lips, and I gasp when his cock pulses inside me. Hot spikes of cum hit my cervix, and I watch as his jaw slackens, as his eyes flutter, as his nails almost break the skin of my thigh because he's holding on so tight.

"Orion, I'm—"

Everything draws up tight inside me, and one swipe of his thumb against my clit sends my orgasm bursting through me.

A crescendo of ecstasy propels through me, and I squeeze my eyes shut. My toes curl inside my pointe shoes, and little pulses of pleasure run through me for over a minute. His breathing steadies, and when he pulls back, he looks disoriented.

His heart beats erratically against my chest, our bodies fused by my legs tightly wrapped around his waist. He doesn't pull out, but instead, he continues kissing me. After a minute, he sets me down, quickly cleaning me with some tissues; running them through my folds and kissing me as he goes.

And other than being a little more rumpled than normal from discarding it onto the floor a few minutes ago, the custom-made costume is fine, so I hang it up for dry-cleaning, removing my pointe shoes and ripped tights.

Then Orion helps me into my underwear, sweat-pants, and sweatshirt.

I place the tiara on the vanity—only a small piece broke off the band, so I hope it's an easy fix—and scribble an apology to the seamstress. By the time I grab my things to leave, Orion has his helmet in his arms and his other hand out for me.

————

Five minutes later, he hands me the helmet he's been carrying and unlocks his from under the bike seat.

I stand straighter, surprised, and more uncertain than ever. "I drove here—"

"We can come get your car tomorrow." I stare at him, tongue-tied, and he sighs. "Put the helmet on, Layla."

I reach out for the helmet and inspect it. "How?"

He chuckles. "Put it on like a hat. I'll make sure it's tight."

I hold it over my head and lower it down, and everything is suddenly muffled. Orion takes a step closer and flips the visor up, smirking as he turns some dial near the base of my neck until it fits snugly on my skull.

"There."

He removes his leather jacket and hands it to me. "Wear this. For protection, but also so you don't get cold."

I arch a brow when I take in his gray T-shirt. "Won't you be cold?"

He pops his helmet on, and *my God* ... he's truly a work of art with that biker helmet and tattoos on display. "No, I'll have my girl wrapped around me like a koala."

My girl.

I'm grinning by the time he lifts one leg over the bike, and after I zip his leather jacket up over the top half of my body, he helps me on behind him. My thighs squeeze his hips from behind, and I wrap my arms around his chest.

"Hold on," he says, voice muffled.

I squeal as we move forward, as the lights of Los Angeles pass us by. At every traffic light, he reaches a hand out to my thigh and rubs it, a nonverbal gesture to make sure I'm okay.

I can't stop laughing as we merge onto the freeway, and though he's very safe, it still feels like we're breaking rules to be riding out in the open like this.

I keep my visor open, and the wind against my face is refreshing. I can't stop smiling the entire way.

Twenty minutes later, I'm too distracted by the motorcycle ride to notice we're heading to Los Feliz rather than Crestwood. When he pulls off at my exit, I tap on his shoulder once we get to the light. Flipping my visor open, he does the same.

"Where are we going? Is the AC fixed?" I ask, feeling slightly disappointed that I won't be going home with him tonight.

"It is. He finished a few hours ago."

"What about Sparrow?"

"You're not staying at your house tonight. The paint fumes still need a day to air out."

My brow creases in confusion. "What paint?"

He smirks, but we're peeling away at the green light before he answers.

Once we arrive at my house, he parks his bike in my driveway. I remove the helmet and adjust my crossbody bag, and then he removes a familiar black box from a storage compartment on the side of his bike.

"Hey," I tease, snatching the belated birthday present from his hands. "Did you take this from your apartment?"

His lips tug into a devilish smile. "Didn't you know that presents are meant to be opened?"

I roll my eyes. "Yeah, yeah. I was waiting for the perfect time."

"Which is when we get inside."

"Fine."

He chuckles as we make our way to the front door. I

remember the last time we were here last week. How we had a moment of something.

He waits for me to unlock the door, and when I do, cool air greets me.

"Ah," I say, smiling, walking over to the thermostat. I turn it off since I won't be staying the night. "You know I'm going to pay you back, right?" I ask, referring to the new unit he had installed for me.

"Sure." His arms are crossed, and he's standing by the hallway looking … nervous? "Come here. I want to show you something. Bring your present."

Setting my bag down, I carry the black box to the first door. My library. Also known as, the bane of my existence. Orion switches the light on, and I nearly drop the box.

The walls are painted a robin's egg blue, which reminds me of Felicity. I picked it out six months ago because of that, but of course hadn't had time to actually paint other than half a wall.

The dark wood built-in shelves that line the room are stained with a gorgeous walnut color, but that's not what catches my attention.

The shelves are carefully organized by author.

He did this. He organized my books.

Emotion catches in my throat as I walk around, taking everything else in. Fairy lights are delicately draped along the top of the shelves, casting a gentle glow that dances off the books and gives the room a magical ambience. In one corner, a plush reading chair with oversized pillows beckons, all in muted tones of cream and white that complement the wall color. A throw blanket is casually draped over one side.

A small wooden side table holds a few miscellaneous books, and a floor lamp with a soft yellow shade stands nearby. A thick Persian rug covers the floor, somehow complementing the blue, brown, and cream. A few houseplants are strategically placed around the room on various shelves.

My eyes brim with tears by the time I turn to face Orion. "You did this?"

He dips his chin and points at the black box in my hands.

I sit down on the chair and untie the satin ribbon. Then I lift the lid. Inside is something wrapped in bubble wrap, and my hands are shaking as I turn it over and over, revealing—

I gasp.

"Oh my God."

The Phantom of the Opera.

"A first edition?" My shaking hands flip to the copyright page, and sure enough ...

Press of Braunworth & Co. Bookbinders and Printers Brooklyn, N. Y.

First Edition, 1909.

I set the book down on my lap. "Orion, this book is so, so rare. The dust jacket design with the Phantom on the stairwell? Only one of three total physical copies of the book is known to have retained the dust jacket in the whole *world*."

I'd done a lot of research.

"Wait, did you pay thirty-two thousand dollars for this?" I ask, breathless.

He shrugs. "It doesn't matter."

I wrap the book back up carefully, placing the box on an empty shelf before I walk back over to Orion.

"It does matter," I murmur, placing a hand on his face. "Thank you. I don't think anyone will ever be able to top this gift."

He smirks, kissing the inside of my wrist. "Good. I will endeavor to always be the best gift-giver."

Laughing, we spend a few minutes in the library, and Orion tells me about the painstakingly meticulous method he used to organize my books by author. I kiss him—a lot.

And then I grab a few extra things before we lock up and head back to his bike.

"How long do you want to stay at my place?" he asks, handing my helmet to me.

I shrug. "I don't know, but we should probably come up with a system now that I'm your *girlfriend*."

"Well, since the theater is closer to my apartment, technically, you could stay there on performance nights. It'd be easy since I'll be there too, and I can drive you to my place. We'll need to figure out shared custody of Sparrow, though. He's sort of growing on me."

Suddenly, a future I'd never considered opens up before me.

Spending the warm, summer days by his pool, writhing underneath him in his large, fancy bed. Showering with him—gripping his waist as he drives us through Southern California on his motorcycle. Dinners at my dad's. Playing together and doing scenes at Inferno. Double dates with Liam and Zoe, and Miles and Stella.

I swallow. "That sounds great."

"And then, of course, I'll stay with you the other nights."

I laugh as I pull my helmet on, climbing behind him. "Only if you don't mind that I'll be reading in that amazing library every night."

"As long as I'm with you, it doesn't matter."

A thought snags in my mind, and I gasp just before we shut our visors. "Oh God."

"What?" he asks, twisting to face me.

"We're going to have to tell my dad about us." Orion shakes his head as his eyes drift to my lips, a smile tugging on his mouth. "What?" I press, sensing something off. He looks away guiltily. "Orion, what did you do?"

"I'm pretty sure Scott already knows."

"How?" I ask, a bite to my voice.

Looking back at me with an impish smile, he pops his visor closed.

"Orion! Tell me."

But before I can demand an answer again, he grabs my arms and wraps them around his waist.

"Hold on, Little Dancer."

The engine roars to life beneath us, and we speed off into the horizon.

EPILOGUE
THE MASK

ORION

One and a half years later

Sliding the balaclava down over my face, I adjust it and wait in the shadows of the apartment. It's late, and the only light coming in through the large windows is the light from Downtown Crestwood. The ding of the elevator sounds through the quiet apartment, and just as Layla steps out of the elevator, my breath hitches in my chest.

She sets her bag down on the table and kicks off her boots, rolling her ankles a few times before she cracks her neck. Rummaging around her bag for her phone, she glances down at it. I see the minute she digests the words on her screen—the words I'd sent only a minute ago.

STARBOY1997

Ten seconds.

Her head pops up and she looks around the dark apartment, and her hand comes to her neck as she slowly scans the atmosphere.

I count down in my head.

10 ...

9 ...

8 ...

7 ...

6 ...

She walks farther into the room, unintentionally getting closer to me. She's facing away, looking around as if she can find me, but she won't. Not in the next five seconds, at least.

5 ...

4 ...

3 ...

2 ...

1 ...

Her breathing turns ragged when I move from behind her, lunging forward and pulling her roughly against my chest. One of my hands flies over her mouth, and she bites down on the leather of my gloves.

"Ah, ah, Little Dancer," I growl, keeping my voice low. "That's not very nice." She fights against me, but I don't relent. I hold her close as she thrashes. "You remember what we had planned, don't you?"

She whimpers.

I want one night with Starboy, and I don't want it to feel consensual.

It took over a year for her to admit that little fantasy to me—to confess that her ultimate, deep, dark secret involved being ambushed and forced.

It was her way of working through her trauma, of giving herself power over what happened.

"You remember your safe word, both the verbal and nonverbal one. Use it." I reach into my hoodie pocket and pull out my keys. "And since you'll be restrained, here are my keys. Drop them if you need to get my attention."

She kicks backward, but her hands clasp around the heavy key ring.

"Good girl." I walk her over to the nearby couch, bending her over the back of it. When I drop my hand from her mouth, she hisses.

"Who are you? And what do you want?"

I smirk at the way she's playing along. "I'm your worst nightmare, darling."

Holding her hands together behind her back with one hand, I use my other hand to pull her sweatpants down to her ankles. Then I kick her feet apart.

Her hands grip the keys, and I know I have several safety measures in place now.

"That's not an answer," she grumbles, attempting to pull out of my grip.

I smack her ass, and she arches her back. "*You* decide how much this will hurt. Is that understood?"

"How did you get in here, anyway? My boyfriend will be back any second."

"Too bad for him, because I don't share."

I use my teeth to pull the glove off the hand not restraining her. Running that hand down her ass crack until I meet her overeager core, I push into her tight cunt with my middle finger.

"Fuck you," she says on a gasp, pulling against where I have her restrained.

"Trust me. I plan to."

———

Layla

"Let me go." I grind against Starboy's hand, rolling my hips and trying not to smile.

"Not a chance."

He pushes another finger inside me, and I groan, hands curling around the keys.

"Stop," I whimper, pulling away from him.

"You don't really want me to stop, do you? Be a good little cumslut and *take it*." He growls the last two words, shoving his fingers so deep into me that I see stars.

My God.

Just as I open my mouth to scream, he removes his fingers. The sound of a zipper reverberates through the dark apartment. I gasp when something warm presses against my opening, and in my peripheral, I see the second glove fall to the floor.

"Beg for it."

"No," I yell, thrashing.

His other hand grabs my hair and yanks my head back. "I said, *beg for it.*"

I release a sob, but it doesn't feel genuine to me. It's better than laughing or moaning. Because right now? I'm so fucking turned on.

He slides his cock along my seam, coating the head of his shaft in my wetness.

"Do you feel how wet you are for me? My little whore loves this, don't you?"

My chest heaves. "No."

He trusts me to use my safe word, and I have more than enough ways to tell him to stop. My fingers curl around the keys, and he's left my mouth unbound.

For now.

"Are you going to behave? Or do I have to spank you again? Perhaps I can have you lick my shoes, or perhaps I could spit into your mouth? What do you think, Little Dancer?"

"No, please—"

"Then beg me for my cock."

I release a sharp breath, pulling away from him as much as possible. "Make me."

He goes rigid, and a thrill works through me. I open my mouth to snark some more, but he knocks my knees farther apart and pistons right into me.

I scream, and he groans.

I'm too wet for it to hurt, and my eyes roll back as he shudders behind me.

"I knew you'd have a tight little fuckhole," he

murmurs, pulling out and driving back into me. "I bet your asshole is just as tight, too. So wound up. So innocent. I plan to ravage you. Break you. *Ruin* you."

A whimper escapes my lips, and he chuckles behind me. "Mmm. I think you like this," he says, voice hoarse. "I think you enjoy being fucked against a couch by a stranger like a whore."

I inhale sharply as he thrusts into me—*hard*.

"You're so wet. Your greedy cunt is begging me for more, isn't it?"

I groan as he pulls out slowly and punches into me again, harder than last time.

A smack against my ass has me seeing stars, and I can feel my arousal gathering inside me, making every muscle tense and pull tight.

He spanks me again—on the other cheek this time.

"Ow! That hurt," I say, letting the pain slide through me.

"Good."

He spanks the other cheek, and I keen.

"You have a perfect little cunt," he says, fisting my hair.

My eyes roll back as he fucks me, as he takes whatever he needs from me.

As he uses me.

"You are mine," he growls, and I nod out of instinct.

I'm close, and it's hard not to know it's Orion fucking me from behind.

Orion, who fulfilled this years-long fantasy.

Orion, who always keeps me on my toes.

"Do you understand? *Mine.*"

I arch my back and meet his thrusts with my hips. I'm not even trying to hide my impending climax.

He yanks on my hair, and the stinging sensation causes white-hot heat to flare through me.

It's unstoppable—like a dam breaking. The maelstrom of heat doesn't relent, and my eyes roll back as a sudden, strong orgasm rocks through me. Despite the scene, he mutters something affectionate into my ear, but I don't hear it. I can't.

Just as I start to come down, he pulls out of me.

"I didn't say you could come."

Twisting me around, he pulls me close and lifts one of my legs, wrapping it around his hips. I stare up at his masked face, still in a post-orgasm daze, and my mouth drops open as he pushes his cock into me.

His eyes don't leave my face as he slowly fucks me.

It's a different pace from earlier, and one of his hands comes to my neck. His thumb brushes against my throat.

He's still wearing the mask, but the scene feels over. His touches are different—lighter, gentler. Even the way he's fucking me feels personal.

I reach for his mask and pull it off, admiring the messy hair and tortured look on his face.

"Orion," I whisper, pleasure coiling inside me again as his cock slides in and out of me with a delicious friction.

"Layla," he hisses. "Fuck, I want to feel you come again."

I nod eagerly, and the hand on my throat moves

down between us. Using two fingers, he slides them along the sides of my piercing, pulling the skin and causing me to jerk away from the pain.

"Good, I felt that—"

He tugs on the metal jewelry. Gently—so gently—but it's enough.

I squeeze my eyes shut as my stomach muscles contract, and then I *shatter*.

"Fuck, Layla." His cock thickens, stretching me as he empties inside me, warmth flooding my core. We stare at each other as we come. My lips part as his mouth drops open, and neither of us looks away. Neither of us *can* look away—it's intense and wonderful all at once.

I could watch him fall apart like this all damn day.

When I stop jerking, he pulls out, and I go limp against him.

He helps me lower my leg, pulling my pants back on as we disentangle ourselves from the intense scene. That mixed with my performance tonight means I'm exhausted, and Orion must notice.

"To bed," he says, pointing in the direction of his bedroom.

"But—"

"I made soup."

My lips twitch. "Soup."

"Yes. I'm trying out a new recipe for the restaurant."

"Soup sounds delicious."

The restaurant.

Orion has been talking about opening it for over a year, always sketching out plans, dreaming out loud when he thought no one was really listening. But it was only recently—just a few weeks ago—that everything finally started falling into place. He's poured his heart into it, and the grand opening is just around the corner. Next week, in fact. He's been testing recipes nonstop, refining every detail. The Orion of a few years ago would've been too caught up in the whirlwind of life to commit to something like this, but now ... now he's different. Calmer, more focused.

The kind of man who tells me to go to bed and then makes me soup, apparently.

He cocks his head and nods toward the hallway. "Don't make me ask you twice."

"I can help you—"

He steps forward and places his hands on my shoulders. "Go. I'll be right there. Let me take care of you."

I lean closer and give him a peck on the lips. "Fine."

"I love you, Little Dancer."

Those words. He first told me a week after I moved in, and they were the best words to hear. I never tire of hearing them.

"I love you too," I say. "Always."

As I walk into the bedroom and settle onto the bed, the sounds of him moving around the kitchen filter through the hallway, and I realize just how much this moment, this simple gesture, means to me. It's not just about the soup or the restaurant. It's about him showing me that he's changed, that he's capable of being the person I need him to be.

I take a deep breath, sinking into the pillows, and let

the warmth of the moment wash over me. It's like everything is finally coming together, for both of us.

Especially since I'm in the process of opening my own dance studio for teenagers.

As much as I love performing, it won't last forever, and I want to have something lined up for when that day comes.

I hear Orion humming softly to himself in the kitchen, and I can't help but grin as I pull my Kindle off my bedside table, opening another dark romance book and settling into the cozy bedding.

Sparrow hops up beside me, purring as he falls asleep against my ribs.

This—with the sounds of my boyfriend making me food in the kitchen, a smutty book on my Kindle, and a cat purring at my side—is everything I ever could've wanted. It's the kind of peace and contentment I never thought I'd have, the quiet, perfect moments I used to dream about when I was alone. It's the feeling of being right where I'm meant to be.

————

Orion

Is it normal to watch your girlfriend sleep? I'm not sure. All I know is I've gotten a lot less sleep since we started dating. I find that I'd rather watch her than dream of whatever my mind cooks up. I'd rather trace a finger along her spine and watch her skin pebble. I'd rather watch the steady rise and fall of her chest, or play with her copper hair, or place my lips on her neck and inhale her delicious scent.

Maybe it's not normal for a girlfriend, but for a fiancée? Perhaps.

I suppose I should find out because I'm finally ready to give her *the* ring.

Never in a million years did I think I'd actually get the chance to give it to her.

Never in a million years did I think she'd ever be in a position to say yes.

Three years ago, I walked by it and purchased it on the spot. It was always hers, and it will always *be* hers.

I planned it all out. Afternoon flight to Paris. Early morning arrival the next day. *Phantom of the Opera*, lots of fancy Parisian sex, and then I would be taking her on a road trip to Château de Sourches, home of the Conservatoire de la Pivoine—a privately owned château outside of Le Mans, France. Over 3,000 varieties of peonies are planted in the deep moat at Sourches, making it one of the largest peony collections in the world.

It's there that I plan to drop to one knee.

I would ask her to marry me with the ring she's already seen, the one that kick-started our entire relationship.

After that ... I have no idea.

We haven't really talked about marriage or children, other than knowing we want to get married and that we might want kids in about ten years. Neither of us is in any rush to reproduce, though I will have fun trying.

I gently kiss her forehead and place my mouth against her temple.

"Thank you for choosing me," I whisper.

At the end of the day, it doesn't matter what happens as long as *she's* the one standing next to me.

I'd never needed anything but her—and yes, it was unhealthy, and I was perhaps a little bit problematic and possessive at times. Things like my job and my family brought me joy, but Layla?

She's my center, the constant in a world of change.

She always has been—ever since the day I met her.

Every moment without her over the last decade felt like a fragment of a life I couldn't fully live.

Not until she was back in it.

She keeps the brute in me steady and grounded.

She's the reason I find meaning in every day.

She is the axis around which my universe spins, and I would never apologize for that.

Not when her love is the one thing I'll always crave and cherish.

————

Thank you so much for reading Layla and Orion's story! Are you ready to get a glimpse into what Malakai's life is like with *both* Julian and Sophie? ;)

Preorder Holy Hearts:

mybook.to/HolyHearts

If you want to sign up for Ravaged Castle release news and updates, as well as receive excerpts and teasers before anyone else, be sure that you're subscribed to my mailing list. It's the best place to follow me!

www.authoramandarichardson.com/newsletter
(Psst... you also get a free student/teacher novella as a thank you for joining!)

ACKNOWLEDGMENTS

Orion and Layla's story has been a long time coming! I know you're all excited to read the youngest Ravage brother's book, especially since you've been getting glimpses of him in all of the previous books.

This book surprised me in the best way. I went into it expecting a completely unhinged, jealous, dark antihero who was ready and willing to drag his stepsister into the depths of hell with him. But when I started writing, a total cinnamon roll and simp for Layla came out, and I found that Orion had already unintentionally healed off page. Forcing him into an unhealthy situation didn't feel true to his character. Maybe after I'd written *Prey Tell*, when he was still drinking and partying, it would've been different.

But he'd slowly been growing as a character, and that was especially evident in *Ward Willing* (if you know, you know). So, while it was confusing to write (what do you mean you're going to be mature about this, Orion?!), at least I can say that every page of this book stays true to the person he eventually becomes, and I grew to love these characters so much. So, I've coined the unofficial subtitle of this book: "Adults Communicating in an

Adult-Like Way," unlike some of my other books. *Cough *literally all of my other books* cough*

This book wouldn't be what it is without the help of a LOT of people!

Always my #1, my husband. A small part of this book was inspired by our story—of two immature young adults who grew apart and came back together much more level-headed and ready to *talk about our damn feelings and communicate!* I love you so much. At least 50% of this book was fueled by meals you brought up to my office, so you can all thank Mr. Richardson for that. Thanks for giving me the most beautiful life with our boys.

To all of my early readers: Erica, Brittni, Macie, Kerrie, Jasmine, Jess... thank you all for your input!

To Marion and Jenny, thank you for the flawless edits!

To Shelbe, for all of your help spreading the word about this book, and for just generally being so organised and willing to help me.

To Emma, aka Moonstruck Cover Design, you are a true gem for getting the new title to me in less than ten minutes. That has to be a record! Thank you!

To Rafa for the gorgeous photo I bought a year and a half ago, knowing Ignatio would make the *perfect* Orion.

Michele, thank you for the proofreads!

To Zoe York for all of your help when Amazon was being a PITA and cancelled the preorder of this book, that was originally called *Step Brute.* Your sound advice kept me from rocking in a corner and giving up. Also, to everyone else who reached out to me personally when I didn't know what to do. You're all the true MVPs.

And last but not least, the author friends who were there with me while I wrote this book, either in sprint rooms or any of our various chats on social media/text message. To the authors who are reading this series and drop into my DM's to tell me how much you love it, you have no idea how much that makes me smile. You all inspire me so much, and I could not do this job without the amazing community of fellow authors lifting me up. Rising tides lift all boats, and we're all so fucking badass. ILY.

ABOUT THE AUTHOR

Amanda Richardson writes from her chaotic dining room table in Yorkshire, England, often distracted by her husband and two adorable sons. When she's not writing contemporary and dark, twisted romance, she enjoys coffee (a little too much) and collecting house plants like they're going out of style.

You can visit my website here:
www.authoramandarichardson.com

ALSO BY AMANDA RICHARDSON

For a complete and updated list of my currently published books, you can visit my website here:

www.authoramandarichardson.com/books

Made in the USA
Las Vegas, NV
06 October 2024

96387145R10277